CYCLOPS

CYC

A NOVEL BY CLIVE

LOPS

CUSSLER

HAMISH HAMILTON

LONDON

First published in Great Britain 1986
by Hamish Hamilton Ltd
Garden House 57–59 Long Acre London WC2E 9JZ

This novel is a work of fiction. Names, characters, places and incidents are either the
product of the author's imagination or are used fictitiously. Any resemblance to actual
events or locales or persons, living or dead, is entirely coincidental.

The author is grateful for permission to reprint lines from the following songs:
'Supercalifragilisticexpialidocious.' Words and music by Richard M. Sherman and Robert
B. Sherman. Copyright © 1963 by Wonderland Music Company, Inc.
'Yankee Doodle Boy' (George M. Cohan). Used by permission of George M. Cohan Music
Publishing Company

British Library Cataloguing in Publication Data

Cussler, Clive
  Cyclops.
  I. Title
  813'.54[F]   PS3553.U75
  ISBN 0-241-11842-5

Printed and bound in Great Britain by
Richard Clay (The Chaucer Press) Ltd, Bungay, Suffolk

To the eight hundred American men
who were lost with the *Leopoldville*
Christmas Eve 1944 near Cherbourg, France.
Forgotten by many, remembered by few.

Prologue

The *Cyclops* had less than one hour to live. In forty-eight minutes she would become a mass tomb for her 309 passengers and crew— a tragedy unforeseen and unheralded by ominous premonitions, mocked by an empty sea and a diamond-clear sky. Even the seagulls that had haunted her wake for the past week darted and soared in languid indifference, their keen instincts dulled by the mild weather.

There was a slight breeze from the southeast that barely curled the American flag on her stern. At three-thirty in the morning, most of the off-duty crewmen and passengers were asleep. A few, unable to drift off under the oppressive heat of the trade winds, stood around on the upper deck, leaning over the railing and watching the ship's bow hiss and lift over the high rolling swells. The main surge of the sea seemed to be moving beneath the smooth surface, while massive forces were building in the depths below.

Inside the *Cyclops'* wheelhouse, Lieutenant John Church stared vacantly through one of the large circular ports. He had the midnight to 4 A.M. dog watch, and it was all he could do to stay awake. He vaguely noticed the increasing height of the waves, but as long as they remained wide-spaced and their slopes gentle he saw no reason to reduce speed.

Nudged by a friendly current, the heavily loaded collier was plodding along at only nine knots. Her machinery was badly in need of overhaul and even now she was steaming on just her port engine. Shortly after departing Rio de Janeiro, the starboard engine broke

11

down and the chief engineer reported it could not be repaired until they reached port in Baltimore.

Lieutenant Church had worked his way up through the ranks to commissioned officer. He was a thin, prematurely gray-haired man a few months shy of thirty. He had been assigned to many different ships and had sailed around the world four times. But the *Cyclops* was the strangest vessel he'd ever encountered during his twelve years in the Navy. This was his first voyage on the eight-year-old vessel and it was not without its odd events.

Since leaving home port, a seaman who fell overboard was battered into pulp by the port propeller. Next came a collision with the cruiser *Raleigh* that caused minor damage to both ships. The brig was filled with five prisoners. One of them, convicted in the brutal murder of a shipmate, was being transported to the naval prison at Portsmouth, New Hampshire. Outside the entrance to Rio Harbor, the ship came within a hair of running onto a reef, and when the executive officer accused the captain of endangering the ship by altering course, he was placed under arrest and confined to quarters. Finally, there was a malcontent crew, a problem-plagued starboard engine, and a captain who was drinking himself into oblivion. When Church summed up the luckless incidents, he felt as if he were standing watch over a disaster waiting to happen.

His gloomy reverie was interrupted by the sound of heavy footsteps behind him. He turned and stiffened as the captain came through the door of the wheelhouse.

Lieutenant Commander George Worley was a character straight out of *Treasure Island.* All that was missing was an eye patch and a pegleg. He was a bull of a man. His neck was almost nonexistent, his massive head seemed to erupt from his shoulders. The hands that hung at his sides were the largest Church had ever seen. They were as long and thick as a volume out of an encyclopedia. Never a stickler for Navy regulations, Worley's uniform aboard ship usually consisted of bedroom slippers, derby hat, and long-john underwear. Church had never seen the captain in a dress uniform except when the *Cyclops* was in port and Worley went ashore on official business.

With merely a grunt of a greeting, Worley walked over and rapped the barometer with a beefy knuckle. He studied the needle and nodded.

"Not too bad," he said with a slight German accent. "Looks good for the next twenty-four hours. With luck it'll be a smooth sail, at

12

least until we catch hell passing Cape Hatteras."

"Every ship catches hell off Cape Hatteras," said Church flatly.

Worley walked into the chart room and peered at the penciled line showing the *Cyclops'* course and approximate position.

"Alter course five degrees north," he said as he returned to the wheelhouse. "We'll skirt the Great Bahama Bank."

"We're already twenty miles west of the main channel," said Church.

"I have my reasons for avoiding the shipping lanes," Worley responded gruffly.

Church simply nodded at the helmsman, and the *Cyclops* came around. The slight alteration brought the swells running against her port bow and her motion changed. She began to roll heavily.

"I don't much care for the look of the sea," said Church. "The waves are getting a bit steep."

"Not uncommon in these waters," replied Worley. "We're nearing the area where the North Equatorial Current meets the Gulf Stream. I've seen the surface as flat as a desert dry lake, other times I've seen waves twenty feet high, nice easy rollers that slide under the keel."

Church started to say something, but paused, listening. The sound of metal scraping against metal rasped through the wheelhouse. Worley acted as though he hadn't heard anything, but Church walked to the rear bulkhead and looked out over the long cargo deck of the *Cyclops.*

She was a large ship for her day, with an overall length of 542 feet and a 65-foot beam. Built in Philadelphia in 1910, she operated with the Naval Auxiliary Service, Atlantic Fleet. Her seven cavernous holds could handle 10,500 tons of coal, but this trip she was carrying 11,000 tons of manganese. Her hull was settled deep in the water a good foot over her Plimsoll mark. To Church's mind the ship was dangerously overloaded.

Staring astern, Church could see the twenty-four coaling derricks looming through the darkness, their giant clamshell buckets secured for rough weather. He could also make out something else.

The deck amidships appeared to be lifting and dropping in unison with the swells as they passed under the keel.

"My God," he muttered, "the hull is bending with the sea."

Worley didn't bother to look. "Nothing to concern yourself over, son. She's used to a little stress."

"I've never seen a ship twist like this," Church persisted.

Worley dropped into a large wicker chair he kept on the bridge

13

and propped his feet on the binnacle. "Son, no need to worry about the old *Cyclops*. She'll be sailing the seas long after you and me are gone."

Church's apprehension was not soothed by the captain's unconcern. If anything, his sense of foreboding deepened.

After Church turned over the next watch to a fellow officer, he left the bridge and stopped by the radio room to have a cup of coffee with the operator on duty. Sparks, as every wireless man aboard every ship at sea was called, looked up as he entered.

"Mornin', Lieutenant."

"Any interesting news from nearby vessels?"

Sparks lifted his headset from one ear. "Sorry?"

Church repeated the question.

"Only a couple of radiomen on a pair of merchant ships exchanging chess moves."

"You should join in to avoid the monotony."

"Checkers is my game," said Sparks.

"How close are those two merchantmen?"

"Their signals are pretty weak...probably a good hundred miles away."

Church straddled a chair and leaned his arms and chin on the backrest. "Give them a call and ask what sort of sea they're encountering."

Sparks gave a helpless shrug. "I can't."

"Your transmitter acting up?"

"She's fit as a sixteen-year-old Havana whore."

"I don't understand."

"Captain Worley's orders," answered Sparks. "When we left Rio, he called me to his quarters and said not to transmit any messages without his direct order before we dock in Baltimore."

"He give a reason?"

"No, sir."

"Damned odd."

"My hunch is it has something to do with that bigwig we took on as a passenger in Rio."

"The consul general?"

"I received my orders right after he came on board—"

Sparks broke off and pressed the headset to his ears. Then he began

14

scribbling an incoming message on a pad of paper. After a few moments he turned, his face grim.

"A distress signal."

Church stood up. "What position?"

"Twenty miles southeast of the Anguilla Cays."

Church mentally calculated. "That puts them about fifty miles off our bow. What else?"

"Name of vessel, *Crogan Castle*. Prow stove in. Superstructure heavily damaged. Taking on water. Require immediate assistance."

"Prow stove in?" Church repeated in a puzzled tone. "From what?"

"They didn't say, Lieutenant."

Church started for the door. "I'll inform the captain. Tell the *Crogan Castle* we're coming at full steam."

Sparks's face took on a pained look. "Please, sir, I can't."

"Do it!" Church commanded. "I'll take full responsibility."

He turned and ran down the alleyway and up the ladder to the wheelhouse. Worley was still sitting in the wicker chair, swaying with the roll of the ship. His spectacles were dipped low on his nose and he was reading a dog-eared *Liberty* magazine.

"Sparks has picked up an SOS," Church announced. "Less than fifty miles away. I ordered him to acknowledge the call and say we were altering course to assist."

Worley's eyes went wide and he launched himself out of the chair and clutched a startled Church by the upper arms. "Are you crazy?" he roared. "Who in hell gave you the authority to countermand my orders?"

Pain erupted in Church's arms. The viselike pressure from those huge hands felt as if it were squeezing his biceps into pulp. "Good God, Captain, we can't ignore another vessel in distress."

"We damn well can if I say so!"

Church was stunned at Worley's outburst. He could see the reddened, unfocused eyes and smell the breath reeking of whisky. "A basic rule of the sea," Church persisted. "We must render assistance."

"Are they sinking?"

"The message said 'taking on water.'"

Worley shoved Church away. "The hell you say. Let the bastards man the pumps until their ass is saved by any ship but the *Cyclops*."

The helmsman and the duty officer looked on in amazed silence as Church and Worley faced each other with unblinking eyes, the atmosphere in the wheelhouse charged with tension. Any rift that

15

was between them in the past weeks was hurled wide open.

The duty officer made a move as if to intervene. Worley twisted his head and snarled, "Keep to your business and mind the helm."

Church rubbed his bruised arms and glared at the captain. "I protest your refusal to respond to an SOS and I insist it be entered in the ship's log."

"I warn you—"

"I also wish it noted that you ordered the radio operator not to transmit."

"You're out of bounds, mister." Worley spoke coldly, his lips compressed in a tight line, his face bathed in sweat. "Consider yourself under arrest and confined to quarters."

"You arrest any more of your officers," Church snapped, his anger out of control, "and you'll have to run this jinx ship by yourself."

Suddenly, before Worley could reply, the *Cyclops* lurched downward into a deep trough between the swells. From instinct, honed by years at sea, everyone in the wheelhouse automatically grabbed at the nearest secure object to keep his footing. The hull plates groaned under the stress and they could hear several cracking noises.

"Mother of God," muttered the helmsman, his voice edged with panic.

"Shut up!" Worley growled as the *Cyclops* righted herself. "She's seen worse seas than this."

A sickening realization struck Church. "The *Crogan Castle*, the ship that sent the distress signal, said her prow was stove in and her superstructure damaged."

Worley stared at him. "So what?"

"Don't you see, she must have been struck by a giant, rogue wave."

"You talk like a crazy man. Go to your cabin, mister. I don't want to see your face until we reach port."

Church hesitated, his fists clenched. Then slowly his hands relaxed as he realized any further argument with Worley was a waste of breath. He turned without a word and left the wheelhouse.

He stepped onto the deck and stared out over the bow. The sea appeared deceptively mild. The waves had diminished to ten feet and no water was coming over the deck. He made his way aft and saw that the steam lines that ran the winches and auxiliary equipment were scraping against the bulwarks as the ship rose and fell with the long, slow swells.

Then Church went below and checked two of the ore holds, probing his flashlight at the heavy shorings and stanchions installed to

16

keep the manganese cargo from shifting. They groaned and creaked under the stress, but they seemed firm and secure. He could not see any sign of trickling grit from the ship's motion.

Still, he felt uneasy, and he was tired. It took all his willpower to keep from heading to the snug confines of his bunk and gratefully closing his eyes to the grim set of problems surrounding the ship. One more inspection tour down to the engine room to see if any water was reported rising in the bilges. A trip that proved negative, seeming to confirm Worley's faith in the *Cyclops*.

As he was walking down a passageway toward the wardroom for a cup of coffee a cabin door opened and the American consul general to Brazil, Alfred Gottschalk, hesitated on the threshold, talking to someone inside. Church peered over Gottschalk's shoulder and saw the ship's doctor bent over a man lying in a bunk. The patient's face looked tired and yellow-skinned, a youngish face that belied the thick forest of white hair above. The eyes were open and reflected fear mingled with suffering and hardship, eyes that had seen too much. The scene was only one more strange element to be added to the voyage of the *Cyclops*.

As officer of the deck before the ship departed Rio de Janeiro, Church had observed a motor caravan arrive on the dock. The consul general had stepped out of a chauffeur-driven town car and directed the loading of his steamer trunks and suitcases. Then he looked up, taking in every detail of the *Cyclops* from her ungainly straight-up-and-down bow to the graceful curve of her champagne-glass stern. Despite his short, rotund, and almost comical frame, he radiated that indefinable air of someone accustomed to the upper rungs of authority. He wore his silver-yellow hair cropped excessively short, Prussian style. His narrow eyebrows very nearly matched his clipped moustache.

The second vehicle in the caravan was an ambulance. Church watched as a figure on a stretcher was lifted out and carried on board, but he failed to discern any features because of heavy mosquito netting that covered the face. Though the person on the stretcher was obviously part of his entourage, Gottschalk took little notice, turning his attention instead to the chain-drive Mack truck that brought up the rear.

He gazed anxiously as a large oblong crate was hoisted in the air by one of the ship's loading booms and swung into the forward cargo compartment. As if on cue, Worley appeared and personally supervised the battening down of the hatch. Then he greeted Gottschalk

17

and escorted him to his quarters. Almost immediately, the mooring lines were cast off and the ship got under way and was heading out to sea through the harbor entrance.

Gottschalk turned and noticed Church standing in the passageway. He stepped from the cabin and closed the door behind him, his eyes narrowed with suspicion. "Something I can help you with, Lieutenant..."

"Church, sir. I was just finishing an inspection of the ship and heading for the wardroom for a cup of coffee. Would you care to join me?"

A faint expression of relief passed over the consul general's face and he smiled. "Might as well. I can never sleep more than a few hours at a stretch. Drives my wife crazy."

"She remain in Rio this trip?"

"No, I sent her on ahead to our home in Maryland. I terminated my assignment in Brazil. I hope to spend the rest of my State Department service in Washington."

Gottschalk appeared unduly nervous to Church. His eyes darted up and down the passageway, and he constantly dabbed a linen handkerchief at his small mouth. He took Church by the arm.

"Before we have coffee, would you be so kind, Lieutenant, as to escort me to the baggage cargo hold?"

Church stared at him. "Yes, sir, if you wish."

"Thank you," said Gottschalk. "I need something from one of my trunks."

If Church thought the request unusual, he said nothing, simply nodded and started off toward the forward part of the ship with the fat little consul general huffing in his wake. They made their way topside and walked along the runway leading from the aft deckhouses toward the forecastle, passing under the bridge superstructure awkwardly suspended on steel stiltlike stanchions. The steaming light, suspended between the two forward masts that formed a support for the skeletal grid connecting the coaling derricks, cast a weird glow that was reflected by the eerie radiance of the approaching swells.

Stopping at a hatch, Church undogged the latches and motioned Gottschalk down a ladder, illuminating the way with his flashlight. When they reached the bottom deck of the cargo hold, Church found the switch and flicked on the overhead lights, which lit the area with an unearthly yellow glow.

Gottschalk shouldered past Church and walked directly to the crate, which was secured by chains whose end links were padlocked into

18

eyebolts protruding from the deck. He stood there for a few moments, a reverent expression on his face as he stared at it, his thoughts wandering in another place, another time.

Church studied the crate up close for the first time. There were no markings on the stout wooden sides. He judged its measurements at nine feet long by three feet high by four feet wide. He couldn't begin to guess the weight, but knew the contents were heavy. He recalled how the winch had strained when it hoisted the crate on board. Curiosity overcame his mask of unconcern.

"Mind if I ask what's inside?"

Gottschalk's gaze remained on the crate. "An archeological artifact on its way to a museum," he said vaguely.

"Must be valuable," Church probed.

Gottschalk did not answer. Something along the edge of the lid struck his eye. He pulled out a pair of reading spectacles and peered through the lenses. His hands trembled and his body stiffened.

"It's been opened!" he gasped.

"Not possible," said Church. "The top is so tightly secured by chains that the links have made indentations on the edges of the wood."

"But look here," he said, pointing. "You can see the pry marks where the lid was forced up."

"Those scratches were probably caused when the crate was sealed."

"They were not there when I checked the crate two days ago," said Gottschalk firmly. "Someone in your crew had tampered with it."

"You're unduly concerned. What crew member would have any interest in an old artifact that must weigh at least two tons? Besides, who else but you has the key to the padlocks?"

Gottschalk dropped to his knees and jerked one of the locks. The shackle came off in his hand. Instead of steel, it was carved from wood. He looked frightened now. As if hypnotized, he slowly rose, looked wildly about the cargo compartment, and uttered one word.

"Zanona."

It was as if he triggered a nightmare. The next sixty seconds were locked in horror. The murder of the consul general happened so quickly that Church could only stand frozen in shock, his mind uncomprehending of what his eyes witnessed.

A figure leaped from the shadows onto the top of the crate. He was dressed in the uniform of a Navy seaman, but there was no denying the racial characteristics of his coarse, straight black hair, the prom-

19

inent cheekbones, the unusually dark, expressionless eyes.

Without uttering a sound, the South American Indian plunged a spearlike shaft through Gottschalk's chest until the barbed point protruded nearly a foot beyond the shoulder blades. The consul general did not immediately fall. He slowly turned his head and stared at Church, his eyes wide and devoid of recognition. He tried to say something, but no words came out, only a sickening, gurgling kind of cough that turned his lips and chin red. As he began to sag the Indian put a foot on his chest and yanked out the spear.

Church had never seen the assassin before. The Indian was not one of the *Cyclops'* crew and could only be a stowaway. There was no malevolence in the brown face, no anger or hate, only an inscrutable expression of total blankness. He grasped the spear almost negligently and silently jumped from the crate.

Church braced himself for the onslaught. He deftly sidestepped the spear's thrust and hurled the flashlight at the Indian's face. There was a soft thud as the metal tube smashed into the right jaw, breaking the bone and loosening several teeth. Then he lashed out with his fist and struck the Indian's throat. The spear dropped onto the deck and Church snatched up the wooden shaft and lifted it above his head.

Suddenly, the world inside the cargo compartment went mad and Church found himself fighting to keep his balance as the deck canted nearly sixty degrees. He somehow kept his footing, running downhill with gravity until he reached the slanting forward bulkhead. The Indian's inert body rolled after him, coming to rest at his feet. Then he watched in helpless terror as the crate, unbound by its locks, hurtled across the deck, crushing the Indian and pinning Church's legs against the steel wall. The impact caused the lid to twist half off the crate, revealing the contents.

Church dazedly stared inside. The incredible sight that met his eyes under the flickering overhead lights was the final image burned into his mind during the fractional seconds that separated him from death.

In the wheelhouse, Captain Worley was witnessing an even more awesome sight. It was as though the *Cyclops* had abruptly dropped into a fathomless hole. Her bow pitched sharply into an immense trough and her stern rose steeply into the air until her propellers came clear of the water. Through the gloom ahead, the *Cyclops'* steaming lights reflected on a seething black wall that rose up and blotted out the stars.

20

Deep in the bowels of the cargo holds came a dreadful rumbling that felt and sounded like an earthquake, causing the entire ship to shudder from stem to stern. Worley never had time to voice the alarm that flashed through his mind. The shorings had given way and the shifting manganese ore increased the *Cyclops'* downward momentum.

The helmsman stared out the bridge port in mute astonishment as the towering column, the height of a ten-story building, roared toward them with the speed of an avalanche. The top half crested and curled under. A million tons of water crashed savagely into the forward part of the ship, completely inundating the bow and superstructure. The doors to the bridge wings shattered and water shot into the wheelhouse. Worley gripped the counter railing, his paralyzed mind unable to visualize the inevitable.

The wave swept over the ship. The entire bow section twisted away as steel beams snapped and the keel buckled. The heavy riveted hull plates were ripped away as if they were paper. The *Cyclops* plunged deeper under the immense pressure of the wave. Her propellers bit the water again and helped impel her into the waiting depths. The *Cyclops* could not come back.

She kept on going, down, down, until her shattered hull and the people it imprisoned fell against the restless sands of the sea floor below, leaving only a flight of bewildered seagulls to mark her fateful passage.

PART I

The Prosperteer

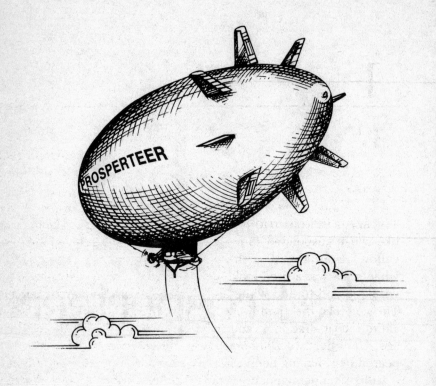

1

October 10, 1989
Key West, Florida

THE BLIMP HUNG MOTIONLESS in the tropical air, poised and tranquil, like a fish suspended in an aquarium. Her bow nudged against a yellow mooring mast as she balanced daintily on a single landing wheel. She was a tired-looking old airship; her once silver skin had wrinkled and turned white and was spotted by numerous patches. The gondola, the control car that hung beneath her belly, wore an antique boat—like look, and its glass windows were yellowed with age. Only her two 200-horsepower Wright Whirlwind engines appeared new, having been carefully restored to pristine condition.

Unlike her younger sister ships that plied the skies above football stadiums, her gas-tight envelope was made from aluminum with riveted seams instead of rubber-coated polyester and was supported by twelve circular frames like the back of a fish. Her cigar shape was 149 feet in length and held 200,000 cubic feet of helium, and if no headwinds attacked her rotund nose, she could barrel through the clouds at sixty-two miles an hour. Her original designation was ZMC-2, Zeppelin Metal Clad Number Two, and she had been constructed in Detroit and turned over to the United States Navy in 1929. Unlike most airships with four massive stabilizing fins, she sported eight small fins on her tapered tail. Very advanced for her era, she had given solid and dependable service until 1942, when she was dismantled and forgotten.

For forty-seven years the ZMC-2 languished in an abandoned hangar along the runway of a deserted naval air station near Key West, Florida. Then in 1988, the property was sold by the government to a financial conglomerate headed by a wealthy publisher, Raymond LeBaron, who intended to develop it as a resort.

Shortly after arriving from his corporate headquarters in Chicago to inspect the newly purchased naval base, LeBaron stumbled onto the dusty and corroded remains of the ZMC-2 and became intrigued. Charging it off to promotion, he had the old lighter-than-air craft reassembled and the engines rebuilt, calling her the *Prosperteer* after the business magazine that was the base of his financial empire, and emblazoning the name in huge red letters on the side of the envelope.

LeBaron learned to fly the *Prosperteer*, mastering the fickle moods of the craft and the constant adjustments required to maintain steady flight under the capricious nature of the wind. There was no autopilot to relieve the chore of dipping the bow against a sudden gust and lifting it when the breeze slackened. The near-neutral buoyancy varied greatly with the atmosphere. Residue from a light rain could add hundreds of pounds to the blimp's vast skin, decreasing her ability to lift, while dry air blowing down from the northwest forced the pilot to fight the craft's insistence on rising to an undesired altitude.

LeBaron reveled in the challenge. The exhilaration of second-guessing the moods of the antique gas bag and wrestling with her aerodynamic whims far exceeded any enjoyment he received from flying any of the five jet aircraft belonging to his corporate holdings. He sneaked away from the boardroom at every opportunity to travel to Key West so he could island-hop around the Caribbean. The *Prosperteer* soon became a familiar sight over the Bahama Islands. A native worker, laboring in a sugarcane field, looked up at the blimp and promptly described her as a "little pig running backwards."

LeBaron, however, like most entrepreneurs of the power elite, suffered from a restless mind and a driving urge to tackle a new project lying over the next hill. After nearly a year his interest in the old blimp began to wane.

Then one evening in a waterfront saloon he met an old beach rat by the name of Buck Caesar, who operated a backwater salvage company with the grandiloquent title "Exotic Artifact Ventures, Inc."

During a conversation over several rounds of iced rum, Caesar spoke the magic word that has fired the human mind into insanity for five thousand years and probably caused more grief than half the wars: *treasure*.

After listening to Caesar spin tales of Spanish galleons littering

26

the waters of the Caribbean, their cargoes of gold and silver mingled with the coral, even a shrewd financial manipulator with the acute business sense of LeBaron was hooked. With a handshake they formed a partnership.

LeBaron's interest in the *Prosperteer* was revived. The blimp made a perfect platform for spotting potential shipwreck sites from the air. Airplanes moved too fast for aerial survey, while helicopters had a limited flying time and churned up the surface of the water with wash from their rotor blades. The blimp could remain airborne for two days and cruise at a walk. From an altitude of 400 feet, the straight lines of a man-made object could be detected by a sharp eye a hundred feet beneath a calm and clear sea.

Dawn was crawling over the Florida Straits as the ten-man ground crew assembled around the *Prosperteer* and began a preflight inspection. The new sun caught the huge envelope covered by morning dew, giving off an iridescent effect like that from a soap bubble. The blimp stood in the center of a concrete runway whose expansion cracks were lined with weeds. A slight breeze blew in from the straits and she swung around the mooring mast until her bulbous nose faced into it.

Most of the ground crew were young, deeply tanned, and casually dressed in an assortment of shorts, bathing suits, and denim cutoffs. They took scant notice as a Cadillac stretch limousine drove across the runway and stopped at the large truck that served as the blimp's repair shop, crew chief's office, and communications room.

The chauffeur opened the door and LeBaron unlimbered from the rear seat, followed by Buck Caesar, who immediately made for the blimp's gondola with a roll of nautical charts tucked under one arm. LeBaron, looking a very trim and healthy sixty-five, towered above everyone at six foot seven. His eyes were the color of light oak, the graying hair combed just so, and he possessed the distant, preoccupied gaze of a man whose thoughts were several hours in the future.

He bent down and spoke for a few moments to an attractive woman who leaned from the car. He kissed her lightly on the cheek, closed the car door, and began walking toward the *Prosperteer.*

The crew chief, a studious-looking man wearing a spotless white shop coat, came over and shook LeBaron's outstretched hand. "Fuel tanks are topped off, Mr. LeBaron. The preflight check list is completed."

"How's the buoyancy?"

27

"You'll have to adjust for an extra five hundred pounds from the dampness."

LeBaron nodded thoughtfully. "She'll lighten in the heat of the day."

"The controls should feel more responsive. The elevator cables were showing signs of rust, so I had them replaced."

"What's the weather look like?"

"Low scattered clouds most of the day. Little chance of rain. You'll be bucking a five-mile-an-hour head wind from the southeast on the way out."

"And a tail wind on the return trip. I prefer that."

"Same radio frequency as the last trip?"

"Yes, we'll report our position and condition, using normal voice communication, every half hour. If we spot a promising target we'll transmit in code."

The crew chief nodded. "Understood."

Without further conversation LeBaron climbed the ladder to the gondola and settled in the pilot's seat. He was joined by his copilot, Joe Cavilla, a sixty-year-old, sad-eyed, dour individual who seldom opened his mouth except to yawn or sneeze. His family had immigrated to America from Brazil when he was sixteen and he had joined the Navy, flying blimps until the last airship unit was formally disbanded in 1964. Cavilla had simply showed up one day, impressed LeBaron with his expertise in lighter-than-air craft, and was hired.

The third member of the crew was Buck Caesar. He wore a constant smile on a gentle, middle-aged face that had the texture of cowhide, but his gaze was shrewd, and the body held the firmness of boxer. He sat hunched over a small table contemplating his charts, drawing a series of squares near a sector of the Bahama Channel.

Blue smoke burst from the exhaust stacks as LeBaron turned over the engines. The ground crew untied a number of canvas sacks containing ballast shot from the gondola. One crewman, the "butterfly catcher," held up a windsock on a long pole so LeBaron could note the exact direction of the wind.

LeBaron gave a hand signal to the crew chief. A wooden chock was pulled from the landing wheel, the nose coupling was released from the mooring mast, and the men holding the bow ropes heaved to one side and let go. When the airship was free and clear of the mast, LeBaron eased the throttles forward and spun the large elevator wheel next to his seat. The *Prosperteer* pointed her comic-opera snout upward at a fifty-degree angle and slowly drove into the sky.

The ground crew watched until the huge airship gradually faded from view over the blue-green waters of the straits. Then their interest turned briefly to the limousine and the vague feminine shape behind the tinted windows.

Jessie LeBaron shared her husband's passion for outdoor adventure, but she was an orderly woman, who preferred organizing charity balls and political fund raisers over a time-wasting hunt for dubious treasure. Vibrant and bouncy, with a mouth that had a repertory of a dozen different smiles, she was six months past fifty but looked closer to thirty-seven. Jessie was slightly heavy-bodied but firm, her facial skin was creamy smooth, and she had allowed her hair to turn a natural salt-and-pepper. The eyes were large and dark and bore no trace of the blank look usually left by plastic surgery.

When she could no longer see the blimp, Jessie spoke into the limousine's intercom. "Angelo, please drive back to the hotel."

The chauffeur, a somber Cuban with the etched face of a postage stamp engraving, touched two fingers to the brim of his cap and nodded.

The ground crew watched the long Cadillac turn and head through the deserted front gate of the former naval base. Then someone produced a volleyball. Quickly they drew out the boundaries and set up a net. After choosing up sides, they began batting the ball back and forth to fight the boredom of waiting.

Inside the air-conditioned truck, the crew chief and a radio operator acknowledged and recorded the reports from the blimp. LeBaron religiously transmitted every thirty minutes, never varying more than a few seconds, describing his approximate position, any changes in weather, and vessels passing below.

Then, at half past two in the afternoon, the reports stopped. The radio operator tried to raise the *Prosperteer,* but there was no response. Five o'clock came and went with still no word. Outside, the ground crew wearily ceased their play and crowded around the door to the radio compartment as the uneasiness inside began to grow. At six o'clock, with no sign of the blimp over the sea, the crew chief put in a call to the Coast Guard.

What no one knew, or possibly suspected, was that Raymond LeBaron and his friends on board the *Prosperteer* had vanished in a mystery that went far beyond any mere treasure hunt.

2

TEN DAYS LATER, the President of the United States stared pensively out the window of his limousine at the passing landscape and idly drummed his fingers on one knee. His eyes didn't see the picturesque estates amid the horse country of Potomac, Maryland. He took scant notice of the sun gleaming on the coats of the Thoroughbreds roaming the rolling pastures. The images that reflected in his mind coursed around the strange events that had literally hurled him into the White House.

As the Vice President he was sworn into the nation's highest office when his predecessor was forced to resign after admitting to a mental illness. Mercifully, the news media did not launch a full-blown investigation. Of course there were the routine interviews with White House aides, congressional leaders, and noted psychiatrists, but nothing smelling of intrigue or conspiracy emerged. The former President left Washington and retired to his farm in New Mexico, still respected with great sympathy from the public, and the truth remained locked in the minds of a very few.

The new Chief Executive was an energetic man who stood slightly over six feet and weighed a solid two hundred pounds. His face was square-jawed, with firm features and a brow that was usually furrowed in a thoughtful frown, yet his intense gray eyes could be deceptively limpid. The silver hair was always neatly trimmed and parted on the right side in the homespun style of a Kansas banker.

He was not handsome or flamboyant in the eyes of the public, but emitted an appealing style and charm. Though he was a professional politician, he somewhat naïvely viewed the government as a giant team with himself as the coach who sent in plays during the game. Highly regarded as a mover and shaker, he surrounded himself with a cabinet and staff of gifted men and women who made every effort to work in harmony with Congress rather than enlisting a band of cronies who were more concerned with fortifying their personal power base.

His thoughts slowly focused on the local scenery as his Secret Service driver slowed down and turned off River Road North through a large stone gate bordered by a white rail fence. A uniformed security guard and a Secret Service agent wearing the standard dark sunglasses and business suit stepped from the gatehouse. They simply peered in the car and nodded in recognition. The agent spoke into a small radio transmitter strapped to his wrist like a watch.

"The Boss is on his way."

The limousine rolled up the tree-lined circular drive of the Congressional Country Club, past the tennis courts on the left teeming with the staring wives of the members, and eased to a stop under the portico of the clubhouse.

Elmer Hoskins, the advance man, stepped forward and opened the rear door. "Looks like a good day for golf, Mr. President."

"My game couldn't get worse if we were standing in snow," the President said, smiling.

"I wish I could shoot in the low eighties."

"So do I," said the President as he followed Hoskins around the side of the clubhouse and down to the pro shop. "I've added five strokes to my score since taking over the Oval Office."

"Still, not bad for someone who only plays once a week."

"That and the fact it becomes increasingly difficult to keep my mind on the game."

The club pro came over and shook his hand. "Reggie has your clubs and is waiting on the first tee."

The President nodded and they climbed into a golf cart and set off over a path that curved around a large pond and onto one of the longest golf courses in the nation. Reggie Salazar, a short, wiry Hispanic, stood leaning on a huge leather bag packed with golf clubs that came up to his chest.

Salazar's appearance was deceiving. Like a small Andes Mountains burro, he could lug a fifty-pound bag of irons around eighteen holes without losing a breath or showing a drop of sweat. When he was only a boy of thirteen he had carried his ailing mother in his arms with a three-year-old sister strapped to his back across the California/ Baja border thirty miles to San Diego. After the illegal alien amnesty was granted in 1985 he worked around golf courses, becoming a top caddy on the professional tour. He was a genius at learning the rhythm

31

of a course, claiming it spoke to him, and unerringly picking the right club for a difficult shot. Salazar was also a wit and a philosopher, blurting adages that would have made Casey Stengel envious. The President had drawn him in a congressional tournament five years before and they became good friends.

Salazar always dressed like a field laborer—denim jeans, western shirt, GI boots, and a rancher's wide-brimmed straw hat. It was his trademark.

"*Saludos*, Mr. President," he greeted in border English, his dark coffee-brown eyes glistening. "Do you wish to walk or ride the cart?"

The President pressed Salazar's outstretched hand. "I could use the exercise, so let's walk for a while and maybe ride the back nine."

He teed off and hit a lofting ball with a slight hook that stopped rolling 180 yards up and near the border of the fairway. As he strolled from the tee the problems of running the country melted away and his mind began planning the next shot.

He played in silence until he dropped his putt in the cup for a par. Then he relaxed and handed his putter to Salazar. "Well, Reggie, any suggestions for dealing with Capitol Hill?"

"Too many black·ants," Salazar replied with an elastic grin.

"Black ants?"

"Everyone wear dark suits and run crazy. All they make is paper and wave tongues. Me, I'd write law saying congresspeople could only meet every other year. That way they'd cause less trouble."

The President laughed. "I can think of at least two hundred million voters who would applaud your idea."

They continued along the course, followed at a discreet distance by two Secret Service agents in a golf cart while at least a dozen others prowled the course grounds. The banter remained cheerful as the President's game went smoothly. After he retrieved the ball from the cup on the ninth green, his score tallied thirty-nine. He considered it a minor triumph.

"Let's take a break before we attack the back nine," said the President. "I'm going to celebrate with a beer. Care to join me?"

"No, thank you, sir. I'll use the time to clean grass and dirt from your clubs."

The President handed him the putter. "Suit yourself. But I must insist you join me for a drink after we finish the eighteenth."

Salazar beamed like a lighthouse. "An honor, Mr. President." Then he trotted off toward the caddy shack.

Twenty minutes later, after returning a call from his chief of staff and downing a bottle of Coors, the President left the clubhouse and joined Salazar, who was sitting slouched in a golf cart on the tenth tee, the wide brim of his straw hat pulled low over his forehead. His hands hung loosely draped on the steering wheel and were now encased in a pair of leather work gloves.

"Well, let's see if I can break eighty," said the President, his eyes glistening in anticipation of a good game.

Salazar said nothing and simply held out a driver.

The President took the club and looked at it, puzzled. "This is a short hole. Don't you think a number three wood should do the job?"

Staring at the ground, the hat hiding any facial expression, Salazar silently shook his head.

"You know best," the President said agreeably. He approached the ball, flexed his hands on the club, arched into a back swing, and brought the head down gracefully but entered into a rather awkward follow-through. The ball sailed straight over the fairway and landed a considerable distance beyond the green.

A perplexed expression spread across the President's face as he retrieved his tee and climbed in the seat of the electric cart. "That's the first time I've ever see you call the wrong club."

The caddy did not reply. He pressed the battery pedal and steered the cart toward the tenth green. About halfway down the fairway he reached over and placed a small package on the dashboard shelf directly in front of the President.

"Bringing along a snack in case you get hungry?" asked the President good-naturedly.

"No, sir, it's a bomb."

The President's eyebrows pinched a fraction in irritation. "Not a funny joke, Reggie—"

His words suddenly choked off as the straw hat rose and he found himself staring into the indigo-blue eyes of a total stranger.

3

"PLEASE KEEP YOUR ARMS in their present position," said the stranger conversationally. "I am aware of the hand signal you were advised to give your Secret Service people if you thought your life was endangered."

The President sat like a dead tree, disbelieving, more curious than afraid. He couldn't trust himself to speak at first, to assemble the right words. His eyes remained locked on the package.

"A stupid act," he said finally. "You won't live to enjoy it."

"This is not an assassination. You will not be harmed if you follow my instructions. Do you accept that?"

"You've got guts, mister."

The stranger ignored the remark and kept talking in the tone of a schoolteacher reciting class rules of conduct. "The bomb is a fragmentation type that will shred any flesh and bone within twenty yards. If you attempt to alert your bodyguards I will detonate it with an electronic control strapped to my wrist. Please continue your golf game as if nothing is out of the ordinary."

He stopped the cart several feet from the ball, stepped to the grass, and glanced warily at the Secret Service agents, satisfying himself that they appeared more intent on scanning the woods around the course. Then he reached in the bag and pulled out a six iron.

"It's obvious you don't know crap about golf," said the President, mildly pleased at gaining a small measure of control. "This calls for a chip shot. Hand me a nine iron."

The intruder obliged and stood by while the President chipped onto the green and putted into the cup. When they set off for the next tee, he studied the man seated beside him.

The few strands of gray hair that strayed beneath the straw hat and the lines bordering the eyes revealed an age in the late fifties. The

34

body was slender, almost frail, the hips slim, a good match for Reggie Salazar except this man was a good three inches taller. The facial features were narrow and vaguely Scandinavian. The voice was educated, the cool manner and the squared shoulders suggested someone who was used to authority, yet there was no hint of viciousness or evil.

"I get the crazy impression," said the President calmly, "that you staged this intrusion to make a point."

"Not so crazy. You're very astute. But I would expect no less from a man with your power."

"Who the hell *are* you?"

"For the sake of conversation call me Joe. And I'll save you asking what this is all about as soon as we reach the tee. There is a restroom there." He paused and removed a folder from inside his shirt, sliding it across the seat to the President. "Enter and quickly scan the contents. Take no more than eight minutes. Linger beyond that time and you might arouse the suspicions of your bodyguards. I needn't describe the consequences."

The electric cart slowly eased to a halt. Without a word the President entered the restroom, sat down on the john, and began reading. Precisely eight minutes later he came out, his face a mask of confusion.

"What kind of insane trick have you hatched?"

"No trick."

"I don't understand why you went to such elaborate lengths to force me to read comic-book science fiction."

"Not fiction."

"Then it has to be some sort of con job."

"The Jersey Colony exists," said Joe patiently.

"Yes, and so does Atlantis."

Joe smiled wryly. "You've just been inducted into a very exclusive club. You're only the second President ever to be briefed on the project. Now I suggest you tee off and I'll flesh out the picture as you continue playing around the course. It won't be a complete picture because there is too little time. Also, some details are not necessary for you to know."

"First, one question. You owe me that."

"All right."

"Reggie Salazar?"

"Sleeping soundly in the caddy shack."

"God help you if you're lying."

35

"Which club?" Joe asked blithely.

"A short hole. Give me a four iron."

The President swung mechanically, but the ball flew straight and true, landing and rolling to within ten feet of the cup. He tossed the club at Joe and sat heavily in the cart, waiting.

"Well, then..." Joe began as he accelerated toward the green. "In 1963, only two months before his death, President Kennedy met with a group of nine men at his home in Hyannis Port who proposed a highly secret leapfrog project to be developed behind the scenes of the fledgling man-in-space program. They were an 'inner core' of brilliant young scientists, corporate businessmen, engineers, and politicians who had achieved extraordinary success in their respective fields. Kennedy bought their idea and went so far as to launch a government agency that acted as a front to siphon federal tax money for what was to be code-named Jersey Colony. The pot was also sweetened by the businessmen, who set up a fund to match the government dollar for dollar. Research facilities were created in existing buildings, usually old warehouses, scattered around the country. Millions were saved in start-up costs, while eliminating questions by the curious over new construction of one vast development center."

"How was the operation kept secret?" the President asked. "Surely there were leaks."

Joe shrugged. "A simple technique. The research teams had their own pet projects. Each worked at a different location. The old act of one hand not knowing what the other was doing. The hardware was farmed out to small manufacturers. It was that elementary. The difficult part was coordinating the efforts under NASA's nose without letting their people know what was going on. So phony military officers were moved into the space centers at Cape Canaveral and Houston, also one at the Pentagon to backstop any embarrassing probes."

"Are you saying the Defense Department knows nothing of this?"

Joe smiled. "The easiest part. One member of the 'inner core' was a high-ranking staff officer, whose name is of no importance to you. He had no problem burying another military mission in the labyrinth of the Pentagon."

Joe paused as they pulled up beside the ball. The President played another shot as if he were sleepwalking. He returned to the cart and stared at Joe.

"Doesn't seem possible NASA could be so completely hoodwinked."

"Again, one of the Space Administration's key directors belonged to the 'inner core.' His vision was also that of a permanent base with limitless opportunity instead of focusing on a few temporary manned landings on the lunar surface. But he realized NASA couldn't do two complicated and expensive programs at the same time, so he became a member of the Jersey Colony. The project was kept secret so there would be no interference from the Executive Office, Congress, or the military. As things turned out, it was a wise decision."

"And the bottom line is that the United States has a solid foot on the moon."

Joe nodded solemnly. "Yes, Mr. President, that is correct."

The President could not fully comprehend the enormity of the concept. "Incredible that a project so vast could be carried off behind an impenetrable curtain of security, unknown and undiscovered for twenty-six years."

Joe stared down the fairway. "It would take me a month to describe the problems, the setbacks, and the tragedies that were suffered. The scientific and engineering breakthroughs in developing a hydrogen-reduction process for making water, an oxygen-extraction apparatus, and a power-generating plant whose turbine is driven by liquid nitrogen. The accumulation of materials and equipment launched into designated orbit by a private space agency sponsored by the 'inner core.' The construction of a lunar transfer vehicle designed to ferry it all from earth orbit to the Jersey Colony."

"And this was done under the nose of our entire space program?"

"What was advertised as large communication satellites were disguised sections of the lunar transfer vehicle, each containing a man in an internal capsule. I won't go into the ten years of planning for that moment or the remarkable complexity of their linkup with each other and one of our abandoned space laboratories that was used as a base for the vehicle's assembly. Or the breakthrough in designing a lightweight, efficient solar electric engine using oxygen as the propulsion fuel. But the job was accomplished."

Joe stopped to allow the President to hit another shot. "Then it was a matter of gathering up the life-support systems and supplies already sent into orbit and transporting all of it, actually towing it like a tugboat, to the predetermined site on the moon. Even an old Soviet orbiting laboratory and any useful piece of space junk were pulled to the Jersey Colony. From the beginning, it's been a no-frills operation, the pioneering trek of man from his home on earth, the most important evolutionary step since the first fish struggled onto land over 300 million years ago. But by God, we did it. As we sit here and talk ten men are living and working in a hostile environment 240,000 miles away."

As Joe spoke his eyes took on the look of a messiah. Then the vision faded and he glanced at his watch. "We'd better hurry along before the Secret Service wonders why we're lagging. Anyway, that's the gist of it. I'll try to answer your questions while you play."

The President stared at him in awe. "Jesus," he groaned. "I don't think I can absorb all this."

"My apologies for throwing so much at you in so short a time," said Joe swiftly. "But it was necessary."

"Where exactly on the moon is this Jersey Colony?"

"After studying the photographs from the Lunar Orbiter probes and Apollo missions, we detected a geyser of vapor issuing from a volcanic region in the southern hemisphere of the moon's far side. Closer examination showed it to be a large cavern, perfect shelter for locating the initial installation."

"You said ten men are up there?"

"Yes."

"What about rotation, replacements?"

"No rotation."

"God, that means the original crew who assembled the lunar transport have been in space six years."

"That's true," acknowledged Joe. "One died and seven were added as the base was expanded to support more life."

"What about their families?"

"All bachelors. All knew and accepted the hardship and risk."

"You say I'm only the second President to learn of the project?"

"That's correct."

"Not allowing the nation's Chief Executive to share in the project is an insult to the office."

Joe's dark blue eyes deepened even more; he stared at the President with stern malice. "Presidents are political animals. Votes become more precious than treasure. Nixon might have used the Jersey Colony as a smokescreen to bail himself out of Watergate. Same with Carter and the Iranian hostage fiasco. Reagan to enhance his image while lording it over the Russians. What's even more deplorable is the thought of what Congress would do with the project, the partisan politics that would come into play as debate raged to no good purpose over whether the money would be better spent on defense or feeding

38

the poor. I love my country, Mr. President, and consider myself a better patriot than most, but I no longer have any faith in the government."

"You took the people's tax dollars."

"Which will be repaid with interest from scientific benefits. But do not forget, private individuals and their corporations contributed half the money, and, I might add, without any thought of profit or personal gain. Defense and space contractors cannot make that claim."

The President did not argue. He quietly set his ball on a tee and socked the ball toward the eighteenth green.

"If you distrust Presidents so much," he said bitterly, "why did you drop out of the heavens to tell *me* all this?"

"We may have a problem." Joe slipped a photograph from the back of the folder and held it up. "Through our connections I've obtained a picture taken from an Air Force stealth aircraft making surveillance flights over Cuba."

The President knew better than to ask how it came to be in Joe's hands. "So what am I looking for?"

"Please study the area above the northern coast of the island and below the Florida Keys."

The President took a pair of glasses from his shirt pocket and peered at the image in the photo. "Looks like the Goodyear blimp."

"No, it's the *Prosperteer*, an old airship belonging to Raymond LeBaron."

"I thought he was lost over the Caribbean two weeks ago."

"Ten days to be exact, along with the blimp and two crewmen."

"Then this photo was taken before he disappeared."

"No, the film came off the aircraft only eight hours ago."

"Then LeBaron must be alive."

"I'd like to think so, but all attempts to raise the *Prosperteer* by radio have gone unanswered."

"What's LeBaron's connection with the Jersey Colony?"

"He was a member of the 'inner core.'"

The President leaned close. "And you, Joe, are you one of the original nine men who conceived the project?"

Joe didn't answer. He didn't have to. The President, staring at him, knew without a doubt.

Satisfied, he sat back and relaxed. "Okay, so what's your problem?"

"In ten days the Soviets will take their newest heavy-lift launch vehicle out of the barn and send it into space with a manned lunar

39

lander that's six times the size and weight of the module used by our astronauts during the Apollo program. You know the details from CIA intelligence reports."

"I've been briefed on their lunar mission," the President agreed.

"And you're also aware that over the past two years they've sent three unmanned probes in orbit around the moon to survey and photograph landing sites. The third and last crashed onto the moon's surface. The second had an engine malfunction and its fuel exploded. The first probe, however, performed successfully, at least in the beginning. It circled the moon twelve times. Then something went wrong. After returning to earth orbit prior to reentry it suddenly refused all commands from the ground. For the next eighteen months, Soviet space controllers worked at bringing the craft down intact. Whether or not they were able to retrieve its visual data, we have no way of knowing. Finally, they managed to fire the retro-rockets. But instead of Siberia, their lunar probe, Selenos 4, landed in the Caribbean Sea."

"What has this to do with LeBaron?"

"He went searching for the Soviet moon probe."

A doubtful look crossed the President's face. "According to CIA reports, the Russians retrieved the craft in deep water off Cuba."

"A smokescreen. They even put on a good show of raising the craft. But in reality, they were never able to find it."

"And your people think they know where it lies?"

"We have a site pinpointed, yes."

"Why would you want to beat the Russians out of a few pictures of the moon? There are thousands of photos available to anybody who wants to study them."

"Those were all taken before Jersey Colony was established. The new Russian survey will no doubt reveal the location."

"What harm could it do?"

"I believe that if the Kremlin discovers the truth, the USSR's first mission to the moon will be to attack, capture our colony, and use it for their own purposes."

"I don't buy that. The Kremlin would be laying their entire space program open for retaliation by our side."

"You forget, Mr. President, our lunar project is blanketed in secrecy. No one can charge the Russians with stealing something that isn't supposed to exist."

"You're stabbing in the dark," the President said sharply.

Joe's eyes hardened. "No matter. Our astronauts were the first to step on the lunar surface. We were the first to colonize it. The moon belongs to the United States and we shall fight any intrusion."

"This isn't the fourteenth century," said the President, shocked. "We can't take up arms and keep the Soviets or anyone else off the moon. Besides, the United Nations ruled that no country had jurisdiction over the moon and planets."

"Would the Kremlin heed U.N. policy if they were in our shoes? I think not." Joe twisted in the seat and extracted a putter from the bag. "The eighteenth green. Your final play, Mr. President."

Dazedly, the President lined up the lay of the green and sank a twenty-foot putt. "I could stop you," he said coldly.

"How? NASA has no ready hardware to land a platoon of Marines on the lunar surface. Thanks to the shortsightedness of you and your predecessors, their efforts are wrapped up in the orbiting space station."

"I can't stand by and allow you to start a war in space that might spill over on earth."

"Your hands are tied."

"You could be wrong about the Russians."

"Let us hope so," said Joe. "But I suspect they may have already killed Raymond LeBaron."

"And this is why you've taken me into your confidence?"

"If the worst happens, at least you have been alerted to the facts and can prepare your strategy for the bedlam to follow."

"Suppose I have my bodyguards arrest you as a crackpot assassin, and then blow the lid off Jersey Colony?"

"Arrest me and Reggie Salazar dies. Expose the project and all the behind-the-scenes double-dealing, the backstabbing, the fraud and the lies, and, yes, the deaths that took place to accomplish what has been achieved, will be laid on your political doorstep, beginning when you were sworn into the Senate. You'll get bounced out of the White House under a bigger cloud than Nixon, providing, of course, you live that long."

"You're threatening me with blackmail?" So far the President had kept his anger under control but now he was seething with fury. "Salazar's life would be a small price to pay to preserve the integrity of the presidency."

"Two weeks, then you can announce the existence of the Jersey Colony to the world. With trumpets sounding and drums beating you can play the big political hero. Two weeks, and you can demonstrate proof of this century's greatest scientific achievement."

41

"After all this time, why then?"

"Because that's when we've scheduled the original crew to leave Jersey Colony and return to earth with the accumulation of two decades of space research—reports on meteorological and lunar probes; the scientific results on thousands of biological, chemical, and atmospheric experiments; uncountable photographs and miles of video records of the first human establishment of a planetary civilization. The first phase of the project is completed. The dream of the 'inner core' is finished. Jersey Colony now belongs to the American people."

The President toyed with his putter thoughtfully. Then he asked, "Who are you?"

"Look to your memory. We knew each other many years ago."

"How am I to contact you?"

"I'll arrange another meeting when I feel it's required." Joe lifted the clubs from the cart's rack and began walking along a narrow path toward the clubhouse. Then he stopped and came back.

"By the way, I lied. That's not a bomb, but a present from the 'inner core'—a new box of golf balls."

The President gazed at him in frustration. "Burn in hell, Joe."

"Oh, and one more thing... congratulations."

"Congratulations?"

Joe handed him the scorecard. "I kept track of your play. You hit a seventy-nine."

4

THE SLEEK HULL of the sailboard skimmed the choppy water with
the graceful elegance of an arrow shot through mist. Its slick and
delicately curved shape was as visually pleasing to the eye as it was
efficient in achieving great speed over the waves. Perhaps the sim-
plest of all sailing systems, the board was built with a polyethylene
shell molded over an inner core of rigid plastic foam to give it light-
ness and flexibility. A small skeg or fin protruded from below the
stern for lateral control, while a daggerboard hung down near the
middle to prevent the board from being swept sideways by the wind.

A triangular sail, dyed purple with a broad turquoise stripe, clung
to an aluminum mast that was mounted onto the board by a universal
joint. An oval tubular wishbone or boom circled the mast and sail,
and was tightly gripped by long, slender hands that were coarse-
skinned and callused.

Dirk Pitt was tired, more tired than his dulled mind could accept.
The muscles of his arms and legs felt as though they were sheathed
in lead and the ache in his back and shoulders grew more intense
with each maneuver of the sailboard. For at least the third time in
the last hour he fought off a growing urge to head for the nearest
beach and stretch out in the sand.

Through the clear window of the sail he studied the orange buoy
marking the final windward leg of the thirty-mile boardsailing marathon race around Biscayne Bay to the Cape Florida lighthouse on
Key Biscayne. Carefully, he chose his position to arc around the buoy.
Deciding on a jibe, the most graceful maneuver in windsurfing, he
threaded his way through the heavy traffic, weighted down the stern
of his board, and aimed the bow on the new course. Then, gripping
the mast with one hand, he swung the rigging to windward, shifted
his feet, and released the boom with his other hand. Next he pulled

the fluttering sail against the wind and caught the boom at the precise moment. Propelled by a fresh twenty-knot breeze from the north, the sailboard sped through the choppy sea and soon gained a speed of nearly thirty miles an hour.

Pitt was mildly surprised to see that out of a field of forty-one racers, most of them at least fifteen years younger, he was in third place, only twenty yards behind the leaders.

The multicolored sails from the fleet of windsurfers flashed across the blue-green water like a prism gone mad. The finish at the lighthouse was in sight now. Pitt closely watched the boardsailer ahead of him, waiting for the right moment to attack. But before he attempted to pass, his opponent miscalculated a wave and fell. Now Pitt was second, with only half a mile to go.

Then, ominously, a dark shadow in a cloudless sky passed overhead and he heard the exhaust of propeller-driven aircraft engines above and slightly to his left. He stared upward and his eyes widened in disbelief.

No more than a hundred yards away, shielding the sun like an eclipse, a blimp was descending from the sky, her great bow set on a collision course with the sailboard fleet. She appeared to be drifting out of control. Her two engines were barely turning over at idle speed, but she was swept through the air by the strong breeze. The sailboarders watched helplessly as the giant intruder crossed their path.

The gondola struck the crest of a wave and the blimp bounced back into the air, leveling off five feet above the water in front of the lead boardsailer. Unable to turn in time, the young boy, no more than seventeen, dove from his board an instant before his mast and sail were minced to shreds under the blimp's starboard propeller.

Pitt nimbly carved a sharp tack and swung on a parallel course with the rampaging airship. From the corner of his eye he noted the name, *Prosperteer,* in huge red letters on her side. The gondola door was open, but he couldn't make out any movement inside. He shouted, but his voice was lost in the exhaust of the engines and rush of the wind. The ungainly craft skidded across the sea as though it had a mind of its own.

Suddenly, Pitt felt the prickle of disaster in the small of his back. The *Prosperteer* was moving toward the beach, only a quarter mile away, and headed directly at the broad terraced side of the Sonesta Beach Hotel. Though the impact of a lighter-than-air ship against a solid structure would cause little damage, there was the ugly certainty of fire from ruptured fuel tanks spilling into the rooms of dozing guests or falling onto the diners on the patio below.

Ignoring the numbing drain of exhaustion, Pitt angled his sailboard on a course that would cross under the great rounded nose. The gondola danced into another swell and a spinning propeller whipped a cloud of salt spray into his eyes. His vision blurred momentarily and he came within inches of losing his balance. He settled in a squatting stance and steadied his tiny craft as he narrowed the distance. Crowds of sunbathers gestured excitedly at the strange sight rapidly approaching the hotel's sloping beach.

Pitt's timing would have to be near perfect; there would be no second attempt. If he missed, there was every chance his body would end up in pieces behind the propellers. He was beginning to feel lightheaded. His strength was nearly sapped. He sensed that his muscles were taking longer to respond to the demands of his brain. He braced himself as his sailboard streaked under the blimp's nose.

Then he leaped.

His hands grasped one of the *Prosperteer*'s bow ropes but slipped on the wet surface, scraping the skin from his fingers and palms. Desperately he swung a leg around the line and held on with every scrap of energy he had left. His weight pulled down the bow and he was dragged under the surface. He clawed up the rope until his head broke free. Then he was gulping air and spitting out seawater. The pursuer had become the captive.

The drag from Pitt's body wasn't nearly enough to stop the air monster, much less slow its momentum from the wind. He was about to release his precarious hold when his feet touched bottom. The blimp carried him through the surge of the surf and he felt like he was riding a roller coaster. Then he was hurtled onto the warm sands of the beach. He looked up and saw the low seawall of the hotel looming a scant hundred feet away.

My God! he thought, this is it—in a few seconds the *Prosperteer* would crash into the hotel and possibly explode. And there was something else. The whirling propellers would shatter on impact, their metal fragments spraying the awestruck crowds with a force as deadly as shrapnel.

"For God's sake, help me!" Pitt shouted.

The mass of people on the beach stood frozen, their mouths gaping, held stupefied in childlike fascination by the strange spectacle. Suddenly two teenage girls and a boy sprang forward and grabbed one of the other tow ropes. Next came a lifeguard, followed by an elderly

45

heavyset woman. Then the dam broke and twenty onlookers surged forward and gathered in the trailing lines. It was as though a tribe of half-naked natives had challenged a maddened brontosaurus to a tug-of-war.

Bare feet dug into the sand, plowing furrows as the stubborn mass above their heads tugged them across the beach. The drag on the bow lines caused the hull to pivot, and the huge finned tail swung around in a 180-degree arc until it was pointing at the hotel, the wheel on the bottom of the gondola scraping through the bushes growing from the top of the seawall, the propellers missing the concrete by inches and chopping through the branches and leaves.

A strong gust of wind blew in from the sea, shoving the *Prosperteer* over the patio, smashing umbrellas and tables, driving her stern toward the fifth story of the hotel. Lines were torn from hands and a wave of helplessness swept over the beach. The battle seemed lost.

Pitt struggled to his feet and half ran, half staggered to a nearby palm tree. In a final desperate act he coiled his line around the slender trunk, feverishly praying it wouldn't snap from the strain.

The line took up the slack and stretched taut. The fifty-foot palm shuddered, swayed, and bent for several seconds. The crowd collectively held its breath. Then with agonizing slowness, the tree gradually straightened into its former upright position. The shallow roots held firm and the blimp stopped, its fins less than six feet from the east wall of the hotel.

Two hundred people gave out a rousing cheer and began applauding. The women jumped up and down and laughed while the men roared and thrust out their hands in the thumbs-up position. No winning team ever received a more spontaneous ovation. The hotel security guards materialized and kept stray onlookers away from the still-turning propellers.

Sand coated Pitt's wet body as he stood there catching his breath, becoming conscious of the pain from his rope-burned hands. Staring up at the *Prosperteer*, he had his first solid look at the airship and was fascinated by the antiquated design. It was obvious she predated the modern Goodyear blimps.

He made his way around the scattered tables and chairs on the patio and climbed into the gondola. The crew were still strapped in their seats, unmoving, unspeaking. Pitt leaned over the pilot, found the ignition switches, and turned them off. The engines popped softly once or twice and went silent as their propellers gave a final twitch and came to rest.

46

The quiet was tomblike.

Pitt grimaced and scanned the interior of the gondola. There was no sign of damage, the instruments and controls appeared to be in operating order. But it was the extensive electronics that amazed him. Gradiometers for detecting iron, side-scan sonar and sub-bottom profiler to sweep the sea floor, everything for an underwater search expedition.

He wasn't aware of the sea of faces peering up into the open door of the gondola, nor did he hear the pulsating scream of approaching sirens. He felt detached and momentarily disoriented. The hot, humid atmosphere was heavy with a morbid eeriness and the sickening stench of human decay.

One of the crewmen was slouched over a small table, head resting on arms as if he were asleep. His clothes were damp and stained. Pitt placed his hand on a shoulder and gave a slight shake. There was no firmness to the flesh. It felt soft and pulpy. An icy shroud fell over him that lifted goose bumps on every inch of his skin, yet the sweat was trickling down his body in streams.

He turned his attention to the ghastly apparitions seated at the controls. Their faces were covered by a blanket of flies, and decomposition was eating away all traces of life. The skin was slipping from the flesh like broken blisters on burns. Jaws hung slack with mouths agape, the lips and tongues swollen and parched. Eyes were open and staring into nothingness, eyeballs opaque and clouded over. Hands still hung on the controls, their fingernails turned blue. Unchecked by enzymes, bacteria had formed gases that grotesquely bloated the stomachs. The damp air and the high temperatures of the tropics were greatly speeding the process of putrefaction.

The rotting corpses inside the *Prosperteer* had flown from some unknown grave, a macabre crew in a charnel airship on a ghostly mission.

5

THE NAKED CORPSE of an adult black woman lay stretched on an examining table under the glaring lights of the autopsy room. Preservation was excellent, no visible injuries due to violence. To the trained eye the state of rigor mortis indicated she had been dead less than seven hours. Her age appeared to be somewhere between twenty-five and thirty. The body might have drawn male stares once, but now it lay undernourished, wasted, and ravaged by a decade of drug intake.

The Dade County coroner, Dr. Calvin Rooney, wasn't too pleased about doing the autopsy. There were enough deaths in Miami to keep his staff working around the clock, and he preferred to spend his time on the more dramatic and puzzling postmortem examinations. A garden-variety drug overdose held little interest for him. But this one was found dumped on a county commissioner's front lawn, and it wouldn't do to send in a third-string quarterback.

Wearing a blue lab coat because he detested the standard white issue, Rooney, a home-grown Floridian, U.S. Army veteran, and Harvard Medical School graduate, slipped a new cassette in a portable tape recorder and dryly commented on the general condition of the body.

He picked up a scalpel and bent over for the dissection, starting a few inches under the chin and slicing downward toward the pubic bone. Suddenly Rooney halted the incision over the chest cavity and leaned closer, squinting through a pair of wide-lensed, horn-rimmed glasses. In the next fifteen minutes, he removed and examined the heart while delivering a running monologue into the tape recorder.

Rooney was in the midst of making a last-minute observation when Sheriff Tyler Sweat entered the autopsy room. He was a medium-built, brooding man, slightly round-shouldered, his face a blend of

48

melancholy and brutish determination. Methodical and shrewdly earnest, he enjoyed great respect from the men and women under him.

He threw an expressionless glance at the opened cadaver and then nodded a greeting to Rooney. "New piece of meat?"

"The woman from the commissioner's yard," answered Rooney.

"Another OD?"

"No such luck. More work for homicide. She was murdered. I found three punctures in the heart."

"Ice pick?"

"From all indications."

Sweat peered at the balding little chief medical examiner, whose benign appearance seemed better suited to a parish priest. "They can't fool you, Doc."

"What brings the master scourge of evildoers to the forensic palace?" Rooney asked amiably. "You slumming?"

"No, an identification by VIPs. I'd like you in on it."

"The bodies from the blimp," Rooney deduced.

Sweat nodded. "Mrs. LeBaron is here to view the remains."

"I don't recommend it. What's left of her husband isn't a pretty sight to someone who doesn't see death every day."

"I tried to tell her that identification of his effects would satisfy legal requirements, but she persisted. Even brought along an aide from the governor's office to grease the way."

"Where are they?"

"Waiting in the morgue office."

"News media?"

"An entire regiment of TV and press reporters running around like crazy people. I've ordered my deputies to keep them confined to the lobby."

"Strange how the world works," said Rooney in one of his philosophical moods. "The renowned Raymond LeBaron gets front-page headlines while this poor baggage gets a column inch next to classified advertising." Then he sighed, removed his lab coat, and threw it over a chair. "Let's get it over with. I've got two more postmortems to conduct this afternoon."

As he spoke a tropical storm passed over and the sound of thunder rumbled through the walls. Rooney slipped on a sports jacket and straightened his tie. They fell into step, Sweat staring down pensively at the design in the hallway carpet.

"Any idea on the cause of LeBaron's death?" asked the sheriff.

49

"Too soon to tell. The lab results were inconclusive. I want to run some more tests. Too many things don't add up. I don't mind admitting, this one is a puzzler."

"No guesses?"

"Nothing I'd put on paper. Problem is the incredibly rapid rate of decomposition. I've seldom seen tissue disintegrate so fast, except maybe once back in 1974."

Before Sweat could prod Rooney's recollection, they reached the morgue office and entered. The governor's aide, a slippery type in a three-piece suit, jumped up. Even before he opened his mouth, Rooney classified him as a jerk.

"Can we please get the show on the road, Sheriff. Mrs. LeBaron is most uncomfortable and would like to return to her hotel as soon as possible."

"I sympathize with her," the sheriff drawled. "But I shouldn't have to remind a public servant that there are certain laws we must follow."

"And I needn't remind you, the governor expects your department to extend every courtesy to ease her grief."

Rooney marveled at Sweat's stony patience. The sheriff simply brushed by the aide as though he were walking past trash on a sidewalk.

"This is our chief medical examiner, Dr. Rooney. He will assist with the identification."

Jessie LeBaron didn't look the least bit uncomfortable. She sat in an orange plastic contour chair, poised, cool, head held high. And yet Rooney sensed a fragility that was held together by discipline and nerve. He was an old hand at presiding over corpse identification by relatives. He'd suffered through the ordeal hundreds of times in his career and instinctively spoke softly and in a gentle manner.

"Mrs. LeBaron, I understand what you're going through and will make this as painless as possible. But first, I wish to make it clear that by simply identifying the effects found on the bodies you will satisfy the laws set down by the state and county. Second, any physical characteristics you can recall, such as scars, dental work, bone fractures, or surgical incisions, will be of great help in my own identification. And third, I respectfully beg you not to view the remains. Though facial features are still recognizable, decomposition has done its work. I think you'd be happier remembering Mr. LeBaron as he was in life rather than how he looks in a morgue."

"Thank you, Dr. Rooney," said Jessie. "I'm grateful for your concern. But I must be certain my husband is truly dead."

Rooney nodded miserably, and then gestured at a worktable containing several pieces of clothing, wallets, wristwatches, and other personal articles. "You've identified Mr. LeBaron's effects?"

"Yes, I have sorted through them."

"And you're satisfied they belonged to him?"

"There can be no doubt about the wallet and its contents. The watch was a gift from me on our first anniversary."

Rooney walked over and held it up. "A gold Cartier with matching band and roman numerals marked in ... am I correct in saying they're diamonds?"

"Yes, a rare form of black diamond. It was his birthstone."

"April, I believe."

She merely nodded.

"Besides your husband's personal articles, Mrs. LeBaron, do you recognize anything belonging to Buck Caesar or Joseph Cavilla?"

"I don't recall the jewelry they wore, but I'm certain the other clothing items are what Buck and Joe were wearing when I last saw them."

"Our investigators can find no next of kin of Caesar and Cavilla," said Sweat. "It would be most helpful if you can point out which articles of clothing belonged to whom."

For the first time Jessie LeBaron faltered. "I'm not sure ... I think the denim shorts and flowered shirt are Buck's. The other things probably belonged to Joe Cavilla." She paused. "May we view my husband's body now?"

"I can't change your mind?" Rooney asked in a sympathetic voice.

"No, I must insist."

"You'd best do what Mrs. LeBaron asks," said the governor's aide, who had yet to introduce himself.

Rooney looked at Sweat and shrugged in resignation. "If you will please follow me. The remains are kept in the refrigeration room."

Obediently, everyone trailed him to a thick door with a small window set at eye level and stood in silence as he yanked on a heavy latch. Cold air spilled over the threshold and Jessie involuntarily shivered as Rooney motioned them inside. A morgue attendant appeared and led the way to one of the square doors along the wall. He swung it open, pulled out a sliding stainless steel table, and stood aside.

Rooney took one corner of the sheet covering the corpse and hesitated. This was the only part of his job he hated. The reaction to viewing the dead usually fell into four categories. Those who vom-

51

ited, those who passed out cold, those who broke into hysterics. But it was the last type that intrigued Rooney. The ones who stood as if turned to stone and showed no emotion at all. He would have given a month's salary to know the thoughts circulating through their minds.

He lifted the sheet.

The governor's aide took one look, made a pathetic groaning sound, and passed out into the arms of the sheriff. The grisly work of decay was revealed in all its horror.

Rooney was astonished by Jessie's response. She stared long and hard at the grotesque thing that lay rotting on the table. She sucked in her breath and her whole body went taut. Then she raised her eyes, not blinking, and spoke in a calm, controlled voice.

"*That* is not my husband!"

"Are you positive?" Rooney asked softly.

"Look for yourself," she said in a flat monotone. "The hairline is wrong. So is the bone structure. Raymond had an angular face. This one is more round."

"Decomposition of the flesh distorts facial features," Rooney explained.

"Please study the teeth."

Rooney looked down. "What about them?"

"They have silver fillings."

"I don't follow."

"My husband's fillings were gold."

There was no arguing with her on that score, thought Rooney. A man of Raymond LeBaron's wealth wouldn't have settled for cheap dental work.

"But the watch, the clothing, you identified them as his."

"I don't give a damn what I said!" she cried. "This loathsome thing is not Raymond LeBaron."

Rooney was stunned at her fury. He stood dazed and unable to speak as she stormed from the icy room. The sheriff handed the limp aide to the morgue attendant and turned to the coroner.

"What in hell do you make of that?"

Rooney shook his head. "I don't know."

"My guess is, she went into shock. Probably fell over the edge and began raving. You know better than I, most people can't accept the death of a loved one. She closed her mind and refused to accept the truth."

"She wasn't raving."

Sweat looked at him. "What do you call it?"

52

"Shrewd acting."

"How did you pick that out of the air?"

"The wristwatch," answered Rooney. "One of my staff worked nights as a jeweler to put himself through medical school. He spotted it right off. The expensive Cartier watch Mrs. LeBaron gave her husband on their anniversary is a fake, one of those inexpensive reproductions that are illegally manufactured in Taiwan or Mexico."

"Why would a woman who could write a check for a million dollars give her husband a cheap imitation?"

"Raymond LeBaron was no slouch when it came to style and taste. He must have recognized it for what it was. Better to ask the question, Why did he stoop to wearing it?"

"So you think she put on an act and lied about the body ID?"

"My gut reaction is that she prepared herself for what to expect," Rooney replied. "And I'd go so far as to bet my new Mercedes-Benz that genetic tracing, the dental report, and the results of the rubber casts I made from what remained of the fingerprints and sent to the FBI lab will prove she was right." He turned and peered at the corpse. "That *isn't* Raymond LeBaron lying there on the slab."

6

DETECTIVE LIEUTENANT HARRY VICTOR, a lead investigator for the Metro Dade County Police Department, sat back in a swivel chair and studied several photographs taken inside the *Prosperteer*'s control cabin. After several minutes, he raised a pair of rimless glasses over a forehead that slipped under a blond hairpiece and rubbed his eyes.

Victor was a tidy man, everything in its correct pigeonhole, neatly alphabetized and consecutively numbered, the only cop in the memory of the department who actually enjoyed making out reports. When most men watched sports on television on weekends or relaxed around a resort swimming pool on vacations, reading Rex Burns detective novels, Victor reviewed files on unsolved cases. A diehard, he was more fanatical about tying up loose ends than obtaining a conviction.

The *Prosperteer* case was unlike any he'd faced in his eighteen years on the force. Three dead men falling out of the sky in an antique blimp didn't exactly lend itself to routine police investigation. Leads were nonexistent. The three bodies in the morgue revealed no clues to where they had been hiding for a week and a half.

He lowered his glasses and was attacking the photographs again when the desk phone buzzed. He lifted the receiver and said pensively, "Yes?"

"You have a witness to see you about a statement," answered the receptionist.

"Send him on back," said Victor.

He closed the file containing the photographs and laid it on the metal desk, whose surface was antiseptic except for a small sign with his name and the telephone. He held the receiver to his ear as though receiving a call and swiveled sideways, looking across the spacious

54

homicide office, keeping his eyes focused at an angle toward the door leading to the corridor.

A uniformed receptionist appeared at the threshold and pointed in Victor's direction. A tall man nodded, eased past her, and approached. Victor gestured to a chair opposite the desk and began muttering in a one-way conversation with the dial tone. It was an old interrogation ploy that gave him an uninterrupted minute to inspect a witness or suspect and mentally construct a profile. Most important, it was an opportunity to observe habits and odd mannerisms that could be used for leverage later.

The male seated across from Victor was about thirty-seven or thirty-eight, approximately six foot three, weight 185, give or take five pounds, black hair tending to be a bit wavy, with no indication of gray. Skin darkened from year-round exposure to the sun. Eyebrows dark and slightly bushy. Straight, narrow nose, lips firm with corners turned up in a slight but fixed grin. Wearing light blue sports coat and off-white slacks, pale yellow polo shirt with collar open. Good taste, casual but not ultraexpensive, probably purchased at Saks rather than a plush men's store. Nonsmoker, as there was no evidence of cigarette package bulge in coat or shirt. Arms were folded, suggesting calm and indifference, and the hands were narrow, long and weathered. No rings or other jewelry, only an old orange-faced diver's watch with a heavy stainless steel band.

This one didn't follow the general pattern. The others who had sat in that chair turned fidgety after a while. Some masked nervousness with arrogance, most restlessly stared around the office, through the windows, at pictures on the walls, at the other officers working their cases, changing position, crossing and recrossing their legs. For the first time Victor could recall, he felt uncomfortable and at a disadvantage. His routine was sidetracked, his act rapidly washing out.

The visitor wasn't the least bit ruffled. He stared at Victor with bemused interest through opaline green eyes that possessed a mesmeric quality. They seemed to pass right through the detective, and finding nothing of interest, examined the paint on the wall behind. Then they dropped to the telephone.

"Most police departments use the Horizon Communications System," he said in an even tone. "If you wish to speak to someone on the other end, I suggest you push a button for an open line."

Victor looked down. One of his four buttons was lit but not punched. "You're very astute, Mr. . . ."

"Pitt, Dirk Pitt. If you're Lieutenant Victor, we had an appointment."

"I'm Victor." He paused to replace the receiver in its cradle. "You were the first person inside the control car of the *Prosperteer* blimp?"

"That's right."

"Thank you for coming in, especially so early on a Sunday. I'd appreciate your cooperation in clearing up a few questions."

"Not at all. Will it take long?"

"Twenty minutes, maybe half an hour. Do you have to be somewhere?"

"I'm booked on a plane for Washington in two hours."

Victor nodded. "I'll get you on your way in plenty of time." He pulled open a drawer and took out a portable tape recorder. "Let's go somewhere more private."

He led Pitt down a long hallway to a small interview room. The interior was spartan, only a desk, two chairs, and an ashtray. Victor sat down and fed a new cassette into the recorder.

"Mind if I put our conversation on tape? I'm a terrible note taker. None of the secretaries can decipher my handwriting."

Pitt shrugged agreeably.

Victor moved the machine to the center of the desk and pressed the red Record button.

"Your name?"

"Dirk Pitt."

"Middle initial?"

"E for Eric."

"Address?"

"266 Airport Place, Washington, D.C. 20001."

"Telephone where you can be reached?"

Pitt gave Victor the phone number of his office.

"Occupation?"

"Special projects director for the National Underwater and Marine Agency."

"Can you describe the event you witnessed on the afternoon of Saturday, October 20?"

Pitt told Victor of his sighting the out-of-control blimp during the sailboard marathon race, the mad ride while clinging to the mooring line, and the last-second capture only a few feet away from potential disaster, ending with his entry into the gondola.

"Did you touch anything?"

"Only the ignition and battery switches. And I laid my hand on the shoulder of the corpse seated at the navigator's table."

"Nothing else?"

"The only other place I might have left a fingerprint was on the boarding ladder."

"And the backrest of the copilot's seat," said Victor with a smug smile. "No doubt when you leaned over and turned off the switches."

"Fast work. Next time I'll wear surgical gloves."

"The FBI was most cooperative."

"I admire competence."

"Did you take anything?"

Pitt shot Victor a sharp look. "No."

"Could anyone else have entered and removed any objects?"

Pitt shook his head. "After I left, the hotel security guards sealed off the gondola. The next person inside was a uniformed police officer."

"Then what did you do?"

"I paid one of the hotel lifeguards to swim out and retrieve my sailboard. He owned a small pickup truck and was kind enough to run me back to the house where I was staying with friends."

"In Miami?"

"Coral Gables."

"Mind if I ask what you were doing in town?"

"I wound up an offshore exploration project for NUMA and decided to take a week's vacation."

"Did you recognize any of the bodies?"

"Not damned likely. I couldn't identify my own father in that condition."

"Any idea who they might be?"

"I assume one of them was Raymond LeBaron."

"You're familiar with the disappearance of the *Prosperteer*?"

"The news media covered the disappearance in great depth. Only a backwoods recluse could have missed it."

"Any pet theories on where the blimp and its crew were buried for ten days?"

"I haven't a clue."

"Not even a wild idea?" Victor persisted.

"Could be a colossal publicity stunt, a media campaign to promote LeBaron's publishing empire."

Interest grew in Victor's eyes. "Go on."

"Or maybe an ingenious scheme to manipulate LeBaron conglomerate stock prices. Sell large blocks before he disappears and buy when prices tumble afterward. And sell again when they rise during his resurrection."

57

"How do you explain their deaths?"

"The plot backfired."

"Why?"

"Ask your coroner."

"I'm asking you."

"They probably ate tainted fish on whatever deserted island they hung out on," said Pitt, tiring of the game. "How would I know? If you want a scenario, hire a screenwriter."

The interest in Victor's eyes blinked out. He relaxed in his chair and sighed dejectedly. "I thought for a second you might have something, a gimmick that could get me and the department off the hook. But your theory went down the drain like all the others."

"I'm not surprised," said Pitt with an indifferent grin.

"How were you able to switch off the power within seconds of entering the control car?" Victor asked, bringing the interrogation back on track.

"After piloting twenty different aircraft during service in the Air Force and civilian life, I knew where to look."

Victor appeared satisfied. "One more question, Mr. Pitt. When you first spotted the blimp, from what direction was she flying?"

"She was drifting with the wind out of the northeast."

Victor reached over and turned off the recorder. "That should do it. Can I reach you at your office number during the day?"

"If I'm not there, my secretary can track me down."

"Thank you for your help."

"Nothing substantial, I'm afraid," said Pitt.

"We have to pull on every thread. Lots of pressure with LeBaron being the bigshot that he was. This has to be the weirdest case the department's ever encountered."

"I don't envy you finding a solution." Pitt glanced at his watch and rose from his chair. "I'd better get a move on for the airport."

Victor stood and reached across the desk to shake hands. "If you should dream up another plot line, Mr. Pitt, please give me a call. I'm always interested in a good fantasy."

Pitt paused in the doorway and turned, a foxlike expression on his face. "You want a lead, Lieutenant? Run this one up the flagpole. Airships need helium for their lift. An old antique like the *Prosperteer* must have required a couple hundred thousand cubic feet of gas to get her in the air. After a week, enough would have leaked out to keep her grounded. Do you follow?"

"Depends on where you're heading."

"There is no way the blimp could have materialized off Miami unless an experienced crew with the necessary supplies reinflated the hull forty-eight hours before."

Victor had the look of a man about to be baptized. "What are you suggesting?"

"That you look for a friendly neighborhood service station that can pump two hundred thousand cubic feet of helium."

Then Pitt turned into the hallway and was gone.

7

"I HATE BOATS," Rooney grumbled. "I can't swim, can't float, and get seasick looking through the window of a washing machine."

Sheriff Sweat handed him a double martini. "Here, this will cure your hangups."

Rooney ruefully eyed the waters of the bay and drained half his drink. "You're not going out in the ocean, I hope."

"No, just a leisurely cruise around the bay." Sweat ducked into the forward cabin of his gleaming white fishing boat and turned over the engine. The single 260-horsepower turbocharged diesel knocked into life. Exhaust rumbled from the stern and the deck throbbed beneath their feet. Then Sweat cast off the lines and eased the boat away from the dock, threading through a maze of moored yachts to Biscayne Bay.

By the time the bow skipped past the channel buoys, Rooney was looking for a second drink. "Where do you keep the courage?"

"Down in the forward cabin. Help yourself. There's ice in the brass diver's helmet."

When Rooney resurfaced he asked, "What's this all about, Tyler? This is Sunday. You didn't drag me away from my season box in the middle of a good football game to show me Miami Beach from the water."

"Truth is, I heard you finished your report on the bodies from the blimp last night."

"Three o'clock this morning, to be exact."

"I thought you might want to tell me something."

"For God's sake, Tyler, what's so damned earthshaking that you couldn't have waited until tomorrow morning?"

"About an hour ago, I got a call from some Fed in Washington." Sweat paused to ease the throttle up a notch. "Said he was with a domestic intelligence agency I'd never heard of. I won't bore you with his downright belligerent talk. Never can understand why everybody up North thinks they can blindside a Southern boy. The upshot was he demanded we turn over the dead from the blimp to federal authorities."

"Which federal authorities?"

"Refused to name them. Got vague as hell when I pushed."

Rooney was suddenly intensely interested. "He give any hint why they wanted the bodies?"

"Claimed it was a security matter."

"You told him no, of course."

"I told him I'd think about it."

The turn of events and the gin combined to make Rooney forget his fear of water. He began to notice the trim lines of the fiberglass craft. It was Sheriff Sweat's second office, occasionally pressed into service as a backup police cruiser, but more often used to entertain county and state officials on weekend fishing trips.

"What do you call her?" Rooney asked.

"Call who?"

"The boat."

"Oh, the *Southern Comfort*. She's a thirty-five-footer, cruises at fifteen knots. Built in Australia by an outfit caled Stebercraft."

"To get back to the LeBaron case," Rooney said, sipping at his martini, "are you going to give in?"

"I'm tempted," said Sweat, smiling. "Homicide has yet to turn up lead one. The news media are making a circus out of it. Everybody from the governor on down is pressuring my ass. And to top it off, there's every likelihood the crime wasn't committed in my jurisdiction. Hell, yes, I'm tempted to pass the buck to Washington. Only I'm just stubborn enough to think we might pull a solution out of this mess."

"All right, what do you want from me?"

The sheriff turned from the helm and looked at him steadily. "I want you to tell me what's in your report."

"My findings made the puzzle worse."

A small sailboat with four teenagers slipped across their bow and Sweat slowed down and gave way. "Tell me about it."

"Let's start at the end and work backwards. Okay with you?"

"Go ahead."

"Threw the hell out of me at first. Mostly because I wasn't looking for it. I had a similar case fifteen years ago. A female body was discovered sitting in a patio chair in her backyard. Her husband claimed they'd been drinking the night before and he'd gone to bed alone, thinking she would follow. When he awoke in the morning and looked around, he found her right where he left her, sitting on the patio, only now she was dead. She had all the appearances of a natural death, no marks of violence, no sign of poison, just a generous amount of alcohol. The organs seemed healthy enough. There were no indications of previous disease or disorder. For a woman of forty she had the body of a twenty-five-year-old. It bugged the hell out of me. Then the pieces began to come together. The postmortem lividity—that's the discoloration of the skin caused by the sinking of blood due to gravity—is usually purplish. Her lividity was cherry pink, which pointed to death from either cyanide or carbon monoxide poisoning or hypothermia. I also discovered hemorrhaging of the pancreas. Through a process of elimination the first two were discarded. The final nail in the coffin was the husband's occupation. The evidence wasn't exactly hard core, but it was enough for the judge to put him away for fifty years."

"What was the husband's line of work?" asked Sweat.

"He drove a truck for a frozen-food company. A neat plan. He pumped booze in her until she passed out. Set her inside his truck, which he always took home nights and weekends, turned up the refrigeration unit, and waited for her to harden. After the poor woman expired, he put her back in the patio chair and went to bed."

Sweat stared blankly. "You're not saying the corpses found in the blimp froze to death."

"I'm saying exactly that."

"No mistake?"

"On a certainty scale from one to ten, I can promise an eight."

"Do you realize how that sounds?"

"Crazy, I would imagine."

"Three men disappear over the Caribbean in ninety-degree weather and freeze to death?" Sweat asked no one in particular. "We'll never make this one stick, Doc. Not without a handy frozen-food truck."

"You've got nothing to stick it to anyway."

"Meaning?"

"The FBI report came in. Jessie LeBaron's ID was on the money. That isn't her husband in the morgue. The other two aren't Buck Caesar or Joseph Cavilla either."

"God, what next," Sweat moaned. "Who are they?"

"There's no record of them in the FBI's fingerprint files. Best guess is they were foreign nationals."

"Did you find anything at all that might give a clue to their identity?"

"I can give you their height and weight. I can show you X rays of their teeth and previous bone fractures. Their livers suggested all three favored generous amounts of hard liquor. The lungs gave away their heavy smoking, teeth and fingertips the fact they smoked unfiltered cigarettes. They were also big eaters. Their last meal consisted of dark bread and various fruits and beets. Two were in their early thirties. One was forty or over. They were in above-average physical condition. Beyond that I can tell you very little that might pin an ID on them."

"It's a start."

"But it still leaves us with LeBaron, Caesar, and Cavilla among the missing."

Before Sweat could reply a female voice rasped out his boat's call sign over the radio speaker. He answered and turned to another channel frequency as instructed.

"Sorry for the interruption," he said to Rooney. "I've got an emergency call over the ship-to-shore phone."

Rooney nodded, went into the forward cabin, and poured himself another drink. A delicious glow coursed through his body. He took a few moments to go to the head. When he returned topside to the wheelhouse, Sweat was hanging up the phone, his face red with anger.

"The rotten bastards!" he hissed.

"What's the problem?" Rooney asked.

"They seized them," Sweat said, pounding the helm with his fist. "The damned Feds walked into the morgue and seized the bodies from the blimp."

"But there are legal procedures to follow," Rooney protested.

"Six men in plainclothes and two federal marshals showed up with the necessary paperwork, stuffed the corpses into three aluminum canisters filled with ice, and took off in a U.S. Navy helicopter."

"When did this happen?"

"Not ten minutes ago. Harry Victor, the lead investigator on the case, says they also rifled his desk in the homicide office when he was in the john and ripped off his files."

"What about my autopsy report?"

"They lifted that too."

The gin had put Rooney in a euphoric mood. "Oh, well, look at it this way. They took you and the department off the hook."

Sweat's anger slowly subsided. "I can't deny they did me a favor, but it's their method that pisses me off."

"There's one small consolation," mumbled Rooney. He was beginning to have trouble standing. "Uncle Sam didn't get everything."

"Like what?"

"Something omitted from my report. One lab result that was too controversial to put on paper, too wild to mention outside a looney house."

"What are you talking about?" Sweat demanded.

"The cause of death."

"You said hypothermia."

"True, but I left out the best part. You see, I neglected to state the time of death." Rooney's speech was becoming slurred.

"Could only be within the last few days."

"Oh, no. Those poor guys froze their guts a long time ago."

"How long?"

"Anywhere from one to two years ago."

Sheriff Sweat stared at Rooney, incredulous. But the coroner stood there grinning like a hyena. He was still grinning when he sagged over the side of the boat and threw up.

8

THE HOME OF DIRK PITT was not on a suburban street or in a high-rise condominium overlooking the jungled treetops of Washington. There was no landscaped yard or next-door neighbors with squealing children and barking dogs. The house was not a house but an old aircraft hangar that stood on the edge of the capital's International Airport.

From the outside it appeared deserted. Weeds surrounded the building and its corrugated walls were weathered and devoid of paint. The only clue remotely suggesting any occupancy was a row of windows running beneath the huge curved roof. Though they were stained and layered with dust, none were shattered like those of an abandoned warehouse.

Pitt thanked the airport maintenance man who had given him a lift from the terminal area. Glancing around to see that he wasn't observed, he took a small transmitter from his coat pocket and issued a series of voice commands that closed down the security systems and opened a side door that looked as if it hadn't swung on its hinges for thirty years.

He entered and stepped onto a polished concrete floor that held nearly three dozen gleaming, classic automobiles, an antique airplane, and a turn-of-the-century railroad car. He paused and stared fondly at the chassis of a French Talbot-Lago sports coupé that was in an early stage of reconstruction. The car had been nearly destroyed in an explosion, and he was determined to restore the twisted remains to their previous elegance and beauty.

He hauled his suitcase and garment bag up a circular staircase to his apartment, elevated against the far wall of the hangar. His watch read 2:15 P.M., but his mind and body felt as though it was closer to midnight. After unpacking his luggage, he decided to spend a few hours working on the Talbot-Lago and take a shower later. He had already donned a pair of old coveralls and his hand was pulling open the drawer of a toolbox, when a loud chime echoed through the hangar. He pulled a cordless phone from a deep pocket.

"Hello."

"Mr. Pitt, please," said a female voice.

"Speaking."

"One moment."

After waiting for nearly two minutes, Pitt cut the connection and began rebuilding the Talbot's distributor. Another five minutes passed before the chime sounded again. He opened the line and said nothing.

"Are you still there, sir?" asked the same voice.

"Yes," Pitt replied indifferently, tucking the phone between his shoulder and ear as he kept working with his hands.

"This is Sandra Cabot, Mrs. Jessie LeBaron's personal secretary. Am I talking to Dirk Pitt?"

Pitt took an instant dislike to people who couldn't dial their own phone calls. "You are."

"Mrs. LeBaron wishes to meet with you. Can you come to the house at four o'clock?"

"Pretty fast off the mark, aren't you?"

"I beg your pardon?"

"Sorry, Miss Cabot, but I have to doctor a sick car. Maybe if Mrs. LeBaron cares to drop by my place, we could talk."

"I'm afraid that won't do. She's holding a formal cocktail party in the greenhouse later in the evening that will be attended by the Secretary of State. She can't possibly break away."

"Some other time then."

There was an icy silence, then Miss Cabot said, "You don't understand."

"You're right, I don't understand."

"Doesn't the name LeBaron mean anything to you?"

"No more than Shagnasty, Quagmire, or Smith," Pitt lied fiendishly.

She seemed lost for a moment. "Mr. LeBaron—"

"We can cut the fun and games," Pitt interrupted. "I'm quite aware of Raymond LeBaron's reputation. And I can save us both time by saying I have nothing to add to the mystery surrounding his disappearance and death. Tell Mrs. LeBaron she has my condolences. That's all I can offer."

Cabot took a deep breath and exhaled. "Please, Mr. Pitt, I know

66

she would be most grateful if you could see her."

Pitt could almost see her speaking the word "please" through clenched teeth. "All right," he said. "I guess I can make it. What's the address?"

The arrogance quickly returned to her tone. "I'll send the chauffeur to pick you up."

"If it's all the same to you, I'd prefer to drive my own car. I get claustrophobic in limousines."

"If you insist," she said stiffly. "You'll find the house at the end of Beacon Drive in Great Falls Estates."

"I'll check a street map."

"By the way, what kind of car do you drive?"

"Why do you want to know?"

"To inform the guard at the gate."

Pitt hesitated and looked across the hangar floor at a car parked by the main door. "An old convertible."

"Old?"

"Yes, a 1951."

"Then would you be so kind to park in the lot by the servants' house. It's to the right as you come up the drive."

"Aren't you ever ashamed of the way you dictate to people?"

"I don't have to be ashamed of anything, Mr. Pitt. We'll expect you at four."

"Will you be through with me before the guests arrive?" asked Pitt, his voice heavy with sarcasm. "I wouldn't want to embarrass anyone by having them see my old junk car littering the grounds."

"Not to worry," she replied testily. "The party doesn't begin until eight. Goodbye."

After Sandra Cabot hung up, Pitt walked over to the convertible, staring at it for several moments. He removed the floorboards under the rear seat and clipped on the cables of a battery charger. Then he returned to the Talbot-Lago and calmly took up where he left off.

At precisely eight-thirty, the security guard at the LeBaron estate's front gate greeted a young couple driving a yellow Ferrari, checked their names on the party list, and waved them through. Next came a Chrysler limousine carrying the President's chief adviser, Daniel Fawcett, and his wife.

The guard was immune to the exotic cars and their celebrity occupants. He raised his hands over his head in a bored stretch and yawned. Then his hands froze in midair and his mouth snapped shut as he found himself staring at the largest car he'd ever seen.

The car was a veritable monster, measuring nearly twenty-two feet from bumper to bumper and weighing well over three tons. The hood and doors were silver-gray and the fenders a metallic maroon. A convertible, its top was completely hidden from view when folded down. The body lines were smooth and elegant in the grand manner, an example of flawless craftsmanship seldom equaled.

"That's some kind of car," the guard finally said. "What is it?"

"A Daimler," replied Pitt.

"Sounds British."

"It is."

The guard shook his head in admiration and looked at his guest list. "Your name, please."

"Pitt."

"I can't seem to find your name. Do you have an invitation?"

"Mrs. LeBaron and I had an earlier appointment."

The guard went into the gatehouse and checked a clipboard. "Yes, sir, your appointment was for four o'clock."

"When I phoned to say I was running late, she said to join the party."

"Well, since she expected you," the guard said, still soaking in the Daimler's lines, "I guess it's all right. Have a good evening."

Pitt nodded a thank-you and eased the immense car silently up the winding drive to the LeBaron residence. The main building sat on a low hill above a tennis court and a swimming pool. The architecture was common to the area, a three-story brick colonial with a series of white columns holding up the roof over a long front porch, the wings extending to each side. To the right a clump of pine trees shielded a carriage house with a garage below, what Pitt assumed were the servants' living quarters. Opposite and to the left of the manor sat a huge glass-enclosed structure, lit by crystal chandeliers hanging from the roof. Exotic flowers and shrubs blossomed around twenty or more dinner tables while a small orchestra played on a stage beneath a waterfall. Pitt was properly impressed. The perfect setting for a party on a brisk October evening. Raymond LeBaron got high marks for originality. He pulled the Daimler up to the front of the greenhouse where a liveried parking valet stood with the awed expression of a carpenter gazing at redwoods.

As he slid from behind the wheel and straightened the jacket of

68

his tuxedo Pitt noticed a crowd beginning to gather behind the transparent wall of the greenhouse, pointing and gesturing at the car. He gave the valet instructions on how to shift the transmission and then passed through the glass doors. The orchestra was playing themes from John Barry scores, light on the brass and heavy on the strings. A woman, elegantly dressed in the latest designer fashion, was standing just inside the entrance, greeting the guests.

He had no doubt she was Jessie LeBaron. Cool composure, the embodiment of grace and style, the living proof women can be beautiful after fifty. She wore a glittery beaded green and silver tunic over a long, slim velvet skirt.

Pitt approached and gave a brief bow. "Good evening," he said, flashing his best gate crasher's smile.

"What is that sensational car?" Jessie asked, peering through the doorway.

"A Daimler powered by a 5.4 liter, straight-eight engine with Hooper coachwork."

She smiled graciously and extended her hand. "Thank you for coming, Mr...." She hesitated, gazing at him curiously. "Forgive me, but I don't seem to recall meeting you before."

"That's because we've never laid eyes on each other," he said, marveling at her throaty voice, almost husky, with a sensual coarseness about it. "My name is Pitt, Dirk Pitt."

Jessie's dark eyes looked at Pitt in a most peculiar way. "You're four and a half hours late, Mr. Pitt. Did you suffer some sort of accidental delay?"

"No accident, Mrs. LeBaron. I planned my arrival most carefully."

"You weren't invited to the party," she said smoothly. "So you'll have to leave."

"A pity," said Pitt mournfully. "I seldom get a chance to wear my tux."

Jessie's face registered scorn. She turned to a prim woman wearing large-lensed glasses and standing slightly to her rear, who Pitt guessed was her secretary, Sandra Cabot.

"Find Angelo and tell him to show this gentleman out."

Pitt's green eyes glinted mischievously. "I seem to have a talent for spreading ill will. Do you wish me to go peacefully or cause a nasty scene?"

"I think peacefully would be best."

"Then why did you ask to meet with me?"

69

"A matter concerning my husband."

"He was a perfect stranger to me. I can't tell you anything about his death that you don't already know."

"Raymond is not dead," she said adamantly.

"When I saw him in the blimp he gave a damn good imitation of it."

"That wasn't him."

Pitt stared at her skeptically, saying nothing.

"You don't believe me, do you?"

"I don't really care."

"I was hoping you'd help me."

"You have a strange way of asking for favors."

"This a formal charity dinner, Mr. Pitt. You don't fit in. We'll set a time to meet tomorrow."

Pitt decided his anger wasn't important, so he shoved it aside. "What was your husband doing when he disappeared?" he asked abruptly.

"Searching for the El Dorado treasure," she replied, looking nervously around the greenhouse at her guests. "He believed it sank on a ship called the *Cyclops*."

Before Pitt could make a comment, Cabot returned with Angelo, the Cuban chauffeur.

"Goodbye, Mr. Pitt," said Jessie, dismissing him and greeting a pair of new arrivals.

Pitt shrugged and offered his arm to Angelo. "Let's make it official. You lead me out." Then he turned to Jessie. "One last thing, Mrs. LeBaron. I don't respond to shabby treatment. You needn't bother to contact me again, ever."

Then Pitt allowed Angelo to escort him from the greenhouse to the driveway where the Daimler was waiting. Jessie watched as the great car disappeared into the night. Then she began mingling with her guests.

Douglas Oates, the Secretary of State, looked over from a conversation he was having with presidential adviser Daniel Fawcett as she approached. "Splendid affair, Jessie."

"Yes indeed," echoed Fawcett. "Nobody in Washington puts on a finer spread."

Jessie's eyes flashed and her full lips curved in a warm smile. "Thank you, gentlemen."

Oates nodded toward the doorway. "Was I imagining things, or did I see Dirk Pitt bounced out the door?"

70

Jessie looked at Oates blankly. "You know him?" she asked, surprised.

"Of course. Pitt is the number two man over at NUMA. He's the guy who raised the *Titanic* for the Defense Department."

"And saved the President's life in Louisiana," added Fawcett.

Jessie noticeably paled. "I had no idea."

"I hope you didn't make him mad," said Oates.

"Perhaps I *was* a bit rude," she conceded.

"Aren't you interested in drilling for offshore oil below San Diego?"

"Yes. Seismic surveys indicate a vast untapped field. One of our companies has the inside track for the drilling rights. Why do you ask?"

"Don't you know who heads up the Senate committee for oil exploration on government lands?"

"Certainly, it's..." Jessie's voice trailed off and her composure melted away.

"Dirk's father," Oates finished. "Senator George Pitt of California. Without his backing and the blessing of NUMA on environmental issues, you don't stand a prayer of winning the drilling rights."

"It would appear," Fawcett said sardonically, "your inside track just washed out."

9

THIRTY MINUTES LATER, Pitt rolled the Daimler into his parking stall in front of the tall, solar-glassed building that housed NUMA headquarters. He signed in at the security desk and took the elevator to the tenth floor. When the doors opened, he stepped into a vast electronic maze, comprising the communications and information network of the marine agency.

Hiram Yaeger looked up from behind a horseshoe-shaped desk, whose surface lay unseen beneath a jungle of computer hardware, and smiled. "Hullo, Dirk. All dressed up and no place to go?"

"The party's hostess decided I was persona non grata and made me walk the plank."

"Anybody I know?"

It was Pitt's turn to smile. He looked down at Yaeger. The computer wizard was a throwback to the hippie days of the early seventies. He wore his blond hair long and tied in a ponytail. His beard was untrimmed and kinky with uncontrolled curls. And his standard uniform for work and play was Levi jacket and pants stuffed into scruffy cowboy boots.

Pitt said, "I can't picture you and Jessie LeBaron traveling in the same social circles."

Yaeger gave out a low whistle. "You got booted from a Jessie LeBaron bash? Man, you're some kind of hero to the downtrodden."

"Are you in the mood for an excavation?"

"On her?"

"On him."

"Her husband? The one who's missing?"

"Raymond LeBaron."

"Another moonlight operation?"

"Whatever you want to call it."

"Dirk," Yaeger said, peering over the rims of his granny glasses, "you are a nosy bastard, but I love you just the same. I'm hired to build a world-class computer network and amass an archive on marine science and history, but every time I belch you turn up, wanting to use my creation for shady purposes. Why do I go along? Okay, I'll tell you why. Larceny flows faster in my veins than yours. Now, how deep do you want me to dig?"

"To the bottom of his past. Where he came from. What was the money base for his empire."

"Raymond LeBaron was pretty secretive about his private life. He may have covered his trail."

"I realize that, but you've pulled skeletons out of the closet before."

Yaeger nodded thoughtfully. "Yes, the Bougainville shipping family a few months ago. A neat little caper, if I do say so."

"One more thing."

"Lay it on me."

"A ship called the *Cyclops*. Could you pull her history for me?"

"No sweat. Anything else?"

"That should do it," Pitt answered.

Yaeger stared at him. "What's going down this time, old friend? I can't believe you're going after the LeBarons because you were dumped at a society party. Take me, I've been thrown out of the worst sleaze joints in town. And I just accept it."

Pitt laughed. "No revenge. I'm just curious. Jessie LeBaron said something that struck me odd about her husband's disappearance."

"I read about it in the *Washington Post*. There was a paragraph mentioning you as the hero of the hour, saving LeBaron's blimp with your rope and palm tree trick. So what's the catch?"

"She claimed that her husband wasn't among the dead I found inside the control cabin."

Yaeger paused, his eyes uncomprehending. "Doesn't make sense. If old man LeBaron flew off in that gas bag, it stands to reason he'd still be inside when it turned up."

"Not according to the bereaved wife."

"Think she's got an angle, insurance or financial?"

"Maybe, maybe not. But there is a chance that because the mystery occurred over water, NUMA will be called in to assist in the investigation."

"And we'll already be on first base."

"Something like that."

"Where does the *Cyclops* fit in the picture?"

"She told me LeBaron was looking for it when he vanished."

Yaeger rose from his chair. "All right then, let's get off the mark. While I design a search program, you study what we have on the ship in our data files."

He led Pitt into a small viewing theater with a large monitor mounted on the far wall and motioned for him to sit behind a console containing a computer keyboard. Then he leaned over Pitt and pressed a series of commands on the keyboard.

"We installed a new system last week. The terminal is hooked into a voice synthesizer."

"A talking computer," said Pitt.

"Yes, it can comprehend over ten thousand verbal commands, make the appropriate reply, and actually carry on a conversation. The voice sounds a little weird, sort of like Hal, the giant computer in the movie *2001*. But you get used to it. We call her Hope."

"Hope?"

"Yeah, we *hope* she'll come up with the right answers."

"Funny."

"I'll be at the main terminal desk if you need help. Just pick up the phone and dial four-seven."

Pitt looked up at the screen. It had a bluish-gray cast. He warily picked up a microphone and spoke into it.

"Hope, my name is Dirk. Are you ready to conduct a search for me?"

God, he felt like an idiot. It was like talking to a tree and expecting a reply.

"Hello, Dirk," replied a vaguely female voice that sounded as if it was coming out of a harmonica. "Ready when you are."

Pitt took a deep breath and made the plunge. "Hope, I'd like you to tell me about a ship named *Cyclops*."

There was a five-second pause, then the computer said, "You will have to be more specific. My memory disks contain data on five different vessels called *Cyclops*."

"This one had treasure on board."

"Sorry, none show any treasure in their cargo manifest."

Sorry? Pitt still couldn't believe he was conversing with a machine. "If I may digress for a moment, Hope, allow me to say you're a very bright and most congenial computer."

"Thank you for the compliment, Dirk. In case you're interested, I can also do sound effects, imitate animals, sing—though not too well—and pronounce 'supercalifragilisticexpialidocious,' even if I haven't been programmed to its exact definition. Would you like me to say it backwards?"

Pitt laughed. "Some other time. Getting back to the *Cyclops*, the one I'm interested in probably sank in the Caribbean."

"That narrows it down to two. A small steamer that ran aground in Montego Bay, Jamaica, 5 May 1968, and a U.S. Navy collier—an ore or coal transport—lost without a trace, between 5 and 10 February 1918."

Raymond LeBaron wouldn't be flying around searching for a ship stranded in a busy harbor only twenty years ago, Pitt reasoned. The tale of the Navy collier came back to him. The loss was touted as one of the great mysteries of the mythical Bermuda Triangle.

"We'll go with the Navy collier," said Pitt.

"If you wish me to print out the data for you, Dirk, press the control button on your keyboard and the letters PT. Also, if you watch the screen I can project whatever photos are available."

Pitt did as he was told and the printer began pounding away. True to her word, Hope flashed a picture of the *Cyclops* lying at anchor in an unnamed port.

Although her hull was slender with its old-fashioned straight-up-and-down bow and graceful champagne-glass stern, her superstructure had the look of a child's erector set gone wild. A maze of derricks, spiderwebbed by cables and laced by overhead supports, rose amidships like a dead forest. A long deckhouse ran along the aft part of the ship above the engine room, its roof festooned with towering twin smokestacks and several tall ventilators. Forward, the wheelhouse perched above the main deck like a vanity table on four legs, spotted with a single row of portholes and open beneath. Two high masts with a crossbar protruded from a bridge that could have passed for a football goalpost. She seemed ungainly, an ugly duckling that never made it to swan.

There was also a ghostly quality about her. At first Pitt couldn't put his finger on it, and then it struck him: oddly, no crew member was visible anywhere on her decks. It was if she were deserted.

Pitt turned from the monitor and scanned the printout of the ship's statistics:

Launched: 7 May 1910 by William Cramp & Sons Shipbuilders, Philadelphia
Tonnage: 19,360 displaced

Length:	542 feet (actually longer than the battleships of her time)
Beam:	65 feet
Draft:	27 feet 8 inches
Speed:	15 knots (3 knots faster than the Liberty ships of World War II)
Armament:	Four 4-inch guns
Crew:	246
Master:	G. W. Worley, Naval Auxiliary Service

Pitt noted that Worley was the *Cyclops'* captain from the time she was placed in service until she disappeared. He sat back, his mind drifting as he studied the picture of the ship.

"Do you have any other photographs of her?" he asked Hope.

"Three from the same angle, one stern shot, and four of the crew."

"Let's have a look at the crew."

The monitor went black for a moment and soon an image of a man, standing at a ship's railing and holding a little girl's hand, came into view.

"Captain Worley with his daughter," explained Hope.

A huge man with thinning hair, neatly trimmed moustache, and massive hands stood in a dark suit, necktie casually askew outside the jacket, shoes highly shined, staring into a camera that froze his image seventy-five years ago. The little blond girl at his side wore a knee-length jumper and a little hat, and gripped what looked to be a very rigid doll in the shape of a bottle.

"Real name was Johann Wichman," Hope briefed without command. "He was born in Germany and illegally entered the United States when he jumped a merchant ship in San Francisco during the year 1878. How he falsified his records is not known. While commanding the *Cyclops*, he lived in Norfolk, Virginia, with his wife and daughter."

"Any possibility he was working for the Germans in 1918?"

"Nothing was ever proven. Would you like the reports from naval investigations of the tragedy?"

"Just print them out. I'll study them later."

"The next photo is of Lieutenant David Forbes, the executive officer," said Hope.

The camera had caught Forbes in dress uniform standing beside what Pitt guessed to be a 1916 Cadillac touring car. He had the face of a greyhound, long, narrow nose, pale eyes whose color could not be determined from the black-and-white photograph. His face was clean-shaven, the eyebrows arched, and he had slightly protruding teeth.

"What sort of man was he?" asked Pitt.

"His naval record was unblemished until Worley put him under ship's arrest for insubordination."

"Reason?"

"Captain Worley altered course from one plotted by Lieutenant Forbes and almost wrecked the ship entering Rio. When Forbes demanded to know why, Worley blew up and confined him to quarters."

"Was Forbes still under arrest during the last voyage?"

"Yes."

"Who's next?"

"Lieutenant John Church, second officer."

The photo showed a small, almost frail-looking man in civilian clothes sitting at a table in a restaurant. His face wore the tired look of a farmer after a long day in the fields, yet his dark eyes seemed to advertise a humorous disposition. The graying hair above a large forehead was brushed back over small ears.

"He seems older than the others," observed Pitt.

"Actually only twenty-nine," said Hope. "Joined the Navy when he was sixteen and worked his way up through the ranks."

"Did he have problems with Worley?"

"Nothing in the file."

The final photograph was of two men standing at attention in a courtroom. There was no sign of apprehension in their faces; if anything, they appeared sullen and defiant. The one on the left was tall and rangy with heavily muscled arms. The other one had the size and shape of a grizzly bear.

"This picture was taken at the court-martial of Fireman First Class James Coker and Fireman Second Class Barney DeVoe for the murder of Fireman Third Class Oscar Stewart. All three men were stationed aboard the U.S. cruiser *Pittsburgh*. Coker, on the left, was sentenced to death by hanging, which was carried out in Brazil. DeVoe, on the right, was sentenced to fifty to ninety-nine years in the naval prison at Portsmouth, New Hampshire."

"What's their connection with the *Cyclops*?" Pitt inquired.

"The *Pittsburgh* was in Rio de Janeiro when the murder occurred.

When Captain Worley reached port, he was instructed to transport DeVoe and four other prisoners in the *Cyclops'* brig to the United States."

"And they were on board at the end."

"Yes."

"No other pictures of the crew?"

"They are probably available in family albums and other private sources, but this is all I have in my library."

"Tell me about the events leading to the disappearance."

"Verbal or print?"

"Can you print it out and talk at the same time?"

"Sorry, I can only perform such functions in sequence. Which do you prefer first?"

"Verbal."

"Very well. One moment while I assemble the data."

Pitt was beginning to feel drowsy. It had been a long day. He used the pause to dial Yaeger and ask for a cup of coffee.

"How are you and Hope getting along?"

"I'm almost beginning to think she's real," Pitt answered.

"Just so long you don't start fantasizing about her nonexistent body."

"I'm not at that stage yet."

"To know her is to love her."

"How are you doing on LeBaron?"

"What I was afraid of," said Yaeger. "He pretty much buried his past. No insight, only statistics up to the time he became the Wall Street whiz."

"Anything interesting?"

"Not really. He came from a fairly affluent family. His father owned a chain of hardware stores. I get the idea Raymond and his father didn't get along. There's no mention of his family in any newspaper biographies after he became the financial whiz."

"Did you find out how he made his first big bucks?"

"That area is pretty vague. He and a partner by the name of Kronberg had a marine salvage company in the middle nineteen-fifties. Seems they scratched along for a few years and then went broke. Two years later, Raymond launched his publication."

"The *Prosperteer.*"

"Right."

"Is there any mention of where his backing came from?"

"None," replied Yaeger. "By the way, Jessie is his second wife. His first was named Hillary. She died a few years ago. Nothing on her at all."

"Keep hunting."

Pitt hung up as Hope said, "I'm ready with the data on the ill-fated final voyage of the *Cyclops*."

"Let's hear it."

"She put to sea from Rio de Janeiro on 16 February 1918, bound for Baltimore, Maryland. On board were her regular crew of 15 officers and 231 men, 57 men from the cruiser *Pittsburgh,* who were being rotated to the Norfolk Naval Base for reassignment, the 5 prisoners including DeVoe, and the American consul general at Rio, Alfred L. Morean Gottschalk, who was returning to Washington. Her cargo was 11,000 tons of manganese ore.

"After a brief call at the port of Bahia to pick up mail, the ship made an unscheduled stop on 4 March, when she entered Carlisle Bay on the island of Barbados and dropped anchor. Here, Worley took on extra coal and provisions, which he claimed were necessary to continue the voyage to Baltimore, but was later considered to be quite excessive. After the ship was lost at sea, the American consul in Barbados reported a number of suspicious rumors regarding Worley's unusual action, strange events on board, and a possible mutiny. The last anyone saw of the *Cyclops* and the men on board was 4 March 1918, when she steamed away from Barbados."

"There was no further contact?" asked Pitt.

"Twenty-four hours later, a lumber freighter called the *Crogan Castle* reported her bow crushed by an immense freak wave. Her radio signals for assistance were answered by the *Cyclops*. The final words from the collier were her call number and the message, 'We are fifty miles due south of you and coming at full steam.'"

"Nothing else?"

"That was it."

"Did the *Crogan Castle* give her position?"

"Yes, it was reported as latitude twenty-three degrees, thirty minutes north by longitude seventy-nine degrees, twenty-one minutes west, which put her about twenty miles southeast from a bank of shallow reefs called the Anguilla Cays."

"Was the *Crogan Castle* lost also?"

"No, the records say she limped into Havana."

"Any wreckage of the *Cyclops* turn up?"

"An extensive search by the Navy found nothing."

79

Pitt hesitated as Yaeger entered the viewing room, set a cup of coffee by the console, and silently retreated. He took a few sips and asked Hope to reshow the photo of the *Cyclops*. The ship materialized on the monitor's screen and he stared at it thoughtfully.

He picked up the phone, punched a number, and waited. A digital clock on the console read 11:55, but the voice that answered sounded bright and cheerful.

"Dirk!" boomed Dr. Raphael O'Meara. "What the hell is going down? You caught me at a good time. I just came home this morning from a dig in Costa Rica."

"Find another truckload of potsherds?"

"Only the richest cache of pre-Columbian art discovered to date. Amazing pieces, some dating back to three hundred B.C."

"Too bad you can't keep them."

"All my finds go to the Museo Nacional de Costa Rica."

"You're a generous man, Raphael."

"I don't donate them, Dirk. The governments where my finds are made preserve the artifacts as part of their national heritage. But why bore an old waterlogged relic like you. To what do I owe the pleasure of your call?"

"I need your expertise on a piece of treasure."

"You know, of course," O'Meara said, his tone edged with a touch of seriousness, "treasure is an unspeakable word to a respected archeologist."

"We all carry an albatross," said Pitt. "Can you meet me for a drink?"

"Now? Do you realize what time it is?"

"I happen to know you're a night owl. Make it easy on yourself. Someplace close to your house."

"How about the Old Angler's Inn on MacArthur Boulevard? Say in half an hour."

"Sounds good."

"Can you tell me what treasure you're interested in?"

"The one everyone dreams about."

"Oh? And which one is that?"

"Tell you when I see you."

Pitt hung up and gazed at the *Cyclops*. There was an eerie loneliness about her. He could not help wondering what secrets she took with her to a watery grave.

"Can I provide any further data?" asked Hope, interrupting his morbid reverie. "Or do you wish to terminate?"

"I think we can call it quits," he replied. "Thank you, Hope. I wish I could give you a big kiss."

"I am grateful for the compliment, Dirk. But I am not physiologically capable of receiving a kiss."

"You're still a sweetheart in my book."

"Come up and use me anytime."

Pitt laughed. "Goodnight, Hope."

"Goodnight, Dirk."

If only she was real, he thought with a dreamy sigh.

10

"JACK DANIEL'S NEAT," Raphael O'Meara said cheerfully. "Make that a double. Best medicine I know to clear the brain of jungle rot."

"How long were you in Costa Rica?" asked Pitt.

"Three months. Rained the whole time."

"Bombay gin on the rocks with a twist," Pitt said to the barmaid.

"So you're joining the greedy ranks of the sea scavengers," O'Meara said, the words emanating through a thick Gabby Hayes beard that hid his face from the nose down. "Dirk Pitt a treasure hunter. I never thought I'd see the day."

"My interest is purely academic."

"Sure, that's what they all say. Take my advice and forget it. More loot has been poured into underwater treasure hunts than was ever found. I can count on one hand the number of lucky discoveries that paid a profit in the last eighty years. The adventure, excitement, and riches, nothing but hype and all myth."

"I agree."

O'Meara's barbed-wire eyebrows narrowed. "So what is it you want to know?"

"You familiar with Raymond LeBaron?"

"Old rich and reckless Raymond, the financial genius who publishes the *Prosperteer?*"

"The same. He disappeared a couple of weeks ago on a blimp flight near the Bahamas."

"How could anybody disappear in a blimp?"

"Somehow he managed. You must have heard or read something about it."

O'Meara shook his head. "I haven't watched TV or seen a newspaper in ninety days."

The drinks were brought, and Pitt briefly explained the strange circumstances surrounding the mystery. The crowd was beginning to thin and they had the bar mostly to themselves.

"And you think LeBaron was flying around in an old gas bag looking for a shipwreck loaded to the gills with the mother lode."

"According to his wife, Jessie."

"What ship?"

"The *Cyclops.*"

"I know about the *Cyclops*. A Navy collier that vanished seventy-one years ago. I don't recall any report of riches on board."

"Apparently LeBaron thought so."

"What sort of treasure?"

"The El Dorado."

"You've got to be kidding."

"I'm only repeating what I was told."

O'Meara went quiet for a long moment, his eyes taking on a faraway look. "*El hombre dorado,*" he said at last. "Spanish for the golden man or the gilded one. The legend—some call it a curse—has fired imaginations for four hundred and fifty years."

"Is there any truth to it?" asked Pitt.

"Every legend is based on fact, but like all the others before and since, this one has been distorted and embellished into a fairy tale. El Dorado has inspired the longest continuing treasure hunt on record. Thousands of men have died searching for a glimpse of it."

"Tell me how the tale originated."

Another Jack Daniel's and Bombay gin arrived. Pitt laughed as O'Meara downed the water chaser first. Then the archeologist made himself comfortable and stared into another time.

"The Spanish conquistadores were the first to hear of a gilded man who ruled an incredibly wealthy kingdom somewhere in the mountainous jungles east of the Andes. Rumors described him as living in a secluded city built of gold with streets paved in emeralds and guarded by a fierce army of beautiful Amazons. Made Oz sound like a slum. Extremely overvalued, of course. But in reality there were a number of El Dorados—a long line of kings who worshiped a demon god who lived in Lake Guatavita, Colombia. When a new monarch took command of the tribal empire, his body was painted with resinous gums and then coated with gold dust, thus the gilded man. Then he was placed on a ceremonial raft, piled high with gold and precious stones, and rowed into the middle of the lake, where he proceeded to pitch the riches into the water as an offering to the god, whose name escapes me."

83

"Was the treasure ever raised?"

"There were any number of attempts to drain the lake, but they all failed. In 1965 the government of Colombia declared Guatavita an area of cultural interest and banned all salvage operations. A pity, when you consider that estimates of the wealth on the bottom of the lake run between one hundred and three hundred million dollars."

"And the golden city?"

"Never found," said O'Meara, signaling the barmaid for another round. "Many looked and many died. Nikolaus Federmann, Ambrosius Dalfinger, Sebastián de Belalcázar, Gonzalo and Hernán Jiménez de Quesada, all sought El Dorado but only found the curse. So did Sir Walter Raleigh. After his second fruitless expedition, King James put his head on the block, literally. The fabulous city of El Dorado and the greatest treasure of them all remained lost."

"Let's back up a minute," said Pitt. "The treasure at the bottom of the lake is not lost."

"That's in scattered pieces," explained O'Meara. "The second one, the grand prize, the bonanza at the end of the rainbow, remains hidden to this day. With maybe two exceptions, no outsider has ever laid eyes on it. The only description came from a monk who wandered out of the jungle into a Spanish settlement on the Orinoco River in 1675. Before dying a week later, he told of being on a Portuguese expedition looking for diamond mines. Out of eighty men, he was the only survivor. He claimed they'd stumbled into a deserted city surrounded by high cliffs and guarded by a tribe who called themselves Zanonas. The party lived in the city for three months, but one by one the men began to die off. Too late they discovered the Zanonas were not as friendly as they made out, but were cannibals, poisoning the Portuguese and eating them. The monk alone managed to escape. He described massive temples and buildings, strange inscriptions, and the legendary treasure that sent so many of its hunters to their graves."

"A true golden man," Pitt speculated. "A statue."

"You're close," said O'Meara. "Damned close, but you missed on the sex."

"Sex?"

"*La mujer dorada*, the golden woman," O'Meara replied. "Or more commonly, La Dorada. You see, the name first applied to a man and a ceremony, later to a city, and finally to an empire. Over the years it became a term for any place where riches could be found on the ground. Like so many descriptions the feminists hate, the masculine myth became generic, while the feminine was forgotten. Ready for another drink?"

"No, thanks. I'll nurse this one."

O'Meara ordered another Jack Daniel's. "Anyway, you know the story behind the Taj Mahal. A Mogul ruler erected the ornate tomb as a monument to his wife. Same with a pre-Columbian, South American king. His name is not recorded, but, so the legend goes, she was the most beloved of the hundreds of women at his court. Then an event occurred in the sky. Probably either an eclipse or Halley's comet. And the priests called on him to sacrifice her to appease the angry gods. Life was no fun in those days. So she was killed, heart torn out in an elaborate ceremony."

"I thought only the Aztecs went in for heart removal."

"The Aztecs didn't have a monopoly on human sacrifice. The upshot was the king called together his artisans and ordered them to build a statue of her likeness so he could elevate her to a god."

"Did the monk describe it?"

"In vivid detail, if his story can be believed. She stands nude, nearly six feet tall, on a pedestal of rose quartz. Her body is solid gold. God, it must weigh at least a ton. Imbedded in the chest, where the heart should be, is a great ruby, judged to be in the neighborhood of twelve hundred carats."

"I don't profess to be an expert," said Pitt, "but I know that rubies are the most valuable of all the gemstones, and one of thirty carats is a rarity. Twelve hundred carats is unbelievable."

"That's not even the half of it," O'Meara continued. "The entire head of the statue is one gigantic carved emerald, deep blue-green and flawless. I can't begin to guess the carat weight, but it would have to hit the scales around thirty pounds."

"More like forty if you include a likeness of the hair."

"What's the largest known emerald?"

Pitt thought a moment. "Certainly no more than ten pounds."

"Can't you just see her standing under spotlights in the main lobby of Washington's Museum of Natural History," O'Meara said wistfully.

"I can only wonder at the value on today's market."

"You could safely say it's priceless."

"There was another man who saw the statue?" Pitt asked.

"Colonel Ralph Morehouse Sigler, a real character from the old explorer school. An engineer in the English army, he tramped around the empire, surveying boundaries and building forts throughout Africa and India. He was also a trained geologist and spent his leave

85

time prospecting. He was either damned lucky or damned good, discovering an extensive chromite deposit in South Africa and several precious gemstone veins in Indochina. He became wealthy but didn't have time to enjoy it. The Kaiser marched into France and he was ordered to the Western Front to build fortifications."

"So he didn't enter South America until after the war."

"No, in the summer of 1916, he stepped off the boat at Georgetown, in what was then British Guiana. It seems some hotshot in the British treasury got the bright idea of sending out expeditions around the world to find and open gold mines to finance the war. Sigler was recalled from the front and ordered into the South American interior."

"You think he knew the monk's story?" Pitt asked.

"Nothing in his diaries or papers indicates he ever believed in a lost city. The guy was no wild-eyed treasure hunter. He was after raw minerals. Historic artifacts never interested him. Are you hungry, Dirk?"

"Yes, come to think of it. I was cheated out of dinner."

"We're long past the dinner hour, but if we ask nice I'm sure the kitchen can rustle up some appetizers."

O'Meara gestured for the barmaid and after pleading his case persuaded her to serve them a platter of shrimp with cocktail sauce.

"Hits the spot," said Pitt.

"I could eat these little devils all day long," O'Meara agreed. "Now, where were we?"

"Sigler was about to find La Dorada."

"Oh, yes. After forming a party of twenty men, mostly British soldiers, Sigler plunged into the uncharted wilds. For months, nothing was heard of them. The British began to sense disaster and sent out several search parties, but none found a trace of the missing men. At last, nearly two years later, an American expedition, surveying for a railroad, stumbled upon Sigler five hundred miles northeast of Rio de Janeiro. He was alone, the only survivor."

"Seems like an incredible distance from British Guiana."

"Almost two thousand miles from his jump-off point as the crow flies."

"What kind of shape was he in?"

"More dead than alive, according to the engineers who found him. They carried Sigler to a village that had a small hospital and sent off a message to the nearest American consulate. A few weeks later a relief party arrived from Rio."

"American or British?"

"An odd twist there," answered O'Meara. "The British consulate claimed they were never notified of Sigler's reappearance. Gossip had it that the American consul general himself showed up to question him. Whatever happened, Sigler dropped from sight. The story is he escaped from the hospital and wandered back into the jungle."

"Doesn't figure that he'd turn his back on civilization after two years of hell," said Pitt.

O'Meara shrugged. "Who can say?"

"Did Sigler give an account of his expedition before he disappeared?"

"Raved in delirium most of the time. Witnesses said afterward that he babbled about finding a huge city surrounded by steep cliffs and overgrown by jungle. His description pretty much matched the Portuguese monk's. He also drew a rough sketch of the golden woman that was saved by a nurse and now lies in Brazil's national library. I had a look at it while researching another project. The real thing must be an awesome sight."

"So it remains buried in the jungle."

"Ah, there's the rub," sighed O'Meara. "Sigler claimed he and his men stole the statue and dragged it twenty miles to a river, fighting off the Zanona Indians the whole trip. By the time they built a raft, heaved La Dorada on board, and pushed off, there were only three of them left. Later one died of his injuries and the other was lost in a stretch of rapids."

Pitt was fascinated by what O'Meara was telling him, but he was having a hard time keeping his eyes open. "The obvious question is, Where did Sigler stash the golden woman?"

"If I only knew," replied O'Meara.

"Didn't he give a clue?"

"The nurse thought he said the raft came apart and the statue dropped into the river a few hundred yards from where the surveyors' party found him. But don't get your hopes up. He was muttering nonsense. Treasure hunters have been dragging metal detectors up and down that river for years without a reading a tick."

Pitt swirled the ice cubes around inside his glass. He knew, he *knew* what happened to Ralph Morehouse Sigler and La Dorada.

"The American consul general," Pitt said slowly, "he was the last person to see Sigler alive?"

"The puzzle gets cloudy at this point, but as near as anyone can tell, the answer is yes."

"Let me see if I can fill in the pieces. This took place in January and February of 1918. Right?"

87

O'Meara nodded, and then he gave Pitt a queer stare.

"And the consul general's name was Alfred Gottschalk, who died a few weeks later on the *Cyclops*. Right?"

"You know this?" said O'Meara, his eyes uncomprehending.

"Gottschalk probably heard of Sigler's mission through his counterpart at the British consulate. When he received the message from the railroad surveyors that Sigler was alive, he kept the news to himself and headed into the interior, hoping to interview the explorer and steal a jump on the British by turning over any valuable information to his own government. What he learned must have shattered any code of ethics he still retained. Gottschalk decided to grab the bonanza for himself.

"He found and raised the golden statue from the river and then transported it, along with Sigler, to Rio de Janeiro. He covered his tracks by buying off anyone who might talk about Sigler, and, if my guess is correct, killing off the men who helped him recover the statue. Then, using his influence with the Navy, he smuggled them both on board the *Cyclops*. The ship was lost and the secret died with her."

O'Meara's eyes deepened in curious interest. "Now *that*," he said, "you can't possibly know."

"Why else would LeBaron be looking for what he thought was La Dorada?"

"You make a good case," O'Meara admitted. "But you left the door open to a moot question. Why didn't Gottschalk simply kill Sigler after he found the statue? Why keep the Englishman alive?"

"Elementary. The consul general was consumed by gold fever. He wanted La Dorada and the emerald city too. Sigler was the only person alive who could give him directions or lead him there."

"I like the way you think, Dirk. Your wild-assed theory calls for another drink."

"Too late, the bar's closed. I think they'd like us to leave so the help can get home to bed."

O'Meara mimicked a crestfallen expression. "That's one nice thing about primitive living. No hours, no curfew." He took a final swallow from his glass. "Well, what are your plans?"

"Nothing complicated," said Pitt, smiling. "I'm going to find the *Cyclops*."

11

THE PRESIDENT WAS AN EARLY RISER, awakening at about 6 A.M. and exercising for thirty minutes before showering and eating a light breakfast. In a ritual going back to the days soon after his honeymoon, he gently eased out of bed and quietly dressed while his wife slept on. She was a night person and could not force herself to rise before 7:30.

He slipped on a sweatsuit and then removed a small leather brief-case from a closet in the adjoining sitting room. After giving his wife a tender kiss on the cheek, he took the back stairway down to the White House gym beneath the west terrace.

The spacious room, containing a variety of exercise equipment, was empty except for a thick-bodied man who lay on his back bench-pressing a set of weights. With each lift he grunted like a woman in childbirth. The sweat beaded from a round head that sprouted a thick mat of ivory hair styled in a short crewcut. The stomach was immense and hairy, the arms and legs protruding like heavy tree limbs. He had the look of a carnival wrestler long past his prime.

"Good morning, Ira," said the President. "I'm glad you could make it."

The fat man set the weight bar on a pair of hooks above his head, rose from the bench, and squeezed the President's hand. "Good to see you, Vince."

The President smiled. No bowing, no scraping, no greeting of "Mr. President." Tough, stoical Ira Hagen, he mused. The gritty old undercover agent never gave an inch to anybody.

"I hope you don't mind meeting like this."

Hagen uttered a coarse laugh that echoed off the gym walls. "I've been briefed in worse places."

"How's the restaurant business?"

"Showing a nice profit since we switched from continental gourmet to downhome American food. Food costs were eating us alive. Twenty entrées with expensive sauces and herbs didn't cut it. So now we specialize in only five menu items the higher-class restaurants don't serve—ham, chicken, fish casserole, stew, and meatloaf."

"You may have something," said the President. "I haven't bitten into a good meatloaf since I was a kid."

"Our customers go for it, especially since we retained the fancy service and intimate atmosphere. My waiters all wear tuxedos, candles on tables, stylish settings, food presented in a continental manner. And the best part is the diners eat faster, so there's a quicker turnover on tables."

"And you're breaking even on the food while taking a profit on the booze and wine, right?"

Hagen laughed again. "Vince, you're okay. I don't care what the news media say about you. When you're an old has-been politician look me up, and we'll open a chain of beaneries together."

"Do you miss criminal investigation, Ira?"

"Sometimes."

"You were the best undercover operative the Justice Department ever had," the President said, "until Martha died."

"Gathering evidence on slime for the government didn't seem to matter anymore. Besides, I had three daughters to raise, and the demands of the job kept me away from home for weeks at a time."

"The girls doing all right?"

"Just fine. As you well know, all three of your nieces have happy marriages and presented me with five grandchildren."

"A pity Martha couldn't have seen them. Of my four sisters and two brothers, she was my favorite."

"You didn't fly me here from Denver on an Air Force jet just to talk old times," said Hagen. "What's going down?"

"Have you lost your touch?"

"Have you forgotten how to ride a bicycle?"

It was the President's turn to laugh. "Ask a stupid question..."

"The reflexes are a mite slower, but the gray matter still turns at a hundred percent."

The President tossed him the briefcase. "Digest this while I hike a couple of miles on the treadmill."

Hagen wiped his sweating brow with a towel and sat on a stationary bicycle, his bulk threatening to bend the frame. He opened the leather

90

case and didn't look up from reading the contents until the President had walked 1.6 miles.

"What do you think?" the President asked finally.

Hagen shrugged, still reading. "Make a great pilot for a TV show. Closet funding, an impenetrable security veil, covert activity on an immense scale, an undetected moon base. The stuff H. G. Wells would have loved."

"Do you figure it's a hoax?"

"Let's say I want to believe it. What flag-waving taxpayer wouldn't? Makes our intelligence community look like deaf and blind mutants. But if it is a hoax, where's the motive?"

"Other than a grand scheme to defraud the government, I can't think of any."

"Let me finish reading. This last file is in longhand."

"My recollection of what was said on the golf course. Sorry about the chicken scratch, but I never learned to type."

Hagen stared at him questioningly. "You've told no one about this, not even your security council?"

"Perhaps I'm paranoid, but this 'Joe' character slipped through my Secret Service cordon like a fox through a barnyard. And he claimed members of the 'inner core' were highly placed at NASA and the Pentagon. It stands to reason they've also penetrated the intelligence agencies and my White House staff as well."

Hagen studied the President's report of the golf course meeting intently, going back occasionally to check the Jersey Colony file. Finally he hoisted his body off the bicycle and sat on a bench, looking at the President.

"This photo blowup of a man sitting next to you in a golf cart. Is that Joe?"

"Yes. When returning to the clubhouse, I spotted a reporter from the *Washington Post* who had been photographing my golf game through a telescopic lens. I asked him to do me a favor and send an enlargement over to the White House so I could autograph it for my caddy."

"Good thinking." Hagen peered closely at the picture and then set it aside. "What do you want me to do, Vince?"

"Dig out the names of the 'inner core.'"

"Nothing else? No information or evidence on the Jersey Colony project?"

"When I know who they are," the President said in a dead voice, "they'll be rounded up and interrogated. Then we'll see how deep their tentacles reach."

"If you want my opinion, I'd pin a medal on every one of those guys."

"I may just do that," the President replied with a cold smile. "But not before I stop them from kicking off a bloody battle for the moon."

"So it adds up to a presidential cutout situation. You can't trust anyone in normal intelligence circles and you're hiring me to be your private field intelligence agent."

"Yes."

"What's my deadline?"

"The Russian spacecraft is set to land on the moon nine days from now. I need every hour I can steal to prevent a fight between their cosmonauts and our moon colonists that might spread into a space conflict that none of us could stop. The 'inner core' must be convinced to back off. I've got to have them under wraps, Ira, at least twenty-four hours before the Russians touch down."

"Eight days isn't much to find nine men."

The President gave a helpless shrug. "Nothing comes easy."

"A certificate saying I'm your brother-in-law won't be enough to pass me through legal and bureaucratic roadblocks. I'll require a concrete cover."

"I leave it to you to create one. An Alpha Two clearance should get you through most doors."

"Not bad," said Hagen. "The Vice President only carries a Three."

"I'll give you the number of a safe phone line. Report to me day or night. Understood?"

"Understood."

"Questions?"

"Raymond LeBaron, dead or alive?"

"Undecided. The wife refused to identify the body found in the blimp as his. She was right. I asked the FBI director, Sam Emmett, to take possession of the remains from Dade County, Florida. They're over at Walter Reed Army Hospital now, undergoing examination."

"Can I see the county coroner's report?"

The President shook his head in wonderment. "You never miss a trick, do you, Ira?"

"Obviously there had to be one."

"I'll see you get a copy."

"And the lab results at Walter Reed."

"That too."

Hagen stuffed the files back into the briefcase, but left out the photo from the golf course. He studied the images for perhaps the fourth time. "You realize, of course, Raymond LeBaron may never be found."

"I've considered that possibility."

"Nine little Indians. And then there were eight...make that seven."

"Seven?"

Hagen held up the photo in front of the President's eyes. "Don't you recognize him?"

"Frankly, no. But he did say we knew each other many years ago."

"Our high school baseball team. You played first base. I was left field and Leonard Hudson caught."

"Hudson!" The President gasped incredulously. "Joe is Leo Hudson. But Leo was a fat kid. Weighed at least two hundred pounds."

"He became a health nut. Lost sixty pounds and ran marathons. You were never sentimental about the old gang. I still keep track of them. Don't you remember? Leo was the school brain. Won all sorts of awards for his science projects. Later he graduated with honors at Stanford and became director of the Harvey Pattenden National Physics Laboratory in Oregon. Invented and pioneered rocket and space systems before anyone else was working in the field."

"Bring him in, Ira. Hudson is the key to the others."

"I'll need a shovel."

"You saying he's buried?"

"Like in dead and buried."

"When?"

"Back in 1965. A light-plane crash in the Columbia River."

"Then who is Joe?"

"Leonard Hudson."

"But you said—"

"His body was never found. Convenient, huh?"

"He faked his death," the President said as if beholding a revelation. "The son of a bitch faked his death so he could go underground to ramrod the Jersey Colony project."

"A brilliant idea when you think about it. No one to answer to. No way he could be tied to a clandestine program. Disguise himself as any character who could be used to his advantage. A nonperson can accomplish far more than the average taxpayer whose name, birthmarks, and nasty habits are stored in a thousand computers."

93

There was a silence, then the President's grim voice: "Find him, Ira. Find and bring Leonard Hudson to me before all hell breaks loose."

Secretary of State Douglas Oates peered through his reading glasses at the last page of a thirty-page letter. He closely examined the structure of each paragraph, trying to read between the lines. At last he looked up at his deputy secretary, Victor Wykoff.

"Looks genuine to me."

"Our experts on the subject think so too," said Wykoff. "The semantics, the rambling flow, the disjointed sentences, all fit the usual pattern."

"No denying it sounds like Fidel all right," Oates said quietly. "However, it's the tone of the letter that bothers me. You almost get the impression he's begging."

"I don't think so. More like he's trying to stress utmost secrecy with a healthy dose of urgency thrown in."

"The consequences of his proposal are staggering."

"My staff has studied it from every angle," said Wykoff. "Castro has nothing to gain from creating a hoax."

"You say he went through devious lengths to get the document into our hands."

Wykoff nodded. "Crazy as it sounds, the two couriers, who delivered it to our field office in Miami, claim they sneaked from Cuba to the United States on board a blimp."

12

THE BARREN MOUNTAINS and the shadowy ridges on the moon's craters leaped out at Anastas Rykov as he peered through the twin lenses of a stereoscope. Beneath the eyes of the Soviet geophysicist the desolate lunar landscape unreeled in three dimensions and vivid color. Taken from thirty-four miles up, the details were strikingly sharp. Solitary pebbles, measuring less than one inch across, were visually distinct.

Rykov lay face downward on a pad, studying the photographic montage that slowly rolled beneath to the stereoscope on two wide reels. The process was similar to a motion picture director editing film, only more comfortable. His hand rested on a small control unit that could stop the reels and magnify whatever area he was scrutinizing.

The images had been received from sophisticated devices on a Russian spacecraft that had circumnavigated the moon. Mirrorlike scanners reflected the lunar surface into a prism that broke it down into spectrum wavelengths that were digitized into 263 different shades of gray: black beginning at 263 and fading to white at zero. Next, the spacecraft's computer converted them into a quiltwork of picture elements on high-density tape. After the data was retrieved from the orbiting spacecraft, it was printed in black-and-white on a negative by laser and filtered with blue, red, and green wavelengths. Then it was computer enhanced in color on two continuous sheets of photographic paper that were overlapped for stereoscopic interpretation.

Rykov raised his glasses and rubbed his bloodshot eyes. He glanced at his wristwatch. It was 11:57 P.M. He'd been analyzing the peaks and valleys of the moon with only a few catnaps for nine days and nights. He readjusted his glasses and ran both hands through a dense carpet of oily black hair, dully realizing he hadn't bathed or changed his clothes since beginning the project.

He shook away the exhaustion and dutifully returned to his work, examining a small area on the far side of the moon that was volcanic in origin. Only two inches of the photo roll remained before it mysteriously ended. He had not been informed by his superiors of the reason for the sudden cutoff, but assumed it was a malfunction of the scanning gear.

The surface was pockmarked and wrinkled, like pimpled skin under a strong magnifying glass, and appeared more beechnut brown than gray in color. The steady bombardment of meteorites through the ages had left crater gouged on crater, scar crossing scar.

Rykov almost missed it. His eyes detected an unnatural oddity, but his tired mind nearly ignored the signal. Wearily he backed the image and magnified a grid on the edge of a steep ridge soaring from the floor of a small crater. Three tiny objects came into crisp focus.

What he saw was unbelievable. Rykov pulled back from the stereoscope and took a deep breath, clearing the creeping fog from his brain. Then he looked again.

They were still there, but one object was a rock. The other two were human figures.

Rykov was transfixed by what he saw. Then the shock set in and his hands began to tremble and his stomach felt as though it had been twisted in a knot. Shaken, he climbed off the pad, walked over to a desk, and opened a small booklet containing private phone numbers of the Soviet Military Space Command. He misdialed twice before he connected with the correct number.

A voice slurred from vodka answered. "What is it?"

"General Maxim Yasenin?"

"Yes, who's this?"

"We've never met. My name is Anastas Rykov. I'm a geophysicist on the Cosmos Lunar Project."

The commander of Soviet military space missions made no attempt to hide his irritation over Rykov's intrusion on his privacy. "Why in hell are you calling me this time of night?"

Rykov fully realized he was overstepping his bounds, but he didn't hesitate. "While analyzing pictures taken by Selenos 4, I've stumbled on something that defies belief. I thought you should be first to be informed."

"Are you drunk, Rykov?"

"No, General. Tired but Siberian sober."

"Unless you are a complete fool, you must know you are in deep trouble for going over the heads of your superiors."

"This is too important to share with anyone beneath your level of authority."

"Sleep on it and you won't be so brash in the morning," said Yasenin. "I'll do you a favor and forget the whole matter. Goodnight."

"Wait!" Rykov demanded, throwing caution aside. "If you dismiss my call, I will have no choice but to turn my discovery over to Vladimir Polevoi."

Rykov's statement was greeted by an icy silence. Finally Yasenin said, "What makes you think the chief of state security would listen to a crazy man?"

"When he checked my dossier, he would find I am a respected party member and a scientist who is far from lunacy."

"Oh?" Yasenin asked, his irritation turning to curiosity. He decided to pin Rykov down. "All right. I'll hear you out. What's so vital to the interest of Mother Russia that it can't go through prescribed channels?"

Rykov spoke very calmly. "I have proof that someone is on the moon."

Forty-five minutes later, General Yasenin strode into the photo analysis laboratory of the Geophysical Space Center. Big, beefy, and red of face, he wore a rumpled uniform that was ablaze with decorations. The hair was smoke-gray, the eyes steady and hard. He walked quietly, his head thrust out as if stalking a prey.

"You Rykov?" he asked without prelude.

"Yes," Rykov said simply but firmly.

They stared at each other a moment, neither making any attempt at shaking hands. Finally, Rykov cleared his throat and motioned toward the stereoscope.

"This way, General," he said. "Please lie prone on the leather cushion and look through the eyepiece."

As Yasenin positioned himself over the photo montage he asked, "What am I searching for?"

"Focus on the small area I've circled," replied Rykov.

The general adjusted the lenses to his vision and peered downward, his face impassive. After a full minute, he looked up strangely, then bent over the stereoscope again. At last he slowly rose and stared at Rykov, eyes stark in open astonishment.

"This is not a photographic trick?" he asked dumbly.

"No, General. What you see is real. Two human forms, wearing encapsulated suits, are aiming some sort of device at Selenos 4."

Yasenin's mind could not accept what his eyes saw to be true. "It's not impossible. Where do they come from?"

Rykov shrugged helplessly. "I don't know. If they're not United States astronauts, they can only be aliens."

"I do not believe in supernatural fairy tales."

"But how could the Americans launch men to the moon without the event leaking to the world news media or our intelligence people?"

"Suppose they left men behind and stockpiled material during the Apollo program. Such an effort might be possible."

"Their last known lunar landing was by Apollo 17 in 1972," Rykov recalled. "No human could survive the harsh lunar conditions for seventeen years without being resupplied."

"I can think of no one else," Yasenin insisted.

He returned to the stereoscope and intently studied the human forms standing in the crater. The sun's glare was coming from the right, throwing their shadows to the left. Their suits were white, and he could make out the dark green viewports on the helmets. They were of a design unfamiliar to him. Yasenin could clearly distinguish footprints leading into a pitch-black shadow cast by the crater's rim.

"I know what you're looking for, General," said Rykov, "but I've already examined the landscape on the floor of the crater and cannot find any sign of their spacecraft."

"Perhaps they climbed down from the top?"

"That's a sheer drop of over a thousand feet."

"I'm at a loss to explain any of this," Yasenin admitted quietly.

"Please look closely at the device they're both holding and pointing at Selenos 4. It seems to be a large camera with an extremely long telephoto lens."

"No," said Yasenin. "You're treading in my territory now. Not a camera but a weapon."

"A laser?"

"Nothing so advanced. Strikes me as a hand-held surface-to-air missile system of American manufacture. A Lariat type 40, I should say. Homes in with a guidance beam, ten-mile range on earth, probably much more in the moon's rarefied atmosphere. Became operational with NATO forces about six years ago. So much for your alien theory."

Rykov was awed. "Every ounce of weight is precious in space

flight. Why carry something so heavy and useless as a rocket launcher?"

"The men in the crater found a purpose. They used it against Selenos 4."

Rykov thought a moment. "That would explain why the scanners stopped operating a minute later. They were damaged—"

"By a hit from a rocket," Yasenin finished.

"We were fortunate the scanners finally relayed the digitized data before it crashed."

"A pity the crew were not so lucky."

Rykov stared at the general, not sure he'd heard right. "Selenos 4 was unmanned."

Yasenin pulled a slim gold case from his coat, selected a cigarette, and lit it with a lighter embedded in the top. Then he slid the case back into a breast pocket.

"Yes, of course, Selenos 4 *was* unmanned."

"But you said—"

Yasenin smiled coldly. "I said nothing."

The message was clear. Rykov valued his position too much to pursue the subject. He simply nodded.

"Do you wish a report on what we've seen here tonight?" Rykov asked.

"The original, no copies, on my desk by ten o'clock tomorrow. And, Rykov, consider this a state secret of the highest priority."

"I will confide in no one but you, General."

"Good man. There may be party honor in this for you."

Rykov wasn't going to hold his breath waiting for the award, yet he could not suppress a glow of pride in his work.

Yasenin returned to the stereoscope, drawn to the image of the intruders on the moon. "So the fabled star wars have begun," he murmured to himself. "And the Americans have launched the first blow."

13

PITT REJECTED ANY THOUGHT of lunch, and opened one of several granola bars he kept in his desk. Fumbling with the wrapper, held over a wastebasket to catch the crumbs, he kept his concentration locked on a large nautical chart spread across the desk. The chart's tendency to curl was held down by a memo pad and two books on historic shipwrecks that were opened to chapters on the *Cyclops*. The chart covered a large area of the Old Bahama Channel, flanked on the south by the Archipelago de Camagüey, a group of scattered islands off the coast of Cuba, and the shallow waters of the Great Bahama Bank to the north. The upper left corner of the chart took in the Cay Sal Bank, whose southeastern tip included the Anguilla Cays.

He sat back and took a bite out of the granola bar. Then he bent over the chart again, sharpened a pencil, and picked up a pair of dividers. Setting the needle tips of the dividers on the scale printed on the bottom of the chart, he measured off twenty nautical miles and carefully marked the distance from the tip of the Anguilla Cays with a penciled dot. Next, he described a short arc another fifty miles to the southeast. He labeled the top dot *Crogan Castle* and the lower arc *Cyclops* with a question mark.

Somewhere above the arc is where the *Cyclops* sank, he reasoned. A logical assumption given the fact of the lumber freighter's position at the time of her distress signal and the *Cyclops'* distance as given in her reply.

The only problem was that Raymond LeBaron's piece of the puzzle didn't fit.

From his experience in searching for shipwrecks, Pitt was convinced LeBaron had performed the same exercise a hundred times, only delving deeper into currents, known weather conditions at the

100

time of the loss, and the projected speed of the Navy collier. But one conclusion always came out the same. The *Cyclops* should have gone down in the middle of the channel under 260 fathoms of water, over 1,500 feet to the bottom. Far too deep to be visible to anything other than a fish.

Pitt relaxed in his chair and stared at the markings on the chart. Unless LeBaron dredged up information nobody else knew about, what was he searching for? Certainly not the *Cyclops*, and certainly not from a blimp. A side-scan survey from a surface craft or a deep-diving submersible would have been better suited for the job.

In addition, the prime search area was only twenty miles off Cuba. Hardly a comfortable place to cruise around in a slow-flying gas bag. Castro's gunboats would have declared open season on such an easy target.

He was sitting lost in contemplation, nibbling on the granola bar, trying to see a probability in Raymond LeBaron's scheme that he had missed, when his desk speaker beeped. He pressed the Talk switch.

"Yes?"

"Sandecker. Can you come up to my office?"

"Five minutes, Admiral."

"Try for two."

Admiral James Sandecker was the director of the National Underwater and Marine Agency. A man in his late fifties, he was of short stature, his body thin and stringy but hard as armor plating. The straight hair and Vandyke beard were blaze red. A fitness freak, he adhered to a strict exercise regimen. His naval career was distinguished more by hard-nosed efficiency than sea combat tactics. And though he wasn't popular in Washington social circles, politicians respected him for his integrity and organizational ability.

The admiral greeted Pitt's entry into his office with nothing more than a curt nod, then gestured to a woman sitting in a leather chair across the room.

"Dirk, I understand you've met Mrs. Jessie LeBaron."

She looked up and smiled, but it was an ingratiating smile. Pitt bowed slightly and pressed her hand.

"Sorry," he said indifferently. "I'd rather forget I know Mrs. LeBaron."

Sandecker's eyebrows pinched together. "Am I missing something?"

"My fault," said Jessie, staring into Pitt's eyes but seeing only green

101

ice. "I was very rude to Mr. Pitt last night. I hope he accepts my apology and forgives my bad manners."

"You needn't act so formal, Mrs. LeBaron. Since we're old pals, I won't throw a tantrum if you call me Dirk. As to forgiving you, how much is it going to cost me?"

"My intent was to hire·*you*," she replied, ignoring the gibe.

He gave Sandecker a bemused look. "Strange, I had this funny idea I worked for NUMA."

"Admiral Sandecker has kindly consented to release you for a few days, providing, of course, you're agreeable," she added.

"To do what?"

"To look for my husband."

"No deal."

"May I ask why?"

"I have other projects."

"You won't work for me because I'm a woman. Is that it?"

"Sex has no bearing on my decision. Let's just say I don't work for someone I can't respect."

There was an embarrassed silence. Pitt looked at the admiral. The lips were turned down in a grimace, but the eyes fairly twinkled. The old bastard was enjoying this, he thought.

"You've misjudged me, Dirk." Jessie's face was flushed in confusion, but her eyes were hard as crystal.

"Please." Sandecker raised both hands. "Let's call a truce. I suggest you two get together some evening and have it out over dinner."

Pitt and Jessie stared at each other for a long moment. Then Pitt's mouth slowly spread in a wide infectious smile. "I'm willing, providing I pay."

Despite herself Jessie had to smile too. "Allow me some self-respect. Let's split the bill?"

"Done."

"Now we can get on with the business at hand," Sandecker said in his no-nonsense way. "Before you arrived, Dirk, we were discussing theories on Mr. LeBaron's disappearance."

Pitt looked at Jessie. "There is no doubt in your mind that the bodies in the blimp were not those of Mr. LeBaron and his crew?"

Jessie shook her head. "None."

"I saw them. There wasn't much left to identify."

"The corpse lying in the morgue was more muscular than Raymond," explained Jessie. "Also, he'd been wearing an imitation of a Cartier wristwatch. One of those cheap replicas made in Taiwan. I'd given my husband an expensive original on our first anniversary."

"I've made a few calls on my own," added Sandecker. "The Miami coroner backed Jessie's judgment. Physical characteristics of the bodies in the morgue didn't match the three men who took off in the *Prosperteer.*"

Pitt looked from Sandecker to Jessie LeBaron, realizing he was getting involved in something he had wished to avoid: the emotional entanglements complicating any project that depended on solid research, practical engineering, and razor-sharp organization.

"Bodies and clothes switched," said Pitt. "Personal jewelry replaced with fakes. Any thoughts on a motive, Mrs. LeBaron?"

"I don't know what to think."

"Did you know that between the time the blimp vanished and when it reappeared in Key Biscayne the gas bags inside the hull would have had to be reinflated with helium?"

She opened her purse, took out a Kleenex, and daintily dabbed at her nose, to give her something to do with her hands. "After the police released the *Prosperteer,* my husband's crew chief inspected every inch of her. I have his report, if you care to see it. You're very perceptive. He found that the gas bags had been refilled. Not with helium, but with hydrogen."

Pitt looked up in surprise. "Hydrogen? That hasn't been used in airships since the *Hindenburg* burned."

"Not to worry," said Sandecker. "The *Prosperteer*'s gas bags have been refilled with helium."

"So what's going down?" Pitt asked cautiously.

Sandecker gave him a hard look. "I hear you want to go after the *Cyclops.*"

"It's no secret," answered Pitt.

"You'd have to do it on your own time without NUMA personnel and equipment. Congress would eat me alive if they learned I sanctioned a treasure hunt with government funds."

"I'm aware of that."

"Will you listen to another proposal?"

"I'll listen."

"I'm not going to hand you a lot of double-talk about doing me a great service by keeping this conversation to yourself. If it gets out I go down the drain, but that's my problem. True?"

"If you say so, yes."

"You were scheduled to direct a survey of the sea floor in the Bering Sea off the Aleutians next month. I'll bring in Jack Harris from the deep-ocean mining project to replace you. To head off any questions or later investigations or bureaucratic wrongdoing, we'll sever your connections with NUMA. As of now, you're on leave of absence until you find Raymond LeBaron."

"Find Raymond LeBaron," Pitt repeated sarcastically. "A piece of cake. The trail is two weeks cold and getting colder by the hour. No motive, no leads, not one clue to why he vanished, who did it, and how. Impossible is an understatement."

"Will you at least give it a try?" asked Sandecker.

Pitt stared at the teakwood planking that made up the floor of the admiral's office, his eyes seeing a tropical sea two thousand miles away. He disliked becoming linked with a riddle without being able to calculate at the very least an approximate solution. He knew Sandecker knew that he would accept the challenge. Chasing after an unknown over the next horizon was a lure Pitt could never resist.

"If I take this on, I'd need NUMA's best scientific team to man a first-rate research vessel. The resources and political clout to back me up. Military support in case of trouble."

"Dirk, my hands are tied. I can offer you nothing."

"What?"

"You heard me. The situation requires the search be conducted as quietly as possible. You'll have to make do without any help from NUMA."

"Have you got both oars in the water?" Pitt demanded. "You expect me, one man working alone, to accomplish what half the Navy, Air Force, and Coast Guard failed to do? Why, hell, they couldn't find a one-hundred-and-fifty-foot airship until it showed up on its own. What am I supposed to use, a dowser and a canoe?"

"The idea," Sandecker explained patiently, "is to fly LeBaron's last known course in the *Prosperteer*."

Pitt slowly sank into an office sofa. "This is the craziest scheme I've ever heard," he said, unbelieving. He turned to Jessie. "Do you go along with this?"

"I'll do whatever it takes to find my husband," she said evenly.

"A cuckoo's nest," Pitt said gravely. He stood and began to pace the room, clasping and unclasping his hands. "Why the secrecy? Your husband was an important man, a celebrity, a confidant of the rich and famous, closely connected with high government officials, a financial guru to executives of major corporations. Why in God's name am I the only man in the country who can search for him?"

"Dirk," Sandecker said softly. "Raymond LeBaron's financial em-

104

pire touches hundreds of thousands of people. Right now, it's hanging in limbo because he's still among the missing. It can't be proven whether he's alive or dead. The government has called off any further hunt, because over five million dollars have been spent by military search and rescue teams without a sighting, without a hint of where he might have disappeared. Budget-conscious congressmen will howl for scalps if more government money is spent on another fruitless effort."

"What about the private sector and LeBaron's own business associates?"

"Many business leaders respected LeBaron, but at one time or another most of them were burned by him in his editorials. They won't spend a dime or go out of their way to look for him. As to the men around him, they have more to gain by his death."

"So does Jessie here," said Pitt, gazing at her.

She smiled thinly. "I can't deny it. But the bulk of his estate goes to charities and other family members. I do, however, receive a substantial inheritance."

"You must own a yacht, Mrs. LeBaron. Why don't you assemble your own crew of investigators and look for your husband?"

"There are reasons, Dirk, why I can't conduct a large publicized effort. Reasons you needn't know. The admiral and I think there is a chance, a very slight chance, that three people can quietly retrace the flight of the *Prosperteer* under the same conditions and discover what happened to Raymond."

"Why bother?" asked Pitt. "All islands and reefs within the blimp's fuel range were covered by the initial search. I'd only be covering the same trail."

"They might have missed something."

"Like maybe Cuba?"

Sandecker shook his head. "Castro would have claimed LeBaron overflew Cuban territory under instructions from the CIA and flaunted the blimp's capture to the world. No, there has to be another answer."

Pitt walked over to the corner windows and gazed longingly down at a fleet of small sailboats that were holding a regatta on the Anacostia River. The white sails gleamed against the dark green water as they raced toward the buoy markers.

"How do we know where to concentrate?" he asked without turning. "We're looking at a search grid as large as a thousand square miles. It would take weeks to cover it properly."

"I have all my husband's records and charts," said Jessie.

105

"He left them behind?"

"No, they were found in the blimp."

Pitt silently watched the sailboats, his arms crossed in front of him. He tried to probe the motives, penetrate the intrigue, lay out the safeguards. He tried to segregate each into an orderly niche.

"When do we go?" he asked finally.

"Sunrise tomorrow morning," Sandecker replied.

"You both still insist I lead the fishing expedition?"

"We do," Jessie said flatly.

"I want two old hands for my crew. They're both on NUMA's payroll. Either I get them or I'll walk."

Sandecker's face clouded. "I've already explained—"

"You've got the moon, Admiral, and you're asking for Mars. We've been friends long enough for you to know I don't operate on a half-assed basis. Put the two men I need on leaves of absence too. I don't care how you do it."

Sandecker wasn't angry, wasn't even annoyed. If there was one man in the country who could pull off the unthinkable, it was Pitt. The admiral had no more cards to play, so he folded.

"All right," he said quietly. "You've got them."

"There's one more thing."

"Which is?" Sandecker demanded.

Pitt turned around with a bleak smile. His gaze went from Jessie to the admiral. Then he shrugged and said, "I've never flown a blimp."

14

"APPEARS TO ME YOU'RE MAKING an end run behind my back," said Sam Emmett, the outspoken chief of the Federal Bureau of Investigation.

The President looked across his desk in the Oval Office and smiled benignly. "You're absolutely right, Sam. I'm doing exactly that."

"I give you credit for laying it on the line."

"Don't get upset, Sam. This in no way reflects any displeasure with you or the FBI."

"Then why can't you tell me what this is all about?" Emmett asked, holding his indignation in check.

"In the first place, it's primarily a foreign affairs matter."

"Has Martin Brogan at CIA been consulted?"

"Martin has not been called in. You have my word on it."

"And in the second place?"

The President was not about to be pushed. "That's my business."

Emmett stiffened. "If the President wishes my resignation—"

"I don't wish anything of the sort," the President cut in. "You're the ablest and best-qualified man to head up the bureau. You've done a magnificent job, and I've always been one of your biggest boosters. However, if you want to pick up your marbles and go home because you think your vanity has been dented, then go right ahead. Prove me wrong about you."

"But if you don't trust—"

"Wait just a damned minute, Sam. Let's not say anything we'll be sorry about tomorrow. I'm not questioning your loyalty or integrity. No one is stabbing you in the back. We aren't talking crime or espionage. This matter doesn't directly concern the FBI or any of the intelligence agencies. The bottom line is that it's you who has to trust me, at least for the next week. Will you do that?"

Emmett's ego was temporarily soothed. He shrugged and then relented. "You win, Mr. President. Status quo. I'll follow your lead."

The President sighed heavily. "I promise I won't let you down, Sam."

"I appreciate that."

"Good. Now let's start at the beginning. What have you got on the dead bodies from Florida?"

The tight uneasiness went out of Emmett's expression, and he noticeably relaxed. He opened his attaché case and handed the President a leather-bound folder.

"Here is a detailed report from the Walter Reed pathology lab. Their examination was most helpful in giving us a lead for identification."

The President looked at him in surprise. "You identified them?"

"It was the analysis of the borscht paste that opened the door."

"Borscht what?"

"You recall that the Dade County coroner fixed death by hypothermia, or freezing?"

"Yes."

"Well, borscht paste is a god-awful food supplement given to Russian cosmonauts. The stomachs of the three corpses were loaded with the stuff."

"You're telling me that Raymond LeBaron and his crew were exchanged for three dead Soviet cosmonauts?"

Emmett nodded. "We were even able to put a name on them through a defector, a former flight surgeon with the Russian space program. He'd examined each of them on several occasions."

"When did he defect?"

"He came over to our side in August of '87."

"A little over two years ago."

"That's correct," Emmett acknowledged. "The names of the cosmonauts found in LeBaron's blimp are Sergei Zochenko, Alexander Yudenich, and Ivan Ronsky. Yudenich was a rookie, but Zochenko and Ronsky were both veterans with two space flights apiece."

"I'd give my next year's salary to know how they came to be inside that damned blimp."

"Regrettably, we turned up nothing concerning that part of the mystery. At the moment, the only Russians circling the earth are four cosmonauts on board the Salyut 9 space station. But the NASA people, who are monitoring the flight, say they're all in good health."

The President nodded. "So that eliminates any Soviet cosmonaut on a space flight and leaves only those on the ground."

"That's the odd twist," Emmett continued. "According to the forensic pathology people at Walter Reed, the three men they examined probably froze to death while in space."

The President's eyebrows raised. "Can they prove it?"

"No, but they say several factors point in that direction, starting with the borscht paste and the analysis of other condensed foods the Soviets are known to consume during space travel. Also evident were physiological signs the men had breathed air of a high oxygen constant and spent considerable time in a weightless environment."

"Wouldn't be the first time the Soviets have launched men into space and failed to retrieve them. They could have been up there for years, and fell to earth only a few weeks ago after their orbit decayed."

"I'm only aware of two instances where the Soviets suffered fatalities," said Emmett. "The cosmonaut whose craft became tangled in the shrouds of its reentry parachute and slammed into Siberia at five hundred miles an hour. And the three Soyuz crewmen who died after a faulty hatch leaked away their oxygen."

"The disasters they couldn't cover up," said the President. "The CIA has recorded at least thirty cosmonaut deaths since the beginning of their space missions. Nine of them are still up there, drifting around in space. We can't advertise the fact on our end because it would jeopardize our intelligence sources."

"We-know-but-they-don't-know-we-know kind of affair."

"Precisely."

"Which brings us back to the three cosmonauts we've got lying here in Washington," said Emmett, clutching his briefcase on his lap.

"And a hundred questions, beginning with, Where did they come from?"

"I did some checking with the Aerospace Defense Command Center. Their technicians say the only spacecraft the Russians have sent aloft large enough to support a manned crew—besides their orbiting station shuttles—were the Selenos lunar probes."

At the word "lunar" something clicked in the President's mind. "What about the Selenos probes?"

"Three went up and none came back. The Defense Command boys thought it highly unusual for the Soviets to screw-up three times in a row on simple moon orbiting flights."

"You think they were manned?"

"I do indeed," said Emmett. "The Soviets wallow in deception.

109

As you suggested, they almost never admit to a space failure. And keeping the buildup for their coming moon landing clouded in secrecy was strictly routine."

"Okay, if we accept the theory the three bodies came from one of the Selenos spacecraft, where did it land? Certainly not through their normal reentry path over the steppes of Kazakhstan."

"My guess is somewhere in or around Cuba."

"Cuba." The President slowly rolled the two syllables from his lips. Then he shook his head. "The Russians would never allow their national heroes, living or dead, to be used for some kind of crazy intelligence scheme."

"Maybe they don't know."

The President looked at Emmett. "Don't know?"

"Let's say for the sake of argument that their spacecraft had a malfunction and fell in or near Cuba during reentry. About the same time, Raymond LeBaron and his blimp show up searching for a treasure ship and are captured. Then, for some unfathomable reason, the Cubans switch the cosmonauts' bodies for LeBaron and his crew and send the blimp back to Florida."

"Do you have any idea how ridiculous that sounds?"

Emmett laughed. "Of course, but considering the known facts, it's the best I can come up with."

The President leaned back and stared at the ornate ceiling. "You know, you just might have struck a vein."

A quizzical look crossed Emmett's face. "How so?"

"Try this on for size. Suppose, just suppose, Fidel Castro is trying to tell us something."

"He picked a strange way to send out a signal."

The President picked up a pen and began doodling on a pad. "Fidel has never been a stickler for diplomatic niceties."

"Do you want me to continue the investigation?" Emmett asked.

"No," the President answered tersely.

"You still insist on keeping the bureau in the dark?"

"This is not a domestic matter for the Justice Department, Sam. I'm grateful for your help, but you've taken it about as far as you can go."

Emmett snapped his attaché case shut and rose to his feet. "Can I ask a touchy question?"

"Shoot."

"Now that we've established a link, regardless of how weak, to a possible abduction of Raymond LeBaron by the Cubans, why is the

110

President of the United States keeping it to himself and forbidding his investigative agencies to follow up?"

"A good question, Sam. Perhaps in a few days we'll both know the answer."

Moments after Emmett left the Oval Office, the President turned in his swivel chair and stared out the window. His mouth went dry and sweat soaked his armpits. He was gripped by foreboding that there was a tie between the Jersey Colony and the Soviet lunar probe disasters.

15

IRA HAGEN STOPPED his rental car at the security gate and displayed a government ID card. The guard made a phone call to the visitors center of the Harvey Pattenden National Physics Laboratory, then waved Hagen through.

He drove up the drive and found an empty space in a sprawling parking lot crowded by a sea of multicolored cars. The grounds surrounding the laboratory were landscaped with clusters of pine trees and moss rock planted amid rolling mounds of grass. The building was typical of tech centers that had mushroomed around the country. Contemporary architecture with heavy use of bronze glass and brick walls curving at the corners.

An attractive receptionist, sitting behind a horseshoe-shaped desk, looked up and smiled as he walked through the lobby. "May I help you?"

"Thomas Judge to see Dr. Mooney."

She went through the phone routine again and nodded. "Yes, Mr. Judge. Please enter the security center to my rear. They'll direct you from there."

"Before I go in, can I borrow your men's room?"

"Certainly," she said, pointing. "The door on the right beneath the mural."

Hagen thanked her and passed under a massive painting of a futuristic starship soaring between a pair of spectral blue-green planets. He went into a stall, closed the door, and sat down on the toilet. Opening a briefcase, he removed a yellow legal pad and turned to the middle. Then, writing on the upper back of the page, he made a series of tiny cryptic notes and diagrams on the security systems he'd observed since entering the building. A good undercover operative would never put anything down on paper, but Hagen could afford to run fast and loose, knowing the President would bail him out if his cover was blown.

A few minutes later he strolled out of the restroom and entered a glass-enclosed room manned by four uniformed security guards, who eyeballed an array of twenty television monitors mounted against one wall. One of the guards rose from a console and approached the counter.

"Sir?"

"I have an appointment with Dr. Mooney."

The guard scanned a visitor list. "Yes, sir, you must be Thomas Judge. May I see some identification, please?"

Hagen showed him his driver's license and government ID. Then he was politely asked to open the briefcase. After a cursory search the guard silently gestured for Hagen to close it, asked him to sign a "time in and out" sheet, and gave him a plastic badge to clip on his breast pocket.

"Dr. Mooney's office is straight down the corridor through the double doors at the end."

In the corridor, Hagen paused to put on his reading glasses and peer at two bronze plaques on the wall. Each bore the raised profile of a man. One was dedicated to Dr. Harvey Pattenden, founder of the laboratory, and gave a brief description of his accomplishments in the field of physics. But it was the other plaque that intriqued Hagen. It read:

In memory of
Dr. Leonard Hudson
1926–1965
Whose creative genius is an
inspiration for all who follow.

Not very original, Hagen thought. But he had to give Hudson credit for playing the dead-man game down to the last detail.

He entered the anteroom and smiled warmly at the secretary, a demure older woman in a mannish navy-blue suit. "Mr. Judge," she said, "please go right in. Dr. Mooney is expecting you."

"Thank you."

Earl J. Mooney was thirty-six, younger than Hagen had expected when he studied a file on the doctor's history. His background was surprisingly similar to Hudson's; same brilliant mind, same high academic record, even the same university. A fat kid who went thin and became director of Pattenden Lab. He stared through pine-green eyes under thunderous eyebrows and above a Pancho Villa mous-tache. Dressed casually in a white sweater and blue jeans, he seemed remote from intellectual rigor.

He came from behind the desk, scattered with papers, notebooks, and empty Pepsi bottles, and pumped Hagen's hand. "Sit down, Mr. Judge, and tell me what I can do for you."

Hagen lowered his bulk into a straight-back chair and said, "As I mentioned over the phone, I'm with the General Accounting Office, and we've had a legislative request to review your accounting sys-tems and audit research funding expenditures."

"Who was the legislator who made the request?"

"Senator Henry Kaltenbach."

"I hope he doesn't think Pattenden Lab is mixed up in fraud," said Mooney defensively.

"Not at all. You know the senator's reputation for smelling out misuse in government funding. His witch-hunts make good publicity for his election campaign. Just between you and me, there're many of us at GAO who wish he'd fall through an open manhole and stop sending us out chasing moonbeams. However, I must admit in all fairness to the senator, we *have* turned up discrepancies at other think tanks."

Mooney was quick to correct him. "We prefer to think of ourselves as a research facility."

"Of course. Anyway, we're making spot checks."

"You must understand, our work here is highly classified."

"The design of nuclear rocketry and third-generation nuclear weapons whose power is focused into narrow radiation beams that travel at the speed of light and can destroy targets deep in space."

Mooney looked at Hagen queerly. "You're very well informed."

Hagen shrugged it off. "A very general description given to me by my superior. I'm an accountant, Doctor, not a physicist. My mind can't function in the abstract. I flunked high school calculus. Your secrets are safe. My job is to help see the taxpayer gets his money's worth out of government-funded programs."

"How can I help you?"

"I'd like to talk to your controller and administration officials. Also, the staff that handles the financial records. My auditing team will arrive from Washington in two weeks. I'd appreciate it if we could set up someplace out of your way, preferably close to where the records are kept."

"You'll have our fullest cooperation. Naturally, I must have security clearances for you and your team."

114

"Naturally."

"I'll take you around personally and introduce you to our controller and accounting staff."

"One more thing," said Hagen. "Do you permit after-hours work?"

Mooney smiled. "Unlike nine-to-five office people, physicists and engineers have no set hours. Many of us work around the clock. I've often put in thirty hours at a stretch. It also helps to stagger the time on our computers."

"Would it be possible for me to do a little preliminary checking from now until, say, about ten o'clock this evening?"

"I don't see why not," Mooney said agreeably. "We have an all-night cafeteria on the lower level if you want to grab a bite. And a security guard is always nearby to point out directions."

"And keep me out of the secret areas." Hagen laughed.

"I'm sure you're familiar with facility security."

"True," Hagen admitted. "I'd be a rich man if I had a dime for every hour I put in auditing different departments of the Pentagon."

"If you'll come this way," said Mooney, heading for the door.

"Just out of curiosity," Hagen said, remaining in his chair. "I've heard of Harvey Pattenden. He worked with Robert Goddard, I believe."

"Yes, Dr. Pattenden invented several of our early rocket engines."

"But Leonard Hudson is unfamiliar to me."

"A pretty bright guy," said Mooney. "He paved the way by design-engineering most of our spacecraft years before they were actually built and sent aloft. If he hadn't died in his prime, there's no telling what he might have achieved."

"How did he die?"

"Light-plane crash. He was flying to a seminar in Seattle with Dr. Gunnar Eriksen when their plane exploded in midair and dropped into the Columbia River."

"Who was Eriksen?"

"A heavy thinker. Perhaps the most brilliant astrophysicist the country ever produced."

A tiny alarm went off in Hagen's mind. "Did he have any particular pursuit?"

"Yes, it was geolunar synoptic morphology for industrialized peoplement."

"Could you translate?"

"Of course." Mooney laughed. "Eriksen was obsessed with the idea of building a colony on the moon."

115

16

TEN HOURS AHEAD IN TIME, 2 A.M. in Moscow, four men were grouped around a fireplace that warmed a small sitting room inside the Kremlin. The room was poorly lit and had a morbid feel about it. Cigarette smoke mingled with that of a single cigar.

Soviet President Georgi Antonov stared thoughtfully at the undulating flames. He had removed his coat after a light dinner and replaced it with an old fisherman's sweater. His shoes were off and his stocking feet casually propped on an embroidered ottoman.

Vladimir Polevoi, head of the Committee for State Security, and Sergei Kornilov, chief of the Soviet space program, wore dark wool suits, custom-tailored in London, while General Yasenin sat in full bemedaled uniform.

Polevoi threw the report and photographs on a low table and shook his head in amazement. "I don't see how they accomplished it without a breach of secrecy."

"Such an extraordinary advance seems inconceivable," Kornilov agreed. "I won't believe it until I see more proof."

"The proof is evident in the photographs," said Yasenin. "Rykov's report leaves no room for doubt. Study the detail. The two figures standing on the moon are real. They're not an illusion cast by shadows or created by a flaw in the scanning system. They exist."

"The space suits do not match those of American astronauts," Kornilov retorted. "The helmets are also designed differently."

"I won't argue over trivials," said Yasenin. "But there is no mistaking the weapon in their hands. I can positively identify it as a surface-to-air missile launcher of American manufacture."

"Then where is their spacecraft?" Kornilov persisted. "Where is their lunar rover? They couldn't just materialize out of nowhere."

"I share your doubts," said Polevoi. "An absolute impossibility for the Americans to put men and supplies on the moon without our intelligence network monitoring the progress. Our tracking stations would have detected any strange movement entering or coming from space."

"Even stranger yet," said Antonov, "is why the Americans have never announced such a momentous achievement. What do they gain by keeping it a secret?"

Kornilov gave a slight nod. "All the more reason to challenge Rykov's report."

"You're all overlooking one important fact," said Yasenin in a level tone. "Selenos 4 went missing immediately after its scanners recorded the figures in the photographs. I say our space probe was damaged by rocket fire which penetrated the hull, drained away the capsule's pressure, and killed our cosmonauts."

Polevoi looked at him, startled. "What cosmonauts?"

Yasenin and Kornilov exchanged bemused looks. "There are some things even the KGB doesn't know," said the general.

Polevoi looked squarely at Kornilov. "Selenos 4 was a manned probe?"

"As were Selenos 5 and 6. Each craft carried three men."

He turned to Antonov, who was calmly puffing on a Havana cigar. "You knew about this?"

Antonov nodded. "Yes, I was briefed. But you must remember, Vladimir, not all matters concerning space fall under state security."

"None of you wasted any time running to me when your precious moon probe fell and vanished in the West Indies," Polevoi said angrily.

"An unforeseen circumstance," Yasenin patiently explained. "After its return from the moon, control could not be established for Selenos 4's earth reentry. The engineers at our space command wrote it off as a dead lunar probe. After orbiting for nearly a year and a half, another attempt was made to establish command. This time the guidance systems responded, but the reentry manuever was only partially successful. Selenos 4 fell ten thousand miles short of its touchdown area. It was imperative we keep the deaths of our cosmonaut heroes secret. Naturally the services of the KGB were required."

"How many lost cosmonauts does that make?" asked Polevoi.

"Sacrifices must be made to ensure Soviet destiny," Antonov murmured philosophically.

"And to cover up blunders in our space program," Polevoi said bitterly.

117

"Let's not argue," cautioned Antonov. "Selenos 4 made a great contribution before it impacted in the Caribbean Sea."

"Where it has yet to be found," Polevoi added.

"True," said Yasenin. "But we retrieved the lunar surface data. That was the main purpose of the mission."

"Don't you think American space surveillance systems tracked its descent and pinpointed the landing position? If they had set their minds on salvaging Selenos 4, they'd already have it sitting hidden away inside a secure facility."

"Of course they tracked the descent trajectory," said Yasenin. "But their intelligence analysts had no reason to believe Selenos 4 was anything but a scientific deep-space probe that was programmed to land in Cuban waters."

"There is a crack in your carefully laid plot," Polevoi argued. "The United States rescue forces made an exhaustive air and sea search for the missing capitalist Raymond LeBaron in the same general area only a few days after Selenos 4 dropped from orbit. I have strong suspicions their search was a decoy to find and retrieve our space-craft."

"I read your report and analysis of the LeBaron disappearance," said Kornilov. "I disagree with your conclusion. Nowhere did I see that they conducted an underwater search. The rescue mission was soon called off. LeBaron and his crew are still listed as missing in the American press and presumed dead. That event was merely a coincidence, nothing more."

"Then we all agree that Selenos 4 and her cosmonauts lie some-where on the bottom of the sea." Antonov paused to blow a smoke ring. "The questions we still face are, Do we concede the probability the Americans may have a base on the moon, and if so, What do we do about it?"

"I believe it exists," Yasenin said with conviction.

"We cannot ignore the possibility," Polevoi granted.

Antonov stared narrowly at Kornilov. "And you, Sergei?"

"Selenos 8, our first manned lunar landing mission, is scheduled for launch in seven days," he answered slowly. "We cannot scrap the mission as we did when the Americans upstaged us with their Apollo program. Because our leaders saw no glory in being the second nation to set men on the moon we tucked our tail between our legs and quit. It was a great mistake to place political ideology above scientific achievement. Now we have a proven heavy-lift launch vehicle ca-pable of placing an entire space station with a crew of eight men on lunar soil. The benefits in terms of propaganda and military rewards are immeasurable. If our ultimate goal is to obtain permanent preeminence in space and beat the Americans to Mars, we must follow through. I vote we program the guidance systems of Selenos 8 to land the crew within walking distance of where the astronauts stood in the crater and eliminate them."

"I am in complete agreement with Kornilov," said Yasenin. "The facts speak for themselves. The Americans are actively engaged in imperialistic aggression in space. The photographs we've studied prove they've already destroyed one of our spacecraft and murdered the crew. And I believe the cosmonauts in Selenos 5 and 6 met the same fate. They have taken their colonialistic designs to the moon and claimed it for their own. The evidence is unequivocal. Our cosmonauts will be attacked and murdered when they attempt to plant the red star on lunar soil."

There was a prolonged hush. No one spoke his thoughts.

Polevoi was the first to break the pensive silence. "So you and Kornilov propose we attack them first."

"Yes," said Yasenin, warming to the subject. "Think of the windfall. By capturing the American moon base and its scientific technology intact, we'd be advancing our own space program by ten years."

"The White House would surely mount a propaganda campaign and condemn us before the world as they did with the KAL Flight 007 incident," protested Polevoi.

"They will remain quiet," Yasenin assured him. "How can they announce the seizure of something that isn't known to exist?"

"The general has a point," said Antonov.

"You realize we could be guilty of launching a war in space," cautioned Polevoi.

"The United States struck first. It is our sacred duty to retaliate." Yasenin turned to Antonov. "The decision must be yours."

The President of the Soviet Union again turned his gaze to the fire. Then he laid the Havana in an ashtray and looked down in wonder at his trembling hands. His face, ordinarily ruddy, was gray. The omen was plain. The demons outnumbered the forces of good. Once the course was set in motion, it would hurtle forward outside his control. Yet he could not allow the country to be slapped in the face by the imperialists. At last he turned back to the other men in the room and wearily nodded.

"For Mother Russia and the party," he said solemnly. "Arm the cosmonauts and order them to strike the Americans."

119

17

EIGHT INTRODUCTIONS and three tiresome conversations after his introduction to Dr. Mooney, Hagen was seated in a small office feverishly pounding an adding machine. Scientists dote on computers and engineers fondle digital calculators, but accountants are a Victorian lot. They still prefer traditional adding machines with thumb-size buttons and paper tapes that spit out printed totals.

The controller was a CPA, a graduate of the University of Texas School of Business, and an ex-Navy man. And he had the engraved degrees and photographs of the ships he'd served on displayed on the oak-paneled wall of his office to prove it. Hagen had detected an uneasiness in the man's eyes, but no more than he'd expect from any corporate finance director who had a government auditor snooping around his private territory.

There had been no suspicious look, no hesitation, when he asked to spot-check the telephone records for the last three years. Though his accounting experience with the Justice Department was limited to photographing ledgers in the dead of night, he knew enough of the jargon to talk a good line. Anyone who happened to glance in his office and saw him scribbling notes and intently examining the tape on the adding machine would have thought he was an old pro.

The numbers on the tape were exactly that, numbers. But the note scribbling consisted of a methodical diagram of the placement and view angles of the security TV cameras between his office and Mooney's. He also wrote out two names and added several notations beside each one. The first was Raymond LeBaron and the second was Leonard Hudson. But now he had a third: Gunnar Eriksen.

He was certain that Eriksen had faked his death along with Hudson and dropped from the living to work on the Jersey Colony project. He also knew Hudson and Eriksen would never completely cut their ties with Pattenden Laboratory. The facility and its high-powered crop of young scientists were too great an asset to ignore. There had to be an underground channel to the "inner core."

The telephone records for a facility with three thousand employees filled several cardboard cartons. Control had been tight. Everyone who used a phone for any purpose, business or personal, had to keep a diary of the calls. Hagen wasn't about to attempt an examintion of each one. That chore would take weeks. He was concerned only with the entries in Mooney's monthly diaries, especially those involving long distance.

Hagen was not psychic, nor was he as exact as some men he knew who had a talent for detecting an irregularity, but he had an eye and a gut instinct for the hidden that seldom failed him.

He copied down six numbers that Mooney had phoned more than once in the past ninety days. Two were itemized as personal calls, four as company calls. Long shots all. Still, it was the only way he might trace a lead to another member of the "inner core."

Playing by the rules, he picked up the phone and punched the Pattenden Lab operator, requesting an open line and promising to record all his calls. The hour was late, and most of the list showed area codes of numbers in the Middle West or in the East Coast. Their time zones were two or three hours ahead and they had likely shut down for the day, but he doggedly began calling anyway.

"Centennial Supply," announced a male in a bored tone.

"Yes, hello, is anyone in this evening?"

"The office is closed. This is the twenty-four-hour order desk."

"My name is Judge, and I'm with the federal government," said Hagen, using his cover in case the phone was tapped. "We're doing an audit of the Pattenden Physics Laboratory in Bend, Oregon."

"You'll have to call back tomorrow morning after the office opens."

"Yes, I'll do that. But can you tell me exactly what kind of business Centennial Supply conducts?"

"We supply specialized parts and electronics for recording systems."

"For what applications?"

"Mostly business. Video for recording executive meetings, laboratory experiments, security systems. And executive audio for secretaries. Stuff like that, you know."

"How many employees do you have?"

"Around twelve."

"Thank you very much," said Hagen. "You've been most helpful.

121

Oh, one more thing. Do you get many orders from Pattenden?"

"Not really. Every couple of months they'll order a part to update or modify their video systems."

"Thanks again. Goodbye."

Hagen scratched that one and tried again. His next two calls reached answering machines. One was a chemical lab at Brandeis University in Waltham and the other an unidentified office at the National Science Foundation in Washington. He checked the latter for a follow-up in the morning and tried an individual's number.

"Hello?"

Hagen looked at the name in Mooney's diary. "Dr. Donald Fremont?"

"Yes."

Hagen went through his routine.

"What do you wish to know, Mr. Judge?" Fremont's voice sounded elderly.

"I'm making a spot check of long-distance telephone calls. Has anyone from Pattenden called you in the last ninety days?" Hagen asked, looking at the dates of the calls and playing dumb.

"Why, yes, Dr. Earl Mooney. He was a student of mine at Stanford. I retired five years ago, but we still keep in touch."

"Did you by chance also have a student by the name of Leonard Hudson?"

"Leonard Hudson," he repeated as if trying to recall. "I met him on two occasions. He wasn't in my class, though. Before my time, or I should say before my tenure at Stanford. I was teaching at USC when he was a student."

"Thank you, Doctor. I won't trouble you further."

"Not at all. Glad to help."

Scratch four. The next name from the diary was an Anson Jones. He tried again, well aware it never came easy and that making a gold strike was 99 percent luck.

"Hello?"

"Mr. Jones, my name is Judge."

"Who?"

"Thomas Judge. I'm with the federal government, and we're running an audit on Pattenden Physics Laboratory."

"I don't know any Pattenden. You must have the wrong number."

"Does the name Dr. Earl Mooney ring a bell?"

"Never heard of him."

122

"He's called your number three times in the last sixty days."

"Must be a phone company foulup."

"You *are* Anson Jones, area code three-zero-three, number five-four-seven—"

"Wrong name, wrong number."

"Before you hang up, I have a message."

"What message?"

Hagen paused, and then leaped. "Tell Leo that Gunnar wants him to pay for the airplane. You got that?"

There was silence on the other end for several moments. Then finally, "Is this a crank call?"

"Goodbye, Mr. Jones."

Pay dirt.

He called the sixth listing just to be on the safe side. An answering service for a stock brokerage firm answered. A dry hole.

Elation, that was what he felt. He became even more elated as he added to his notes. Mooney was not one of the "inner core," but he was connected—one of the subordinate officers under the high command.

Hagen tapped out a number in Chicago and waited. After four rings, a woman answered sweetly. "Drake Hotel."

"Ny name is Thomas Judge and I'd like to confirm a room reservation for tomorrow night."

"One moment and I'll connect you with reservations."

Hagen repeated the request for confirmation with the desk clerk. When asked for a credit card number to hold the room for late arrival, he gave Anson Jones's phone number in reverse

"Your room is confirmed, sir."

"Thank you."

What time was it? A glance at his watch told him it was eight minutes to midnight. He closed the briefcase and wiggled into his coat. Taking a cigarette lighter from one pocket, he slid the interior workings from its case. Next, he removed a thin metal shaft with a dental mirror on one end from a slit in his rear coat flap.

Hagen moved to the doorway. Clutching the briefcase between his knees, he stopped short of the threshold and tilted the tiny mirror up and down the corridor. It was empty. He turned the mirror until it reflected the television monitor above the far end of the corridor. Then he positioned the lighter until it barely protruded around the doorframe and pressed the flint lever.

Inside the security booth behind the main lobby, a screen on one of the TV monitors suddenly turned to snow. The guard at the console quickly began checking the circuit lights.

"I've got a problem with number twelve," he announced.

His supervisor came over from a desk and stared at the monitor. "Interference. The eggheads in the electrophysics lab must be at it again."

Suddenly the interference stopped, only to begin again on another monitor.

"That's funny," said the supervisor. "I've never seen it happen in sequence before."

After a few seconds, the screen cleared, showing nothing but an empty corridor. The two security guards simply looked at each other and shrugged.

Hagen turned off the miniature electrical impulse jammer as soon as he stepped inside and closed the door to Mooney's office. He walked softly over to the window and closed the drapes. He slipped on a pair of thin plastic gloves and turned on the overhead lights.

Hagen was a master at the technique of tossing a room. He didn't bother with the obvious, the drawers, files, address and telephone lists. He went directly to a bookshelf and found what he had hoped to find in less than seven minutes.

Mooney might have been one of the leading physicists in the nation, but Hagen had read him like a pictorial magazine. The small notebook was hidden inside a book entitled *Celestial Mechanics in True Perspective* by Horace DeLiso. The contents were in a code employing equations. It was Greek to Hagen but he wasn't fooled by the significance. Normally he would have photographed the pages and put them back, but this time he simply pocketed them, fully realizing he could never have them deciphered in time.

The guards were still struggling with the monitors when he stepped up to the counter.

"Would you like me to sign out?" he said with a smile.

The head security guard came over, a quizzical expression on his face. "Did you just come from finance?"

"Yes."

"We didn't see you on the security TV."

"I can't help that," said Hagen innocently. "I walked out the door and through the hallways until I came here. I don't know what else to tell you."

"Did you see anyone? Anything unusual?"

124

"No one. But the lights flickered and dimmed a couple of times."

The guard nodded. "Electrical interference from the electrophysics lab. That's what I thought it was."

Hagen signed out and walked into a cloudless night, humming softly to himself.

PART II

The Cyclops

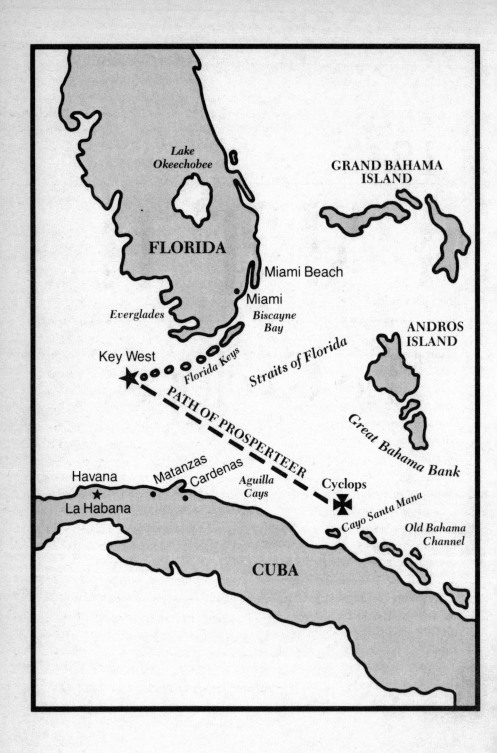

Lake Okeechobee

GRAND BAHAMA ISLAND

FLORIDA

Miami Beach

Miami

Everglades

Biscayne Bay

ANDROS ISLAND

Key West

Florida Keys

Straits of Florida

Great Bahama Bank

PATH OF PROSPERTEER

Havana

Matanzas

Cardenas

Aguilla Cays

Cyclops

La Habana

Cayo Santa Mana

Old Bahama Channel

CUBA

18

October 25, 1989
Key West, Florida

PITT LAY with his back pressed against the cool concrete of the airstrip, looking up at the *Prosperteer.* The sun pushed over the horizon and slowly covered her worn hull in a shroud of pastel orange. The blimp had an eerie quality about it, or so it seemed in Pitt's imagination, an aluminum ghost unsure of where it was supposed to haunt.

He'd been awake most of the time during the flight from Washington to Key West, poring over Buck Caesar's charts of the Old Bahama Channel and retracing Raymond LeBaron's carefully marked flight path. He closed his eyes, trying to get a clear picture of the *Prosperteer*'s spectral wanderings. Unless the gas bags inside the blimp were reinflated from a ship, an extremely unlikely event, the only answer to Raymond LeBaron's whereabouts lay in Cuba.

Something nagged at his mind, a thought that kept returning after he unconsciously brushed it aside, a piece of the picture that became increasingly lucid as he began dwelling on it. And then suddenly it crystallized.

The flight to trace LeBaron's trail was a setup.

A rational and logical conclusion remained a dim outline in a thick mist. The trick was to try to fit it into a pattern. His mind was casting about for directions to explore when he sensed a shadow fall over him.

"Well, well," said a familiar voice, "looks as though Snow White fell for the old apple routine again."

"Either that or he's hibernating," came another voice Pitt recognized.

He opened his eyes, shielded them from the sun with one hand, and looked up at a pair of grinning individuals who stared down. The shorter of the two, a barrel-chested, muscled character with black curly hair and the ironbound look of a man who enjoyed eating bricks for breakfast, was Pitt's old friend and assistant projects director at NUMA, Al Giordino.

Al reached down, grabbed an outstretched hand, and pulled Pitt to his feet as effortlessly as a sanitation worker picking up an empty beer can from park grass.

"Departure time in twelve minutes."

"Our unnamed pilot arrive yet?" Pitt asked.

The other man, slightly taller and much thinner than Giordino, shook his head. "No sign of one."

Rudi Gunn peered through a pair of blue eyes that were magnified by thick-lensed glasses. He had the appearance of an undernourished assistant bookkeeper toiling for a gold watch. The impression was deceptive. Gunn was the overseer of NUMA's oceanographic projects. While Admiral Sandecker waged pitched battles with Congress and the federal bureaucracy, Gunn watched over the agency's day-to-day operation. For Pitt, prying Gunn and Giordino from under Sandecker had been a major victory.

"If we want to match LeBaron's departure time, we'll have to wrestle it aloft ourselves," said Giordino, unconcerned.

"I guess we can manage," said Pitt. "You study the flight manuals?"

Giordino nodded. "Requires fifty hours of instruction and flying time to qualify for a license. The basic control isn't difficult, but the art of keeping that pneumatic scrotum stable in a stiff breeze takes practice."

Pitt couldn't help grinning at Giordino's colorful description. "The equipment loaded on board?"

"Loaded and secured," Gunn assured him.

"Then I guess we might as well shove off."

As they approached the *Prosperteer*, LeBaron's crew chief climbed down the ladder from the control car. He spoke a few words to one of the ground crew and then waved a friendly greeting.

"She's all ready to go, gentlemen."

"How close are we to the actual weather conditions of the previous flight?" asked Pitt.

"Mr. LeBaron was flying against a five-mile-an-hour head wind out of the southeast. You'll buck eight, so figure on compensating. There's a late-season hurricane moving in over the Turks and Caicos

130

Islands. The meteorological guys christened her Little Eva because she's a small blow with a diameter no more than sixty miles wide. The forecasters think she'll swing north toward the Carolinas. If you turn back no later than 1400 hours, Little Eva's outer breeze should provide you with a nice fat tail wind to nudge you home."

"And if we don't?"

"Don't what?"

"Swing back by 1400 hours."

The crew chief smiled thinly. "I don't recommend getting caught in a tropical storm with fifty-mile-an-hour winds, at least not in an airship that's sixty years old."

"You make a strong case," Pitt admitted.

"Allowing for the head wind," said Gunn, "we won't reach the search area until 1030 hours. That doesn't leave us much time to look around."

"Yes," Giordino said, "but LeBaron's known flight path should put us right in the ballpark."

"A tidy package," Pitt mused to no one in particular. "Too tidy."

The three NUMA men were about to climb on board when the LeBaron limousine pulled up beside the blimp. Angelo got out and smartly opened the passenger door. Jessie stepped into the sun and walked over, looking outdoorsy in a designer safari suit with her hair tied in a bright scarf, nineteen-thirties style. She was carrying a suede flight bag.

"Are we ready?" she said brightly, slipping past them and nimbly hustling up the ladder to the control car.

Gunn gave Pitt a grim look. "You didn't tell us we were going on a picnic."

"Nobody told me either," Pitt said, gazing up at Jessie, who had turned and was framed in the doorway.

"My fault," said Jessie. "I forgot to mention that I'm your pilot."

Giordino and Gunn looked as if they had swallowed live squid. Pitt's face wore an amused expression.

He said, "No kidding."

"Raymond taught me to fly the *Prosperteer*," she said. "I've logged over eighty hours at the controls and have a license."

"No kidding," Pitt repeated, becoming intrigued.

Giordino failed to see the humor. "Do you also know how to dive, Mrs. LeBaron?"

"Sky or scuba? I'm certified for both."

"We can't take a woman," said Gunn resolutely.

131

"Please, Mrs. LeBaron," pleaded the crew chief. "We don't know what happened to your husband. The flight might be dangerous."

"We'll use the same communication plan as Raymond's flight," she said, ignoring him. "If we find anything interesting we'll transmit in normal voice. No code this time."

"This is ridiculous," snapped Gunn.

Pitt shrugged. "Oh, I don't know. I'll vote for her."

"You don't really mean it!"

"Why not?" replied Pitt with a sardonic grin. "I firmly believe in equal rights. She has just as much right to get herself killed as we do."

The ground crew stood as silent as pallbearers, their eyes following the old blimp as she lifted into the sunrise. Suddenly she began dropping. They held their breath as the landing wheel touched the crest of a wave. Then she slowly bounced back into the air and struggled to rise.

Someone muttered anxiously, "Lift, baby, lift!"

The *Prosperteer* agonizingly rose a few feet at a time until she finally leveled out at a safe altitude. The ground crew watched motionless, staring until the blimp became a tiny dark speck above the silent horizon. They stood there when she was no longer in view, instinctively quiet, a sense of dread in their hearts. There would be no volleyball game this day. They all herded inside the maintenance truck, overburdening the air conditioning system, clustering around the radio.

The first message came in at 0700 hours. Pitt explained away the shaky liftoff. Jessie had undercompensated for the lack of buoyancy caused by the extra payload Giordino and Gunn had placed on board.

From then on until 1400 hours, Pitt kept the frequency open and maintained a running dialogue, matching his observations with the transcribed report that was recorded during LeBaron's flight.

The crew chief picked up the microphone. "*Prosperteer*, this is Grandma's house. Over."

"Go ahead, Grandma."

"Can you give me your latest VIKOR satellite position."

"Roger. VIKOR reading H3608 by T8090."

The crew chief quickly plotted the position on a chart. "*Prosper-*

teer, you're looking good. I have you five miles due south of Guinchos Cay on the Bahama Bank. Over."

"I read the same, Grandma."

"How are the winds?"

"Judging from the wave crests, I'd say the breeze has picked up to about Force 6 on the Beaufort scale."

"Listen to me, *Prosperteer.* The Coast Guard has issued a new update on Little Eva. She has doubled her speed and swung east. Hurricane warnings are up throughout the southern Bahamas. If she sticks to her present course, she'll strike the east coast of Cuba sometime this evening. I repeat, Little Eva has swung east and is heading in your direction. Call it a day, *Prosperteer,* and beat a course for home."

"Will do, Grandma. Turning onto new course for the Keys."

Pitt was silent for the next half hour. At 1435 hours, the crew chief hailed again.

"*Prosperteer,* come in, please. Over."

No reply.

"Come in, *Prosperteer.* This is Grandma's house. Do you read?"

Still nothing.

The stifling air inside the truck seemed suddenly to turn cold as fear and apprehension gripped the crew. The seconds crawled past and took forever to become minutes as the crew chief tried desperately to raise the blimp.

But the *Prosperteer* did not respond.

The crew chief slammed down the microphone and pushed his way outside the truck through the stunned ground crew. He ran over to the parked limousine and feverishly jerked open a rear door.

"They're gone! We've lost them, the same as the last time!"

The man sitting alone in the rear seat simply nodded. "Keep trying to raise them," he said quietly.

As the crew chief hurried back to the radio, Admiral James Sandecker lifted a telephone receiver from a varnished cabinet and placed a call.

"Mr. President."

"Yes, Admiral."

"They're missing."

"Understood. I've briefed Admiral Clyde Monfort of the Caribbean Joint Task Force. He's already put ships and planes on alert around the Bahamas. As soon as we hang up I'll order him to launch a search and rescue operation."

133

"Please impress upon Monfort the need for speed. I've also been informed the *Prosperteer* disappeared in the predicted path of a hurricane."

"Return to Washington, Admiral, and do not worry. Your people and Mrs. LeBaron should be sighted and picked up within a few hours."

"I'll try to share your optimism, Mr. President. Thank you."

If there was one doctrine Sandecker believed in with all his heart, it was "Never trust a politician's word." He placed another call on the limousine's phone.

"Admiral James Sandecker. I'd like to speak with Admiral Monfort."

"Right away, sir."

"Jim, is that really you?"

"Hello, Clyde. Good to hear your voice."

"Damn, it's been nearly two years. What's on your mind?"

"Tell me, Clyde, have you been alerted for a rescue mission in the Bahamas?"

"Where did you hear that?"

"The rumor mill."

"News to me. Most of our Caribbean forces are conducting an amphibious landing exercise on Jamaica."

"Jamaica?"

"A little muscle-flexing display of military capability to shake up the Soviets and Cubans. Keeps Castro off balance, thinking we're going to invade one of these days."

"Are we?"

"What in hell for? Cuba is the best advertising campaign we've got running that promotes communism as a big economic bust. Besides, better the Soviet Union throws twelve million dollars a day down Castro's toilet than us."

"You've received no orders to keep an eye on a blimp that left on a flight from the Keys this morning?"

There was an ominous silence on the other end of the line.

"I probably shouldn't be telling you this, Jim, but I did receive a verbal order concerning the blimp. I was told to keep our ships and aircraft out of the Bahama Banks and to put a blackout on all communications coming from the area."

"The order come direct from the White House?"

"Don't press your luck, Jim."

"Thanks for setting me straight, Clyde."

134

"Any time. Let's get together next time I'm in Washington."

"I'll look forward to it."

Sandecker hung up, his face red with anger, his eyes fired with fury.

"God help them," he muttered through clenched teeth. "We've all been had."

19

JESSIE'S SMOOTH, HIGH-CHEEKBONED FACE was tense from the strain of fighting the wind gusts and rain squalls that pounded against the skin of the blimp. Her arms and wrists were turning numb as she orchestrated the throttles and the big elevator pitch control. With the added weight from the rain it was becoming nearly impossible to keep the wallowing airship level and steady. She began to feel the icy caress of fear.

"We'll have to head for the nearest land," she said, her voice uneven. "I can't keep her aloft much longer in this turbulence."

Pitt looked at her. "The nearest land is Cuba."

"Better arrested than dead."

"Not yet," Pitt replied from his seat to the right and slightly behind her. "Hang on a little longer. The storm will sweep us back to Key West."

"With the radio out, they won't know where to look if we're forced to ditch in the sea."

"You should have thought of that before you spilled coffee on the transmitter and shorted its circuitry."

She stole a glance at him. God, she thought, it was maddening. He was leaning out the starboard window, nonchalantly peering through a pair of binoculars at the sea below. Giordino was observing out the port side, while Gunn was taking readings off the VIKOR navigating computer and laying out their course on a chart. Every so often, Gunn calmly examined the stylus markings on the recorder of a Schonstedt gradiometer, an instrument for detecting iron by measuring magnetic intensity. All three men looked at though they didn't have a care in the world.

"Didn't you hear what I said?" she asked in exasperation.

"We heard," Pitt replied.

"I can't control her in this wind. She's too heavy. We've got to drop ballast or touch down."

"The last of the ballast was dumped an hour ago."

"Then get rid of that junk you brought on board," she ordered, gesturing to a small mountain of aluminum boxes strapped to the deck.

"Sorry. That junk, as you call it, may come in handy."

"But we're losing lift."

"Do the best you can."

Jessie pointed through the windshield. "The island off to our starboard is Cayo Santa María. The landmass beyond is Cuba. I'm going to bring the blimp around on a southerly course and take our chances with the Cubans."

Pitt swung from the window, his green eyes set and purposeful. "You volunteered for this mission," he said roughly. "You wanted to be one of the boys. Now hang in there."

"Use your head, Pitt," she snapped. "If we wait another half hour the hurricane will tear us to pieces."

"I think I have something," Giordino called.

Pitt moved from his seat over to the port side. "What direction?"

Giordino pointed. "We just passed over it. About two hundred yards off our stern."

"A big one," Gunn said excitedly. "The markings are going off the scale."

"Come about to port," Pitt ordered Jessie. "Take us back over the same course."

Jessie didn't argue. Suddenly caught up in the fervor of the discovery, she felt her exhaustion fall away. She slammed the throttles forward and rolled the blimp to port, using the wind to crab around on a reverse course. A gust slammed into the aluminum envelope, causing a shudder to run through the ship and rocking the control car. Then the buffeting eased and the flight smoothed as the eight tail fins came around and the wind beat from astern.

The interior of the control car was as hushed as the crypt of a cathedral. Gunn unreeled the line from the gradiometer's sensing unit until it dangled four hundred feet below the belly of the blimp and skimmed the rolling swells. Then he turned his attention back to the recorder and waited for the stylus to make a horizontal swing across the graph paper. Soon it began to waver and scratch back and forth.

"Coming up on target," Gunn announced.

137

Giordino and Pitt ignored the wind stream and leaned farther out the windows. The sea was building and foam was spraying from the wave crests, making it difficult to see into the transparent depths. Jessie was having a tougher time of it now, struggling with the controls, trying to reduce the violent shaking and swaying of the blimp, which behaved like a whale fighting its way up the Colorado River rapids.

"I've got her!" Pitt suddenly shouted. "She's lying north and south, about a hundred yards to starboard."

Giordino moved to the opposite side of the control car and gazed down. "Okay, I have her in sight too."

"Can you detect any sign of derricks?" Gunn asked.

"Her outline is distinct, but I can't make out any detail. I'd say she's about eighty feet under the surface."

"More like ninety," said Pitt.

"Is it the *Cyclops*?" Jessie asked anxiously.

"Too early to tell." He turned to Gunn. "Mark the position from the VIKOR."

"Position marked," Gunn acknowledged.

Pitt nodded at Jessie. "All right, pilot, let's make another pass. And this time, as we come about into the wind, try to hover over the target."

"Why don't you ask me to turn lead into gold," she snapped back.

Pitt came over and kissed her lightly on the cheek. "You're doing great. Stick in a little longer and I'll spell you at the controls."

"Don't patronize me," she said testily, but her eyes took on a warm glow and the tension lines around her lips softened. "Just tell me when to stop the bus."

Very self-willed she was, thought Pitt. For the first time he felt himself envying Raymond LeBaron. He returned aft and put a hand on Gunn's shoulder.

"Use the clinometer and see if you can get a rough measurement of her dimensions."

Gunn nodded. "Will do."

"If that's the *Cyclops*," said Giordino happily, "you made a damned good guess."

"A lot of luck mixed with a small amount of hindsight," Pitt admitted. "That, and the fact Raymond LeBaron and Buck Caesar aimed us toward the ballpark. The puzzle is why the *Cyclops* lies outside the main shipping lane."

138

Giordino gave a helpless tilt to his head. "We'll probably never know."

"Coming back on target," Jessie reported.

Gunn set the distance on the clinometer and then sighted through the eyepiece, measuring the length of the shadowy object under the water. He managed to hold the instrument steady as Jessie fought a masterful battle against the wind.

"No way of accurately measuring her beam because it's impossible to see if she lies straight up or on her side," he said, studying the calibrations.

"And the overall length?" asked Pitt.

"Between five hundred thirty and five hundred fifty feet."

"Looking good," Pitt said, visibly relieved. "The *Cyclops* was five hundred and forty-two feet."

"If we drop down closer, I might be able to get a more precise reading," said Gunn.

"One more time, Jessie," Pitt called out.

"I don't think so." She lifted a hand from the controls and pointed out the forward window. "A welcoming committee."

Her expression appeared calm, almost too calm, while the men watched in mild fascination as a helicopter materialized out of the clouds a thousand feet above the blimp. For several seconds it seemed to hang there, fastened in the sky like a hawk eyeing a pigeon. Then it swelled in size as it approached and banked around on a parallel course with the *Prosperteer.* Through the binoculars they could clearly see the grim faces of the pilots and the two pairs of hands grasping the automatic guns that poked through the open side door.

"They brought friends," Gunn said succinctly. He was aiming his binoculars at a Cuban gunboat about four miles away that was planing through the swells, throwing up great wings of sea spray.

Giordino said nothing. He tore the holding straps from the boxes and began throwing the contents on the deck as fast as his hands could move. Gunn joined him as Pitt began assembling a strange-looking screen.

"They're holding up a sign in English," Jessie announced.

"What does it say?" Pitt asked without looking up.

"'Follow us and do not use your radio,'" she read aloud. "What should I do?"

"Obviously we can't use the radio, so smile and wave to them. Let's hope they won't shoot if they see you're a woman."

"I wouldn't count on it," grunted Giordino.

"And keep hovering over the shipwreck," Pitt added.

Jessie didn't like what was going on inside the control car. Her face noticeably paled. She said, "We'd better do what they want."

"Screw them," Pitt said coldly. He unbuckled her seat belt and lifted her away from the controls. Giordino held up a pair of air tanks and Pitt quickly adjusted the straps over her shoulders. Gunn handed her a face mask, swim fins, and a buoyancy compensator vest.

"Quickly," he ordered. "Put these on."

She stood there baffled. "What are you doing?"

"I thought you knew," said Pitt. "We're going for a swim."

"We're what?" The dark gypsy eyes were wide, not so much from alarm as astonishment.

"No time for the defense to make a closing argument," Pitt said calmly. "Call it a wild plan for staying alive and let it go at that. Now do as you're told and lie down on the deck behind the screeen."

Giordino stared dubiously at the inch-thick screen. "Let's hope it does the job. I'd hate to be around if a bullet finds an air tank."

"Fear not," Pitt replied, as the three men hurriedly strapped on their diving gear. "High-tensile plastic. Guaranteed to stop anything up to a twenty-millimeter shell."

With no hands at the controls, the blimp lurched sideways under the onslaught of a fresh gust and pitched downward. Everyone instinctively dropped to the deck and snatched at the nearest handgrip. The boxes that held the equipment skidded madly across the deck and crashed into the pilots' seats.

There was no hesitation, no further attempt at communication. The Cuban commander of the helicopter, thinking the sudden erratic movement of the blimp meant it was trying to escape, ordered his crew to open fire. A storm of bullets struck the starboard side of the *Prosperteer* from no more than thirty yards away. The control car was immediately turned into a shambles. The old yellowed windows melted away in a shower of fragments that splashed cross the deck. The controls and the instrument panel were blasted into twisted junk, filling the shattered cabin with smoke from shorted circuitry.

Pitt lay prone on top of Jessie, Gunn and Giordino blanketing him, listening to the steel-nosed shells thump against the bulletproof screen. Then the gunmen in the helicopter altered their aim and concentrated on the engines. The aluminum cowlings were torn and mangled by the devastating fire until they shredded and blew away in the air stream. The engines coughed and sputtered into silence, their cylinder heads shot away, oil spewing out amid torrents of black smoke.

"The fuel tanks!" Jessie heard herself shouting above the mad din. "They'll explode!"

"The least of our worries," Pitt yelled back in her ear. "The Cubans aren't using incendiary bullets, and the tanks are made out of self-sealing neoprene rubber."

Giordino crawled over to the ripped and jumbled pile of equipment boxes and retrieved what looked to Jessie like some kind of tubular container. He pushed it ahead of him up the steeply tilted deck.

"Need any help?" Pitt yelled.

"If Rudi can brace my legs..." His voice trailed off.

Gunn didn't require a lecture on instructions. He jammed his feet against a bulkhead for support and clutched Giordino around the knees in a vise grip.

The blimp was totally out of control, dead in the sky, the nose pointing at a forty-degree angle toward the sea. All lift was gone and it began to sink from the sky as the Cubans sprayed the plump, exposed envelope. The stabilizer fins still reached for the clouds, but the old *Prosperteer* was in her death throes.

She would not die alone.

Giordino wrestled the tube open, pulled out an M-72 missile launcher, and loaded the 66-millimeter rocket. Slowly, moving with great caution, he eased the snout of the bazookalike weapon over the jagged glass left in the frame of the window and took aim.

To the astonished men in the patrol boat, less than one mile away, the helicopter appeared to disintegrate in a huge mushroom of fire. The sound of the explosion burst through the air like thunder, followed by a flaming rain of twisted metal that hissed and steamed when it hit the water.

The blimp still hung there, pivoting slowly on its axis. Helium surged through gaping rents in the hull. The circular supports inside began snapping like dried sticks. As if heaving out her final breath the *Prosperteer* caved in on herself, collapsing like an eggshell, and fell into the seething whitecaps.

The raging devastation all happened so quickly. In less than twenty seconds both engines were torn from their mounts, and the support beams holding the control car twisted apart, accompanied by a banshee screeching sound. Like a fragile toy thrown on the sidewalk by a destructive child, the rivets burst and the internal structure shrieked in agony as it disintegrated.

The control car kept sinking into the deep, the water flooding through the shattered windows. It was as if a giant hand was pressing the blimp downward until at last she slipped into the depths and disappeared. Then the control car broke free and dropped like a falling leaf, trailed by a confused maze of wire and cable. The remains of the duraluminum envelope followed, flapping wildly like a drunken bat in flight.

A school of yellowtail snappers darted from under the plunging mass an instant before it struck the sea floor, the impact throwing up billowing clouds of fine sand.

Then all was as quiet as a grave, the deathly stillness broken only by the gentle gurgle of escaping air.

On the turbulent surface the stunned crew of the gunboat began sweeping back and forth over the crash sites, searching for any sign of survivors. They only found spreading pools of fuel and oil.

The winds from the approaching hurricane increased to Force 8. The waves reached a height of eighteen feet, making any further search impossible. The boat's captain had no choice but to turn about on a course toward a safe harbor in Cuba, leaving behind a swirling and malignant sea.

20

THE OPAQUE CLOUD OF SILT that hid the shredded remains of the *Prosperteer* was slowly carried away by a weak bottom current. Pitt rose to his hands and knees and looked around the shambles that had been the control car. Gunn was sitting upright on the deck, his back pressed against a buckled bulkhead. His left ankle was swelling into the shape of a coconut, but he sucked on his mouthpiece and raised one hand with the fingers formed in a V.

Giordino doggedly pulled himself upright and tenderly pressed the right side of his chest. One broken ankle and probably a few ribs between them, thought Pitt. It could be worse. He bent over Jessie and lifted her head. Her eyes appeared blank through the lens of the face mask. The hollow hiss of her regulator and the rise and fall of her chest indicated her breathing was normal, if a bit on the rapid side. He ran his fingers over her arms and legs but found no sign of a fracture. Except for a rash of black-and-blue marks that would bloom in the next twenty-four hours, she seemed whole. As if to assure him, she reached out for his arm and gave it a firm squeeze.

Satisfied, Pitt turned his attention to himself. All the joints swiveled properly, the muscles functioned, nothing seemed distorted. Yet he didn't escape unscathed. A purplish lump was rising on his forehead, and he noticed a strange stiffening sensation in his neck. Pitt canceled out the discomfort with the consolation that no one appeared to be bleeding. One hairline brush with death was enough for one day, he mused. The last thing they needed now was a shark attack.

Pitt focused on the next problem: getting out of the control car. The door was jammed, small wonder after the beating it had taken. He sat on his buttocks, grasped both hands on the bent frame, and lashed out with his feet. Lashed out was an exaggeration. The water pressure impeded the thrust of his legs. He felt as though he was trying to kick out the bottom of a huge jar of glue. On the sixth attempt, when the balls and heels of his feet could take no more, the metal seal gave and the door swung outward in slow motion.

Giordino emerged first, his head swathed by a surge of bubbles from his breathing regulator. He reached back inside, dug his feet into the sand, braced himself for the chest pain that was sure to come, and gave a mighty heave. With Pitt and Gunn shoving from the inside, a large, unwieldy bundle slowly squeezed through the door and dropped to the sand. Then eight steel tanks containing 104 cubic feet of air were passed out to the waiting hands of Giordino.

Inside the mangled control car Jessie fought to equalize her ears with the water pressure. The blood roared and a stabbing pain burst in her head, blanking out the trauma of the crash. She pinched her nose and snorted furiously. On the fifth try her ears finally popped, and the relief was so marvelous that tears came to her eyes. She clamped her teeth on the regulator's mouthpiece and sucked in a lungful of air. How beautiful it would be to wake up in her own bed, she thought. Something touched her hand. It was another hand, firm and rough-skinned. She looked up to see Pitt's eyes staring at her through his mask; they seemed crinkled in a smile. He nodded for her to follow him.

He led her outside into the vast liquid void. She gazed up, watching her air bubbles hiss and swirl toward the restless surface. Despite the turbulence above, visibility on the bottom was nearly two hundred feet and she could clearly see the entire length of the airship's main carcass lying a short distance from the control car. Gunn and Giordino were nowhere in sight.

Pitt gestured for her to wait by the air tanks and the strange bundle. He checked the compass on his left wrist and swam off into the blue haze. Jessie drifted, weightless, her head feeling light from a touch of nitrogen narcosis. An overwhelming sense of loneliness closed over her, but quickly evaporated when she saw Pitt retuning. He made a sign for her to follow, and then he turned and slowly paddled away. Pounding her feet against the water resistance, she quickly caught up with him.

The white sandy bottom gave way to clumps of coral inhabited by a variety of oddly shaped fish. Their natural bright colors were deadened to a soft gray by the scattering and absorption of the water particles that filtered out the reds, oranges, and yellows, leaving only dull greens and blues. They pedaled their fins, moving only an arm's length above the weird and exotically molded underwater jungle, observed queerly by a crowd of small angelfish, pufferfish, and trumpetfish. The amusing scene reminded Pitt of children watching the huge ballooned cartoon characters that float down Broadway in Macy's Thanksgiving Day parade.

Suddenly Jessie dug her fingers into Pitt's leg and pointed above and behind. There, swimming in lazy apathy, only twenty feet away, was a school of barracuda. There must have been two hundred of them, none measuring less than four feet in length. They turned as one and began circling the divers while displaying a beady-eyed curiosity. Then, deciding that Pitt and Jessie were not worth lingering over, they flashed away in the wink of an eye and were lost to view.

When Pitt turned back he saw Rudi Gunn materializing out of the smoky blue curtain. Gunn came to a stop and beckoned for them to hurry in his direction. Then he made the V sign of success.

The meaning was clear. Gunn vigorously kicked with one fin, rapidly rising at an angle until he was about thirty feet above the coral landscape, Pitt and Jessie trailing immediately in his wake.

They had traveled nearly a hundred yards when Gunn abruptly slowed and curved his body into a vertical position, one whitened hand held out, slightly bent finger pointing like the grim reaper.

Like a haunted castle looming from the mists of a Yorkshire moor, the phantom shape of the *Cyclops* rose up through the watery gloom, evil and sinister, as though some unspeakable force lurked within her bowels.

21

PITT HAD DIVED on many shipwrecks and he was the first man to view the *Titanic*, but staring at the lost ghost ship of legend left him numb with an almost superstitious awe. The knowledge that she was the tomb for over three hundred men only deepened her malignant aura.

The sunken ship was lying on her port side with a list of about twenty-five degrees, her bow set toward the north. She did not have the look of anything that was supposed to rest on the sea floor, and mother nature had gone to work laying a veil of sediment and marine organisms over the steel intruder.

The entire hull and superstructure were encrusted with sea growth of every imaginable description—sponges, barnacles, flowery anemones, feathery sea ferns, and slender weeds that gracefully swayed with the current like the arms of dancers. Except for the distorted bow and three fallen derricks, the ship was suprisingly intact.

They found Giordino busily scraping the growth from a small section below the stern railing. He turned at their approach and showed off his handiwork. He had exposed the raised letters that spelled out *Cyclops.*

Pitt glanced at his orange-faced Doxa diver's watch. It seemed an eternity since the blimp crashed, but only nine minutes had passed from the moment they swam out of the control car. It was imperative that they conserve their air. They still had to search the wreck and have enough left in the spare tanks for decompression. The safety margin would be cut dangerously thin.

He checked Jessie's air gauge and studied her eyes. They looked clear and bright. She was breathing slowly in a comfortable rhythm. She gave him a thumbs-up sign and then threw him a coquettish wink. Her brush with death in the *Prosperteer* was forgotten for the moment.

146

Pitt winked back. She's actually enjoying this, he thought.

Using hand signals for communication, the four of them fanned out in a line above the fantail and began prowling her length. The doors of the aft deckhouse had rotted away and the teak deck was heavily worm-eaten. Any flat surface was coated by sediment that gave the appearance of a dusty shroud.

The jackstaff stood bare, the United States ensign having rotted away long ago. The two stern guns pointed aft, mute and deserted. The twin smokestacks stood like sentries over the decaying wreckage of ventilators, bollards and railings, rotting coils of wire and cable still hugging rusting winches. Like a shantytown, each piece of debris offered a nesting place for spiny urchins, arrow crabs, and other creatures of the sea.

Pitt knew from studying a diagram of the *Cyclops'* interior that searching the stern section was a waste of time. The smokestacks stood over the engine room and its crew quarters. If they were to find the La Dorada statue it would most likely be in the general cargo compartment beneath the bridge and forecastle. He motioned the others to continue their probe toward the bow.

They swam slowly, carefully along the catwalk that stretched over the sprawling coal hatches, skirting around the great clamshell loading buckets and under the corroded derricks that reached forlornly toward the refracted rays from above. It became apparent to them that the *Cyclops* had died a quick and violent death. The rotting remains of the lifeboats were forever frozen in their davits and much of the superstructure looked as if it had been crushed by a monstrous fist.

The odd boxlike form of the bridge slowly took form out of the blue-green dusk. The two support legs on the starboard side had buckled, but the hull's tilt to port had compensated for the angle. Peculiarly out of kilter with the rest of the ship, the bridge stood on a perfect horizontal plane.

The dark on the other side of the wheelhouse door looked ominous. Pitt switched on his dive light and drifted slowly inside, taking care not to stir up the silt on the deck with his fins. Dim light filtered through the slime-coated portholes on the forward bulkhead. He brushed away the muck from the glass covering the ship's clock. The tarnished hands were frozen at 12:21. He also examined the big upright compass stand. The interior was still watertight and the needle floated free in kerosene, pointing faithfully toward magnetic north. Pitt noted that the ship's heading was 340 degrees.

On opposite sides of the compass, covered over by a colony of sponges that turned vivid red under Pitt's light, were two postlike objects that rose from the deck and fanned out at the top. Curious Pitt wiped the growth from the port one, revealing a glass face, through which he could barely make out the words AHEAD FULL, HALF, SLOW DEAD SLOW, STOP, and FINISHED WITH ENGINES. It was the bridge telegraph to the engine room. He noted that the brass arrow was pointing to FULL. He floated over and cleaned the glass on the starboard telegraph. The pointer was locked on FINISHED WITH ENGINES.

Jessie was about eight feet behind Pitt when she let out a garbled scream that lifted the hair on the nape of his neck. He spun around, half thinking she was being dragged away by a shark, but she was gesturing frantically at a pair of objects protruding from the silt.

Two human skulls, muck up to their nose openings, stared through empty eye sockets. They give Pitt the disconcerting feeling he was being watched. The bones of another crewman rested against the base of the helm, one skeletal arm still wedged between the spokes of the wheel. Pitt wondered if one of them might be the pitiful remains of Captain Worley.

There was nothing else to see, so Pitt led Jessie outside the wheelhouse and down a companionway to the crew and passenger quarters. At almost the same time, Gunn and Giordino disappeared down a hatch leading to a small cargo hold.

The layer of silt was shallow in this section of the ship, no more than an inch deep. The companionway led to a long passageway with small compartments off to the sides. Each one contained bunks, porcelain sinks, scattered personal effects, and the skeletal relics of their occupants. Pitt soon lost count of the dead. He paused and added air to his buoyancy compensator to keep his body balanced in a free-floating, horizontal position. The slightest touch from his fins would stir up large clouds of blinding silt.

Pitt tapped Jessie on the shoulder and shone his light into a small head with a bathtub and two toilets. He made a questioning gesture. She grinned around her mouthpiece and made a comical but negative reply.

He accidentally struck his dive light against a steampipe running along the ceiling and momentarily knocked the switch into the Off position. The sudden realm of utter darkness was as total and stifling as if they were dropped into a coffin and the lid slammed shut. Pitt had no wish to remain surrounded by eternal black within the grave of the *Cyclops*, and he quickly flicked on the light again, exposing

148

a brilliant yellow and red sponge colony that clung to the bulkheads of the passageway.

It soon became obvious they would find no evidence of the La Dorada statue here. They made their way back through the passageway of death and resurfaced on the forecastle deck. Giordino was waiting and motioned toward a hatch that was frozen half open. Pitt squeezed through, clanging his air tanks on the frame, and dropped down a badly eroded ladder.

He swam through what looked like a baggage cargo hold, twisting around the jumbled and decayed rubbish, heading toward the unearthly glow of Gunn's dive light. A pile of unhinged bones passed under him, the jaw of the skull gaping in what seemed in Pitt's imagination a ghastly scream of terror.

He found Gunn intently examining the rotting interior of a large shipping crate. The grisly skeletal remains of two men were wedged between the crate and a bulkhead.

For a brief instant Pitt's heart pounded with excitement and anticipation, his mind certain they had found the most priceless treasure of the sea. Then Gunn looked up, and Pitt saw the bitter disappointment reflected in his eyes.

The crate was empty.

A frustrating search of the cargo hold turned up a startling revelation. Lying in the dark shadows like a collapsed rubber doll was a deep-sea diving suit. The arms were outstretched, the feet encased in Frankenstein-style weighted boots. A tarnished brass diving helmet and breastplate covered the head and neck. Curled off to the side like a dead gray snake was the umbilical line that contained the air hose and lifeline cable. They were severed about six feet from the helmet couplings.

The layer of silt and slime on the diving outfit indicated it had lain there for many years. Pitt removed a knife strapped to his right calf and used it to pry loose the wing nut clamping the helmet's faceplate. It gave slowly at first and then loosened enough to be removed by his fingers. He pulled the faceplate open and aimed the beam of the dive light inside. Protected from the ravages of destructive sea life by the rubber suit and the helmet's safety valves, the head still retained hair and remnants of flesh.

Pitt and his party were not the first to have probed the gruesome secrets of the *Cyclops*. Someone else had already come and gone with the La Dorada treasure.

149

22

Pitt checked his old Doxa watch and calculated their decompression stops. He added an extra minute to each stop as a safety margin to eliminate the gas bubbles from their blood and tissues and prevent the agony of diver's bends.

After leaving the *Cyclops,* they had exchanged the nearly empty air cylinders for their reserve supply stashed beside the control car and began their slow rise to the surface. A few feet away, Gunn and Giordino added air to their buoyancy compensators to maintain the required depth while handling the cumbersome bundle.

Below them in the watery gloom, the *Cyclops* lay desolate and cursed to oblivion. Before another decade passed, her rusting walls would begin to collapse inward, and a century later the restless sea floor would cover her pitiful remains under a shroud of silt, leaving only a few pieces of coral-encrusted debris to mark her grave.

Above them, the surface was a turmoil of quicksilver. At the next decompression stop, they began to feel the crushing momentum from the mountainous swells and fought to hang in the void together. There was no thought of a stop at the twenty-foot level. Their air supply was almost exhausted and only death by drowning waited in the depths. They had no alternative but to surface and take their chances in the tempest above.

Jessie seemed composed and unshaken. Pitt realized that she didn't suspect the danger on the surface. Her only thoughts were of seeing the sky again.

Pitt made one final check of the time and motioned upward with his thumb. They began to ascend as one, Jessie hanging on to Pitt's leg, Gunn and Giordino dragging the bundle. The light increased and when Pitt looked up he was surprised to see a whorl of foam only a few feet above his head.

He surfaced in a trough and was lifted by a vast sloping wall of green that carried him up and over the crest of a high wave as lightly as a bathtub toy. The wind shrieked in his ears and sea spray lashed his cheeks. He pulled up his mask and blinked his eyes. The sky to the east was filled with dark swirling clouds, dark as charcoal as they soared over the gray-green sea. The speed of the approaching storm was uncanny. It seemed to be leaping from one horizon to the next.

Jessie popped up beside him and stared through wide stricken eyes at the blackening overcast bearing down on them. She spit out her mouthpiece. "What is it?"

"The hurricane," Pitt shouted over the wind. "It's coming faster than anyone thought."

"Oh, God!" she gasped.

"Release your weight belt and unstrap your air tanks," he said.

Nothing needed to be said to the others. They had already dropped their gear and were tearing open the bundle. The clouds swept overhead and they were hurled into a twilight world drained of all color. They were stunned at the violent display of atmospheric power. The wind suddenly doubled in strength, filling the air with foam and driving spray and shattering the wave crests into froth.

Abruptly, the bundle that they had so doggedly hauled with them from the *Prosperteer* burst open into an inflatable boat, complete with a compact twenty-horsepower outboard motor encased in a waterproof plastic cover. Giordino rolled over the side, followed by Gunn, and they frantically tore at the motor covering. The savage winds quickly drove the boat away from Pitt and Jessie. The gap began widening at an alarming rate.

"The sea anchor!" Pitt bellowed. "Throw out the sea anchor!"

Gunn barely heard Pitt over the wail of the wind. He heaved a canvas cone-shaped sack over the side that was held open by an iron hoop at the mouth. He then paid it out on a line which he made fast to the bitt on the bow. As the drag on the anchor took hold, the boat's head came around into the wind and slowed its drift.

While Giordino labored over the motor, Gunn threw out a line to Pitt, who tied it under Jessie's arms. As she was towed toward the boat Pitt swam after her, the waves breaking over his head. The mask was torn from his head and the salt spray whipped his eyes. He doubled his effort when he saw that the running sea was carrying away the boat faster than he could swim.

Giordino's muscled arms thrust into the water, closed on Jessie's wrists, and yanked her into the boat as effortlessly as if she were a

151

ten-pound sea bass. Pitt squinted his eyes until they were almost slits. He felt rather than saw the line fall over his shoulder. He could just make out Giordino's grinning face leaning over the side, his great hands winding in the line. Then Pitt was lying in the bottom of the wildly rocking boat, panting and blinking the salt from his eyes.

"Another minute and you'd have been beyond reach of the line," Giordino yelled.

"Time sure flies when you're having fun," Pitt yelled back.

Giordino rolled his eyes at Pitt's cocky reply and went back to laboring over the motor.

The immediate danger facing them now was overturning. Until the motor could be started to provide a small degree of stability, a thrashing wave could flip them upside down. Pitt and Gunn threw over trailing ballast bags, which temporarily reduced the threat.

The strength of the wind was ungodly. It tore at their hair and bodies, the spray felt as abrasive to their skin as if it came from a sand blaster. The little inflatable boat flexed under the stress of the mad sea and reeled in the grip of the gale, but she somehow refused to be tipped over.

Pitt knelt on the hard rubber floorboards, clasping the lifeline with his right hand, and turned his back to the wind. Then he extended his left arm. It was an old seaman's trick that always worked in the Northern Hemisphere. His left hand would be pointing to the center of the storm.

They were slightly outside the center, he judged. There would be no breathing spell from the relative calm of the hurricane's eye. Its main path lay a good forty miles to the northwest. The worst was yet to come.

A wave crashed over them, and then another; two in quick succession that would have broken the back of a larger, more rigid vessel. But the tough, runty inflatable shook off the water and struggled back to the surface like a playful seal. Everyone managed to keep a firm grip and no one was washed overboard.

At last Giordino signaled that he had the motor running. No one could hear it over the howl of the wind. Quickly Pitt and Gunn pulled in the sea anchor and the ballast bags.

Pitt cupped one hand and yelled in Giordino's ear, "Run with the storm!"

To sheer on a sideways course was impossible. The combined force of wind and water would have flung them over. To head into the thrust of the storm bows-on meant a sure battering they could never

152

survive. Their only hope was to ride in the path of the least resistance.

Giordino grimly nodded and pushed the throttle lever. The boat banked around sharply in a trough and surged forward across a sea that had turned completely white from the driving spray. They all flattened themselves against the floorboards except Giordino. He sat with one arm wrapped around a lifeline and gripped the outboard motor's steering lever with his free hand.

The daylight was fading slowly away and night would fall in another hour. The air was hot and stifling, making it difficult to breathe. The almost solid wall of wind-stripped water decreased visibility to less than three hundred yards. Pitt borrowed Gunn's diver's mask and raised his head over the bow. It was like standing under Niagara Falls and staring upward.

Giordino felt icy despair as the hurricane unleashed its full wrath around them. That they had survived this long was just short of a miracle. He was fighting the tumbling sea in a kind of restrained frenzy, struggling desperately to keep their puny oasis from being overwhelmed by a wave. He constantly changed throttle settings, trying to ride just behind the towering crests, warily glancing over his shoulder every few seconds at the gaping trough chasing their stern thirty feet below and behind.

Giordino knew the end was only minutes away, certainly no more than an hour with enormous luck. It would be so easy to swing the boat abeam of the sea and finish it now. He allowed himself a quick look down at the others and saw a broad smile of encouragement on Pitt's lips. If his friend of nearly thirty years felt close to death, he gave no hint of it. Pitt threw a jaunty wave and returned to peering over the bow. Giordino couldn't help wondering what he was looking at.

Pitt was studying the waves. They were piling up higher and more steeply, the wind hurling the foaming white horse at the peaks into the next trough. He estimated the distance between crests and judged that they were packing together like the forward lines of a marching column that was slowing its pace.

The bottom was coming up. The surge was flinging them into shallower water.

Pitt's eyes strained to penetrate the chaotic wall of water. Slowly, as if a black-and-white photograph were being developed, shadowy images began taking shape. The first image that flashed through his mind was that of stained teeth, blackened molars being scrubbed by white toothpaste. The image sharpened into dark rocks with the

153

waves smashing against them in great unending explosions of white. He watched the water shoot skyward as the backwash struck an incoming surge. Then, as the surf momentarily settled, he spotted a low reef extending parallel to the rocks that formed a natural wall in front of a wide, sweeping beach. It had to be the Cuban island of Cayo Santa María, he reckoned.

Pitt had no problem visualizing the probabilities of the new nightmare: bodies torn to shreds on the coral reef or crushed on the jagged rocks. He wiped the salt from the mask lens and stared again. Then he saw it, a thousand-in-one chance to survive the vortex.

Giordino had seen it too—a small inlet between the rocks. He steered for it, knowing he stood a better chance of threading a needle in a thrashing washing machine.

In the next thirty seconds the churning outboard and the storm had carried them a hundred yards. The sea over the reef boiled in a dirty foam and the wind velocity increased to where the driving spray and the darkness made vision almost impossible. Jessie's face went white, her body rigid. Her eyes met Pitt's for an instant, fearful yet trusting. His arm circled her waist and squeezed tight.

A breaker caught and struck them like an avalanche down a mountain. The screw of the outboard raced as it lifted clear of the crest, but its protesting whirr was drowned by the deafening noise of the surf. Gunn opened his mouth to shout a warning, but no sound came. The plunging breaker curled over the boat and smashed down on them with fantastic force. It tore Gunn's hold on the lifeline, and Pitt saw him gyrate through the air like a kite with a broken string.

The boat was driven over the reef, buried in foam. The coral sliced through the rubberized fabric into the air chambers; a field of razor blades couldn't have done it more efficiently. The thickly encrusted bottom swirled past. For several moments they were completely submerged. Then at last the faithful little inflatable wallowed to the surface and they were clear of the reef with only fifty yards of open water separating them from the craggy ramparts, looming dark and wet.

Gunn bobbed up only a few feet away, gasping for breath. Pitt reached way out, grabbed him by the shoulder strap of his buoyancy compensator, and hauled him on board. The rescue didn't come a second too soon. The next breaker came roaring over the reef like a herd of crazed animals running before a forest fire.

Giordino grimly hung on to the motor, which was unfalteringly purring away with every bit of horsepower her pistons could punch

154

out. It didn't take a psychic to know the frail craft was being torn to bits. She was only buoyed up by air still trapped in her chambers.

They were almost within reach of the gap between the rocks when they were caught by the wave. The preceding trough slipped under the base of the breaker, causing it to steepen to twice its height. Its speed increased as it rushed toward the rocky shoreline.

Pitt glanced up. The menacing pinnacles towered above them, water boiling around their foundations like a seething caldron. The boat was thrust up the front of the breaker, and for a brief instant Pitt thought they might be carried over the peak before it broke. But it curled suddenly and toppled forward, striking the rocks opposite the inlet with the shattering crash of thunder, throwing the shredded boat and its occupants into the air, spilling them into the maelstrom.

Pitt heard Jessie scream from far in the distance. It barely pierced his numbed mind, and he struggled to reply, but then everything blurred. The boat fell with such jarring force the motor was ripped from the transom and slung onto the beach.

Pitt remembered nothing after that. A black whirlpool opened up and he was sucked into it.

23

THE MAN WHO WAS THE DRIVING FORCE behind the Jersey Colony lay on an office couch inside the concealed headquarters of the project. He rested his eyes and concentrated on his meeting with the President on the golf course.

Leonard Hudson knew damn well the President wasn't about to sit still and wait patiently for another surprise contact. The Chief Executive was a pusher who never left anything to luck. Although Hudson's sources inside the White House and the intelligence agencies reported no indication of an investigation, he was certain the President was figuring a way to penetrate the curtain around the "inner core."

He could almost feel the net being thrown.

His secretary rapped softly on the door and then opened it. "Excuse me for intruding, but Mr. Steinmetz is on the viewer and wishes to talk to you."

"I'll be there in a minute."

Hudson rearranged his thoughts as he laced his shoes. Like a computer, he logged out of one problem and called up another. He didn't look forward to battling with Steinmetz even if the man *was* a quarter of a million miles away.

Eli Steinmetz was the kind of engineer who overcame an obstacle by designing a mechanical solution and then building it with his own hands. His talent for improvisation was the reason Hudson had chosen him as the leader of the Jersey Colony. A graduate of Caltech with a master's degree from MIT, he had supervised construction projects in half the countries of the world, even Russia.

When approached by the "inner core" to build the first human habitat on lunar soil, Steinmetz had taken nearly a week to make a decision while his mind wrestled with the awesome concept and

156

staggering logistics of such a project. Finally, he accepted, but only on his own terms.

He and only he would select the crew to live on the moon. There would be no pilots or prima donna astronauts in residence. All space flight would be directed by ground control or computers. Only men whose special qualifications were vital in the construction of the base would be included. Besides Steinmetz, the first three to launch the colony were solar and structural engineers. Months later a biologist-doctor, a geochemical engineer, and a horticulturist arrived. Other scientists and technicians followed as their special skills and knowledge were required.

At first Steinmetz had been considered too old. He was fifty-three when he set foot on the moon, and he was fifty-nine now. But Hudson and the other "inner core" members weighed experience over age and never once regretted their selection.

Now Hudson stared into the video monitor at Steinmetz, who was holding up a bottle with a hand-drawn label. Unlike the other colonists', Steinmetz's face sprouted no beard and his head was clean-shaven. His skin had a dusky tint that complemented his slate-black eyes. Steinmetz was a fifth-generation American Jew, but he could have walked unnoticed in a Moslem mosque.

"How's that for self-sufficiency?" said Steinmetz. "Château Lunar Chardonnay, 1989. Not exactly a premier vintage. Only had enough grapes to make four bottles. Should have allowed the vines in the greenhouses to mature another year, but we got impatient."

"I see you even made your own bottle," observed Hudson.

"Yes, our pilot chemical plant is in full operation now. We've increased our output to where we can process almost two tons of lunar-soil materials into two hundred pounds of a bastard metal or five hundred pounds of glass in fifteen days."

Steinmetz appeared to be sitting at a long flat table in the center of a small cave. He was wearing a thin cotton shirt and a pair of jogger's shorts.

"You look cool and comfortable," said Hudson.

"Our first priority when we landed," Steinmetz said, smiling. "Remember?"

"Seal the entrance to the cavern and pressurize its interior so you could work in a comfortable atmosphere without the handicap of encapsulated suits."

"After living in those damned things for eight months, you can't imagine what a relief it was to get back into normal clothing."

157

"Murphy has been closely monitoring your temperatures and he says the walls of the cavern are increasing their rate of heat absorption. He suggests that you send a man out and lower the angle on the solar collectors by half a degree."

"I'll see to it."

Hudson paused. "It won't be long now, Eli."

"Much changed on earth since I left?"

"About the same, only more smog, more traffic, more people."

Steinmetz laughed. "You trying to talk me into another tour of duty, Leo?"

"Wouldn't dream of it. You're going to be the biggest-man-on-campus since Lindbergh when you drop out of the blue."

"I'll have all our records packed and secured in the lunar transfer vehicle twenty-four hours before liftoff."

"I hope you don't have a mind to uncork your lunar vino on the trip home."

"No, we'll hold our farewell party in plenty of time to purge all alcoholic residue."

Hudson had been trying to approach his point sideways, but decided it was better to come right out with it. "You'll have to deal with the Russians shortly before you leave," he said in a monotone.

"We've been through this," Steinmetz replied firmly. "There is no reason to believe they'll land within two thousand miles of the Jersey Colony."

"Then seek them out and destroy them. You have the weapons and equipment for such a hunting expedition. Their scientists won't be armed. The last thing they'd expect is an attack from men already on the moon."

"The boys and I will gladly defend the homestead, but we're not about to go out and shoot down unarmed men who are innocent of any threat."

"Listen to me, Eli," Hudson implored. "There is a threat, a very real one. If the Soviets somehow discover the existence of Jersey Colony, they can move right in. With you and your people returning to earth less than twenty-four hours after the cosmonauts land, the colony will be deserted and everything in it fair game."

"I realize that as well as you," said Steinmetz roughly, "and hate it even worse. But the sad fact is we can't postpone our departure. We've pushed ourselves to the limit and beyond up here. I can't order these men to hang on another six months or a year, or until

158

your friends can whistle up another craft to take us from space to a soft landing on earth. Cross it off to bad luck and the Russians, who leaked their lunar landing schedule after it was too late for us to alter our return flight."

"The moon belongs to us by right of possession," Hudson argued angrily. "Men of the United States were the first to walk on its soil, and we were the first to colonize it. For God's sake, Eli, don't turn it over to a bunch of thieving Communists."

"Dammit, Leo, there's enough moon for everybody. Besides, this isn't exactly a Garden of Eden. Outside this cavern, day and night temperatures can vary as much as two hundred and fifty degrees Celsius. I doubt if even casino gambling could make a go of it here. Look, even if the cosmonauts fall into our colony, they won't strike a gold vein of information. The accumulation of all our data will go back to earth with us. What we leave behind we can destroy."

"Don't be a fool. Why destroy what can be used by the next colonists, permanent colonists, who will need every advantage they can get?"

Viewing the monitor in front of him, Steinmetz could see the flush on Hudson's face 240,000 miles away. "I've made my position clear, Leo. We'll defend Jersey Colony if need be, but don't expect us to form a posse to kill innocent cosmonauts. It's one thing to shoot at an unmanned space probe, but quite another to murder a fellow human being for trespassing on land he has every right to walk on."

There was an uneasy silence after this statement, but it was no less than what Hudson expected from Steinmetz. The man was no coward. Far from it. Hudson had heard reports of many fights and brawls. Steinmetz could be pushed and clubbed to the floor, but when he came to his feet and his rage seethed to a boil, he could fight like ten devils incarnate. Purveyors of his legend had lost count of the backcountry saloon patrons he had mauled.

Hudson broke the spell. "Suppose the Soviet cosmonauts land within fifty miles? Will that prove to you they intend to occupy Jersey Colony?"

Steinmetz shifted in his stone-carved chair, reluctant to make a concession. "We'll have to wait and see."

"Nobody ever won a battle by going on the defensive," Hudson lectured him. "If their landing site is within striking distance and they show every indication of advancing on the colony, will you accept a compromise and attack?"

159

Steinmetz bowed his shaven head in assent. "Since you insist on putting my back to the wall, you don't leave me much choice."

"The stakes are too high," said Hudson. "You have no choice at all."

24

THE FOG IN PITT'S BRAIN LIFTED, and one by one his senses flickered back to life like lights across a circuitboard. He struggled to raise his eyelids and focus on the nearest object. For a good half minute he stared at the water-wrinkled skin of his left hand, then at the orange face of his diver's watch as if it were the first time he had ever laid eyes on it.

In the dim twilight the luminescent hands read 6:34. Only two hours since they had escaped from the wrecked control car. It seemed more like a lifetime, and none of it real.

The wind was still roaring off the sea with the speed of an express train and the sea spray combined with rain to beat against his back. He tried to lift himself to his hands and knees, but his legs felt trapped in concrete. He turned and looked down. They were half buried under the sand by the burrowing action of the ebbing surf line.

Pitt lay there for a few more moments, recharging his strength, an exhausted and battered piece of flotsam thrown on the beach. Boulders rose up on either side of him like tenements overlooking an alley. His first really conscious thought was that Giordino had done it, he had steered them through the needle's eye of the rock barrier.

Then somewhere through the howling wind, he could hear Jessie calling faintly. He dug out his legs and forced himself to his knees, staggering under the gale, retching out the saltwater that had been forced into his nose, mouth, and down his throat.

Half crawling, half stumbling across the stinging sand, he found Jessie sitting dazed, her hair limp and stringy on her shoulders, Gunn's head resting in her lap. She looked up at him through lost eyes that suddenly widened in vast relief.

"Oh, thank God," she murmured, her words drowned out by the storm.

161

Pitt put his arms around her shoulders and gave her a reassuring hug. Then he turned his attention to Gunn.

He was semiconscious. The broken ankle had swelled like a soccer ball. There was an ugly gash above the hairline, and his body was cut in a dozen places from the coral, but he was alive and his breathing was deep and steady.

Pitt shielded his eyes and scanned the beach. Giordino was nowhere in sight. At first Pitt refused to believe it. The seconds passed and he stood rooted, his body leaning into the offshore gale, eyes peering desperately through the torrential dark. He caught a glimpse of orange in the swirl of a dying breaker, and immediately recognized it as the shredded carcass of the inflatable boat. It was caught in the grip of the backwash, drifting out and then swept in again by the next wave.

Pitt lurched into the water up to his hips, oblivious to the spent breakers that rolled around him. He dove under the tattered boat and extended his hands, feeling around like a blind man. His groping fingers found only torn fabric. Moved by some deep urgency to make absolutely sure, he pulled the boat toward the beach.

A large wave caught him unawares and smashed into his back. Somehow he managed to keep his feet under him and drag the boat into shallow water. As the blanket of foam dissolved and was blown away, he saw a pair of legs protruding from under the collapsed boat. Shock, disbelief, and a fanatical refusal to accept Giordino's death flooded through his mind. Frantically, oblivious to the battering of the hurricane, he tore away the sliced remains of the inflatable, revealing Giordino's body floating upright, his head buried inside a buoyancy chamber. Hope came first to Pitt, then optimism that struck him like a punch in the stomach.

Giordino might still be alive.

Pitt stripped away the interior liner and bent over Giordino's face, afraid deep down it would be a lifeless blue. But there was color, and there was breath—ragged and shallow, but there was breath. The brawny little Italian had incredibly survived on air that was trapped inside the buoyancy chamber.

Pitt felt suddenly drained to his bones. Physically and emotionally he was spent. He swayed wearily, the wind trying to beat him flat. Only a firm resolve to save everyone drove him on. Slowly, stiffly from a myriad of cuts and bruises, he slid his arms under Giordino and picked him up. The dead weight of Giordino's solid hundred and seventy-five pounds felt like a ton.

Gunn had come around and was huddled with Jessie. He looked up questioningly at Pitt, who was struggling across the windswept beach under Giordino's inert body.

"We've got to find shelter from the wind," Pitt yelled, his voice rasped by the intake of saltwater. "Can you walk?"

"I'll help him," Jessie yelled in reply. She circled both arms around Gunn's waist, braced her feet in the sand, and shoved him upright.

Panting under his load, Pitt made for a line of palm trees bordering the beach. Every twenty feet he glanced back. Jessie had somehow retained her dive mask, so she was the only one who could keep her eyes open and see straight ahead. She was supporting nearly half of Gunn's weight while he gamely hobbled beside her, eyes shut against the stinging sand, dragging his badly swollen foot.

They made it into the trees but received no mercy from the hurricane. The gale bent the tops of the palms almost to the ground, their fronds splitting like paper in a shredding machine. Coconuts were ripped from their clusters, striking the ground with the velocity of cannonballs and just as deadly. One grazed Pitt's shoulder, its husk tearing his exposed skin. It was as though they were running through the no-man's-land of a battlefield.

Pitt kept his head bent down and squinted sideways, watching the ground directly in front of him. Before he knew it he had walked into a chain link fence. Jessie and Gunn drew up beside him and stopped. He stared to the right and then the left, but found no sign of a break. Trying to climb it was out of the question. The fence was at least ten feet high with a thick angle of barbed wire at the top. Pitt also spotted a small porcelain insulator and realized the chain links were wired for electricity.

"Which way?" Jessie cried.

"You lead," Pitt shouted in her ear. "I can hardly see."

She nodded to the left and set off with Gunn limping along at her side. They staggered onward, beaten every step by the unrelenting force of the wind.

Ten minutes later they had covered only fifty yards. Pitt couldn't push on much longer. His arms were going numb and he was losing his grip on Giordino. He closed his eyes and blindly began to count the steps, staying in a straight line by brushing his right shoulder against the fence, certain the hurricane must have cut off the power source.

He heard Jessie shouting something, and he opened one eye in a narrow slit. She was pointing vigorously ahead. Pitt sank to his knees, gently lowered Giordino to the ground, and looked past Jessie. A palm tree had been uprooted by the insane wind and hurled through the air like some monstrous javelin, landing on the fence and crushing it against the sand.

With appalling abruptness, night closed in and the sky went pitch black. Blindly, they stepped over the flattened fence like sightless drones, reeling and falling, driven on by instinct and some inner discipline that wouldn't allow them to lie down and give up. Jessie gamely kept the lead. Pitt had slung Giordino over a shoulder and held on to the waistband of Gunn's swim trunks, not so much for support as to prevent them from becoming separated.

A hundred yards, then another hundred yards, and suddenly Gunn and Jessie seemed to drop into the ground as if they were swallowed up. Pitt released his grip on Gunn and fell backward, grunting as Giordino's full weight fell across his chest, forcing the air from his lungs. He scrambled from under Giordino and stretched his hand gropingly forward into the dark until he felt nothing there.

Jessie and Gunn had fallen down a steep, eight-foot slope into a sunken road. He could just make out their vague outlines huddled in a heap below.

"Are you injured?" he called.

"We already hurt so much we can't tell." Gunn's voice was muffled by the gale, but not so muffled Pitt couldn't tell it came through clenched teeth.

"Jessie?"

"I'm all right... I think."

"Can you give me a hand with Giordino?"

"I'll try."

"Send him down," said Gunn. "We can manage it."

Pitt eased Giordino's limp figure over the edge of the slope and lowered him gently by the arms. The others held him by the legs until Pitt could scramble down beside them and take up the heavy bulk. Once Giordino was stretched comfortably on the ground, Pitt looked around and took stock.

The sunken road provided a shelter from the gale-force wind. The blowing sand had dropped off and Pitt could finally open his eyes. The road's surface was made up of crushed seashells and appeared hard packed and little used. No sign of light was visible in either direction, which wasn't too surprising when Pitt considered that any local inhabitants would have evacuated the shoreline before the full energy of the hurricane struck.

Both Jessie and Gunn were very nearly played out, their breath coming in short, tortured rasps. Pitt was aware his own breathing was fast and labored, and his heart pounding like a steam engine under full load. Exhausted and battered as they were, Pitt reflected, it still felt like paradise to lie behind a barrier that reduced by half the main drive of the gale.

Two minutes later Giordino began to groan. Then he slowly sat up and looked around, seeing nothing.

"Jesus, it's dark," he muttered to himself, his mind crawling from a woolly mist.

Pitt knelt beside him and said, "Welcome back to the land of the walking dead."

Giordino raised his hand and touched Pitt's face in the darkness. "Dirk?"

"In the flesh."

"Jessie and Rudi?"

"Both right here."

"Where is here?"

"About a mile from the beach." Pitt didn't bother to explain how they survived the landing or how they arrived at the road. That could come later. "Where are you hurt?"

"All over. My rib cage feels like it's on fire. I think my left shoulder is dislocated, one leg feels like it was twisted off at the knee, and the base of my skull where it meets the neck throbs like hell." He swore disgustedly. "Damn, I blew it. I thought I could bring us through the rocks. Forgive me for screwing up."

"Would you believe me if I told you we'd all be fish food if it wasn't for you?" Pitt smiled and then gently probed Giordino's knee, guessing that the injury was a torn tendon. Then he turned his attention to the shoulder. "I can't do anything about your ribs, knee, or thick skull, but your shoulder is out of place, and if you're in the mood I think I can manipulate it back where it belongs."

"Seems I recall you doing that to me when we played football in high school. The team doctor raised holy hell. Said you should have let him do it."

"That's because he was a sadist," Pitt said, grasping Giordino's arm. "Ready?"

"Go on, tear it off."

Pitt yanked and the joint snapped into place with an audible *pop*. Giordino let out a gasp that died into a relieved sigh. Pitt felt around in the dark beside the road until he found a stout branch that had been torn off a small scrub pine, and gave it to Gunn to use as a staff in place of a crutch. Jessie clutched one of Gunn's arms to steady him, while Pitt hoisted Giordino onto his sound leg and supported him with an arm around his waist.

This time Pitt led the way, mentally flipping a coin and heading up the road to their right, plodding close to the high embankment to shelter their progress from the unabating onslaught of the storm. Now the going was easier. No deep sand to wade through, no fallen trees to stumble over, not even the wind-propelled rain to torture them, for the edge of the slope caused it to fly over their heads. Just the graded flat of the road leading off into the stricken darkness.

After an hour had passed, Pitt figured they had hobbled about a mile. He was about to call a rest stop when Giordino suddenly stiffened and stopped so unexpectantly that he lost Pitt's support and toppled to the road.

"Barbecue!" he yelled. "Smell it? Somebody's barbecuing beef."

Pitt sniffed the air. The aroma was faint, but it was there. He lifted Giordino and pushed ahead. The smell of steaks broiling over charcoal grew stronger with every step. In another fifty yards they met with a massive iron gate whose bars were welded in the shape of dolphins. A wall topped by broken glass stretched into the darkness on either side and stood astride a guardhouse. Not surprisingly, in light of the hurricane, it was vacant.

The gate, reaching a good twelve feet toward the ebony sky, was locked, but the outer and inner doors of the guardhouse were open, so they walked through. A short distance beyond, the road ended in a circular drive that passed in front of what seemed in the stormy dark to be a large mound. As they approached, it became a castlelike structure whose roof and three sides were covered over with sandy soil and planted with palmetto trees and native scrub brush. Only the front of the building lay exposed, starkly barren with no windows and only one huge, mahogany door artistically carved with lifelike fish.

"Reminds me of a buried Egyptian temple," said Gunn.

"If it wasn't for the ornate door," said Pitt, "I'd guess it was some kind of military supply depot."

Jessie set them straight. "A subinsulator house. Soil is an ideal insulation against temperatures and weather. Same principle as the sod houses on the early American prairie. I know an architect who specializes in designing them."

"Looks deserted," observed Giordino.

Pitt tried the doorknob. It turned. He eased the door open. The aroma of food wafted out from somewhere within the darkened interior.

"Doesn't smell deserted," said Pitt.

The foyer was paved in tile with a Spanish motif and was lit by several large candles set on a tall stand. The walls were carved blocks of black lava rock and their only decoration was a gruesome painting of a man hanging from the fanged mouth of a snakelike sea monster. They entered and Pitt pulled the door closed behind them.

For some strange reason, the howl of the tempest outside and everyone's weary breathing seemed to add to the deathly stillness of the house.

"Anyone home?" Pitt called out.

He repeated the question twice more, but his only reply was a ghostly silence. A dim corridor beckoned, but Pitt hesitated. Another smell invaded his nostrils. Tobacco smoke. Stronger than the near-lethal gas emitted by Admiral Sandecker's cigars. Pitt was no expert, but he knew that expensive cigars smelled more rotten than the cheap ones. He guessed the smoke must be coming from prime Havanas.

He turned to the others. "What do you think?"

"Do we have a choice?" Giordino asked dumbly.

"Two," replied Pitt. "We can either get out of here while we can and take our chances in the hurricane. Then, when it begins to die down, we can try to steal a boat and head back to Florida—"

"Or throw ourselves on the mercy of the Cubans," Gunn interrupted.

"That's how it boils down."

Jessie shook her head and stared at him through soft, tender eyes. "We can't go back," she said quietly with no trace of fear. "The storm will take days to die, and none of us is in any condition to survive out there another four hours. I vote we take our chances with Castro's government. The very worst they can do is throw us in jail while the State Department negotiates our release."

Pitt looked at Gunn. "Rudi, how say you?"

"We're done in, Dirk. Logic is on Jessie's side."

"Al, how do you see it?"

Giordino shrugged. "Say the word, pal, and I'll swim back to the States." And Pitt knew he meant it too. "But the honest truth is we can't take much more. It pains me to say this, but I think we'd better throw in the towel."

Pitt looked at them and reflected that he couldn't have been blessed

167

with a better team of people to face an unpleasant situation, and it didn't take a visionary to see things were going to become very unpleasant indeed.

"Okay," he said with a grim smile. "Let's crash the party."

They set off down the corridor and soon passed under an archway that opened onto a vast living room decorated in early Spanish antiques. Giant tapestries hung on the walls, depicting galleons sailing sunset seas or being driven helplessly onto reefs by thrashing storms. The furnishings seemed to have a nautical flair; the room was illuminated by ancient ship's lanterns of copper and colored glass. The fireplace was glowing with a crackling fire that warmed the room to hothouse temperatures.

There wasn't a soul to be seen anywhere.

"Ghastly," murmured Jessie. "Our host has simply dreadful taste in decor."

Pitt held up his hand for quiet. "Voices," he said softly. "Coming from that other archway between those two suits of armor."

They moved into another corridor that was dimly lit by candle holders every ten feet. The sounds of laughter and obscure words, from both male and female, became louder. A light loomed from under a curtain ahead. They paused for a second, and then swung it aside and passed through.

They had entered a long dining hall filled with nearly forty people, who stopped in midconversation and stared at Pitt and the others with the awed expression of a group of villagers meeting their first aliens from space.

The women were elegantly dressed in evening gowns, while half the men wore tuxedos and the other half were attired in military uniforms. Several servants waiting on the table stood stock-still like images on motion picture film that was suddenly freeze-framed. The stunned silence was as thick as a wool blanket. A scene straight out of an early thirties Hollywood melodrama.

Pitt realized he and the rest must have made a shocking picture. Soaking wet, their clothing torn and ragged, bruised and gashed skin, torn muscles, broken bones. Hair plastered down around their heads, they must have looked like drowned rats rejected from a polluted river.

Pitt looked at Gunn and said, "How do you say 'Pardon the intrusion' in Spanish?"

"Haven't the vaguest idea. I took French in school."

Then it struck Pitt. Most of the uniformed men were high-ranking

Soviet officers. Only one appeared to be from the Cuban military.

Jessie was in her element. To Pitt she couldn't have looked more regal, even if the designer safari suit hung on her body in tatters.

"Is there a gentleman among you who will offer a lady a chair?" she demanded.

Before she received an answer, ten men with Russian-type machine pistols burst into the room and surrounded them in a loose circle, sphinx-faced men whose weapons were aimed at all four stomachs. Their eyes were icy and their lips set in tight lines. There was little doubt in Pitt's mind that they were highly trained to kill on command.

Giordino, with the appearance of a man run over by a garbage truck, painfully pulled himself to his full height and stared back. "Did you ever see so many smiling faces?" he asked conversationally.

"No," said Pitt with the beginning of a to-hell-with-you grin. "Not since Little Big Horn."

Jessie didn't hear them. As if in a trance she shouldered her way through the armed guards and stopped near the head of the table, staring down at a tall, gray-haired man attired in formal evening wear, who stared back at her in shocked disbelief.

She brushed back her wet, tangled hair and struck a sophisticated, feline pose. Then she spoke in a soft, commanding voice. "Be a dear, Raymond, and pour your wife a glass of wine."

25

HAGEN DROVE NINETEEN MILES east of downtown Colorado Springs on Highway 94 until he came to Enoch Road. Then he turned right and arrived at the main entrance of the Unified Space Operations Center.

The two-billion-dollar project, constructed on 640 acres of land and manned by 5,000 uniformed and civilian personnel, controlled all military space vehicle and shuttle flights as well as satellite monitoring programs. An entire aerospace community mushroomed around the center, covering thousands of acres with residential developments, scientific and industrial parks, high-tech research and manufacturing plants, and Air Force test facilities. In ten short years, what had once been sparse grazing land inhabited by small herds of cattle had become the "Space Capital of the World."

Hagen flashed his security clearance, drove into the parking lot, and stopped opposite a side entrance to the massive building. He did not get out of the car but opened his briefcase and removed his worn legal pad. He turned to a page with three names and added a fourth.

Raymond LeBaron................Whereabouts unknown.
Leonard Hudson...................Same.
Gunnar Eriksen....................Same.
General Clark Fisher............Colorado Springs.

Hagen's call to the Drake Hotel from Pattenden Lab had alerted an old friend at the FBI, who traced the number of Anson Jones to a classified line at an officer's residence on Peterson Air Force Base outside of Colorado Springs. The house was occupied by four-star General Clark Fisher, head of the Joint Military Space Command.

170

Posing as a pest control inspector, Hagen had been given the run of the house by the general's wife. Fortunately for him, she considered his unexpected arrival as a heaven-sent opportunity to complain about an army of spiders that had invaded the premises. He listened attentively and promised to attack the insects with every weapon in his arsenal. Then, while she fussed around in the kitchen with the hired cook, experimenting with a new recipe for apricot sautéd prawns, Hagen tossed the general's study.

His search revealed only that Fisher was a stickler for security. Hagen found nothing in desk drawers, files, or hidden recesses that could prove beneficial to a Soviet agent or himself. He decided to wait it out until the general left for the evening and then search his office at the space center. As he left by the rear door Mrs. Fisher was talking on the telephone and simply waved goodbye. Hagen paused for a moment and overheard her telling the general to stop off on his way home and pick up a bottle of sherry.

Hagen put the legal pad back in the briefcase and took out a can of diet cola and a thick salami sandwich with sliced dill pickle, wrapped in wax paper with a delicatessen's advertising printed on both sides. The Colorado temperature had cooled considerably once the sun had dropped over the Rocky Mountains. The shadow of Pike's Peak stretched out over the plains, casting a dark veil over the treeless landscape.

Hagen didn't notice the scenic beauty unfolding through the windshield. What disturbed him was that he did not have a firm grip on any member of the "inner core." Three of the names on his list remained hidden, God only knew where, and the fourth was still innocent until proven guilty. No hard facts, only a phone number and a gut instinct that Fisher was part of the Jersey Colony conspiracy. He had to be absolutely certain, and most important, he desperately needed to pick up a thread to the next man.

Hagen stopped his mental wanderings, his eyes focused on the rearview mirror. A man in a blue officer's uniform was passing through the side entrance, the door held open by a five-stripe sergeant, or whatever specialist rating the Air Force gave its enlisted men these days. The officer was tall, athletically built, wore four stars on his shoulders, and was quite handsome in a Gregory Peck way. The sergeant accompanied him across a sidewalk to a waiting Air Force blue sedan and smartly opened the rear door.

Something about the scene snapped a string in Hagen's mind. He sat up straight and turned around to stare boldly out the side window. Fisher was in the act of bending over to enter the backseat of his car, holding a briefcase. That was it. The briefcase wasn't held by the handle as it would normally be carried. Fisher was clutching it like a football, under his arm and against the side of his chest.

Hagen had no qualms against changing his carefully laid out plan in midstream. He improvised on the spot, quickly forgetting about searching Fisher's command office. If his sudden creative spark didn't pan out, he could always go back. He started the engine and moved off across the parking lot behind the general's car.

Fisher's driver pulled across the intersection and turned onto Highway 94 under a yellow light. Hagen hung back until the traffic thinned. Then he ran the red light and accelerated until he was close enough behind the Air Force blue car to make out the driver's face in its rearview mirror. He held that position, watching to see if there was any eye contact. There was none. The sergeant was not a suspicious sort and never checked his tail. Hagen rightly assumed the man had no training in defensive driving tactics against possible terrorist attack.

After a slight bend in the highway the lights of a shopping center came into view. Hagen glanced at his speedometer. The sergeant was cruising along five miles an hour below the posted speed limit. Hagen pulled into the outer lane and passed. He speeded up slightly and then slowed down to turn into the driveway of the shopping center, gambling that one of the stores sold liquor, gambling that General Fisher hadn't forgotten his wife's instructions to buy the bottle of sherry.

The Air Force car drove on past.

"Damn!" Hagen muttered to himself. It struck him that any serviceman would have purchased liquor at his base post exchange, where it was sold for much less than at a retail store.

Hagen was stalled for a few seconds behind a woman trying to back out of a parking slot. When he finally broke free, he burned rubber swinging from the driveway onto the road. Luckily, Fisher's driver had caught a red light at the next intersection and Hagen was able to catch and pass him again.

He pressed the accelerator to the floor, trying to put as much distance as he could between them. In two miles he turned into the narrow road leading to the main gate of Peterson Air Force Base. He showed his security clearance to the Air Policeman standing stiffly, wearing a white helmet, matching silk scarf at the neck, and a black leather side holster that contained a pearl-handled revolver.

"Where can I find the PX?" Hagen asked.

The AP pointed up the road. "Straight ahead to the second stop sign. Then left toward the water tower. A large gray building. You can't miss it."

Hagen thanked him and moved away just as Fisher's car pulled up behind and was smartly waved on through the gate. Taking his time, he stayed within the base speed limit and eased into the post exchange parking area only fifty feet ahead of Fisher. He stopped between a Jeep Wagoneer and a Dodge pickup truck with a camper that effectively hid most of his car from view. He slipped from behind the wheel, turning off the lights but keeping the engine running.

The general's car had stopped, and Hagen unhurriedly approached it in a direct line, wondering if Fisher would get out and buy the sherry or send the sergeant to run the errand.

Hagen smiled to himself. He should have known it was a pre-ordained conclusion. The general, of course, sent the sergeant.

Hagen reached the car at nearly the same moment as the sergeant walked through the door into the PX. One quick scan to see if some bored soul waiting in a parked car might be idly staring in his direction or a shopper from the PX pushing a grocery cart close by. The old cliché "The coast is clear" ran through his mind.

Without the slightest hesitation or wasted movement, Hagen slipped a weighted rubber sap from a specially sewn pocket under one arm of his windbreaker, jerked open the rear car door, and swung his arm in a short arc. No words of greeting, no trivial conversation. The sap caught Fisher precisely on the point of his jaw.

Hagen snatched the briefcase from the general's lap, slammed the door, and walked casually back to his car. From start to finish the action had taken no more than four seconds.

As he drove away from the PX toward the main gate he ticked off the timing sequence in his mind. Fisher would be unconscious for twenty minutes, maybe an hour. Give the sergeant four to six minutes to find the shelf with the sherry, pay for it, and return to the car. Another five minutes before an alert was sounded, providing the sergeant even noticed the general had been mugged in the backseat.

Hagen felt pleased with himself. He would be through the main gate and halfway to the Colorado Springs airport before the Air Police realized what had happened.

·   ·   ·

173

An early snow started to fall over southern Colorado shortly after midnight. At first it melted when it met the ground, but soon an icy sheet formed, and then a white blanket began to build. Farther east the winds kicked up, and the Colorado Highway Patrol closed off the smaller county roads due to blizzard conditions.

Inside a small, unmarked Lear jet parked at the far end of the airport terminal, Hagen sat at a desk and studied the contents of General Fisher's briefcase. Most of it was highly classified material concerning day-to-day operations of the space center. One file of papers concerned the flight of the space shuttle *Gettysburg,* which had been launched from Vandenberg Air Force Base in California only two days before. He was amused to find amid the slots of the briefcase a pornographic magazine. But the champion prize was a black leather book that contained a total of thirty-nine names and phone numbers. No addresses or notations, only names and numbers segregated in three sections. The first section gave fourteen; the second, seventeen; and the third, eight.

None of them struck a chord with Hagen. It was possible they were simply friends and associates of Fisher's. He stared at the third list, the printing beginning to blur before his eyes from weariness.

Abruptly the top name leaped out at him. Not the surname, but the first name.

Startled, shocked that he had missed something so simple, a code so obvious that no one would consider it, he copied the list on his legal pad and matched up three of the names by adding the correct ones.

Gunnar Monroe/Eriksen
Irwin Dupuy
Leonard Murphy/Hudson
Daniel Klein
Steve Larson
Ray Sampson/LeBaron
Dean Beagle
Clyde Ward

Eight names instead of nine. Then Hagen shook his head, marveling at his slow grasp of the conspicuous fact that General Clark Fisher would hardly have included his own name on a telephone list.

He was almost home, but his elation was muted by fatigue; he'd

174

had no sleep in the past twenty-two hours. The gamble to snatch General Fisher's briefcase had paid off with unexpected dividends. Instead of one thread, he held five, all the remaining members of the "inner core." Now all he had to do was match up the first names with the phone numbers and he would have a neat and tidy package.

All this was wishful thinking. He had made an amateur's error by mouthing off to General Clark Fisher, alias Anson Jones, over the telephone from Pattenden Lab. He'd tried to write it off as a shrewd move designed to goad the conspirators into making a mistake and give him an opening. But now he realized it was nothing but cockiness mixed with a healthy dose of stupidity.

Fisher would alert the "inner core," if he hadn't already done so. There was nothing Hagen could do now. The damage was done. He was left with no choice but to plunge ahead.

He was staring blankly into the distance when the aircraft pilot entered the main compartment from the cockpit. "Excuse me for interrupting, Mr. Hagen, but the snowstorm is expected to get worse. The control tower just informed me they're going to close down the airport. If we don't take off now, we may not get clearance till tomorrow afternoon."

Hagen nodded. "No sense in hanging around."

"Can you give me a destination?"

There was a short pause as Hagen looked down at his handwritten notes on the legal pad. He decided to leave Hudson until last. Besides, Eriksen, Hudson, and Daniel Klein or whoever, all had the same telephone area code. He recognized the code after Clyde Ward's name and settled on it simply because the location was only a few hundred miles south of Colorado Springs.

"Albuquerque," he said finally.

"Yes, sir," replied the pilot. "If you'll strap yourself in, I'll have us off the ground in five minutes."

As soon as the pilot disappeared into the control cabin, Hagen stripped to his shorts and dropped into a soft berth. He was dead asleep before the wheels left the snow-carpeted runway.

26

THE FEAR THAT the President's chief of staff, Dan Fawcett, inspired inside the White House was immense. His was one of the most powerful positions in Washington. He was the keeper of the sanctum sanctorum. Virtually every document or memo sent to the President had to go through him. And no one, including members of the cabinet and the leaders of Congress, gained entry to the Oval Office unless Fawcett approved it.

The times that someone, high-ranking or low, refused to take no for an answer were nonexistent. So he was uncertain how to react as he looked up from his desk into the smoldering eyes of Admiral Sandecker. Fawcett couldn't remember when he had seen a man seething with so much anger, and he sensed that the admiral was exerting every disciplined resource to hold it under control.

"I'm sorry, Admiral," said Fawcett, "but the President's schedule is airtight. There is no way I can squeeze you in."

"Get me in," Sandecker demanded through tight lips.

"Not possible," replied Fawcett firmly.

Sandecker slowly braced his arms and hands sacrilegiously on the paperwork strewn on Fawcett's desk and leaned over until only a few inches separated their noses.

"You tell the son of a bitch," he snarled, "that he just killed three of my best friends. And unless he gives me a damned good reason why, I'm going to walk out of here, hold a press conference, and reveal enough dirty secrets to scar his precious administration for the rest of his term. Am I getting through to you, Dan?"

Fawcett sat there, rising anger unable to overcome shock. "You'll only destroy your own career. What would be the sense?"

"You're not paying attention. I'll run it by you again. The President is responsible for the deaths of three of my dearest friends. One of them you knew. His name was Dirk Pitt. If it wasn't for Pitt, the President would be resting on the bottom of the sea instead of sitting in the White House. Now, I demand to know for what purpose Pitt died. And if it costs me my career as chief of NUMA, then you can damn well let it."

Sandecker's face was so close that Fawcett could have sworn the admiral's red beard had a life force all its own. "Pitt's dead?" he said dumbly. "I haven't heard—"

"Just tell the President I'm here," Sandecker cut in, his voice turned to steel. "He'll see me."

The news came so abruptly, so coldly, that Fawcett was startled. "I'll inform the President about Pitt," he said slowly.

"Don't bother. If I know, he knows. We're tuned into the same intelligence sources."

"I need time to find out what this is all about," Fawcett said.

"You don't have time," said Sandecker stonily. "The President's nuclear energy bill is coming up for a vote before the Senate tomorrow. Think what might happen if Senator George Pitt is told the President had a hand in murdering his son. I don't have to paint you a picture of what will happen when the senator stops throwing his weight in support of presidential policies and starts opposing them."

Fawcett was shrewd enough to recognize an ambush looming in the distance. He pushed himself back from the desk, clasped his hands and stared at them for a few moments. Then he stood and walked toward the hallway.

"Come with me, Admiral. The President is in a meeting with Defense Secretary Jess Simmons. They should be wrapping up about now."

Sandecker waited outside the Oval Office while Fawcett entered, pardoned himself, and spoke a few whispered words to the President. Two minutes later Jess Simmons came out and exchanged a friendly greeting with the admiral, followed by Fawcett, who motioned for him to come in.

The President came from behind his desk and shook Sandecker's hand. His face was expressionless, his body loose and composed, and his intelligent eyes locked on the hard, burning stare of his visitor.

He turned to Fawcett. "Would you please excuse us, Dan? I'd like to speak with Admiral Sandecker privately."

Wordlessly Fawcett stepped out and closed the door behind him.

The President gestured toward a chair and smiled. "Why don't we sit down and relax."

"I'd rather stand," Sandecker said flatly.

"As you wish." The President eased into an overstuffed armchair and crossed his legs. "I'm sorry about Pitt and the others," he said without preamble. "No one meant for it to happen."

"May I respectfully ask what in hell is going on?"

"Tell me something, Admiral. Would you believe that when I asked for your cooperation in sending out a crew on the blimp it went far beyond a mere hunt for a missing person?"

"Only if there was a solid explanation to back you up."

"And would you also believe that besides looking for her husband, Mrs. LeBaron was part of an elaborate deception to open a direct line of communication between myself and Fidel Castro?"

Sandecker stared at the President, his anger momentarily placed on hold. The admiral was not awed in the least by the nation's leader. He had seen too many Presidents come and go, seen too many of their human frailties. He could not think of one he'd have set on a pedestal.

"No, Mr. President, I can't buy that," he said, his tone sarcastic. "If my memory serves me, you have a very capable Secretary of State in Douglas Oates, who is backed by an occasionally efficient State Department. I'd have to say they're better equipped to communicate with Castro through existing diplomatic channels."

The President smiled wryly. "There are times negotiations between unfriendly countries must deviate from normal standards of statesmanship. Surely, you must believe that."

"I do."

"You don't involve yourself with politics, matters of state, Washington social parties, cronies or cliques, do you, Admiral?"

"That's right."

"But if I gave you an order, you'd obey it."

"Yes, sir, I would," Sandecker replied without hesitation. "Unless, of course, it was illegal, immoral, or unconstitutional."

The President considered that. Then he nodded and held out his hand toward a chair. "Please, Admiral. My time is limited, but I'll briefly explain what's going down." He paused until Sandecker was seated. "Now then...

"Five days ago a highly classified document written by Fidel Castro was smuggled out of Havana to our State Department. Basically

178

it was a proposal for paving the way for positive and constructive relations between Cuba and America."

"What's so startling about that?" Sandecker asked. "He's been angling for closer ties since President Reagan kicked his ass out of Grenada."

"True," the President acknowledged. "Until now the only agreement we've reached over the bargaining table was a deal raising immigration quotas for dissident Cubans coming to America. This new stance, however, went way beyond. Castro wants our help in throwing off the Russian yoke."

Sandecker looked at him, skeptical. "Castro's hatred of the U.S. is an obsession. Why, hell, he still holds rehearsals for an invasion. The Russians aren't about to be shoved out. Cuba represents their only toehold in the Western Hemisphere. Even if they suffered from a moment of madness and yanked their support, the island would sink in an economic quagmire. Cuba can't possibly stand on its own feet, it doesn't have the resources. I wouldn't buy Fidel's act if Christ himself applauded."

"The man is mercurial," admitted the President. "But don't underestimate his intentions. The Soviets are buried in their own economic quagmire. The Kremlin's paranoia against the outside world has driven their military budget to astronomical heights they can no longer afford. Their citizens' standard of living is the worst of any industrialized nation. Their agricultural harvests, industrial goals, and oil exports have all fallen into the cellar. They've lost the means to continue pumping massive aid to the Eastern bloc countries. And in Cuba's situation, the Russians have reached a point where they're demanding more while supplying less. The days of the billion-dollar aid grants, soft loans, and cheap arms supplies have passed. The free ride is over."

Sandecker shook his head. "Still, if I were in Castro's shoes, I'd consider it a bad trade. There is no way Congress would vote billions of dollars to subsidize Cuba, and the island's twelve million people could barely exist without imported goods."

The President glanced at the clock on the mantel. "I've only got another couple of minutes. Anyway, Castro's greatest fear doesn't come from economic chaos or a counterrevolution. It comes from the slow, steady creep of Soviet influence into every corner of his government. The people from Moscow chip off a little here, steal a little there, waiting patiently to make the right moves until they can dominate the government and control the country's resources. Only now

179

has Castro awakened to the fact that his friends in the Kremlin are attempting to steal the country out from under him. His brother, Raúl, was stunned when he became alerted to the heavy infiltration of his officer corps by fellow Cubans who had shifted their loyalty to the Soviet Union."

"I find that surprising. The Cubans detest the Russians. Their viewpoints on life don't mix at all."

"Certainly Cuba never intended to become a Kremlin pawn, but since the revolution thousands of Cuban students have studied in Russian universities. Many, rather than return home and work in a job dictated by the state, a job they might hate or which could lead to a dead end, were swayed by subtle Russian offerings of prestige and money. The canny ones, who placed their future above patriotism, secretly renounced Castro and swore allegiance to the Soviet Union. You have to give the Russians credit. They kept their promises. Using their influence over the Cuban government, they wove their new subjects into positions of power."

"Castro is still revered by the Cuban people," said Sandecker. "I can't see how they could stand by and watch him totally subjugated by Moscow."

The President's expression turned grave. "The very real threat is that the Russians will assassinate the Castro brothers and throw the blame on the CIA. Easy enough to do since the agency is known to have made several attempts on his life back in the sixties."

"And the Kremlin walks through the open door and installs a puppet government."

The President nodded. "Which brings us to his proposed U.S.–Cuban pact. Castro doesn't want to scare the Russians into making their move before we've agreed to back his play to boot them out of the Caribbean. Unfortunately, after making the opening gambit, he has stonewalled all replies from myself and Doug Oates."

"Sounds like the old stick-and-carrot routine to whet your appetite."

"The way I see it too."

"So where do the LeBarons fit into all this?"

"They fell into it," the President said with a touch of irony. "You know the story. Raymond LeBaron flew off in his antique blimp in search of a treasure ship. Actually, he had another target in mind, but that needn't concern NUMA or you personally. As fate would have it, Raúl Castro was on an inspection tour of the island's defense command complex outside of Havana when LeBaron was spotted by

180

their offshore detection systems. The thought struck him that the contact might prove useful. So he ordered his guard forces to intercept the blimp and escort it to an airfield near the city of Cárdenas."

"I can guess the rest," said Sandecker. "The Cubans reinflated the blimp, hid an envoy on board, who was carrying the U.S.–Cuban document, and sent it aloft, figuring prevailing winds would nudge it toward the States."

"You're close," the President acknowledged, smiling. "But they didn't take any chances on fickle winds. A close friend of Fidel's and a pilot sneaked on board with the document. They flew the blimp to Miami, where they jumped into the water a few miles offshore and were picked up by a waiting yacht."

"I'd be curious to learn where the three bodies in the control cabin came from," Sandecker probed.

"A melodramatic display by Castro to prove his good intentions that I haven't got time to go into."

"The Russians haven't become suspicious?"

"Not yet. Their superior attitude over the Cubans prevents them from seeing anything resembling Latin ingenuity."

"So Raymond LeBaron is alive and well somewhere in Cuba."

The President made an open gesture with his hands. "I can only assume that's his situation. CIA sources report that Soviet intelligence demanded to interrogate LeBaron. The Cubans obliged and LeBaron hasn't been seen since."

"Aren't you going to even try to negotiate LeBaron's release?" asked Sandecker.

"The situation is delicate as it is without throwing him on the bargaining table. When we can nail down and sign the U.S.–Cuban pact, I have no doubt that Castro will take custody of LeBaron from the Russians and turn him over to us."

The President paused and stared at the mantel clock. "I'm late for a conference with my budget people." He stood up and started for the door. Then he turned to Sandecker. "I'll wrap this up quickly. Jessie LeBaron was briefed on the situation and memorized our response to Castro. The plan was to have the blimp return with a LeBaron on board. A signal to Castro that my reply was being sent in the same way his proposal was sent out. Something went wrong. You passed Jess Simmons on your way in. He briefed me on the photos taken by our aerial reconnaissance. Instead of stopping the blimp and escorting it to Cárdenas, the Cuban patrol helicopter fired upon it. Then for some unexplained reason the helicopter exploded, and they both crashed into the sea. You must realize, Admiral, I couldn't send rescue forces because of the sensitive nature of the mission. I'm truly sorry about Pitt. I owed him a debt I could never repay. We can only pray that he, Jessie LeBaron, and your other friends somehow survived."

"Nobody could survive a crash in the path of hurricane," Sandecker said caustically. "You'll have to pardon me, Mr. President, but even Mickey Mouse could have put together a better operation."

A pained expression lined the President's face. He started to say something, thought better of it, and pulled open the door. "I'm sorry, Admiral, I'm late for the conference."

The President spoke no more. He walked from the Oval Office and left Sandecker standing confused and alone.

27

THE WORST OF HURRICANE Little Eva skirted the island and turned northeast into the Gulf of Mexico. The winds dropped off to forty miles an hour, but another two days would pass before they were replaced by the gentle trade winds from the south.

Cayo Santa María seemed empty of any life, animal or human. Ten years earlier, in a moment of generous comradeship, Fidel Castro had deeded the island over to his Communist allies as a gesture of goodwill. He then slapped the face of the White House by proclaiming it as a territory of Russia.

The natives were quietly but forcefully relocated onto the mainland, and engineering units of the GRU (Glavnoye Razvedyvatelnoye Upravleniye, or Chief Intelligence Directorate of the Soviet General Staff), the military arm of the KGB, moved in and began building a highly secret underground installation. Working in stages and only under cover of darkness, the complex slowly took shape beneath the sand and palm trees. CIA spy planes monitored the island, but intelligence analysis failed to detect any defense installations or heavy shipment of supplies by sea or air. Enhanced photo examination showed little except a few eroding roads that seemingly went nowhere. Only as a matter of routine was the island studied, but nothing ever turned up that indicated a threat to United States security.

Somewhere beneath the wind-beaten island, Pitt awoke in a small sterile room on a bed with a goosedown mattress under a fluorescent light that blazed continuously. He could not recall if he had ever slept in a feather bed, but he found it most comfortable and made a mental note to look around for one, if and when he ever got back to Washington.

Apart from bruises, sore joints, and a slight throb in his head he felt reasonably fit. He lay there and stared at the gray-painted ceiling, recalling the night before: Jessie's discovery of her husband; the guards escorting Pitt, Giordino, and Gunn to an infirmary, where a female Russian doctor, who was built like a bowling pin, tended to their injuries; a meal of mutton stew in a mess hall that Pitt rated six points below an east Texas truck stop; and finally being locked in a room with a toilet and washbasin, a bed, and a narrow wooden wardrobe.

Slipping his hands under the sheet, he explored his body. Except for several yards of tape and gauze, he was naked. He marveled at the homely doctor's fetish for bandages. He swung his bare feet onto the concrete floor and sat there, pondering his next move. A signal from his bladder reminded him he was still human, so he moved over to the commode and wished he had a cup of coffee. They, whoever they were, had left him his Doxa watch. The dial read 11:55. Since he had never slept more than nine hours in his life, he rightly assumed that it was the following morning.

A minute later he leaned over the basin and splashed cold water on his face. The single towel was coarse and hardly absorbed the moisture. He went over to the wardrobe, pulled it open, and found a khaki shirt and pants on a hanger and a pair of sandals. Before he put them on he removed several bandages over wounds that were already beginning to scab, and flexed the newfound freedom of movement. After he dressed, he tried the heavy iron door. The latch was still locked, so he pounded on the thick metal panel, causing a hollow boom to reverberate around the concrete walls.

A boy who looked no older than nineteen and wearing Soviet army fatigues opened the door and stood back, aiming a machine pistol, no larger than an ordinary household hammer, at Pitt's midsection. He motioned down a long hall to the left, and Pitt obliged. They passed several other iron doors, and Pitt wondered if Gunn and Giordino were behind any of them.

They stopped at an elevator whose doors were held open by another guard. They entered and Pitt felt the slight pressure against his feet as the car rose. He glanced at the indicator above the door and noticed that it showed lights for five levels. A good-sized layout, he thought. The elevator came to a stop and the automatic doors glided open.

Pitt and his guard stepped out into a carpeted room with a vaulted ceiling. The two side walls held shelves stacked with hundreds of books. Most of the books were in English and many of them were by current bestselling American authors. A vast map of North America covered the entire far wall. The room looked to Pitt to be a private study. There was a big, antique carved desk whose marble top was strewn with current issues of the *Washington Post*, the *New York Times*, the *Wall Street Journal*, and *USA Today*. Stacked atop tables on each side of the doorway were piles of technical magazines, including *Computer Technology*, *Science Digest*, and the *Air Force Journal*. The carpet was burgundy red with six green leather chairs spaced evenly about its thick pile.

Maintaining his silence, the guard reentered the elevator and left Pitt standing alone in the empty room.

Must be time to observe the monkey, he mused. Pitt didn't bother to probe the walls for the lens to the video camera. There was little doubt in his mind that it was concealed in the room somewhere, recording his actions. He decided to try for a reaction. He swayed drunkenly for a moment, rolled his eyes upward, and then crumpled onto the carpet.

Within fifteen seconds a hidden door, whose edges perfectly matched latitude and longitude lines of the giant wall map, swung open and a short, trim man in an elegantly tailored Soviet military uniform walked into the room. He knelt down and peered into Pitt's half-open eyes.

"Can you hear me?" he asked in English.

"Yes," Pitt mumbled.

The Russian went over to a table and tilted a crystal decanter over a matching glass. He returned and lifted Pitt's head.

"Drink this," he ordered.

"What is it?"

"Courvoisier cognac with a sharp, biting taste," the Russian officer answered in a flawless American accent. "Good for what ails you."

"I prefer a richer, smoother Rémy Martin," said Pitt, holding up the glass. "Cheers."

He sipped the cognac until it was gone, then rose lightly to his feet, found a chair, and sat down.

The officer smiled with amusement. "You seem to have made a quick recovery, Mr...."

"Snodgrass, Elmer Snodgrass, from Moline, Illinois."

"A nice Midwestern touch," the Russian said, coming around and sitting behind the desk. "I am Peter Velikov."

"General Velikov, if my memory of Russian military insignia is correct."

"Quite correct," Velikov acknowledged. "Would you care for another cognac?"

185

Pitt shook his head and studied the man across the desk. He judged Velikov to be no taller than five foot seven, weighing about a hundred and thirty pounds, and somewhere in his late forties. There was a comfortable friendliness about him, and yet Pitt sensed an underlying coldness. His hair was short and black with only a touch of gray at the sideburns and receding around a peak above the forehead. His eyes were as blue as an alpine lake, and the light-skinned face seemed sculptured more by classic Roman influence than Slavic. Dress him in a toga and set a wreath on his head, Pitt imagined, and Velikov could have posed for a marble bust of Julius Caesar.

"I hope you don't mind if I ask you a few questions," said Velikov politely.

"Not at all. I have no pressing engagements for the rest of the day. My time is yours."

A look of ice glinted in Velikov's eyes for an instant and then quickly faded. "Suppose you tell me how you came to be on Cayo Santa María."

Pitt held out his hands in a helpless gesture. "No sense in wasting your time. I might as well make a clean breast of it. I'm president of the Central Intelligence Agency. My board of directors and I thought it would be a great promotional idea to charter a blimp and drop redeemable coupons for toilet paper over the length of Cuba. I'm told there's an acute shortage down here. Unfortunately, the Cubans didn't agree with our marketing strategy and shot us down."

General Velikov gave Pitt a tolerant but irritated look. He perched a pair of reading glasses on his nose and opened a file on his desk.

"I see by your dossier, Mr. Pitt—Dirk Pitt, if I read it right—that your character profile mentions a drift toward dry wit."

"Does it also tell you I'm a pathological liar?"

"No, but it seems you have a most fascinating history. A pity you aren't on our side."

"Come now, General, what future could a nonconformist possibly have in Moscow?"

"A short one, I'm afraid."

"I compliment your honesty."

"Why not tell me the truth?"

"Only if you're willing to believe it."

"You don't think I can?"

"Not if you adhere to the Communist mania of seeing a CIA plot under every rock."

"Seems you have a high disregard for the Soviet Union."

186

"Name one thing you people have ever done in the last seventy years to earn a humanity award. What is baffling as hell is why the Russians have never wised up to the fact they're the laughing stock of the world. Your empire is history's most pathetic joke. The twenty-first century is just around the corner and your government operates as though it never advanced past the nineteen-thirties."

Velikov didn't bat an eyelid, but Pitt detected a slight redness in his face. It was clear the general wasn't used to being lectured by a man he looked down upon as an enemy of the state. His eyes examined Pitt with the unmistakable gaze of a judge who was weighing a convicted murderer's life in the balance. Then his gaze turned speculative.

"I'll see that your comments are passed on to the Politburo," he said dryly. "Now if you're through with the speech, Mr. Pitt, I'd be interested in hearing how you came to be here."

Pitt nodded toward the table with the decanter. "I think I'd like that cognac now."

"Help yourself."

Pitt half filled his glass and returned to the chair. "What I'm about to tell you is the straight truth. I want you to understand I have no reason to lie. To the best of my knowledge I am not on any sort of intelligence mission for my government. Do you understand me so far, General?"

"I do."

"Is your hidden tape recorder running?"

Velikov had the courtesy to nod. "It is."

Pitt then related in detail his discovery of the runaway blimp, the meeting with Jessie LeBaron in Admiral Sandecker's office, the final flight of the *Prosperteer,* and finally the narrow escape from the hurricane, omitting any mention of Giordino's downing of the patrol helicopter or the dive on the *Cyclops.*

Velikov did not look up when Pitt finished speaking. He sifted through the dossier without a flicker of change in his expression. The general acted as if his mind were light-years away and he hadn't heard a word.

Pitt could play the game too. He took his cognac glass and rose from his chair. Picking up a copy of the *Washington Post,* he noted with mild surprise that the masthead carried that day's date.

"You must have an efficient courier system," he said.

"Sorry?"

"Your newspapers are only a few hours old."

187

"Five hours, to be exact."

The cognac fairly glowed on Pitt's empty stomach. The awkward consequences of his predicament mellowed after his third drink. He went on the attack.

"Why are you holding Raymond LeBaron?" he asked.

"At the moment he is a house guest."

"That doesn't explain why his existence has been kept quiet for two weeks."

"I don't have to explain anything to you, Mr. Pitt."

"How is it LeBaron receives gourmet dinners in formal dress, while my friends and I are forced to eat and dress like common prisoners."

"Because that is precisely what you all are, Mr. Pitt, common prisoners. Mr. LeBaron is a very wealthy and powerful man whose dialogue is most enlightening. You, on the other hand, are merely an inconvenience. Does that satisfy your curiosity?"

"It doesn't satisfy a thing," Pitt said, yawning.

"How did you destroy the patrol helicopter?" Velikov asked suddenly.

"We threw our shoes at it," Pitt fired back testily. "What did you expect from four civilians, one of whom was a woman, flying in a forty-year-old gas bag?"

"Helicopters don't blow up in midair for no reason."

"Maybe it was struck by lightning."

"Well, then, Mr. Pitt, if you were on a simple search mission to locate a clue to Mr. LeBaron's disappearance and hunt for treasure, how do you explain the report from the captain of the patrol boat, who stated that the blimp's control car was so shattered by shellfire that no one could have survived, and that a streak of light issued from the blimp an instant before the helicopter exploded, and that a thorough search over the crash site showed no signs of survivors? Yet you all appear like magic on this island in the middle of a hurricane, when the security patrols were taking shelter from the winds. Most opportune, wouldn't you say?"

"How do you read it?"

"The blimp was either remote controlled or another crew was killed by the gunners on board the helicopter. You and Mrs. LeBaron were brought close to shore by submarine, but during the landing everyone was thrown onto the rocks and injured."

"You get a passing grade for creativity, General, but you fail accuracy. Only the landing part is correct. You forgot the most important ingredient, a motive. Why would four unarmed castaways attack whatever it is you've got here?"

"I don't have the answers yet," said Velikov with a disarming smile.

"But you intend to get them."

"I'm not a man who accepts failure, Mr. Pitt. Your story, though imaginative, does not wash." He pressed a button on the desk intercom. "We'll talk again soon."

"When can we expect you to contact our government so they can begin negotiations for our release?"

Velikov gave Pitt a patronizing look. "My apologies. I neglected to mention that your government was notified only an hour ago."

"Of our rescue?"

"No, of your deaths."

For a long second it didn't dawn on Pitt. Then it slowly began to register. His jaw stiffened and his eyes bored into Velikov.

"Spell it out, General."

"Very simple," said Velikov in a manner as friendly as if he were passing the time of day with a mailman. "Whether by accident or by design, you have stumbled onto our most sensitive military installation outside the Soviet Union. You cannot be permitted to leave. After I learn the true facts, you will all have to die."

28

INDULGING IN HIS FAVORITE PASTIME—eating—Hagen stole an hour to enjoy a Mexican lunch of flat enchiladas topped with an egg followed by sopaipillas and washed down with a tequila sour. He paid the check, left the restaurant, and drove to the address assigned to Clyde Ward. His source with the telephone company had traced the number in General Fisher's black book to a public phone in a gas station. He marked the time. In another six minutes his pilot would call the number from the parked jet.

He found the gas station in an industrial area near the rail yards. It was self-serve, selling an unknown independent brand. He pulled up to a pump whose red paint was heavily coated by grime and inserted the nozzle into the car's fuel spout, careful to avoid looking toward the pay phone inside the station's office.

Shortly after landing at the Albuquerque airport, Hagen had rented a car and siphoned ten gallons of fuel from the tank so his pit stop would appear genuine. The trapped air pockets inside the tank gurgled and he screwed on the cap and replaced the nozzle. He entered the office and was fumbling with his wallet when the pay phone mounted on the wall began to ring.

The only attendant on duty, who was in the act of repairing a flat tire, wiped his hands on a rag and picked up the receiver. Hagen tuned in on the one-way conversation.

"Mel's Service.... Who?... There ain't no Clyde here.... Yeah, I'm sure. You got the wrong number.... That's the right number, but I've worked here for six years and I ain't never heard of no Clyde."

He hung up and stepped up to the cash register and smiled at Hagen. "How much you get?"

"Ten point two gallons. Thirteen dollars and fifty-seven cents."

While the attendant made change for a twenty, Hagen scanned the

190

station. He couldn't help admiring the professionalism that went into setting up the stage, because that's what it was, a stage setting. The office and lube bay floors hadn't seen a mop in years. Cobwebs hung from the ceilings, the tools had more rust than oil on them, and the attendant's palms and fingernails didn't look as if they had ever seen grease. But it was the surveillance system that astounded him. His trained eye picked out subtly placed electrical wiring that didn't belong in a run-of-the-mill service station. He sensed rather spotted the bugs and cameras.

"Could you do me a favor?" Hagen ask the attendant as he received his change.

"Whatta you need?"

"I've got a funny noise in the engine. Could you take a look under the hood and tell me what might be wrong?"

"Sure, why not. Ain't got much else to do."

Hagen noticed the attendant's designer hair style and doubted if it had ever been touched by the neighborhood barber. He also caught the slight bulge in the pants leg, on the outer right calf just above the ankle.

Hagen had parked the car on the opposite side of the second gas-pump island away from the station building. He started the engine and pulled the hood latch. The attendant put his foot on the front bumper and peered over the radiator.

"I don't hear nothin'."

"Come around on this side," said Hagen. "It's louder over here." He stood with his back to the street, shielded from any electronic observation by the pumps, the car, and its raised hood.

As the attendant leaned over the fender and poked his head into the engine compartment, Hagen slipped a gun from a belt holster behind his back and pushed the muzzle between the man's buttocks.

"This is a two-and-a-half-inch-barreled combat magnum .357 shoved up your ass and it's loaded with wad cutters. Do you understand?"

The attendant tensed, but he did not show fear. "Yes, I read you, friend."

"And do you know what a wad cutter can do at close range?"

"I'm aware of what a wad cutter is."

"Good, then you know it'll make a nice tunnel from your asshole to your brain if I pull the trigger."

"What are you after, friend?"

"What happened to your phony jerkwater accent?" Hagen asked.

"It comes and goes."

Hagen reached down with his free hand and removed a small Beretta .38-caliber automatic from under the attendant's pants leg. "Okay, *friend*, where can I find Clyde?"

"Never heard of him."

Hagen rammed the muzzle of the magnum up against the base of the spine with such force the fabric on the seat of the attendant's pants split and he grunted in agony.

"Who are you working for?" he gasped.

"The 'inner core,'" answered Hagen.

"You can't be."

Hagen gave an upward thrust with the snub-nosed gun barrel again. The attendant's face contorted and he moaned as his lower body burned with the jarring pain.

"Who is Clyde?" Hagen demanded.

"Clyde Booth," the attendant muttered through clenched teeth.

"I can't hear you, friend."

"His name is Clyde Booth."

"Tell me about him."

"He's supposed to be some kind of genius. Invents and manufactures scientific gadgets used in space. Secret systems for the government. I don't know exactly, I'm only a member of the security staff."

"Location?"

"The plant is ten miles west of Santa Fe. It's called QB-Tech."

"What's the QB stand for?"

"Quarter Back," the attendant answered. "Booth was an all-American football player for Arizona State."

"You knew I would show up?"

"We were told to be on the lookout for a fat man."

"How many others positioned around the station?" asked Hagen.

"Three. One down the street in the tow truck, one on the roof of the warehouse behind the station, one in the red van parked beside the western bar and diner next door."

"Why haven't they made their move?"

"Our orders were only to follow you."

Hagen eased the pressure and reholstered his revolver. Then he removed the shells from the attendant's automatic, dropped it on the ground, and kicked it under the car.

"Okay," said Hagen. "Now walk, don't run, back inside the station."

Before the attendant was halfway across the station drive, Hagen had turned the corner a block away. He made four more quick turns to lose the tow truck and the van, and then sped toward the airport.

29

LEONARD HUDSON STEPPED OUT of the elevator that lowered him into the heart of the Jersey Colony headquarters. He carried an umbrella that was dripping from the rain outside, and a fancy briefcase of highly polished walnut.

He looked neither right nor left and acknowledged the greetings from his staff with a curt wave. Hudson was not the nervous type, nor was he a worrier, but he was concerned. The reports coming in from other members of the "inner core" spelled danger. Someone was methodically tracking each of them down. An outsider had breached their carefully devised cover operations.

Now the whole lunar base effort—the ingenuity, the planning, the lives, the money, and the manpower that had gone into the Jersey Colony—was in jeopardy because of an unknown intruder.

He walked into his large but austere office and found Gunnar Eriksen waiting for him.

Eriksen was sitting on a couch, sipping a cup of hot coffee and smoking a curved pipe. His round, unlined face wore a somber look and his eyes had a benign glow. He was dressed casually, but unrumpled, in an expensive cashmere sports jacket and a tan V-neck sweater over matching woolen slacks. He would not look out of place selling Jaguars or Ferraris.

"You talked to Fisher and Booth," said Hudson, hanging up the umbrella and setting the briefcase beside the desk.

"I have."

"Any idea who it might be?"

"None."

"Strange that he never leaves fingerprints," said Hudson, sitting on the couch with Eriksen and pouring himself a cup of coffee from a glass pot.

193

Eriksen sent a puff of smoke toward the ceiling. "Stranger yet that every image we have of him on videotape is a blur."

"He must carry some sort of electronic erasing device."

"Obviously not your ordinary private investigator," Eriksen mused. "A top-of-the-line professional with heavy backing."

"He knows his way around, produces all the correct identification papers and security clearances. The story he handed Mooney about being an auditor with the General Accounting Office was first-rate. I'd have swallowed it myself."

"What have we got on him?"

"Only a stack of descriptions that don't agree on anything except his size. They're unanimous in referring to him as a fat man."

"Could be the President has turned an intelligence agency loose on us."

"If that were the case," said Hudson doubtfully, "we'd be looking at an army of undercover agents. This man appears to work alone."

"Did you consider the possibility the President might have quietly hired an agent outside the government?" asked Eriksen.

"The thought crossed my mind, but I'm not completely sold on it. Our friend in the White House is tapped into the Oval Office. Everyone who calls or walks in and out of the executive wing is accounted for. Of course, there's always the President's private line, but I don't think this is the sort of mission he could instigate over the telephone."

"Interesting," said Eriksen. "The fat man started his probe at the facility where we first created the idea of the Jersey Colony."

"That's right," Hudson acknowledged. "He rifled Earl Mooney's office at Pattenden Lab and traced a phone call to General Fisher, even made some remark about you wanting me to pay for the airplane."

"An obvious reference to our advertised deaths," Eriksen said thoughtfully. "That means he's tied us together."

"Then he turned up in Colorado and mugged Fisher, stealing a notebook with the names and numbers of the top people on the Jersey Colony project, including those of the 'inner core.' Then he must have seen through the trap we laid to trail him from New Mexico and escaped. We got a small break when one our security men who was watching the Albuquerque airport spotted a fat man arrive in an unmarked private jet and take off again only two hours later."

"He must have rented a car, used some sort of identification."

Hudson shook his head. "Nothing of any use. He showed a driver's license and a credit card from a George Goodfly of New Orleans, who doesn't exist."

Eriksen tapped the ashes from his pipe into a glass dish. "Seems odd he didn't drive to Santa Fe and attempt to penetrate Clyde Booth's operation."

"My guess is he's only on a fact-finding hunt."

"But who is paying him? The Russians?"

"Certainly not the KGB," said Hudson. "They don't send subtle messages over the phone or move around the country in a private jet. No, this man moves fast. I'd say he's running on a tight deadline."

Eriksen stared into his coffee cup. "The Soviet lunar mission is scheduled to set down on the moon in five days. That has to be his deadline."

"I believe you may be right."

Eriksen stared at him. "You realize now that the power behind the intruder has to be the President," he said quietly.

Hudson nodded slowly. "I blinded myself to the possibility," he said in a distant voice. "I wanted to believe he would back the security of the Jersey Colony from Russian penetration."

"From what you told me of your meeting, he wasn't about to condone a battle on the moon between our people and Soviet cosmonauts. Nor would he be overjoyed to learn Steinmetz destroyed three Soviet spacecraft."

"The point that bothers me," said Hudson, "is if we accept the President's interference, why, with all of his resources, would he send only one man?"

"Because once he accepted the Jersey Colony as a reality, he realized our supporters cover his every move, and he rightly assumed we could throw a school of red herrings across our trail to mislead any investigation. A wise man, the President. He brought in a ringer from left field who cracked our walls before we knew what was happening."

"There may still be time to send him on the wrong scent."

"Too late. The fat man has Fisher's notebook," said Eriksen. "He knows who we are and where to find us. He is a very real threat. He started at the tail and now he's working toward the head. When the fat man comes through this door, Leo, the President will surely move to stop any confrontation between the Soviet cosmonauts and our people in the Jersey Colony."

"Are you hinting we eliminate the fat man?" asked Hudson.

195

"No," Eriksen replied. "Better not to antagonize the President. We'll merely put him on ice for a few days."

"I wonder where he'll turn up next," Hudson pondered.

Eriksen methodically reloaded his pipe. "He began his witch-hunt in Oregon and from there to Colorado and then New Mexico. My guess is his next stop will be Texas, at the office of our man with NASA in Houston."

Hudson punched a number on his desk phone. "A pity I can't be there when we snare the bastard."

30

PITT SPENT THE NEXT TWO HOURS on his back in bed, listening to the sounds of metal doors being opened and closed, tuning in on the footsteps heard outside his cell. The youthful guard brought lunch and waited while Pitt ate, making sure all the utensils were accounted for when he left. This time the guard seemed in a better humor and was unarmed. He also left the door open during the meal, giving Pitt a chance to study the latch.

He was surprised to see that it was an ordinary doorknob lock instead of a heavy-security or mortice throw bolt. His cell was never meant to serve as a jail. It was mostly likely intended as a storeroom.

Pitt stirred a spoon over a bowl of foul-smelling fish stew and handed it back, more interested in the closing of the door than eating slop that he knew was the first step of a psychological ploy to lower his mental defense mechanisms. The guard stepped back and yanked the iron door shut. Pitt cocked his ear and caught a single, decisive click immediately after the slam.

He knelt and closely examined the crack between the door and the strike. The gap was ⅙ inch across. Then he scoured the cell, searching for an object thin enough to slip between the crack so he could jimmy the latch.

The bunk supporting the down mattress was made of wood with grooved joints. No metal or hard, flat surface there. The faucets and spouts on the sink were ceramic and the plumbing underneath and in the toilet tank offered nothing he could mold with his hands. He got lucky with the wardrobe. Any one of the hinges would work perfectly, except he could not remove the screws with his fingernails.

He was pondering this problem when the door swung open and the guard stood in the entrance. His eyes cautiously scanned the cell for a moment. Then he brusquely motioned Pitt outside, led him through a maze of gray concrete corridors, stopping finally outside a door marked with the numeral 6.

Pitt was roughly shoved into a small boxlike room with a sickly stench about it. The floor was cement with a drain in its center. The walls were painted a dreary shade of red that ominously matched the pattern of stains that were splattered on them. The only illumination came from a dull yellow bulb hanging by a cord from the ceiling. It was the most depressing room Pitt had ever entered.

The only furniture was a cheap, deeply scarred wooden chair. But it was the man seated in the chair that Pitt's eyes focused on. The eyes that stared back were as expressionless as ice cubes. Pitt could not tell the stranger's height, but his chest and shoulders were so ponderous they seemed deformed, the look of a body builder who had spent thousands of hours of sweat and effort. The head was completely shaven, and the face might have been considered almost handsome but for the large misshapen nose that was totally out of place with its surroundings. He was wearing only a pair of rubber boots and tropical shorts. Except for a Bismarck moustache, he looked strangely familiar to Pitt.

Without looking up he began reading off a list of crimes Pitt was accused of. They began with violating Cuban air space, shooting down a helicopter, murdering its crew, working as an agent for the Central Intelligence Agency, entering the country illegally. The accusations droned on until they ended at last with unlawful entry into a forbidden military zone. The voice spoke in pure American with a trace of a Western accent.

"How do you respond?"

"Guilty as sin."

A piece of paper and a pen were held out by an enormous hand. "Please sign the confession."

Pitt took the pen and signed the paper against a wall without reading the wording.

The interrogator stared at the signature broodingly. "I think you've made a mistake."

"How so?"

"Your name is not Benedict Arnold."

Pitt snapped his fingers. "By God, you're right. That was last week. This week I'm Millard Fillmore."

"Very amusing."

"Since General Velikov has already informed American officials of my death," said Pitt seriously, "I fail to see any good of a confession.

Seems to me it's like injecting penicillin into a skeleton. What purpose can it possibly serve?"

"Insurance against an incident, propaganda reasons, even a bargaining position," answered the interrogator amiably. "There could be any number of reasons." He paused and read from a file on the desk. "I see from the dossier General Velikov gave me that you directed a salvage project on the *Empress of Ireland* shipwreck in the Saint Lawrence River."

"That is correct."

"I believe I was on the same project."

Pitt stared at him. There was a familiarity, but it wouldn't frame in his mind. He shook his head. "I don't recall you working on my team. What's your name?"

"Foss Gly," he said slowly. "I worked with the Canadians to disrupt your operations."

A scene burst within Pitt's mind of a tugboat tied to a dock in Rimouski, Quebec. He had saved the life of a British secret agent by braining Gly on the head with a wrench. He also remembered with great relief that Gly's back had been turned and he had not seen Pitt's approach.

"Then we've never met face to face," Pitt said calmly. He watched for a faint sign of recognition from Gly, but he didn't bat an eye.

"Probably not."

"You're a long way from home."

Gly shrugged his great shoulders. "I work for whoever pays top dollar for my special services."

"In this case the money machine spits out rubles."

"Converted into gold," Gly added. He sighed and pulled himself to a standing position and stretched. The skin was so taut, the veins so pronounced, they actually looked grotesque. He rose from the chair and looked up, the smooth dome of his head on a level with Pitt's chin. "I'd like to continue the small talk about past events, Mr. Pitt, but I must have the answers to several questions and your signature on the confession."

"I'll discuss whatever subject that interests you when I'm assured the LeBarons and my friends will not be harmed."

Gly did not reply, only stared with a look that bordered on indifference.

Pitt sensed a blow was coming and tensed his body to roll with it. But Gly did not cooperate. Instead, he slowly reached out with one hand and gripped Pitt at the base of the neck on the soft part of the

199

shoulder. At first the pressure was light, a squeeze, and then a gradual tightening until the pain erupted like fire.

Pitt clutched Gly's wrist with both hands and tried to wrench away the ironlike claw, but he might as well have tried to pull a twenty-foot oak out of the ground by the roots. He ground his teeth together until he thought they would crack. Dimly through the bursting fireworks in his brain, he could hear Gly's voice.

"Okay, Pitt, you don't have to go through this. Just tell me who masterminded your intrusion on this island and why. No need to suffer unless you're a professional masochist. Believe me, you won't find the experience enjoyable. Tell the general what he wants to know. Whatever you're hiding won't change the course of history. Thousands of lives won't hang in the balance. Why feel your body being pulped day after day until all bones are crushed, all joints are cracked, your sinews reduced to the consistency of mashed potatoes. Because that is exactly what will happen if you don't play ball. You understand?"

The ungodly agony eased as Gly released his grip. Pitt swayed on his feet and stared through half-open eyes at his tormentor, one hand massaging the ugly bruise that was spreading on his shoulder. He realized that whatever story he told, true or fabricated, would never be accepted. The torture would continue until his physical resources finally gave in and numbed to it.

He asked politely, "Do you get a bonus for every confession?"

"I do not work on commission," said Gly with friendly humor.

"You win," said Pitt easily. "I have a low threshold of pain. What do you want me to confess to, attempting to assassinate Fidel Castro or plotting to convert Russian advisers to democrats?"

"Merely the truth, Mr. Pitt."

"I've already told General Velikov."

"Yes, I have your recorded words."

"Then you know that Mrs. LeBaron, Al Giordino, Rudi Gunn, and I were trying to find a clue to the disappearance of Raymond LeBaron while searching for a shipwreck supposedly containing treasure. What's so sinister about that?"

"General Velikov sees it as a front for a more classified mission."

"For instance?"

"An attempt to communicate with the Castros."

"Ridiculous is the first word that comes to mind. There must be easier ways for our governments to negotiate with each other."

"Gunn has told us everything," said Gly. "You were to head the operation to stray into Cuban waters, where you were to be captured by their patrol craft and escorted to the mainland. Once there, you were to turn over vital information dealing with secret U.S.–Cuban relations."

Pitt was genuinely at a loss. This was all Greek to him. "That has to be the dumbest cock-and-bull tale I've ever heard."

"Then why were you armed and able to destroy the Cuban patrol helicopter?"

"We carried no arms," Pitt lied. "The helicopter suddenly exploded in our faces. I can't give you a reason."

"Then explain why the Cuban patrol boat could find no survivors at the crash site."

"We were in the water. It was dark and the seas were rough. They didn't spot us."

"Yet you were able to swim six miles through the violent water of a hurricane, all four of you keeping together as a group, and landing intact on Cayo Santa María. How was it possible?"

"Just lucky, I guess."

"Now who's telling a dumb cock-and-bull tale?"

Pitt never got a chance to answer. Without a flicker of warning, Gly swung and rammed a fist into the side of Pitt's body near the left kidney.

The pain and the sudden understanding burst within him at the same time. As he sank into the black pool of unconsciousness he reached out for Jessie, but she laughed and made no effort to reach back.

31

A DEEP, RESONANT VOICE was saying something, almost in his ear. The words were vague and distant. An army of scorpions crept over the edge of the bed and began thrusting their poisoned tails in his side. He opened his eyes. The bright fluorescent light above blinded him, so he closed them again. His face felt wet and he thought he might be swimming and threw out his arms. Then the voice beside him spoke more distinctly.

"Lie easy, partner. I'm just sponging off your face."

Pitt reopened his eyes and focused them on the face of an older, gray-haired man with soft, concerned eyes in a warm, scholarly face. The eyes met his and he smiled.

"Are you in much pain?"

"It smarts a bit."

"Would you like some water?"

"Yes, please."

When the man stood up, the hair on his head nearly touched the ceiling. He produced a cup from a small canvas bag and filled it from the washbasin.

Pitt clutched his side and eased very slowly to a sitting position. He felt rotten and realized he was ravenously hungry. When was the last time he'd eaten? His drowsy mind couldn't recall. He accepted the water thankfully and quickly downed it. Then he looked up at his benefactor.

"Old rich and reckless Raymond, I presume."

LeBaron smiled tightly. "Not a title I'm fond of."

"You're not an easy man to locate."

"My wife has told me how you saved her life. I wish to thank you."

"According to General Velikov, the rescue is only temporary."

LeBaron's smile vanished. "What did he tell you?"

"He said, and I quote, 'You all have to die.'"

"Did he give you a reason?"

"The story he handed me was that we had stumbled into a most sensitive Soviet military installation."

A pensive look crossed LeBaron's face. Then he said, "Velikov was lying. Originally this place was built to gather communications data from microwave transmissions around the U.S., but the rapid development of eavesdropping satellites made it obsolete before it was completed."

"How do you know that?"

"They've allowed me the run of the island. Something impossible if the area was highly secret. I've seen no evidence of sophisticated communications equipment or antennas anywhere. I've also become friendly with a number of Cuban visitors who let slip bits and pieces of information. The best I can figure is that this place is like a businessmen's retreat, a hideaway where corporate executives go to discuss and plan marketing strategy for the coming year. Only here, high-ranking Soviet and Cuban officials meet to create political and military policy."

It was difficult for Pitt to concentrate. His left kidney hurt like hell and he felt drowsy. He staggered over to the commode. His urine was pink with blood, but not very much, and he didn't feel the damage was serious.

"We had best not continue this conversation," said Pitt. "My cell is probably bugged."

LeBaron shook his head. "No, I don't think so. This level of the compound wasn't constructed for maximum security detention because there is no way out. It's like the old French penal colony at Devil's Island; impossible to escape from. The Cuban mainland is over twenty miles away. The water teems with sharks, and the currents sweep out to sea. In the other direction the nearest landfall is in the Bahamas, a hundred and ten miles to the northeast. If you're thinking of escape, my advice is to forget it."

Pitt gingerly settled back on his bed. "Have you seen the others?"

"Yes."

"Their condition?"

"Giordino and Gunn are together in a room thirty feet down the corridor. Because of their injuries they've been spared a visit to room number six. Until now, they've been treated quite well."

"Jessie?"

LeBaron's face tensed very slightly. "General Velikov has graciously allowed us a VIP room to ourselves. We're even permitted to dine with the officers."

"I'm glad to hear you've both been spared a trip to room six."

"Yes, Jessie and I are lucky our treatment is humanly decent."

LeBaron's tone seemed unconvincing, his words spoken in a flat monotone. There was no light in his eyes. This wasn't the man who was famous for his audacious and freewheeling adventures and flamboyant fiascos in and out of the business world. He seemed completely out of character with the prodigious dynamo whose advice was sought by financiers and world leaders. He struck Pitt as a beaten farmer, forced off his land by an unscrupulous banker.

"And the status of Buck Caesar and Joe Cavilla?" Pitt asked.

LeBaron shrugged sadly. "Buck eluded his guards during an exercise period outside the compound and tried to swim for it, using the trunk of a fallen palm tree as a raft. His body, or what was left after the sharks were through with it, drifted onto the beach three days later. As for Joe, after several sessions in room six, he went into a coma and died. A great pity. There was no reason for him not to cooperate with General Velikov."

"You've never paid a visit to Foss Gly?"

"No, I've been spared the experience. Why, I can't say. Perhaps General Velikov thinks I'm too valuable as a bargaining tool."

"So I've been elected," said Pitt grimly.

"I wish I could help you, but General Velikov ignored all my pleas to save Joe. He is equally cold in your case."

Pitt idly found himself wondering why LeBaron always referred to Velikov with due respect to the Russian's military rank. "I don't understand the brutal interrogation. What was to be gained by killing Cavilla? What do they hope to get out of me?"

"The truth," LeBaron said simply.

Pitt gave him a sharp look. "The truth as I know it is, you and your team searched for the *Cyclops* and vanished. Your wife and the rest of us went after the shipwreck in hopes we could get a clue as to what happened to you. Tell me where it rings false."

LeBaron wiped newly formed sweat from his forehead with his sleeve. "No use in arguing with me, Dirk, I'm not the one who doesn't believe you. The Russian mentality thinks there is a lie behind every truth."

"You've talked with Jessie. Surely she explained how we happened to find the *Cyclops* and land on the island."

LeBaron visibly winced at Pitt's mention of the *Cyclops*. He suddenly seemed to recoil from Pitt. He picked up his canvas bag and pounded on the door. It swung open almost immediately and he was gone.

Foss Gly was waiting when LeBaron entered room six. He sat there, a brooding evil, a human murder machine immune to suffering or death. He smelled of decayed meat.

LeBaron stood trembling and silently handed over the canvas bag. Gly rummaged inside and drew out a small recorder and rewound the tape. He listened for a few seconds to satisfy himself that the voices were distinct.

"Did he confide in you?" asked Gly.

"Yes, he made no attempt to hide anything."

"Is he working for the CIA?"

"I don't believe so. His landing on the island was merely an accident."

Gly came from behind the desk and grabbed the loose skin on the side of LeBaron's waist, squeezing and twisting in the same motion. The publisher's eyes bulged, gasping as the agony pierced his body. He slowly sank to his knees on the concrete.

Gly bent down until he stared with frozen malignancy scant inches from LeBaron's eyes. "Do not screw with me, scum," he said menacingly, "or your sweet wife will be the next one who pays with a mutilated body."

32

IRA HAGEN THREW Hudson and Eriksen a curve and bypassed Houston. There was no need for the trip. The computer on board his jet told him all he needed to know. A trace of the Texas phone number in General Fisher's black book led to the office of the director of NASA's Flight Operations, Irwin Mitchell, alias Irwin Dupuy. A check of another name on the list, Steve Larson, turned up Steve Busche, who was director of NASA's Flight Research Center in California.

Nine little Indians, and then there were four...

Hagen's tally of the "inner core" now read:

Raymond LeBaron............Last reported in Cuba.
General Mark Fisher.........Colorado Springs.
Clyde Booth...................Albuquerque.
Irwin Mitchell ....Houston.
Steve Busche..................California.
Dean Beagle (?)...............Philadelphia. (ID and location
                            not proven)
Daniel Klein (?)...............Washington, D.C. (ditto)
Leonard Hudson..............Maryland. (location not
                            proven)
Gunnar Eriksen...............Maryland. (ditto)

His deadline was only sixty-six hours away. He had kept the President advised of his progress and warned him that his investigation would be cutting it thin. Already, the President was putting together a trusted team to gather up members of the "inner core" and transport them to a location the President had yet to specify. Hagen's ace card was the proximity of the last three names on the list. He was gambling they were all sitting in the same basket.

Hagen altered his routine and did not waste time renting a car when his plane landed at Philadelphia International Airport. His pilot had called ahead, and a Lincoln limousine was waiting when he stepped down the stairway. During the twenty-four-mile drive along the Schuylkill River to Valley Forge State Park, he worked on his report to the President and formulated a plan to speed the discovery of Hudson and Eriksen, whose joint phone number turned out to be a disconnected number in an empty house near Washington.

He closed his briefcase as the car rolled past the park where George Washington's army had camped during the winter of 1777–78. Many of the trees still bore golden leaves and the rolling hills had yet to turn brown. The driver turned onto a road that wound around a hill overlooking the park and was bordered on both sides by old stone walls.

The historic Horse and Artillery Inn was built in 1790 as a stagecoach stop and tavern for colonial travelers and sat amid sweeping lawns and a grove of shade trees. It was a picturesque three-story building with blue shutters and a stately front porch. The inn was an original example of early limestone farm architecture and bore a plaque designating it as listed on the National Register of Historic Places.

Hagen left the limousine, climbed the steps to the porch furnished with old-fashioned rockers, and passed into a lobby filled with antique furniture clustered around a cozy fireplace containing a crackling log. In the dining room he was shown to a table by a girl dressed in colonial costume.

"Is Dean around?" he asked casually.

"Yes, sir," answered the girl brightly. "The Senator is in the kitchen. Would you like to see him?"

"I'd be grateful if he could spare me a few minutes."

"Would you like to see a menu in the meantime?"

"Yes, please."

Hagen scanned the menu and found the list of early American dishes to be quite tempting. But his mind didn't really dwell on food. Was it possible, he thought, that Dean Beagle was Senator Dean Porter, who once chaired the powerful Foreign Relations Committee and narrowly lost a presidential primary race to George McGovern? A member of the Senate for nearly thirty years, Porter had left an indelible mark on American politics before he had retired two years ago.

A baldheaded man in his late seventies walked through a swinging door from the kitchen, wiping his hands on the lower edge of an apron. An unimpressive figure with a grandfatherly face. He stopped at Hagen's table and looked down without expression. "You wish to see me?"

Hagen came to his feet. "Senator Porter."

"Yes."

"My name is Ira Hagen. I'm a restaurateur myself, specializing in American dishes, but not nearly as creative as your recipes."

"Leo told me you might walk through my door," Porter said bluntly.

"Won't you please sit down."

"You staying for dinner, Mr. Hagen?"

"That was my plan."

"Then permit me to offer you a bottle of local wine on the house."

"Thank you."

Porter called over his waitress and gave the order. Then he turned back to Hagen and looked him solidly in the eye. "How many of us have you tagged?"

"You make six," Hagen answered.

"You're lucky you didn't go to Houston. Leo had a reception committee waiting for you."

"Were you a member of the 'inner core' from the beginning, Senator?"

"I came on board in 1964 and helped set up the undercover financing."

"I compliment you on a first-rate job."

"You're working for the President, I take it."

"Correct."

"What does he intend to do with us?"

"Eventually hand out the honors you all so richly deserve. But his main concern is stopping your people on the moon from starting a war."

Porter paused when the waitress brought over a bottle of chilled white wine. He expertly pulled the cork and poured one glass. He took a large sip and swished the wine around in his mouth and nodded. "Quite good." Then he filled Hagen's glass.

"Fifteen years ago, Mr. Hagen, our government made a stupid mistake and gave away our space technology in a sucker play that was heralded as a 'handshake in space.' If you remember, it was a much publicized joint venture between American and Russian space programs that called for our Apollo astronauts to team up and meet with the Soyuz cosmonauts in orbit. I was against it from the beginning, but the event occurred during the détente years and my voice was only a cry in the wilderness. I didn't trust the Russians then and I don't trust them now. Their whole space program was built on political propaganda and damned little technical achievement. We exposed the Russians to American technology that was twenty years ahead of theirs. After all this time Soviet space hardware is still crap next to anything we've created. We blew four hundred million dollars on a scientific giveaway. The fact we kissed the Russians' asses while they reamed ours only proves Barnum's moral about 'one born every minute.' I made up my mind to never let it happen again. That's why I won't stand dumb and let the Russians steal the fruits of the Jersey Colony. If they were technically superior to us, there is no doubt in my mind they would bar us from the moon."

"So you agree with Leo that the first Russians to land on the moon must be eliminated."

"They'll do everything in their power to grab every scientific wind-fall from our moon base they can touch. Face reality, Mr. Hagen. You don't see our secret agents buying Russian high technology and smuggling it to the West. The Soviets have to rely on our progress because they're too stupid and nearsighted to create it on their own."

"You don't have a very high regard for the Russians," said Hagen.

"When the Kremlin decides to build a better world rather than divide and dictate to it, I might change my mind."

"Will you help me find Leo?"

"No," the senator said simply.

"The least the 'inner core' can do is listen while the President pleads his case."

"Is that why he sent you?"

"He hoped I could find all of you while there is still time."

"Time for what?"

"In less than four days the first Soviet cosmonauts land on the moon. If your Jersey Colony people murder them their government might feel justified in shooting down a space shuttle or the space lab."

The senator looked at Hagen, his eyes turning to ice. "An interesting conjecture. I guess we'll just have to wait and see, won't we?"

33

PITT USED THE CATCH from his watchband as a screwdriver to remove the screws holding the hinges to the wardrobe. He then slid the flat side of one hinge between the door latch and the strike. It was a near perfect fit. Now all he had to do was wait until the guard showed up with his dinner.

He yawned and lay on the bed, his thoughts turning to Raymond LeBaron. His image of the famous publisher-tycoon was chipped and cracked. LeBaron did not measure up to his hard reputation. He gave the appearance of a man who was running scared. Not once did he quote Jessie, Al, or Rudi. Surely they would have relayed a message of encouragement. There was something very fishy about LeBaron's actions.

He sat up at the sound of the door latch turning. The guard entered, holding a tray in one hand. He held it out to Pitt, who set it on his lap.

"What gourmet delight have you brought this evening?" Pitt inquired cheerfully.

The guard gave a distasteful twist of his lips and shrugged indifferently. Pitt couldn't blame him. The tray held a small loaf of doughy, tasteless bread and a bowl of god-awful chicken stew.

Pitt was hungry, but more important he needed to keep his strength. He forced the slop down, somehow managing to keep from gagging. Finally he passed the tray back to the guard, who silently took it and then pulled the door closed as he stepped into the corridor.

Pitt leaped from the bed, dropped to his knees, and slipped one of the wardrobe hinges between the latch and the doorjamb, preventing the bolt from passing through the strike into the catch. In almost the same motion he pressed his shoulder against the door and

210

tapped the second hinge on it to imitate the click of the latch snapping into place.

As soon as he heard the guard's footsteps fade down the corridor he eased open the door slightly, peeled a piece of tape from a bandage covering a cut on his arm, and stuck it over the latch shaft so the door would remain unlocked.

Removing his sandals and stuffing them into his waistband, he eased the door closed, taped a hair across the crack, and soundlessly padded down the empty corridor, pressing his body close against the wall. There was no sign of any guards or security equipment.

Pitt's first goal was to find his friends and plan an escape, but twenty yards down the corridor he discovered a narrow, circular emergency shaft with a ladder that led upward into darkness. He decided to see where it went. The climb seemed endless and he realized it was taking him past the upper levels of the underground facility. At last his groping hands touched a wooden cover above his head. He leaned his upper back against it and slowly applied pressure. The cover creaked loudly as it lifted.

Pitt sucked in his breath and froze. Five minutes came and went and nothing happened, nobody shouted, and when he finally eased the cover high enough, he found himself looking out across the concrete floor of a garage containing several military and construction vehicles. The structure was large, eighty by a hundred feet and perhaps fifteen feet to a ceiling supported by row of steel girders. The parking area was dark, but there was an office at one end whose interior was brightly lit. Two Russians in Army fatigues were sitting at a table playing chess.

Pitt snaked from the exit shaft, skirted behind the parked vehicles, and crawled under the windows of the office until he reached the main entry door. Coming this far from his cell was surprisingly easy but now defeat had arrived where he least expected it. The door was electric. There was no way he could activate it without alerting the chess players.

Staying in the shadows, he moved along the walls searching for another entrance. In his mind he knew it was a lost cause. If this building was on the surface it was probably another covered mound with the large vehicle entry door as the only means of getting in and out.

He made a complete circuit of the walls and returned to the spot where he started. Disheartened, he was about to give up when he

211

looked upward and spotted an air vent mounted on the roof. It appeared large enough to squeeze through.

Pitt quietly climbed on top of a truck, reached over his head, and pulled himself onto a support girder. Then he inched his way about thirty feet to the vent and squirmed his way to the outside. The rush of fresh, humid air felt invigorating. He guessed that the dying wind of the hurricane was only blowing at about twenty miles an hour. The sky was only partially overcast and there was a quarter moon that provided enough visibility to vaguely make out objects within a hundred feet.

His next problem was to get beyond the high wall enclosing the compound. The guardhouse by the gate was manned, so there would be no repeat of his entry two nights ago.

In the end, luck came to his aid once again. He walked along a small drainage culvert that passed under the wall. He ducked under but was brought up short by a row of iron bars. Fortunately they were badly rusted from the tropical salt air and he easily bent them apart.

Three minutes later Pitt was well clear of the installation, jogging through the palm trees lining the sunken road. There were no signs of guards or electronic surveillance cameras and the low shrubs helped conceal his silhouette against the light-colored sand. He ran at an angle toward the beach until he was up against the electrified fence.

Eventually, he came to the section damaged by the hurricane. It had been repaired, but he knew it was the correct spot because the fallen palm tree that had caused the break was lying nearby. He dropped to his knees and began scooping the sand from under the fence. The deeper he dug the more the walls of his trench kept sliding and filling in the bottom. Nearly an hour passed before he formed a crater deep enough for him to wiggle on his back through to the other side.

His shoulder and kidney ached and he was sweating like a soaked sponge. He tried to retrace his steps to the landing site by the rocks on the beach. None of the landscape seemed the same under the dim light of the moon, not that he could recall how it looked when beaten flat by hurricane winds and with his eyes mostly closed.

Pitt wandered up and down the beach, probing between the rock formations. He was almost ready to give up and quit when his eye caught the moon's glint on an object in the sand. His hands reached out and touched the fuel tank of the inflatable boat's outboard motor. The shaft and propeller were buried in the sand about thirty feet

212

from the high-tide line. He dug away the damp sand until he could pull the motor free. Then he hoisted it over his shoulder and began walking down the beach away from the Russian compound.

Pitt had no idea where he was going or where he was going to hide the motor. His feet dug into the sand and the burden of sixty pounds made it tough going. He had to stop every few hundred yards and rest.

He had walked about two miles when he met a weed-covered road that passed through several rows of deserted and decaying houses. Most of them were little more than shacks and they nestled around a small lagoon. It must have once been a fishing village, Pitt thought. He could not know it was one of the settlements whose residents had been forcefully uprooted to the mainland during the Soviet take-over.

He gratefully shrugged off the motor and began rummaging in the houses. The walls and roofing were made from corrugated iron sheets and scrap wood. Little of the furnishings remained. He found a boat pulled up on the beach, but any hope of using it was crushed. The bottom was rotted away.

Pitt considered building a raft, but it would take too long, and he couldn't run the risk of putting together something under the double handicap of working in darkness with no tools. The end result would not offer much peace of mind in rough water.

The luminous dial on his watch read 1:30. If he wanted to find and talk to Giordino and Gunn, he'd have to get a move on. He wondered what to do about fuel for the outboard motor, but there was no time to search now. He calculated it would take him a good hour to regain his cell.

He found an old cast-iron bathtub lying outside a collapsed shed. He placed the outboard motor on the ground and turned the tub upside down over it. Then he threw some tires and a rotting mattress on top and walked backward, brushing sand over his footprints with a palm frond until he stood a good seventy-five feet away.

Sneaking back in went more smoothly than sneaking out. All he had to remember was to restraighten the bars in the culvert. Belatedly, he wondered why the island compound wasn't crawling with security guards, but then it came to him that the area was constantly overflown by American spy planes whose cameras had the uncanny ability to produce photographs that could read the name on a golf ball from ninety thousand feet.

The Soviets must have figured it was better to trade heavy security

213

for the appearance of a lifeless, abandoned island. Cuban dissidents fleeing Castro's government would ignore it and any Cuban exile commandos would certainly bypass it for the mainland. With no one landing and no one escaping, the Russians had nothing to guard against.

Pitt dropped through the air ventilator and stealthily made his way back across the garage and down the exit shaft. The corridor was still quiet. He checked his door and saw the hair was still in place.

His plan now was to find Gunn and Giordino. But he didn't want to crowd his luck. Although their imprisonment was lax, there was always the problem of a chance discovery. If Pitt was caught outside his cell now, it would spell the end. Velikov and Gly were sure to keep him tightly locked away if they didn't outright execute him.

He felt he had to risk it. There might not be another opportunity. Any sound echoed throughout the concrete corridor. He would be able to hear footsteps in plenty of time to regain his cell if he didn't probe too far.

The room next to his was a paint locker. He searched it for a few minutes but found nothing useful. Two rooms across the corridor were empty. The third held plumbing supplies. Then he unlatched another door and found himself staring into the surprised faces of Gunn and Giordino. He quickly slipped inside, careful to keep the door's bolt from engaging.

"Dirk!" Giordino cried.

"Keep it down," Pitt whispered.

"Good to see you, buddy."

"Have you checked this place for ears?" Pitt asked.

"Thirty seconds after they pitched us in," answered Gunn. "The room is clean."

It was then Pitt saw the dark shades of purple around Giordino's eyes. "I see you've met with Foss Gly in room six."

"We had an interesting conversation. Pretty much one-sided, though."

Pitt looked at Gunn but saw no marks. "What about you?"

"He's too smart to beat my brains out," said Gunn with a taut smile. He pointed to his broken ankle. The cast was gone. "He gets his kicks by twisting my foot."

"What about Jessie?"

Gunn and Giordino exchanged grim looks. "We fear the worst," said Gunn. "Al and I heard a woman's screams late in the afternoon as we stepped out of the elevator."

"We were coming from an interrogation by that slimy bastard Velikov."

"Their system," explained Pitt. "The general uses the velvet glove and then turns you over to Gly for the iron fist treatment." He angrily paced the tiny room. "We've got to find Jessie and get the hell out of here."

"How?" asked Giordino. "LeBaron has paid a visit and made a point of stressing the hopelessness of escaping the island."

"I don't trust rich and reckless Raymond as far as I can throw this building," said Pitt acidly. "I think Gly has beaten him into jelly."

"Agreed."

Gunn twisted to his side in his bunk, favoring the broken ankle. "How do you intend on leaving the island?"

"I found and stashed the outboard motor for insurance if I can't steal a boat."

"What?" Giordino stared at Pitt increduously. "You walked out of here?"

"Not exactly a garden stroll," Pitt replied. "But I scouted an escape route to the beach."

"Stealing a boat is impossible," Gunn said flatly.

"You know something I don't."

"My smattering of Russian came in handy. I've begun developing a prison grapevine through the guards. I was also able to glean a few details from Velikov's papers in his office. One item of interesting information is that the island is supplied at night by submarine."

"Why so complicated?" muttered Giordino. "Seems to me surface transportation would be more efficient."

"That calls for docking facilities that can be seen from the air," explained Gunn. "Whatever is going on around here, they want to keep it damned quiet."

"I'll second that," said Pitt. "The Russians have gone to a lot of work to make the island look deserted."

"No wonder it shook them up when we walked through the front door," Giordino said thoughtfully. "That explains the interrogation and torture."

"All the more reason to make a break and save our lives."

"And alert our intelligence agencies," Gunn added.

"When do you plan to cut out?" asked Giordino.

"Tomorrow night, right after the guard brings dinner."

Gun gave Pitt a long, hard stare. "You'll have to go it alone, Dirk."

"We came together, we'll leave together."

Giordino shook his head. "You can't carry Jessie and us on your back too."

"He's right," said Gunn. "Al and I are in no condition to crawl fifty feet. Better we stay than foul your chances. Take the LeBarons and swim like hell for the States."

"I can't risk taking Raymond LeBaron into our confidence. I'm positive he would inform on us. He lied up a storm claiming the island is nothing but a businessmen's retreat."

Gunn shook his head in disbelief. "Whoever heard of a retreat run by the military that tortured its guests."

"Forget LeBaron." Giordino's eyes went black with fury. "But for God's sake, save Jessie before that son of a bitch Gly kills her."

Pitt stood there confused. "I can't go off and leave you two behind to die."

"If you don't," said Gunn gravely, "you'll die too, and no one will be left alive to tell what's happening here."

34

THE MOOD WAS SOMBER but softened by the long gap in time. No more than one hundred people had assembled for the early morning ceremony. In spite of the President's presence, only one network bothered to send a television crew. The small crowd stood quietly in a secluded corner of Rock Creek Park and listened to the conclusion of the President's brief address.

"...and so we have gathered this morning to pay belated tribute to the eight hundred American men who died when their troopship, the *Leopoldville*, was torpedoed off the port of Cherbourg, France, on Christmas Eve of 1944.

"Never has such a wartime tragedy been denied the honor it deserved. Never has such a tragedy been so completely ignored."

He paused and nodded toward a veiled statue. The shroud was pulled away, revealing a solitary figure of a soldier, standing brave with grim determination in the eyes, wearing a GI overcoat and full field gear with an M-1 carbine slung over one shoulder. There was a pained dignity about the life-sized bronze fighting man, heightened by the wave of water that lapped around his ankles.

After a minute of applause, the President, who had served in Korea as a lieutenant in an artillery company of the Marine Corps, began pumping hands with survivors of the *Leopoldville* and other veterans of the Panther Division. As he worked his way toward the White House limousine he suddenly stiffened when he shook the hand of the tenth man in line.

"A moving speech, Mr. President," said a recognizable voice. "May we talk in private?"

Leonard Hudson's lips were spread in an ironic smile. He bore no resemblance to Reggie Salazar the caddy. His hair was thick and gray and matched a Satan-style beard. He wore a wool turtleneck sweater

217

under a tweed jacket. The flannel slacks were a dark coffee color and the English leather shoes were highly polished. He looked as though he had stepped out of a cognac ad in *Town & Country* magazine.

The President turned and spoke to a Secret Service agent who stood less than a foot from his elbow. "This man will be accompanying me back to the White House."

"A great honor, sir," said Hudson.

The President stared at him for a moment and decided to carry on the charade. His face broke into a friendly grin. "I can't miss an opportunity to swap war stories with an old buddy, can I, *Joe?*"

The presidential motorcade turned onto Massachusetts Avenue, red lights flashing, sirens cutting the rush-hour traffic sounds. Neither man spoke for nearly two minutes. At last Hudson made the opening play.

"Have you recalled where we first knew each other?"

"No," the President lied. "You don't look the least bit familiar to me."

"I suppose you meet so many people..."

"Frankly, I've had more important matters on my mind."

Hudson brushed aside the President's seeming hostility. "Like throwing me in prison?"

"I thought something more along the lines of a sewer."

"You're not the spider, Mr. President, and I'm not the fly. It may look like I've walked into a trap, in this case a car surrounded by an army of Secret Service bodyguards, but my peaceful exit is guaranteed."

"The old phony bomb trick again?"

"A different twist. A plastic explosive is attached to the bottom of a table in one of the city's four-star restaurants. Precisely eight minutes ago Senator Adrian Gorman and Secretary of State Douglas Oates sat down at that table for a breakfast meeting."

"You're bluffing."

"Maybe, but if I'm not, my capture would hardly be worth the carnage inside a crowded restaurant."

"What do you want this time?"

"Call off your bloodhound."

"Make sense, for Christ's sake."

"Get Ira Hagen off my back while he can still breathe."

218

"Who?"

"Ira Hagen, an old school chum of yours who used to be with the Justice Department."

The President stared unseeing out the window as if recalling. "Seems like a lifetime since I've talked to Ira."

"No need to lie, Mr. President. You hired him to track down the 'inner core.'"

"I what?" The President acted genuinely surprised. Then he laughed. "You forget who I am. With one phone call I could have the entire capabilities of the FBI, CIA, and at least five other intelligence services on your ass."

"Then why haven't you?"

"Because I've questioned my science advisers and some pretty respected people in our space program. They agreed unanimously. The Jersey Colony is a pipedream. You talk a good scheme, Joe, but you're nothing but a fraud who sells hallucinations."

Hudson was caught off base. "I swear to God, Jersey Colony is a reality."

"Yes, it sits midway between Oz and Shangri-la."

"Believe me, Vince, when our first colonists return from the moon, your announcement will fire the imagination of the world."

The President ignored the presumptuous use of his first name. "What you'd really like me to announce is a make-believe battle with the Russians over the moon. Just what is your angle? Are you some kind of Hollywood publicity flack who's trying to hype a space movie, or are you an escaped mental patient?"

Hudson could not suppress a flash of fury. "You idiot!" he snapped. "You can't turn your back on the greatest scientific achievement in history."

"Watch me." The President picked up the car phone. "Roger, pull up and stop. My guest is getting out."

On the other side of the glass divider, the Secret Service chauffeur raised one hand from the wheel and nodded in understanding. Then he notified the other vehicles of the President's order. A minute later the motorcade turned onto a quiet residential side street and stopped at the curb.

The President reached over and opened the door. "The end of the line, Joe. I don't know what your fantasy is with Ira Hagen, but if I hear of his death, I'll be the first to testify at your trial that you threatened his life. That is, of course, if your execution hasn't already been carried out for committing mass murder in a swank restaurant."

219

In an angry daze, Hudson slowly climbed from the limousine. He hesitated, bent half in, half out of the car. "You're making a terrible mistake," he said accusingly.

"It won't be a new experience," the President said, dismissing him.

The President leaned back in his seat and smiled smugly to himself. A masterful performance, he thought. Hudson was off balance and building barricades on the wrong streets. Moving up the unveiling of the *Leopoldville* memorial by a week was a shrewd move. An inconvenience to the veterans who attended perhaps, but a boon to an old spook like Hagen.

Hudson stood on a grassy parkway and watched the motorcade grow smaller before turning on the next cross street, his mind confused and disoriented. "Goddamned mud-brained bureaucrat!" he shouted in frustration.

A woman walking her dog on the sidewalk gave him a distasteful look indeed.

An unmarked Ford van eased to a stop, and Hudson climbed inside. The interior was plush with leather captain's chairs spaced around a highly polished redwood table. Two men, impeccably dressed in business suits, looked at him expectantly as he slipped tiredly into a chair.

"How did it go?" asked one.

"The dumb bastard threw me out," he said in exasperation. "Claims he hasn't seen Ira Hagen in years and couldn't care less if we killed him and blew up the restaurant."

"I'm not surprised," said an intense-looking man with a square red face and a condor nose. "The guy is pragmatic as hell."

Gunnar Eriksen sat with a dead pipe stuck between his lips. "What else?" he asked.

"Said he believed the Jersey Colony was a hoax."

"Did he recognize you?"

"I don't think so. He still called me Joe."

"Could be an act."

"He was pretty convincing."

Eriksen turned to the other man. "How do you read it?"

"Hagen is a puzzle. I've closely monitored the President and haven't detected any contact between them."

"You don't think Hagen was brought in by any of the intelligence directors?" asked Eriksen.

"Certainly not through ordinary channels. The only meeting the

President has had with any intelligence people was a briefing by Sam Emmett of the FBI. I couldn't get my hands on the report, but it had to do with the three bodies found in LeBaron's blimp. Beyond that, he's done nothing."

"No, he's most certainly done something." Hudson's voice was quiet but positive. "I fear we've underestimated his shrewdness."

"In what way?"

"He knew I would make contact again and warn him to call off Hagen."

"What brought you to that conclusion?" asked Condor Nose.

"Hagen," replied Hudson. "No good undercover operative calls attention to himself. And Hagen was one of the best. He had to have a good reason for advertising his presence by that phone call to General Fisher and his little face-to-face chat with Senator Porter."

"But what was the President's purpose in forcing our hand if he made no demands, no requests?" asked Eriksen.

Hudson shook his head. "That's what scares me, Gunnar. I can't see for the life of me what he had to gain."

Unnoticed in the downtown traffic, an old dusty camper with Georgia license plates kept a discreet distance behind the van. In the back, Ira Hagen sat at a small dining table with earphones and a microphone clamped to his head and uncorked a bottle of Martin Ray Cabernet Sauvignon. He let the opened bottle sit while he made an adjustment with the voice-tone knob on a microwave receiving set that was plugged into reel-to-reel tape decks.

Then he raised his headset to expose one ear. "They're fading. Close up a bit."

The driver, wearing a fake scraggly beard and an Atlanta Braves baseball cap, replied without looking back. "I had to drop off when a taxi cut in front of me. I'll make up the distance in the next block."

"Keep them in sight until they park."

"What's going down, a drug bust?"

"Nothing that exotic," replied Hagen. "They're suspected of working a traveling poker game."

"Big deal," grunted the driver without realizing the pun.

"Gambling is still illegal."

"So is prostitution and it's a helluva lot more fun."

"Just keep your eyes glued on the van," Hagen said in an official tone. "And don't let it get more than a block away."

The radio crackled. "T-bone, this is Porterhouse."

"I hear you, Porterhouse."

"We have Sirloin in visual but would prefer a lower altitude. If he should happen to merge with another similar-colored vehicle under trees or behind a building, we could lose him."

Hagen turned and stared upward from the camper's rear window at the helicopter above. "What's your height?"

"The limit for aircraft over this section of the city is thirteen hundred feet. But that's only half the problem. Sirloin is heading for the Capitol mall. We're not allowed to fly over that area."

"Stand by, Porterhouse. I'll get you an exemption."

Hagen made a call over a cellular telephone and was back to the helicopter pilot in less than a minute. "This is T-bone, Porterhouse. You are cleared for any altitude over the city so long as you do not endanger lives. Do you read?"

"Man, you must carry some kind of heavy weight."

"My boss knows all the right people. Don't take your eyes off Sirloin."

Hagen lifted the lid of an expensive picnic basket from Abercrombie & Fitch and pried open a can of goose liver pâté. Then he poured the wine and returned to listening in on the conversation ahead.

There was no doubt that Leonard Hudson was one of the men in the van. And Gunnar Eriksen was mentioned by his first name. But the identity of the third man remained a mystery.

Hagen was dogged by an unknown. Eight men of the "inner core" were accounted for, but number nine was still lost in the fog. The men in the van were heading... where? What kind of facility housed the headquarters for the Jersey Colony project? A dumb name, the Jersey Colony. What was the significance? Some connection with the state of New Jersey? There must be something that could be comprehended, that might explain how none of the information on the establishment of the moon base ever came to the attention of a high government official. Someone with more power than Hudson or Eriksen had to be the key. The last name on the "inner core" list perhaps.

"This is Porterhouse. Sirloin has turned northeast onto Rhode Island Avenue."

"I copy," answered Hagen.

He spread a map of the District of Columbia on the table and unfolded a map of Maryland. He began tracing a line with a red grease pencil, extending it as they crossed from the District into

Prince Georges County. Rhode Island Avenue became U.S. Highway 1 and swung north toward Baltimore.

"Got any idea where they're heading?" asked the driver.

"Not the slightest," replied Hagen. "Unless..." he muttered under his breath. The University of Maryland. Not twelve miles from downtown Washington. Hudson and Eriksen would hang close to an academic institution to take advantage of the research facilities.

Hagen spoke into the mike. "Porterhouse, keep a sharp eye. Sirloin may be heading for the university."

"Understood, T-bone."

Five minutes later the van turned off the highway and passed through the small city of College Park. Then after about a mile it pulled into a large shopping center, anchored on both ends by well-known department stores. The several acres of parking space were filled with shoppers' cars. All conversation had died inside the van, and Hagen was caught off guard.

"Damn!" Hagen swore.

"Porterhouse," came the voice of the helicopter pilot.

"I read you."

"Sirloin just pulled under a big projection in front of the main entrance. I have no visual contact."

"Wait until he appears again," ordered Hagen, "and then stay on his tail." He rose from the table and stepped behind the driver. "Pull up on his ass."

"I can't. There are at least six cars between him and me."

"Did anybody get out and enter the stores?"

"Hard to tell in the crush of people. But it looked like two, maybe three heads ducked out of the van."

"Did you get a good look at the guy who was picked up in town?" asked Hagen.

"Gray hair and beard. Thin, about five nine. Turtleneck, tweed coat, brown pants. Yeah, I'd recognize him."

"Circle the parking lot and watch for him. He and his pals may be switching cars. I'm going inside the shopping mall."

"Sirloin is moving," announced the helicopter pilot.

"Stick with him, Porterhouse," said Hagen. "I'm going off the air for a while."

"I read you."

Hagen jumped out of the camper and rushed through the crowd of shoppers into the interior mall. It was like looking for three needles

223

hidden inside a straw in a haystack. He knew what Hudson looked like, and he had obtained photographs of Gunnar Eriksen, but either one or both might still be in the van.

Frantically he rushed from store to store, searching the faces, staring at any male head that showed above the mob of female shoppers. Why did it have to be a weekend, he thought. He could have shot a cannon through the mall at this early hour on a weekday and not hit anybody. After nearly an hour of fruitless searching, he went outside and stopped the camper.

"Spot them?" he questioned, knowing the answer.

The driver shook his head. "Takes me almost ten minutes to make a full circuit. The traffic is too thick and most of them drive like zombies when they're looking for a parking space. Your suspects could have easily come out another exit and driven off while I was on the opposite side of the building."

Hagen pounded his fist against the camper in frustration. He had come so close, so damned close, only to stumble at the finish line.

35

PITT SOLVED THE PROBLEM of sleeping without the constant glare from the fluorescent light by simply climbing on top of the wardrobe and disconnecting the tubes. He did not wake up until the guard brought him breakfast. He felt refreshed and dug into the thick gruel as if it were his favorite dish. The guard seemed upset at finding the light fixture dark, but Pitt simply held up his hands in a helpless gesture of ignorance and finished his gruel.

Two hours later he was escorted to General Velikov's office. There was the expected interminable wait to crack his emotional barriers. God, but the Russians were transparent. He played along by pacing the floor and acting nervous.

The next twenty-four hours were, to say the least, critical. He was confident that he could escape the compound again, but he could not predict any new obstacles that might be thrown in his way, or whether he would be capable of physical exertion after another interview with Foss Gly.

There could be no postponement, no falling back. He had to somehow leave the island tonight.

Velikov finally entered the room and studied Pitt for several moments before addressing him. There was a noticeable coldness about the general, an unmistakable toughness in his eyes. He nodded for Pitt to sit on a hard chair that hadn't been in the room during the last meeting. When he spoke, his tone was menacing.

"Will you sign a valid confession to being a spy?"

"If it will make you happy."

"It will not pay you to act clever with me, Mr. Pitt."

Pitt could not contain his anger and it overpowered his common sense. "I do not take kindly to scum who torture women."

Velikov's eyebrows raised. "Explain."

Pitt repeated Gunn's and Giordino's words as though they were his. "Sound carries in concrete hallways. I've heard Jessie LeBaron's screams."

"Have you now?" Velikov brushed at his hair in a practiced gesture. "It seems to me you should see the advantages of cooperating. If you tell me the truth, I might see my way clear to relax the discomfort of your friends."

"You know the truth. That's why you've reached a dead end. Four people have given you identical stories. Doesn't that seem odd to a professional interrogator like yourself? Four people who have been physically tortured in separate sessions, and yet give the same answers to the same questions. The utter lack of depth in the Russian mentality equals your fossilized infatuation with confessions. If I signed a confession for espionage, you'd demand another for crimes against your precious state, followed up with one for spitting on a public sidewalk. Your tactics are as unsophisticated as your architecture and gourmet recipes. One demand comes on the heels of another. The truth? You wouldn't accept the truth if it rose up out of the ground and bit you in the balls."

Velikov sat silent and examined Pitt with the contempt only a Slav could show to a Mongol. "I'll ask you again to cooperate."

"I'm only a marine engineer. I don't know any military secrets."

"My only interest is what your superiors told you about this island and how you came to be here."

"What are the percentages? You've already made it clear my friends and I are to die."

"Perhaps your future can be extended."

"Makes no difference. We've already told you all we know."

Velikov drummed his fingers on the desktop. "You still claim you landed on Cayo Santa María purely by chance?"

"I do."

"And you expect me to believe that of all the islands and all the beaches in Cuba Mrs. LeBaron came ashore at the exact spot—without any prior knowledge, I might add—where her husband was residing?"

"Frankly, I'd have a tough time believing it too. But that's exactly how it happened."

Velikov glared at Pitt, but he seemed to sense an integrity that he could not bring himself to approve. "I have all the time in the world, Mr. Pitt. I'm convinced you're withholding vital information. We'll talk again when you're not so arrogant." He pushed a button on his

226

desk that summoned the guard. There was a smile on his face, but there was no satisfaction, no hint of pleasure. If anything, the smile was sad.

"You must excuse me for being so abrupt," said Foss Gly. "Experience has taught me that the unexpected produces more effective results than lengthy anticipation."

No word had been spoken when Pitt entered room six. He had taken only one step over the threshold when Gly, who was standing behind the half-opened door, struck him in the small of his back just above the kidney. He gasped in agony and nearly blacked out but somehow remained standing.

"So, Mr. Pitt, now that I have your attention, perhaps there is something you wish to say to me."

"Did anybody ever tell you you're a psycho case?" Pitt muttered through pressed lips.

He saw the fist lashing out, expected it, and rolled with the punch, reeling backward into a wall and melting to the floor, feigning unconsciousness. He tasted the blood inside his mouth and felt a numbness creeping over the left side of his face. He kept his eyes closed and lay limp. He had to feel his way with this sadistic hulk of slime, assess Gly's reaction to answers and attitude, and predict when and where the next blow would strike. There would be no stopping the brutality. His only objective was to survive the interrogation without a crippling injury.

Gly went over to a dirty washbasin, filled a bucket of water, and splashed it on Pitt. "Come now, Mr. Pitt. If I'm any judge of men, you can take a punch better than that."

Pitt struggled to his hands and knees, spit blood on the cement floor, and groaned convincingly, almost pitiable. "I can't tell you any more than I already have," he mumbled.

Gly picked him up as if he were a small child and dropped him in a chair. Out of the corner of one eye Pitt caught Gly's right fist coming at him in a vicious swing. He rode the impact as best he could, catching the blow just above the cheekbone under the temple. For a few seconds he absorbed the stunning pain and then pretended to pass out again.

Another bucket of water and he went through his moaning routine. Gly leaned down until they were face to face. "Who are you working for?"

227

Pitt raised his hands and clutched his throbbing head. "I was hired by Jessie LeBaron to find out what happened to her husband."

"You landed from a submarine."

"We left the Florida Keys in a blimp."

"Your purpose in coming here was to gather information on the transfer of power in Cuba."

Pitt furrowed his brow in confusion. "Transfer of power? I don't know what you're talking about."

This time Gly struck Pitt in the upper stomach, knocking every cubic inch of wind from him. Then he calmly sat down and watched the reaction.

Pitt went rigid as he fought for breath. He felt as if his heart had stopped. He could taste the bile in his throat, feel the sweat seep from his forehead, and his lungs seemed to be twisted in knots. The walls of the room wavered and swam before his eyes. Gly looked to be smiling wickedly at the end of a long tunnel.

"What were your orders once you arrived on Cayo Santa María?"

"No orders," Pitt rasped.

Gly rose and approached to strike again. Pitt drunkenly came to his feet, swayed for a moment, and began to sag, his head drooping to one side. He had Gly's measure now. He recognized a weak point. Like most sadists, Gly was basically a coward. He would flinch and be thrown off his track if he was evenly matched.

Gly flexed his body to swing, but suddenly froze in stunned astonishment. Bringing up his fist from the floor and pivoting his shoulder, Pitt threw a right-hand cross that carried every ounce of power he could muster. He connected with Gly's nose, mashing the cartilage and breaking the bone. Then he followed up with two left jabs and a solid hook to the body. He might as well have attacked the cornerstone of the Empire State Building.

Any other man would have fallen flat on his back. Gly staggered back a few feet and stood there with his face slowly reddening in rage. The blood streamed from his nose but he took no notice of it. He raised one fist and shook it at Pitt. "I'll kill you for that," he said.

"Stick it in your ear," Pitt replied sullenly. He grabbed the chair and threw it across the room. Gly merely smashed it aside with his arm. Pitt caught the shift of the eyes and realized his whiplash speed was about to lose out to brute strength.

Gly tore the washbasin from the wall, literally ripped it from its plumbing, and lifted it over his head. He took three steps and heaved

228

it in Pitt's direction. Pitt jumped sideways and ducked around in one convulsive motion. As the sink sailed toward him like a safe falling from a high building, he knew his reaction came a split second too late. He threw up his hands instinctively in a hopeless gesture to ward off the flying mass of iron and porcelain.

Pitt's salvation came from the door. The latch caught the main crush from one corner of the washbasin and was smashed out of its catch. The door burst open and Pitt was knocked backward into the hallway, crashing in a heap at the feet of the startled guard. A shooting pain in his groin and right arm compounded the agonies already piercing his side and head. Gray-faced, waves of nausea sweeping over him, he shook away the beckoning unconsciousness and came to his feet, his hands spread on the wall for support.

Gly tore the sink from the doorway where it had become jammed and stared at Pitt with a look that could only be described as murderous. "You're a dead man, Pitt. You're going to die slowly, an inch at a time, begging to be put out of your agony. The next time we meet I'll snap every bone in your body and tear your heart out."

There was no fear in Pitt's eyes. The pain was draining away, to be replaced with elation. He had survived. He hurt, but the way was clear.

"The next time we meet," he said vengefully, "I'll carry a big club."

36

PITT SLEPT after the guard helped him back to his cell. When he woke up it was three hours later. He lay there for several minutes until his mind slowly shifted into gear. His body and face were an unending sea of contusions, but no bones were broken. He had survived.

He sat up and swung his feet to the floor, waiting for a few moments of dizziness to pass. He pushed himself to his feet and began doing stretching exercises to ease the stiffness. A wave of weakness swept over him, but he willed himself to reject it, continuing the drill until his muscles and joints became limber.

The guard came and went with dinner, and Pitt adroitly jammed the latch again, a maneuver he had honed so there would be no fumbling, no last-minute bungle. He paused, and hearing no footsteps or voices, stepped into the corridor.

Time was a luxury. There was too much to accomplish and too few hours of darkness to manage it. He regretfully wished he could say his farewells to Giordino and Gunn, but every minute he lingered in the compound depleted his odds of success. The first order of business was to find Jessie and take her with him.

She was behind the fifth door he tried, lying on the concrete floor with nothing under her but a dirty blanket. Her naked body was completely unmarked, but her once lovely face was grotesquely swollen with purplish bruises. Gly had shrewdly worked his evil by humiliating her virtue and brutalizing a beautiful woman's most valued asset—her face.

Pitt bent over and cradled her head in his arms, his expression tender, but his eyes insane with rage. He was consumed with revenge. He shook with a madness for savage vengeance that went far beyond anything he had experienced before. He gritted his teeth and gently shook her awake.

"Jessie. Jessie, can you hear me?"

Her mouth trembled open as her eyes focused on him. "Dirk," she moaned. "Is it you?"

"Yes, I'm taking you out of here."

"Taking...how?"

"I've found a way for us to escape the compound."

"But the island. Raymond said it's impossible to escape from the island."

"I've hidden the outboard motor from the inflatable boat. If I can build a small raft—"

"No!" she whispered adamantly.

She struggled to sit up, a look of concentration crossing the swollen mask that was her face. He lightly gripped her by the shoulders and held her down.

"Don't move," he said.

"You must go alone," she said.

"I won't leave you like this."

She shook her head weakly. "No. I would only increase your chances of getting caught."

"Sorry," Pitt said flatly. "Like it or not, you're coming."

"Don't you understand," she pleaded. "You're the only hope for saving all of us. If you make it back to the States and tell the President what's happening here, Velikov will have to keep us alive."

"What does the President have to do with this?"

"More than you know."

"Then Velikov was right. There is a conspiracy."

"Don't waste time conjecturing. Go, please go. By saving yourself you can save all of us."

Pitt felt an overwhelming surge of admiration for Jessie. She looked like a discarded doll now, battered and helpless, but he realized her outer beauty was matched by an inner one that was brave and resolute. He leaned over and kissed her lightly on puffed and split lips.

"I'll make it," he said confidently. "Promise me you'll hang on till I get back."

She tried to smile, but her mouth couldn't respond. "You crazy clown. You can't return to Cuba."

"Watch me."

"Good luck," she murmured softly. "Forgive me for messing up your life."

Pitt grinned, but the tears were welling in his eyes. "That's what men like about women. They never let us get bored."

231

He kissed her again on the forehead and turned away, his tanned fists white-knuckled by his side.

The climb up the emergency-shaft ladder made Pitt's arms ache, and when he reached the top he rested for a minute before pushing the lid aside and crouching in the darkness of the garage. The two soldiers were still engaged in a game of chess. It seemed to be a nightly routine to pass the boring hours of standby duty. They seldom bothered to glance at the vehicles parked outside their office. There was no reason to anticipate trouble. They were probably mechanics, Pitt reasoned, not security guards.

He reconnoitered the garage area: tool benches, lubrication racks, oil and parts storage, trucks, and construction equipment. The trucks had spare five-gallon fuel cans attached to their beds. Pitt lightly tapped the cans until he found one that was full. The rest were all half empty or less. He groped around a tool bench until he found a rubber tube and used it to siphon gas from one of the truck's tanks. Two cans containing ten gallons were all he could carry. The problem he faced now was getting them through the vent in the roof.

Pitt took a towrope that was hanging from one wall and tied the ends to the handles on the gas cans. Holding the middle in a loop, he climbed to the support girders. Slowly, watching to see that the mechanics kept their attention on the chess game, he pulled the cans to the roof one at a time and pushed them ahead of him into the vent.

In another two minutes he was lugging them across the yard into the culvert that ran under the wall. He quickly spread the bars apart and hurried outside.

The sky was clear and the quarter-moon floated in a sea of stars. There was only a whisper of wind and the night air was cool. He fervently hoped the sea was calm.

For no particular reason he skirted the opposite side of the road this time. It was slow going. The heavy cans soon made his arms feel as though they were separating at the joints. His feet sank into the soft sand, and he had to stop every two hundred yards to catch his breath and allow the growing ache in his hands and arms to subside.

Pitt tripped and sprawled on the edge of a wide clearing surrounded by a thick grove of palm trees, so thick their trunks almost touched each other. He reached out and swept around with his hands. They touched a metal network that blended into the sand and became nearly invisible.

232

Curious, he left the gas cans and crawled cautiously around the edge of the clearing. The metal grid rose two inches off the ground and extended across the entire diameter. The center dropped away until it became concave like a bowl. He ran his hands over the trunks of the palm trees circling the rim.

They were fake. The trunks and fronds were constructed out of aluminum tubes and covered with realistic sheathing made from sanded plastic. There were over fifty of them, painted with camouflage to deceive American spy planes and their penetrating cameras.

The bowl was a giant dish-shaped radio and television antenna and the bogus palm trees were hydraulic arms that raised and lowered it. Pitt was stunned at the implication of what he had accidentally discovered. He knew now that buried under the sands of the island was a vast communications center.

But for exactly what purpose?

Pitt had no time to reflect. But he was determined more than ever to get free. He continued walking in the shadows. The village was farther than he remembered. He was a mass of sweat and panted heavily from exhaustion when he finally stumbled into the yard where he'd hidden the outboard motor under the bathtub. He thankfully dropped the gas cans and lay down on the old mattress and dozed for an hour.

Although he could not afford the time, the short rest refreshed him considerably. It also allowed his mind to create. An idea crystallized that was so incredibly simple in concept he couldn't believe he hadn't thought of it before.

He carried the gas cans down to the lagoon. Then he returned for the outboard. Looking through piles of trash, he located a short plank that showed no rot. The last chore was the hardest. Necessity was the mother of invention, Pitt kept telling himself.

Forty-five minutes later, he had dragged the old bathtub from its resting place in the yard down the road to the water's edge.

Using the plank as a transom, Pitt bolted the outboard to the rear of the tub. Next he cleaned out the fuel filter and blew out the lines. A piece of tin bent in a cone served as a funnel to fill the outboard's tank. By holding his thumb over the bottom hole he could also use it for a bailing can. His final act before stuffing a rag plug in the drain was to knock off the bathtub's four webbed feet with an iron bar.

He pulled at the starter cord twelve times before the motor sputtered, caught, and began to purr. He shoved the tub into deeper water until it floated. Then he climbed in. The ballast weight of his body and the two full gas cans made it surprisingly stable. He lowered the propeller shaft into the water and pushed the gear lever to Forward.

The oddball craft slowly moved out into the lagoon and headed for the main channel. A shaft of moonlight showed the sea was calm, the swells no more than two feet. Pitt concentrated on the surf. He had to pass through the breaking waves and place as much distance between himself and the island by sunrise as possible.

He slowed the motor and timed the breakers, counting them. Nine heavies crashed one behind the other, leaving a long trough separating the tenth. Pitt pushed the throttle to Full and settled in the stern of the tub. The next wave was low and crashed immediately in front of him. He took the impact of the churning foam bow-on and plowed through. The tub staggered, then the propeller bit the water and it surged over the crest of the following wave before it curled.

Pitt let out a hoarse shout as he broke free. The worst was over. He knew he could only be discovered by sheer accident. The bathtub was too small to be picked up by radar. He eased up on the throttle to conserve the motor and the fuel. Dragging his hand in the water, he guessed his speed at about four knots. He should be well clear of Cuban waters by morning.

He looked up at the heavens, took his bearings, picked out a star to steer by, and set a course for the Bahama Channel.

PART III

Selenos 8

37

WITH A FIREBALL BRIGHTER than the Siberian sun, Selenos 8 rose into a chilly blue sky carrying the 110-ton manned lunar station. The super rocket and four strap-on boosters, generating 14 million pounds of thrust, threw out a tail of orange-yellow flame 1,000 feet long and 300 feet wide. White smoke burst around the launch pad and the rumble from the engines rattled glass twelve miles away. At first it lifted so ponderously that it hardly seemed to be moving at all. Then it picked up speed and thundered skyward.

Soviet President Antonov observed the liftoff from an armored glass bunker through a pair of large binoculars mounted on a tripod. Sergei Kornilov and General Yasenin stood beside him, intently monitoring voice communications between the cosmonauts and the space control center.

"An inspiring sight," Antonov muttered in awe.

"A textbook launch," Kornilov said. "They'll reach escape velocity in four minutes."

"Does all go well?"

"Yes, Comrade President. All systems are functioning normally. And they are exactly on track."

Antonov gazed at the long tongue of flame until it finally vanished. Only then did he sigh and step away from the binoculars. "Well, gentlemen, this space spectacular should take the world's eyes off the next American shuttle flight to their new orbital station."

Yasenin nodded in agreement and gripped Kornilov's shoulder.

237

"My congratulations, Sergei. You stole the Yankee triumph for the Soviet Union."

"No brilliance on my part," said Kornilov. "Because of orbital mechanics, our lunar launch window happened to be open for an advantageous shot several hours ahead of their scheduled launch."

Antonov stared into the sky as if mesmerized. "I assume American intelligence isn't privy to the fact our cosmonauts are not what they seem."

"A flawless deception," Yasenin said without reservation. "The switch of five space scientists for specially trained soldiers shortly before liftoff went smoothly."

"I hope we can say the same about the crash program to replace test equipment with weapons," said Kornilov. "The scientists whose experiments were canceled nearly caused a riot. And the engineers, who were ordered to redesign the interior of the station to accommodate new weight factors and weapon storage requirements, became angry at not being told the reason behind the last-minute changes. Their displeasure will most certainly be leaked."

"Don't lose any sleep over it," Yasenin laughed. "The American space authorities will suspect nothing until communication with their precious moon base goes dead."

"Who is in command of our assault team?" asked Antonov.

"Major Grigory Leuchenko. An expert on guerrilla warfare. The major won many victories against the rebels in Afghanistan. I can personally vouch for his qualities as a loyal and outstanding soldier."

Antonov nodded thoughtfully. "A good choice, General. He should find the lunar surface little different from that of Afghanistan."

"There is no question that Major Leuchenko will conduct a successful operation."

"You forget the American astronauts, General," said Kornilov.

"What about them?"

"The photographs demonstrate they have weapons too. I pray they are not fanatics who will wage a strong fight to protect their facility."

Yasenin smiled indulgently. "Pray, Sergei? Pray to whom? Certainly not to any God. He won't help the Americans once Leuchenko and his men begin their attack. The outcome is a foregone conclusion. Scientists cannot stand up against professional soldiers trained to kill."

"Do not underrate them. That's all I have to say."

"Enough!" Antonov said loudly. "I'll hear no more of this defeatist talk. Major Leuchenko has the double advantage of surprise and superior weaponry. Less than sixty hours from now the first real battle for space will begin. And I do not expect the Soviet Union to lose it."

In Moscow, Vladimir Polevoi sat at his desk in the KGB center on Dzerzhinski Square, reading a report from General Velikov. He did not glance up as Lyev Maisky strode into the room and sat down without an invitation. Maisky's face was common, blank and one-dimensional like his personality. He was Polevoi's deputy head of the First Chief Directorate, the foreign operations arm of the KGB. Maisky's relations with Polevoi were restrained, but they complemented each other.

Finally, Polevoi's eyes bored through Maisky. "I'd like an explanation."

"The LeBarons' presence was unforeseen," Maisky said tersely.

"Mrs. LeBaron and her crew of treasure hunters, perhaps, but certainly not her husband. Why did Velikov take him from the Cubans?"

"The general thought Raymond LeBaron might be a useful pawn in negotiations with the U.S. State Department after the Castros were removed."

"His good intentions have made for a dangerous game," said Polevoi.

"Velikov assures me that LeBaron is kept under strict security and fed false information."

"Still, there is always a small chance LeBaron might discover the true function of Cayo Santa María."

"Then he would simply be erased."

"And Jessie LeBaron?"

"My personal thoughts are that she and her friends will prove useful dupes in laying the blame for our projected disaster on the CIA's doorstep."

"Has Velikov or our resident agents in Washington uncovered any plans by American intelligence to infiltrate the island?"

"Negative," Maisky answered. "A check on the blimp's crew showed none have current ties with the CIA or the military."

"I want no screw-ups," said Polevoi firmly. "We're too close to success. You pass my words on to Velikov."

"He shall be instructed."

There was a knock on the door and Polevoi's secretary entered. Without a word she handed him a paper and left the room.

Sudden anger reddened Polevoi's face. "Damn! Speak of a threat, and it becomes a reality."

"Sir?"

"A priority signal from Velikov. One of the prisoners has escaped."

Maisky made a nervous movement with his hands. "It is impossible. There are no boats on Cayo Santa María, and if he is foolish enough to swim, he'll either drown or be eaten by sharks. Whoever it is won't get far."

"His name is Dirk Pitt, and according to Velikov he's the most dangerous of the lot."

"Dangerous or not—"

Polevoi waved him to silence and began pacing the carpet, his face reflecting deep agitation. "We cannot afford the unexpected. The deadline for our Cuban adventure must be moved up a week."

Maisky shook his head in disagreement. "The ships would never reach Havana in time. Also, we can't change the dates of the celebration. Fidel and every high-ranking member of his government will be on hand for the speechmaking. The wheels of the explosion are set in motion. Nothing can be done to alter the timing. Rum and Cola must either be called off or continue as scheduled."

Polevoi clasped and unclasped his hands in an agony of indecision. "Rum and Cola, a stupid name for an operation of such magnitude."

"Another reason to push on. Our disinformation program has already begun spreading rumors of a CIA plot to launch devastation in Cuba. The phrase 'Rum and Cola' is patently American. No foreign government would suspect it as being hatched in Moscow."

Polevoi shrugged in assent. "Very well, but I don't want to think about the consequences if this Pitt fellow by some miracle survives and makes it back to the United States."

"He is already dead," Maisky announced boldly. "I am sure of it."

38

THE PRESIDENT LEANED into Daniel Fawcett's office and waved. "Don't get up. Just wanted you to know I'm going upstairs for a quiet lunch with my wife."

"Don't forget we have a meeting with the intelligence chiefs and Doug Oates in forty-five minutes," Fawcett reminded him.

"I promise to be on time."

The President turned and took the elevator to his living quarters on the second floor of the White House. Ira Hagen was waiting for him in the Lincoln suite.

"You look tired, Ira."

Hagen smiled. "I'm behind on my sack time."

"How do we stand?"

"I've accounted for the identities of all nine members of the 'inner core.' Seven are pinpointed. Only Leonard Hudson and Gunnar Eriksen remain outside the net."

"You haven't picked up their trail from the shopping center?"

Hagen hesitated. "Nothing that panned out."

"The Soviet moon station was launched eight hours ago," said the President. "I can't delay any longer. Orders will go out this afternoon to round up as many of the 'inner core' as we can."

"Army or FBI?"

"Neither. An old buddy in the Marine Corps has the honors. I've already supplied him with your list of names and locations." The President paused and stared at Hagen. "You said you accounted for the identities of all nine men, Ira, but your report only gave eight names."

Hagen seemed reluctant, but he reached inside his coat and withdrew a sheet of folded paper. "I was saving the last man until I could be absolutely certain. A voice analyzer confirmed my suspicions."

241

The President took the paper from Hagen's hand, unfolded it, and read the single hand-printed name. He removed his glasses and wearily wiped the lenses as if he didn't trust his eyes. Then he slipped the paper into his pocket.

"I suppose I knew all along but couldn't bring myself to believe his complicity."

"Do not judge harshly, Vince. These men are patriots, not traitors. Their only crime is silence. Take the case of Hudson and Eriksen. Pretending to be dead all these years. Think of the agony that must have caused their friends and families. The nation can never compensate them for their sacrifices or fully comprehend the rewards of their accomplishment."

"Are you lecturing me, Ira?"

"Yes, sir, I am."

The President suddenly became aware of Hagen's inner struggle. He understood that his friend's heart wasn't in the final confrontation. Hagen's loyalty was balanced on a razor's edge.

"You're holding out on me, Ira."

"I won't lie to you, Vince."

"You know where Hudson and Eriksen are hiding."

"Let's say I have a damned solid hunch."

"Can I trust you to bring them in?"

"Yes."

"You're a good scout, Ira."

"Where do you want them delivered, and when?"

"Camp David," the President replied. "Eight o'clock tomorrow morning."

"We'll be there."

"I can't include you, Ira."

"The decent thing to do on your part, Vince. Call it a repayment of sorts. You owe it to me to be in on the finish."

The President considered that. "You're right. It's the very least I can do."

Martin Brogan, director of the CIA, Sam Emmett of the FBI, and Secretary of State Douglas Oates came to their feet as the President entered the conference room with Dan Fawcett on his heels.

"Please be seated, gentlemen," the President said, smiling.

There were a few minutes of small talk until Alan Mercier, the national security adviser, entered. "Sorry for being late," he said,

242

quickly sliding into a chair. "I haven't even had time to think of a good excuse."

"An honest man," Brogan said, laughing. "How disgusting."

The President poised a pen above a note pad. "Where do we stand on the Cuban pact?" he asked, looking at Oates.

"Until we can open a secret dialogue with Castro, it's pretty much on the back burner."

"Is there a remote possibility Jessie LeBaron might have gotten through with our latest reply?"

Brogan shook his head. "I feel it's very doubtful she made contact. Our sources have had no word since the blimp was shot down. The consensus is she's dead."

"Any word at all from the Castros?"

"None."

"What do you hear from the Kremlin?"

"The internal struggle going on between Castro and Antonov is about to break out in the open," said Mercier. "Our people inside the Cuban war ministry say that Castro is going to pull his troops out of Afghanistan."

"That clinches it," said Fawcett. "Antonov won't stand idle and allow that to happen."

Emmett leaned forward and folded his hands on the table. "It all goes back to four years ago when Castro begged off making even a token payment on the ten billion dollars owned to the Soviet Union on loans constantly 'rolled over' since the nineteen-sixties. He painted himself into an economic corner and had to knuckle under when Antonov demanded he send troops to fight in Afghanistan. Not simply a few small companies, but nearly twenty thousand men."

"What estimate does the CIA have of casualties?" asked the President, turning to Brogan.

"Our figures show approximately sixteen hundred dead, two thousand wounded, and over five hundred missing."

"Good lord, that's better than twenty percent."

"Another reason the Cuban people detest the Russians," Brogan continued. "Castro is like a drowning man, sinking between a leaking rowboat whose crew is pointing a gun at him and a luxury yacht whose passengers are waving champagne bottles. If we throw him the rope, the crew in the Kremlin will blast him."

"Actually, they're planning on blasting him anyway," Emmett added.

"Do we have any idea how or when the assassination will take place?" asked the President.

243

Brogan shifted in his chair uneasily. "Our sources have been unable to turn up a timetable."

"Their security on the subject is as tight as anything I've ever seen," said Mercier. "Our computers have failed to decode any data from our space listening systems tuned to the operation. Only a few bits and pieces that fail to give us a concrete fix on their plans."

"Do you know who is in charge of it?" the President persisted.

"General Peter Velikov, GRU, considered something of a wizard at third-world government infiltration and manipulation. He was the architect of the Nigerian overthrow two years ago. Fortunately, the Marxist government he set up didn't last."

"Is he operating out of Havana?"

"He's secretive as hell," replied Brogan. "The perfect image of the man who isn't there. Velikov hasn't been seen in public in the past four years. We're dead certain he's directing the show from a hidden location."

The President's eyes seemed to darken. "All we have here is a vague theory that the Kremlin plans to assassinate Fidel and Raúl Castro, fix the blame on us, then take over the government using Cuban stooges who receive their orders straight from Moscow. Come now, gentlemen, I can't act on what-ifs. I need facts."

"It's a projection based on known facts," Brogan explained heavily. "We have the names of the Cubans who are on the Soviet payroll and waiting on the sidelines to assume power. Our information fully supports the Kremlin's intent to murder the Castros. The CIA makes the perfect scapegoat because the Cuban people have not forgotten the Bay of Pigs or the agency's fumbling plots to assassinate Fidel by the Mafia during the Kennedy administration. I assure you, Mr. President, I have given this every priority. Sixty agents on every level in and out of Cuba are concentrating on penetrating Velikov's wall of secrecy."

"And yet we can't reach Castro for an open dialogue to help each other."

"No, sir," said Oates. "He's resisting any contact through official channels."

"Doesn't he realize his time may be running out?" asked the President.

"He's wandering in a vacuum," Oates replied. "On one hand he feels secure in knowing the great mass of Cubans idolize him. Few national leaders can command the awe and affection he enjoys from his people. And yet on the other, he cannot fully comprehend the

244

dead seriousness of the Soviet threat on his life and government."

"So what you're telling me," said the President gravely, "is that unless we can make an intelligence breakthrough or get someone into Castro's hideout who can make him listen to reason, we can only sit back and watch Cuba sink under total Soviet domination."

"Yes, Mr. President," said Brogan. "That is exactly what we're telling you."

39

HAGEN WAS DOING some browsing. He wandered through the mall of the shopping center, casually eyeing the merchandise in the stores. The smell of roasted peanuts reminded him that he was hungry. He stopped at a gaily painted wagon and bought a bag of roasted cashews.

Resting his feet for a few minutes, Hagen sat on a couch in an appliance store and watched an entire wall of twenty television sets all tuned to the same channel. The pictures showed an hour-old rerun of the space shuttle *Gettysburg* as it lifted off from California. Over three hundred people had been launched into space since the shuttle's first flight in 1981, and except for the news media, nobody paid much attention anymore.

Hagen wandered up and down, pausing to gawk through a large window at a disk jockey spinning records for a radio station that was located in the mall. He rubbed shoulders with the crowds of female shoppers, but he concentrated on the occasional man. Most seemed to be on their lunch break, probing the counters and racks, usually buying the first thing they saw, in contrast to the women, who preferred to keep searching in the forlorn hope they could find something better at a cheaper price.

He spotted two men eating submarine sandwiches at a fast-food restaurant. They were not carrying any purchase bags, nor were they dressed like store clerks. They wore the same casual style as Dr. Mooney at the Pattenden Lab.

Hagen followed them into a large department store. They took the escalator down to the basement, passed through the shopping area, and entered a rear hallway marked with a sign that read "Employees Only."

A warning bell went off inside Hagen's head. He returned to a counter stacked with bed sheets, removed his coat, and stuck a pencil

246

behind one ear. Then he waited until the clerk was busy with a customer before picking up a pile of sheets and heading back into the hallway.

Three doors led to stock rooms, two to restrooms, and one was marked "Danger—High Voltage." He yanked open the latter door and rushed inside. A startled security guard sitting at a desk looked up. "Hey, you're not supposed to be—"

That was as far as he got before Hagen threw the sheets in his face and judo-chopped him on the side of the neck. There were two security guards behind a second door, and Hagen put them both down in less than four seconds. He crouched and whipped around in anticipation of another threat.

A hundred pairs of eyes stared at him in blank astonishment.

Hagen was confronted by a room that seemed to stretch into infinity. From wall to wall it was filled with people, offices, computer and communications equipment. For a long second, he stood stunned by the vastness of it all. Then he took a step forward and grabbed a terrified secretary by the arms and lifted her out of a chair.

"Leonard Hudson!" he snapped. "Where can I find him?"

Fear shone from her eyes like twin spotlights. She tilted her head to the right. "Th-the office w-with the blue d-door," she stammered.

"Thank you very much," he said with a broad smile.

Hagen released the girl and walked swiftly through the hushed complex. His face was twisted with malevolence, as if daring anyone to stop him.

No one made the slightest attempt. The growing crowd of people parted like the Red Sea as he passed down a main aisle.

When he came to the blue door, Hagen stopped and turned around, surveying the brain trust and communications center of the Jersey Colony program. He had to admire Hudson. It was an imaginative cover. Excavated during the construction of the shopping center, it would have attracted little or no suspicion. The scientists, engineers, and secretaries could come and go amid the shoppers, and their cars simply melted into hundreds of others in the parking lot. The radio station was also a work of genius. Who would suspect they were transmitting and receiving messages from the moon while broadcasting Top 40 records to the surrounding college community.

Hagen pushed inside the door and entered what seemed to be a studio control booth.

Hudson and Eriksen sat with their backs to him, staring up at a large video monitor that reflected the face and shaven head of a man

247

who stopped speaking in midsentence and then said, "Who is that man behind you?"

Hudson made a cursory glance over his shoulder. "Hello, Ira." The voice mirrored the eyes; Hagen could almost hear the cracking of ice cubes. "I wondered when you'd show up."

"Come in," said Eriksen in an equally frigid tone. "You're just in time to talk to our man on the moon."

40

PITT HAD CLEARED Cuban waters and was well into the main shipping lane of the Bahama Channel. But his luck was running out. The only ships that came within sight failed to spot him. A large tanker flying the Panamanian flag steamed by no more than a mile away. He stood as high as he dared without tipping over the tub and waved his shirt, but his little vessel went unnoticed by the crew.

For a watch officer on the bridge to aim his binoculars at the precise spot at the precise instant when the bathtub rose out of a trough and climbed the crest of a swell before dropping from sight again was a bet no self-respecting bookie would make. The awful truth plagued Pitt: he made too small a target.

Pitt's movements were becoming mechanical. His legs had gone numb after rolling around the sea in the cramped bathtub for nearly twenty hours, and the constant friction of his buttocks against the hard surface had raised painful blisters. The tropical sun beat on him, but he wore a good tan and the least of his problems was sunburn.

The sea remained calm, but still it was a continuous effort to keep the bow of the tub straight into the swells and bail out the water at the same time. He had emptied the final drops from the fuel cans into the outboard motor before refilling them with seawater for ballast.

Another fifteen or twenty minutes, that was all he could expect the motor to keep running before it starved for gas. Then it would be all over. Without control, the tub would soon swamp and sink.

His mind began to slip away; he hadn't slept in thirty-six hours. He fought to stay awake, steering and bailing with leaden arms and water-wrinkled hands. For hour after endless hour his eyes swept the horizon, seeing nothing that was traveling toward his tiny area of the sea. A few sharks had bumped the bottom of the slow-moving tub; one made the mistake of coming too close to the spinning propeller and got his fin chewed up. Pitt eyed them with a detached air. He dumbly planned to beat them out of a meal by opening his mouth and drowning, before realizing it was a stupid thought and brushing it aside.

The wind gently began to rise. A squall passed overhead and deposited an inch of water in the tub. It wasn't the cleanest, but it was better than nothing. He scooped up a few handfuls and gratefully gulped it down, feeling refreshed.

Pitt looked up at the shimmering horizon to the west. Night would fall in another hour. His last spark of hope was dying with the setting sun. Even if he somehow kept afloat, he could never be seen in the darkness.

Hindsight, he mused. If only he'd stolen a flashlight.

Suddenly, the outboard sputtered and then caught again. He slowed the throttle as much as he dared, knowing he was only pushing off the inevitable by a minute or two.

Pitt fought off the cloud of morale collapse and steeled himself to bail until his arms gave out or a wave struck the drifting, helpless little tub on the beam and swamped her. He emptied one of the gas cans of seawater. When the tub sank, he reasoned, he would use the can as a float. So long as he could move a muscle, he wasn't about to give up.

The faithful little outboard coughed once, twice, and then died. After hearing the beat of the exhaust since the night before, Pitt felt smothered by the abrupt silence. He sat there in a doomed little craft on a vast and indifferent sea under a clear and cloudless sky.

He kept her afloat for another hour into the twilight. He was so tired, so physically exhausted that he missed a small movement five hundred yards away.

Commander Kermit Fulton pulled back from the periscope eyepiece, his face wearing a questioning expression. He looked across the control room of the attack submarine *Denver* at his executive officer. "Any contact on our sensors?"

The exec spoke into one of the control room phones. "Nothing on radar, skipper. Sonar reports a small contact, but it stopped about a minute ago."

"What do they make of it?"

The answer was slow in coming and the question was repeated.

"Sonar says it sounded like a small outboard motor, no more than twenty horsepower."

"There's something mighty peculiar out there," said Fulton. "I want to check it out. Slow speed to one-third and come left five degrees."

He pressed his forehead against the periscope eyepiece again and increased the magnification. Slowly, wonderingly, he pulled back. "Give the order to surface."

"You see something?" asked the executive officer.

He nodded silently.

Everyone in the control room stared at Fulton expectantly. The exec took the initiative. "Mind letting us in on it, skipper?"

"Twenty-three years at sea," said Fulton, "and I thought I'd seen almost everything. But damned if there isn't a man up there, almost a hundred miles from the nearest land, floating in a bathtub."

41

SINCE THE BLIMP'S DISAPPEARANCE, Admiral Sandecker had rarely left his office. He buried himself in work that soon lost all meaning. His parents, though quite elderly, were still alive, and so were his brother and sister. Sandecker had never really tasted personal tragedy before.

During his years in the Navy, he was infected with dedication. There was little time for a deep relationship with a woman, and he counted few good friends, mostly Navy acquaintances. He built a wall around him between superiors and subordinates and walked the middle ground. He made flag rank before he was fifty, but he was stagnating.

When Congress approved his appointment as chief of the National Underwater and Marine Agency, he came back to life. He formed warm friendships with three unlikely people, who looked up to him with respect but treated him no differently than the man on the next bar stool.

The challenges facing NUMA had drawn them together. Al Giordino, an extrovert who took a strange glee in volunteering for the dirtiest projects and stealing Sandecker's expensive cigars. Rudi Gunn, driven to accomplish nothing less than perfection, a natural at organizing programs, who couldn't make an enemy if he tried. And then there was Pitt, who had done more than anyone to revive Sandecker's creative spirit. They soon became as close as father and son.

Pitt's freewheeling attitude toward life and his sarcastic wit trailed behind him like a comet's tail. He couldn't enter a room without livening it up. Sandecker tried but failed to blot out the memories, to unchain himself from the past. He leaned back in the desk chair and closed his eyes and gave in to the sorrow. To lose all three of them at one time stunned him beyond comprehension.

While Pitt was in his thoughts, the light blinked and a muted chime came from his private phone line. He massaged his temples briefly and picked up the receiver.

"Yes?"

"Jim, is that you? I got your private number from a mutual friend at the Pentagon."

"I'm sorry. My mind was wandering. I don't recognize the voice."

"This is Clyde. Clyde Monfort."

Sandecker tensed. "Clyde, what's up?"

"A signal from one of our attack subs returning from the Jamaican landing exercise just came across my desk."

"How does that concern me?"

"The sub's commander reports picking up a castaway no more than twenty minutes ago. Not exactly standard procedure for our nuclear sub forces to take strangers on board, but his guy claimed he worked for you and got pretty nasty when the skipper refused to allow him to send a message."

"Pitt!"

"You got it," answered Monfort. "That's the name he gave. Dirk Pitt. How'd you know?"

"Thank God!"

"Does he check out?"

"Yes, yes, he's bona fide," Sandecker said impatiently. "What about the others?"

"No others. Pitt was alone in a bathtub."

"Say again."

"The skipper swears it was a bathtub with an outboard motor."

Knowing Pitt, Sandecker didn't doubt the story for a second. "How soon can you have him picked up by helicopter and dropped at the nearest airfield for transport to Washington?"

"You know that's not possible, Jim. I can't have him cleared and released until after the sub docks at its base in Charleston."

"Hang on, Clyde. I'll call the White House on another line and get the authorization."

"You got that kind of clout?" Monfort asked incredulously.

"That and more."

"Can you tell me what's going down, Jim?"

"Take my word for it. You don't want to get involved."

● ● ●

They gathered at a White House dinner party to honor the Prime Minister of India, Rajiv Gandhi, who was on a goodwill tour of the United States. Actors and labor leaders, athletes and billionaires, they all shed their opinions, their differences, and mingled like neighbors at a Sunday social.

Former Presidents Ronald Reagan and Jimmy Carter conversed and acted as though they had never left the West Wing. Standing in a corner filled with flowers, Secretary of State Douglas Oates swapped war stories with Henry Kissinger, while the Super Bowl champion quarterback of the Houston Oilers stood in front of the fireplace and peered openly at the breasts of ABC news anchor Sandra Malone.

The President shared a toast with Prime Minister Gandhi and then introduced him to Charles Murphy, who had recently flown over Antarctica in a hot-air balloon. The President's wife came over, took her husband's arm, and pulled him toward the dance floor of the state dining room.

A White House aide caught Dan Fawcett's eye and nodded toward the doorway. Fawcett went over, heard him out, then approached the President. The chain of command was well oiled.

"My apologies, Mr. President, but a courier has just arrived with a congressional bill that requires your signature before midnight."

The President nodded in understanding. There was no bill to sign. It was a code for an urgent message. He excused himself to his wife and went across the hall to a small private office. He paused until Fawcett closed the door before picking up the phone.

"This is the President."

"Admiral Sandecker, sir."

"Yes, Admiral, what is it?"

"I have the Chief of Naval Forces in the Caribbean on another line. He has just informed me that one of my people, who vanished with Jessie LeBaron, has been rescued by one of our submarines."

"Has he been identified?"

"It's Dirk Pitt."

"The man must be either indestructible or very lucky," the President said with a touch of relief in his voice. "How soon can we get him here?"

"Admiral Clyde Monfort is holding on the line for authorization to provide priority transport."

"Can you connect me to him?"

"Hold on, sir." There was a second's pause followed by a click.

The President said, "Admiral Monfort, can you hear me?"

"I hear you."

"This is the President. Do you recognize my voice?"

"Yes, sir, I do."

"I want Pitt in Washington as fast as you can possibly get him here. Understood?"

"I read you, Mr. President. I'll see that a Navy jet lands him at Andrews Air Force Base before daybreak."

"Spread a security net on this affair, Admiral. Keep the submarine at sea and place the pilots, or anyone else who comes within a hundred yards of Pitt, under confinement for three days."

There was a slight hesitation. "Your orders will be carried out."

"Thank you. Now please let me speak to Admiral Sandecker."

"I'm here, Mr. President."

"You heard? Admiral Monfort will have Pitt at Andrews before dawn."

"I'll personally be on hand to meet him."

"Good. Take him by helicopter to CIA headquarters in Langley. Martin Brogan and representatives from my office and the State Department will be waiting to debrief him."

"He may not be able to shed light on anything."

"You're probably right," said the President wearily. "I'm expecting too much. I guess I always expect too much."

He hung up and sighed heavily. He collected his thoughts for a moment and then shelved them in a mental niche for later retrieval, a technique mastered sooner or later by every President. Shifting the mind from crisis to trivial routine and back again to crisis like the flick of a light switch was a requirement that went with the job.

Fawcett knew the President's every mood and patiently waited. Finally he said, "It might not be a bad idea if I attended the debriefing."

The President looked up at him sadly. "You'll be going with me to Camp David at sunup."

Fawcett looked blank. "I have nothing on your schedule that includes a trip to Camp David. Most of the morning is taken up by meetings with congressional leaders over the proposed budget."

"They will have to wait. I have a more important conference tomorrow."

"As your chief of staff may I ask who you're conferring with?"

"A group of men who call themselves the 'inner core.'"

Fawcett stared at the President, his mouth slowly tightening. "I don't understand."

"You should, Dan. You're one of them."

Before a dazed Fawcett could reply, the President left the office and rejoined the dinner party.

42

THE THUMP OF THE LANDING WHEELS woke Pitt up. Outside the twin-engined Navy jet the sky was still dark. Through a small window he could see the first streaks of orange spearheading the new day.

The blisters caused by the friction from the bathtub made sitting almost impossible, and he had slept in a cramped position on his side. He felt generally awful, and he was thirsty for something besides the fruit juices forced down his stomach in endless quantities by an overly concerned doctor on the submarine.

He wondered what he would do if he ever met up with Foss Gly again. Whatever fiendish punishment he created in his mind didn't seem excessive enough. The thought of the agony Gly was inflicting on Jessie, Giordino, and Gunn haunted him. He felt guilty for having escaped.

The whine of the jet engines faded and the door was opened. He walked stiffly down the stairs and was embraced by Sandecker. The admiral rarely shook hands, and the unexpected display of affection surprised Pitt.

"I guess what they say about a bad penny is true," said Sandecker hoarsely, groping for words.

"Better to turn up than not," Pitt replied, smiling.

Sandecker took him by the arm and led him over to a waiting car. "They're waiting at CIA headquarters in Langley to question you."

Pitt suddenly stopped. "They're alive," he announced briefly.

"Alive?" said Sandecker, stunned. "All of them?"

"Imprisoned by the Russians and tortured by a defector."

Incomprehension showed on Sandecker's face. "You were in Cuba?"

"On one of the outer islands," Pitt explained. "We've got to apprise the Russians of my rescue as quickly as possible to stop them from—"

"Slow down," Sandecker interrupted. "I'm losing you. Better yet, wait and tell the whole story when we get to Langley. I suspect you may have fallen in the creek and come up with a pocketful of trout."

On the flight across the city it began to rain. Pitt gazed through the plexiglass windshield at the 219 wooded acres surrounding the sprawling gray marble and concrete structure that was the home of America's cloak-and-dagger army. From the air it seemed deserted, no people were visible on the grounds. Even the parking lot was only one quarter full. The only human shape Pitt could detect was a statue of the nation's most famous spy, Nathan Hale, who had made the mistake of getting caught and was hanged.

Two senior officials were waiting at the helipad with umbrellas. Everyone hurried into the building, and Pitt and Sandecker were shown into a large conference room. There were six men and one woman present. Martin Brogan came over and shook Pitt's hand and introduced the others. Pitt simply nodded and promptly forgot their names.

Brogan said, "I hear you've had a rough trip."

"Not one I'd recommend to tourists," Pitt replied.

"Can I get you something to eat or drink?" Brogan offered graciously. "A cup of coffee or breakfast maybe?"

"If you could find a bottle of cold beer..."

"Of course." Brogan picked up the phone and said something. "Be here in a minute."

The conference room was plain by business-office standards. The walls were a neutral beige color, the carpet the same, and the furniture looked as though it came from a discount store. No pictures, no decorations of any kind gave it life. A room whose only function was to serve as a place to work.

Pitt was offered a chair at one end of the table, but declined. His rear end did not feel up to sitting just yet. Every eye in the room stared at him, and he began to feel like an inmate at the zoo on a Sunday afternoon.

Brogan gave him a relaxed smile. "Please tell us everything you've heard and observed from the beginning. Your account will be recorded and transcribed. Afterward, we'll go for questions and answers. All right with you?"

The beer came. Pitt took a long pull, relaxed, and then started relating the events from the takeoff in Key West to elatedly seeing the submarine rise out of the water a few yards from his sinking tub. He left out nothing and took his time, going into every detail, no matter how minor, he could recall. It took him nearly an hour and a half, but they listened attentively without question or interruption. When he finally finished, he gently eased his aching body into a chair and calmly watched everyone check over their notes.

Brogan declared a short break while aerial photographs of Cayo Santa María, files on Velikov and Gly, and the copies of the transcription were brought in. After forty minutes of study, Brogan kicked off the questioning.

"You carried weapons in the blimp. Why?"

"Projections of the *Cyclops'* wreck site indicated it lay in Cuban waters. It seemed appropriate to carry a bulletproof shield and a missile launcher for protective insurance."

"You realize, of course, your unwarranted attack on the Cuban patrol helicopter was a breach of government policy." This from a man Pitt remembered as working for the State Department.

"I followed a higher law," said Pitt with a sardonic grin.

"And what law, may I ask, is that?"

"Comes from the Old West, something they called self-preservation. The Cubans fired first, about a thousand rounds, I would judge, before Al Giordino blew it away."

Brogan smiled. He could see Pitt was a man after his own heart. "Our main concern here is with your description of the Russians' installation on the island. You say the island is unguarded."

"Above ground the only guards I saw were stationed at the gate of the compound. None were patrolling the roads or the beaches. The only security measure was an electrified fence."

"That explains why infrared photography hasn't detected any signs of human activity," said an analyst eyeballing the photos.

"Unlike the Russians to step out of character," mused another CIA official. "They almost always give away a secret base by going overboard on security."

"Not this time," said Pitt. "They've gone to opposite extremes and it's paid off for them. General Velikov stated that it was the most sensitive military installation outside the Soviet Union. And I gather that no one in your agency was aware of it until now."

"I admit, we may have been taken in," said Brogan. "Providing what you've described to us is true."

259

Pitt gave Brogan a cold stare. Then he painfully rose from his chair and started for the door. "All right, have it your way. I lied. Thanks for the beer."

"May I ask where you're going?"

"To call a press conference," Pitt said, addressing Brogan directly. "I'm wasting precious time for your benefit. The sooner I announce my escape and demand the release of the LeBarons, Giordino, and Gunn, the sooner Velikov will be forced to halt their torture and execution."

There was a shocked quiet. None of the people at the conference table could believe Pitt was walking out, none except Sandecker. He sat there and smiled like the owner of a winning ball club. "You'd better pull your act together, Martin. You've just been presented with a top-of-the-line intelligence coup, and if no one in this room can recognize it, I suggest you all find another line of work."

Brogan may have been a brusque egotist, but he was no fool. He quickly rose and stopped Pitt at the doorway. "Forgive an old Irishman who's been burned more times than he can count. Thirty years in this business and you just naturally become a doubting Thomas. Please help us to fit the puzzle together. Then we'll discuss what's to be done for your friends and the LeBarons."

"It'll cost you another beer," Pitt said.

Brogan and the others laughed then. The ice was broken, and the questioning was resumed from all sides of the table.

"Is this Velikov?" asked an analyst, holding up a photograph.

"Yes, General Peter Velikov. His American-accented English was letter perfect. I almost forgot, he had my dossier, including a personality profile."

Sandecker looked at Brogan. "Sounds like Sam Emmett has a mole in his FBI records department."

Brogan smiled sarcastically. "Sam won't be happy to learn of it."

"We could write a book on Velikov's exploits," said a heavy man facing Pitt. "At a later time I'd like you to give me a profile of his mannerisms."

"Glad to," said Pitt.

"And this is the interrogator with the heavy hand, Foss Gly?"

Pitt nodded at the second photograph. "He's a good ten years older than the face in the picture, but that's him."

"An American mercenary, born in Arizona," said the analyst. "You say you two met before?"

260

"Yes, during the *Empress of Ireland* project in search of the North American Treaty. I think you may recall it."

Brogan nodded. "Indeed I do."

"Getting back to the layout of the installation," said the woman. "Levels of the compound?"

"According to the elevator indicator, five, all underground."

"Idea as to extent?"

"All I saw was my cell, the hallway, Velikov's office, and a motor pool. Oh, yes, and the entry to the upper living quarters, which was decorated like a Spanish castle."

"Wall thickness?"

"About two feet."

"Quality of construction?"

"Good. No leakage or noticeable cracking of the concrete."

"Type of vehicles in the motor pool?"

"Two military trucks. The rest construction—a bulldozer, a back hoe, and a cherry picker."

The woman looked up from her notes. "Excuse me. The last one?"

"Cherry picker," Pitt explained. "A special truck with a telescoping platform to work at heights. You see them used by tree trimmers and telephone linemen."

"Approximate dimensions of the antenna dish?"

"Difficult to measure in the dark. Approximately three hundred yards long by two hundred yards wide. It lifts into position by hydraulic arms camouflaged as palm trees."

"Solid or grid?"

"Grid."

"Circuitry, junction boxes, relays?"

"Didn't see any, which doesn't mean they weren't there."

Brogan had followed the questions without intruding. Now he held up a hand and stared at a studious-looking man seated halfway down the table. "What do you make of it, Charlie?"

"Not enough technical detail to pinpoint an exact purpose. But there are three possibilities. One is that it's a listening station capable of intercepting telephone, radio, and radar signals across the United States. Two, a powerful jamming facility, just sitting there waiting for a crucial moment, like a nuclear first strike when it is suddenly activated, scrambling all our vital military and commercial communications. The third prospect is that it might have the capability to transmit and feed false information throughout our communications

261

systems. Most worrisome, the size and elaborate antenna design suggests the ability to perform the functions of all three."

The muscles in Brogan's face went taut. The fact that such a super-secret spy operation had been constructed less than two hundred miles from the shores of the United States did not exactly thrill the chief of the Central Intelligence Agency.

"If worse comes to worse, what are we looking at?"

"What I'm afraid we're looking at," answered Charlie, "is an electronically advanced and powerful facility capable of intercepting radio or phone communications and then using time-lag technology to allow a new-generation computerized synthesizer to imitate the callers' voices and alter the conversation. You'd be amazed how your words can be manipulated over a telephone to another party without your detecting the change. As a matter of fact, the National Security Agency has the same type of equipment on board a ship."

"So the Russians have caught up with us," said Brogan.

"Their technology is probably cruder than ours, but it seems they've gone a step further and expanded it on a grander scale."

The woman intelligence official looked at Pitt. "You said the island is supplied by submarine."

"So Raymond LeBaron informed me," said Pitt. "And what little I saw of the shoreline didn't include a docking area."

Sandecker played with one of his cigars but didn't light it. He pointed one end at Brogan. "Appears the Soviets have gone to unusual lengths to throw your Cuban surveillence off the track, Martin."

"The fear of exposure came out during the interrogation," said Pitt. "Velikov insisted we were agents on your payroll."

"Can't really blame the bastard," said Brogan. "Your entrance must have shocked the hell out of him."

"Mr. Pitt, could you describe the people at the dinner party when you entered?" asked an scholarly-looking man in an argyle sweater.

"Roughly I'd say there were sixteen women and two dozen men—"

"You did say women?"

"I did."

"What type?" asked the only woman in the room.

Pitt had to ask. "Define type."

"You know," she answered seriously. "Wives, nice single ladies, or hookers?"

"Definitely not hookers. Most were in uniform, probably part of Velikov's staff. The ones wearing wedding rings appeared to be wives

262

of the Cuban civilians and military officers who were present."

"What in hell is Velikov thinking?" Brogan asked no one in particular. "Cubans and their wives at a top-secret installation? None of this makes any sense."

Sandecker stared pensively at the tabletop. "Makes sense to me, if Velikov is using Cayo Santa María for something besides electronic espionage."

"What are you hinting at, Jim?" asked Brogan.

"The island would make a perfect base of operations for the overthrow of the Castro government."

Brogan looked at him in astonishment. "How do you know about that?"

"The President briefed me," Sandecker replied loftily.

"I see." But it was clear Brogan didn't see.

"Look, I realize this is all highly important," said Pitt, "but every minute we spend speculating puts Jessie, Al, and Rudi that much closer to death. I expect you people to pull out all the stops to save them. You can begin by notifying the Russians that you're aware of their captivity because of my rescue."

Pitt's demand was met with an odd quiet. Nobody except Sandecker looked at him. The CIA people, especially, avoided his eyes.

"Forgive me," said Brogan stonily. "I don't think that would be a smart move."

Sandecker's eyes suddenly flashed with anger. "Watch what you say, Martin. I know there's a Machiavellian plot jelling in your mind. But take warning, my friend. You've got me to deal with, and I'm not about to let my friends be literally thrown to the sharks."

"We're looking at a high-stakes game," said Brogan. "Keeping Velikov in the dark may prove most advantageous."

"And sacrifice several lives for an intelligence gamble?" said Pitt bitterly. "No way."

"Please bear with me a moment," Brogan pleaded. "I'll agree to leak a story saying we know the LeBarons and your NUMA people are alive. Next, we'll accuse the Cubans of imprisoning them in Havana."

"How can Velikov be expected to fall for something he knows is crap?"

"I don't expect him to fall for it. He's no cretin. He'll smell a rat and wonder how much we know about his island. And that's all he can do—wonder. We'll also muddy the waters by claiming our knowledge comes from photographic evidence showing your inflatable

263

boat washed up on the main island of Cuba. That should take the pressure off our captives and keep Velikov guessing. The *pièce de résistance* will be the discovery of Pitt's body by a Bahamian fisherman."

"What in hell are you proposing?" Sandecker demanded.

"I haven't thought it through yet," Brogan admitted. "But the basic idea is to sneak Pitt back on the island."

As soon as Pitt's debriefing had concluded, Brogan returned to his office and picked up the phone. His call went through the usual batting order of buffers before the President came on.

"Please make it quick, Martin. I'm about to leave for Camp David."

"We've just finished interrogating Dirk Pitt."

"Could he fill in any pieces?"

"Pitt gave us the intelligence breakthrough we discussed."

"Velikov's headquarters?"

"He led us straight to the mother lode."

"Nice work. Now your people can launch an infiltration operation."

"I think a more permanent solution would be in order."

"You mean offset its threat by exposing its existence to the world press?"

"No. I mean go in and destroy it."

43

THE PRESIDENT HAD A LIGHT BREAKFAST after reaching Camp David. The weather was unseasonably warm, there was Indian summer in the air, and he was dressed in cotton slacks and short-sleeved sweater.

He sat in a large wing chair with several file folders in his lap and studied the personal histories of the "inner core." After reading the last file he closed his eyes, pondering his options, wondering what he would say to the men who were waiting in the camp's main dining room.

Hagen entered the study and stood quietly until the President opened his eyes.

"Ready when you are, Vince."

The President slowly pushed himself from the chair. "Might as well get on with it then."

They were waiting around the long dining table as the President had arranged. No guards were present, none were required. These were honorable men who had no intent to commit crime. They respectfully rose to their feet as he entered the room, but he waved them down.

Eight were present and accounted for: General Fisher, Booth, Mitchell, and Busche sat on one side of the table opposite Eriksen, Senator Porter, and Dan Fawcett. Hudson was seated by himself at the far end. Only Raymond LeBaron was missing.

They were dressed casually, sitting comfortably like golfers in a clubhouse, relaxed, supremely confident and showing no signs of tension.

"Good morning, Mr. President," greeted Senator Porter cheerfully. "To what do we owe the honor of this mysterious summons?"

The President cleared his throat. "You all know why I've brought you here. So we don't have to play games."

265

"You don't want to congratulate us?" asked Clyde Booth sarcastically.

"Tributes may or may not be offered," said the President coldly. "That will depend."

"Depend on what?" Gunnar Eriksen demanded rudely.

"I believe what the President is fishing for," said Hudson, "is our blessing for allowing the Russians to claim a share of the moon."

"That and a confession of mass murder."

The tables were turned. They just sat there, eyes with the look of fish in a freezer, staring at the President.

Senator Porter, a fast thinker, launched his attack first. "Execution gangland style or *Arsenic and Old Lace* poison in the tea? If I may ask, Mr. President, what in hell are you talking about?"

"A small matter of nine dead Soviet cosmonauts."

"Those lost during the early Soyuz missions?" asked Dan Fawcett.

"No," answered the President. "The nine Russians who were killed on the Selenos lunar probes."

Hudson gripped the edge of the table and stared as if he had been electrocuted. "The Selenos spacecraft were unmanned."

"The Russians wanted the world to think so, but in reality they each carried three men. We have one of the crews on ice in the Walter Reed hospital morgue, if you care to examine the remains."

No one would have thought it to look at them. They considered themselves moral-minded citizens doing a job for their country. The last thing any of them expected to see in a mirror was the reflection of a cold-blooded killer. To say that the President had his audience in the palm of his hand would be an understatement.

Hagen sat fascinated. This was all news to him.

"If you'll bear with me," the President continued, "I'll indulge in mixing facts with speculation. To begin with, you and your moon colonists have accomplished an incredible achievement. I compliment you on your perseverance and genius, as will the world in the coming weeks. However, you have unwittingly made a terrible error that could easily stain your accomplishment.

"In your zeal to wave the Stars and Stripes you have ignored the international space law treaty governing activities on the moon, which was ratified by the United States, the Soviet Union, and three other countries in 1984. Then you took it upon yourselves to claim the moon as a sovereign possession and, figuratively speaking, posted 'Trespassers Will Be Shot' signs. Only you backed it up by somehow destroying three Soviet lunar probes. One of them, Selenos 4, man-

266

aged to return to earth, where it orbited for eighteen months before control was reestablished. Soviet space engineers attempted to bring it down in the steppes of Kazakhstan, but the craft was damaged and it fell near Cuba instead.

"Under the guise of a treasure hunt, you sent Raymond LeBaron to find it before the Russians. Telltale marks of damage inflicted by your colonists had to be obliterated. But the Cubans beat you both to the downed craft and retrieved it. You weren't aware of that until now, and the Russians still don't know. Unless..."

The President hung on the word. "Unless Raymond LeBaron has spilled his knowledge of the Jersey Colony under torture. I have it on good authority he was captured by the Cubans and turned over to Soviet military intelligence, the GRU."

"Raymond won't talk," Hudson said wrathfully.

"He may not have to," the President replied. "A few hours ago intelligence analysts, whom I asked to reexamine Soviet space signals received during Selenos 4's reentry orbits, have discovered that its data on the lunar surface were transmitted to a ground tracking station on the island of Socotra, near Yemen. Do you comprehend the consequences, gentlemen?"

"We comprehend what you're driving at." It was General Fisher who spoke, his voice reflective. "The Soviets may have visual proof of the Jersey Colony."

"Yes, and they've probably put two and two together and figured your people up there had something to do with the Selenos disasters. You can be sure they will retaliate. No calls on the hot line, no messages slipped through diplomatic channels, no announcements in TASS or *Pravda*. The battle for the moon will be kept secret by both sides. When you total the score, gentlemen, the result is you have launched a war that may prove impossible to stop."

The men seated around the table were shocked and confused, dazed and angry. But they were angry only because of a miscalculation of an event that was beyond their knowledge. The awful truth took several moments to register.

"You speak of Soviet retaliation, Mr. President," said Fawcett. "Do you have any insight on the possibility?"

"Put yourself in Soviet shoes. They were on to you a good week before their Selenos 8 lunar station was launched. If I were President Antonov, I'd have ordered the mission converted from scientific exploration to a military operation. There is little doubt in my mind that when Selenos 8 touches down on the moon twenty hours from

267

now, a special team of Soviet commandos will encircle and attack the Jersey Colony. Now you tell me, can the base defend itself?"

General Fisher looked at Hudson, then turned to the President and shrugged his shoulders. "I can't say. We've never made contingency plans for an armed assault on the colony. As I recall, their only weapons are two handguns and a missile launcher."

"Incidentally, when were your colonists scheduled to leave the moon?"

"They should lift off in about thirty-six hours," answered Hudson.

"I'm curious," said the President. "How do they intend to return through earth's atmosphere? Certainly their lunar transport vehicle doesn't have the capability."

Hudson smiled. "They'll return to the Kennedy spaceport at Cape Canaveral on the shuttle."

The President sighed. "The *Gettysburg*. Stupid of me not to think of it. She's already docked at our space station."

"Her crew hasn't been advised yet," said Steve Busche of NASA, "but once they get over the shock of seeing the colonists suddenly show up on the transport vehicle, they'll be more than willing to take on extra passengers."

The President paused and stared at the members of the "inner core," his expression suddenly bleak. "The burning question we all have to face, gentlemen, is whether the Jersey colonists will survive to make the trip."

44

"DO YOU REALLY EXPECT to get away with it?" Pitt asked.

Colonel Ramon Kleist, U.S. Marine Corps, Retired, rocked on his heels and scratched an itch on his back with a swagger stick. "So long as we can withdraw as a unit with our casualties, yes, I believe the mission can be pulled off successfully."

"Nothing this complicated can go letter perfect," said Pitt. "Destroying the compound and the antenna, plus killing off Velikov and his entire staff, sound to me like you're biting off more than you can chew."

"Your eyewitness observation and our stealth aircraft photos corroborate the light defensive measures."

"How many men make up your team?" asked Pitt.

"Thirty-one including yourself."

"The Russians are bound to find out who trashed their secret base. You'll be kicking a hornet's nest."

"All part of the plan," Kleist said airily.

Kleist stood ramrod straight, his chest threatening to burst from a flowered shirt. Pitt guessed his age as late fifties. He was a medium-skinned black, born in Argentina, the only child of a former SS officer who had fled Germany after the war and the daughter of a Liberian diplomat. Sent to a private school in New York, he decided to drop out and make a career in the Marines.

"I thought there was an unwritten agreement between the CIA and the KGB: we won't waste your agents if you don't waste ours."

The colonel gave Pitt an innocent look. "Whatever gave you the idea our side will do the dirty work?"

Pitt did not reply, only stared at Kleist, waiting.

"The mission will be conducted by Cuban Special Security Forces," he explained. "Their equivalent to our SEALS. Or to be honest, expertly trained exiles dressed in genuine Cuban battle fatigues. Even their underwear and socks will be standard Cuban military issue. Weapons, wristwatches, and other equipment will be of Soviet manufacture. And, just so we keep up appearances, the landing will come from the Cuban side of the island."

"All neat and tidy."

"We try to be efficient."

"Are you leading the mission?"

Kleist smiled. "No, I'm getting too old to leap out of the surf onto beaches. The assault team will be led by Major Angelo Quintana. You'll meet him at our camp in San Salvador. I'll be standing by on the SPUT."

"Say again."

"Special-purpose undersea transport," answered Kleist, "a vessel constructed expressly for missions of this kind. Most people don't know they exist. You'll find it most interesting."

"I'm not what you'd call trained for combat."

"Your job is purely to guide the team into the compound and show them the ventilator access to the garage area. Then you're to return to the beach and stay under cover until the mission is completed."

"Do you have a timetable for the raid?"

Kleist had a pained expression. "We prefer to call it a covert operation."

"Sorry, I've never read your bureaucratic manual on semantics."

"In answer to your question, the landing is set for 0200 four days from now."

"Four days may be too late to save my friends."

Kleist looked genuinely concerned. "We're already working on short notice and cutting our practice exercises razor thin. We need time to cover every uncertainty, every freak event. The plan has to be as airtight as our computer's tactical programs can make it."

"And if there's a human flaw in your plan?"

Any expression of friendly warmth left Kleist's face and was replaced with a cold, hard look. "If there is a human flaw, Mr. Pitt, is you. Barring divine intervention, the success or failure of this mission will rest heaviest on *your* shoulders,"

The CIA people were thorough. Pitt was shuffled from office to office, interview to interview, with stopwatch precision. The plans to neutralize Cayo Santa María progressed with prairie-fire swiftness.

270

His briefing by Colonel Kleist took place less than three hours after he was interrogated by Martin Brogan. He came to realize there were thousands of contingency plans to invade every island in the Caribbean and every nation in Central and South America. Computerized war games created a series of options. All the covert-operation experts had to do was select the program that came closest to fitting the objective, and then refine it.

Pitt endured a thorough physical examination before he was allowed lunch. The physician pronounced him fit, pumped him full of high-potency vitamins, and prescribed an early bedtime before Pitt's drowsy mind turned to mush.

A tall, high-cheekboned woman with braided hair was assigned as his nursemaid, escorting him to the proper room at the proper time. She introduced herself as Alice, no surname, no title. She wore a soft tan suit over a lace blouse. Pitt thought her rather pretty and found himself wondering what she would look like curled up on satin sheets.

"Mr. Brogan has arranged for you to eat in the executive dining room," she said in perfect tour-guide fashion. "We'll take the elevator."

Pitt suddenly remembered something. "I'd like the use of a telephone."

"Sorry, not possible."

"Mind if I ask why?"

"Have you forgotten you're supposed to be dead?" Alice asked matter-of-factly. "One phone call to a friend or a lover and you could blow the entire operation."

"Yes, 'The slip of a lip may sink a ship,'" Pitt said cynically. "Look, I need some information from a total stranger. I'll hand him a phony name."

"Sorry, not possible."

A scratched phonograph record came to Pitt's mind. "Give me a phone or I'll do something nasty."

She looked at him quizzically. "Like what?"

"Go home," he said simply.

"Mr. Brogan's orders. You're not to leave the building until your flight to our camp in San Salvador. He'd have you in a straitjacket before you reached the front door."

Pitt hung back as they walked down a hallway. Then he suddenly turned and entered an anteroom whose door was unmarked. He calmly walked past a startled secretary and entered the inner office. A short

271

man with cropped white hair, a cigarette dangling from his lips, and making strange markings on a graph, looked up in amused surprise.

Pitt flashed his best politician's smile and said, "I beg your pardon, may I borrow your phone?"

"If you work here, you know that using an unauthorized phone is against agency regulations."

"Then I'm safe," said Pitt. "I don't work here."

"You'll never get an outside line," said old White Hair.

"Watch me."

Pitt picked up the phone and asked the operator for Martin Brogan's office. In a few seconds Brogan's private secretary came on the line.

"My name is Dirk Pitt. Please inform Mr. Brogan that if I don't get the use of a telephone in one minute I'm going to cause a terrible scene."

"Who is this?"

"I told you."

Pitt was obstinate. Stoutly refusing to take no for an answer, it took him another twenty minutes of cursing, shouting, and generally being obnoxious before Brogan consented to a call outside the building, but only if Alice stood by and monitored the conversation.

She showed him to a small private office and pointed to the phone. "We have an internal operator standing by. Give her your number and she'll put it through."

Pitt spoke into the receiver. "Operator, what's your name?"

"Jennie Murphy," replied a sexy voice.

"Jennie, let's start with Baltimore information. I'd like the number of Weehawken Marine Products."

"Just a sec. I'll get it for you."

Jennie got the number from the Baltimore information operator and placed the call.

After explaining his problem to four different people, Pitt was finally connected to the executive chairman of the board—a title generally bestowed on old company heads who were eased out of the corporate mainstream.

"I'm Bob Conde. What can I do for you?"

Pitt looked at Alice and winked. "Jack Farmer, Mr. Conde. I'm with a federal archeological survey and I've discovered an old diving helmet in a shipwreck I hope you might identify."

"I'll do my best. My grandfather started the business nearly eighty years ago. We've kept fairly tight records. Have you got a serial number?"

"Yes, it was on a data plate attached to the front of the breastplate." Pitt closed his eyes and visualized the helmet on the corpse inside the *Cyclops*. "It read, 'Weehawken Products, Inc., Mark V, Serial Number 58-67-C.'"

"The Navy standard diving helmet," Conde said without hesitation. "We've been making them since 1916. Constructed of spun copper with bronze fittings. Has four sealed glass viewports."

"You sold it to the Navy?"

"Most of our orders came from the Navy. Still do, as a matter of fact. The Mark V, Mod 1 is still popular for certain types of surface-supplied-air diving operations. But this helmet was sold to a commercial customer."

"If you'll forgive me for asking, how do you know?"

"The serial number. Fifty-eight is the year it was manufactured. Sixty-seven is the number produced, and C stands for commercial sale. In other words, it was the sixty-seventh helmet to come out of our factory in 1958 and was sold to a commercial salvage company."

"Any chance of digging back and finding who bought it?"

"Might take a good half hour. We haven't bothered putting the old records on computer disks. I'd better call you back."

Alice shook her head.

"The government can afford the phone service, Mr. Conde. I'll hang on the line."

"Suit yourself."

Conde was as good as his word. He came back in thirty-one minutes. "Mr. Farmer, one of the bookkeepers found what you were looking for."

"I'm ready."

"The helmet along with a diving suit and hose equipment were sold to a private individual. Coincidentally, I knew him. Name was Hans Kronberg. A diver from the old school. Caught the bends more than anybody I ever knew. Hans was badly crippled, but it never stopped him from diving."

"Do you know what became of him?"

"As I recall, he purchased the equipment for a salvage job somewhere around Cuba. Rumor was the bends finally put him away for good."

"You don't remember who hired him?"

"No, it was too long ago," said Conde. "I think he found himself a partner who had a few bucks. Hans's regular diving gear was old and worn. His suit must have had fifty patches on it. He worked

273

hand to mouth, barely earned enough to make a decent living. Then one day he walks in here, buys all new equipment, and pays cash."

"I appreciate your help," said Pitt.

"Not at all. Glad you called. Interesting you should call. May I ask where you found his helmet?"

"Inside an old steel wreck near the Bahamas."

Conde got the picture. He was quiet for a moment. Then he said, "So old Hans never surfaced. Well, I guess he would have preferred it to passing away in bed."

"Can you think of anyone else who might remember Hans?"

"Not really. All the hard-hat divers from the old days are gone now. The only lead I can think of is Hans's widow. She still sends me Christmas cards. She lives in a rest home."

"Do you know the name of the rest home or where it's located?"

"I believe it's in Leesburg, Virginia. Haven't a clue to the name. Speaking of names, hers is Hilda."

"Thank you, Mr. Conde. You've been a great help."

"If you're ever in Baltimore, Mr. Farmer, drop in and say hello. Got plenty of time to talk about the old days since my sons aced me out of the company helm."

"I'd like that," said Pitt. "Goodbye."

Pitt cut the connection and rang Jennie Murphy. He asked her to call senior citizen rest homes around the Leesburg area until she hit on the one that housed Hilda Kronberg.

"What are you after?" demanded Alice.

Pitt smiled. "I'm looking for El Dorado."

"Very funny."

"That's the trouble with CIA types," said Pitt. "They can't take a joke."

45

THE FORD DELIVERY TRUCK rolled up the driveway of the Winthrop Manor Nursing Home and stopped at the service entrance. The truck was painted a bright blue with illustrations of floral arrangements on the sides. Gold lettering advertised Mother's House of Flowers.

"Please don't dally," said Alice impatiently. "You have to be in San Salvador four hours from now."

"Do my best," Pitt said as he jumped from the truck, wearing a driver's uniform and carrying a bouquet of roses.

"A mystery to me how you talked Mr. Brogan into this private excursion."

Pitt smiled as he closed the door. "A simple matter of extortion."

The Winthrop Manor Nursing Home was an idyllic setting for the sunset years. There was a nine-hole golf course, tropical indoor swimming pool, an elegant dining room, and lush landscaped gardens. The main building was designed more along the lines of a five-star hotel than a drab sanatorium.

No ramshackle home for the aged poor, thought Pitt. Winthrop Manor radiated first-class taste for wealthy senior citizens. He began to wonder how the widow of a diver who struggled to make ends meet could afford to live in such luxury.

He came through a side door, walked up to a reception desk, and held up the flowers. "I have a delivery for Mrs. Hilda Kronberg."

The receptionist gave him a direct gaze and smiled. Pitt found her quite attractive, dark red hair, long and gleaming, gray-blue eyes set in a narrow face.

"Just leave them on the counter," she said sweetly. "I'll have an attendant give them to her."

"I have to deliver them personally," Pitt said. "They come with a verbal message."

275

She nodded and pointed to a side door. "You'll probably find Mrs. Kronberg out by the pool. Don't expect her to be lucid, she drifts in and out of reality."

Pitt thanked her and felt remiss for not making a try for a dinner date. He walked through the door and down a ramp. The glassed-in pool was designed like a Hawaiian garden with black lava rock and a waterfall.

After asking two elderly women for Hilda Kronberg, he found her sitting in a wheelchair, her eyes staring into the water, her mind elsewhere.

"Mrs. Kronberg?"

She shaded her eyes with one hand and looked up. "Yes?"

"My dame is Dirk Pitt, and I wonder if I might ask you a few questions?"

"Mr. Pitt, is it?" she asked in a soft voice. She studied his uniform and the flowers. "Why would a florist's delivery boy want to ask me questions?"

Pitt smiled at her use of "boy" and handed her the flowers. "It concerns your late husband, Hans."

"Are you with *him*?" she asked suspiciously.

"No, I'm quite alone."

Hilda was sickly thin and her skin was as transparent as tissue paper. Her face was heavily made up and her hair skillfully dyed. Her diamond rings would have bought a small fleet of Rolls-Royces. Pitt guessed her age was a good fifteen years younger than the seventy-five she appeared. Hilda Kronberg was a woman waiting to die. Yet when she smiled at the mention of her husband's name, her eyes seemed to smile too.

"You look too young to have known Hans," she said.

"Mr. Conde of Weehawken Marine told me about him."

"Bob Conde, of course. He and Hans were old poker pals."

"You never remarried after his death?"

"Yes, I remarried."

"Yet you still use his name?"

"A long story that wouldn't interest you."

"When was the last time you saw Hans?"

"It was a Thursday. I saw him off on the steamship *Monterey*, bound for Havana, on December 10, 1958. Hans was always chasing rainbows. He and his partner were off on another treasure hunt. He swore they would find enough gold to buy me the dream house I always wanted. Sadly, he never came back."

"Do you recall who his partner was?"

Her gentle features suddenly turned hard. "What are you after, Mr. Pitt? Who do you represent?"

"I'm a special projects director for the National Underwater and Marine Agency," he replied. "During a survey on a sunken ship called the *Cyclops*, I discovered what I believe to be the remains of your husband."

"You found Hans?" she asked, surprised.

"I didn't make positive identification, but the diver's helmet on the body was traced to him."

"Hans was a good man," she said wistfully. "Not a good provider, perhaps, but we had a good life together until... well, until he died."

"You asked me if I was with *him*?" he prompted gently.

"A family skeleton, Mr. Pitt. I'm taken good care of. He watches over me. I've no complaints. My retreat from the real world is my own choosing..." Her voice trailed off and her stare grew distant.

Pitt had to catch her before she retreated into a self-induced shell. "Did *he* tell you Hans was murdered?"

Hilda's eyes flickered for an instant, and then she shook her head silently.

Pitt knelt beside her and held her hand. "His lifeline and air hose were cut while he was working underwater."

She noticeably trembled. "Why are you telling me this?"

"Because it's the truth, Mrs. Kronberg. I give you my word. Whoever worked with Hans probably killed him so he could steal Hans's share of the treasure."

Hilda sat there in trancelike confusion for nearly a minute. "You know about the La Dorada treasure," she said at last.

"Yes," Pitt answered. "I know how it came to be on the *Cyclops*. I also know Hans and his partner salvaged it."

Hilda began toying with one of the diamond rings on her hand. "Deep down I always suspected that Ray killed Hans."

The delayed shock of understanding slowly fell over Pitt's face. He cautiously played a wild card. "You think that Hans was murdered by Ray LeBaron?"

She nodded.

The unexpected revelation caught Pitt unawares, and it took him a few moments to come back on track. "The motive was the treasure?" he asked softly.

"No. The motive was me." She shook her head.

Pitt did not reply, only waited quietly.

277

"Things happen," she began in a whisper. "I was young and pretty in those days. Can you believe I was once pretty, Mr. Pitt?"

"You're still very pretty."

"I think you may need glasses, but thank you for the compliment."

"You also have a quick mind."

She gestured toward the main building. "Did they tell you I was a bit balmy?"

"The receptionist insinuated you weren't quite together."

"A little act I love to put on. Keeps everyone guessing." Her eyes sparkled briefly and then they took on a faraway look. "Hans was a nice man who was seventeen years older than me. My love for him was mixed with compassion because of his crippled body. We had been married about three years when he brought Ray home for dinner one evening. The three of us soon became close friends, the men forming a partnership to salvage artifacts from old shipwrecks and sell them to antique dealers and marine collectors. Ray was handsome and dashing in those days, and it wasn't long before he and I entered into an affair." She hesitated and stared at Pitt. "Have you ever deeply loved two women at the same time, Mr. Pitt?"

"I'm afraid the experience has eluded me."

"The strange part was that I didn't feel any guilt. Deceiving Hans became an exciting adventure. It was not that I was a dishonest person. It was just that I had never lied to somebody close to me before and remorse never entered my mind. Now I thank God that Hans didn't find out before he died."

"Can you tell me about the La Dorada treasure?"

"After graduating from Stanford, Ray spent a couple years tramping through the jungles of Brazil, hunting for gold. He first heard of the La Dorada from an American surveyor. I don't remember the details, but he was sure it was on board the *Cyclops* when it disappeared. He and Hans spent two years dragging some sort of instrument that detected iron up and down the Caribbean. Finally, they found the wreck. Ray borrowed some money from his mother to buy diving equipment and a small salvage boat. He sailed ahead to Cuba to set up a base of operations while Hans was finishing up a job off New Jersey."

"Did you ever receive a letter or a phone call from Hans after he sailed on the *Monterey*?"

"He called once from Cuba. All he said was that he and Ray were leaving for the wreck site the next day. Two weeks later, Ray returned and told me Hans had died from the bends and was buried at sea."

"And the treasure?"

"Ray described it as a huge golden statue," she replied. "He somehow raised it onto the salvage boat and took it to Cuba."

Pitt stood, stretched, and knelt beside Hilda again. "Odd that he didn't bring the statue back to the States."

"He was afraid that Brazil, the state of Florida, the federal government, other treasure hunters and marine archeologists would confiscate or tie up the La Dorada in court claims and eventually leave him nothing. Then, of course, there was always the Internal Revenue Service. Ray couldn't see giving away millions of dollars in taxes if he could get around it. So he told no one but me of the discovery."

"What ever became of it?"

"Ray removed a giant ruby from the statue's heart, cut it up into small stones, and sold them piecemeal."

"And that was the beginning of the LeBaron financial empire," said Pitt.

"Yes, but before Ray could cut up the emerald head or melt down the gold, Castro came to power and he was forced to hide the statue. He never told me where he hid it."

"Then the La Dorada is still buried somewhere in Cuba."

"I'm certain Ray was never able to return and retrieve it."

"Did you see Mr. LeBaron after that?"

"Oh my, yes," she said brightly. "We were married."

"You were the first Mrs. LeBaron?" Pitt asked, astonished.

"For thirty-three years."

"But the records say his first wife's name was Hillary and she died some years ago."

"Ray preferred Hillary over Hilda when he became wealthy. Thought it had more class. My death was a convenient arrangement for him when I became ill—divorcing an invalid was abhorrent to him. So he buried Hillary LeBaron, while Hilda Kronberg withers away here."

"That strikes me as inhumanly cruel."

"My husband was generous if not compassionate. We lived two different lives. But I don't mind. Jessie comes to see me occasionally."

"The second Mrs. LeBaron?"

"A very charming and thoughtful person."

"How can she be married to him if you're still alive?"

279

She smiled brightly. "The one time Ray made a bad deal. The doctors told him I had only a few months to live. But I fooled them all and have hung on for seven years."

"That makes him a bigamist as well as a murderer and a thief."

Hilda did not argue. "Ray is a complicated man. He takes far more than he gives."

"If I were you I'd nail him to the nearest cross."

"Too late for me, Mr. Pitt." She looked up at him, a sudden twinkle in her eyes. "But you could do something in my place."

"Name it."

"Find the La Dorada," she said fervently. "Find the statue and give it to the world. See that it's displayed to the public. That would hurt Ray more than losing his magazine. But more important, it's what Hans would have wanted."

Pitt took her hand and held it. "Hilda," he said softly, "I'll do my damnedest."

46

HUDSON ADJUSTED THE CLARITY of the image and nodded a greeting at the face staring back. "Eli, I have someone who has asked to talk to you."

"Always happy to see a new face," Steinmetz replied cheerfully.

Another man took Hudson's place beneath the video camera and monitor. He gazed in fascination for a few moments before speaking.

"Are you really on the moon?" he asked finally.

"Show time," Steinmetz said with an agreeable smile. He moved offscreen and lifted the portable camera from its tripod and panned it through a quartz window at the lunar landscape. "Sorry I can't show you earth, but we're on the wrong side of the ball."

"I believe you."

Steinmetz replaced the camera and moved in front of it again. He leaned forward and stared into his monitor. His smile slowly faded and his eyes took on a questioning look. "Are you who I think you are?"

"Do you recognize me?"

"You look and sound like the President."

It was the President's turn to smile. "I wasn't sure you were aware, knowing that I was a senator when you left earth, and newspapers aren't delivered in your neighborhood."

"When the moon's orbit around the earth is in the proper position we can tap into most communication satellites. During the crew's last rest break, they watched the latest Paul Newman movie on Home Box Office. We also devour the Cable News Network programs like starving dogs."

"The Jersey Colony is an incredible achievement. A grateful nation will forever be in your debt."

"Thank you, Mr. President, though it comes as a surprise that Leo

281

jumped the gun and announced the success of the project before our return to earth. That wasn't part of the plan."

"There has been no public announcement," said the President, becoming serious. "Next to you and your colony people, I am the only one outside the 'inner core' who is aware of your existence, except maybe the Russians."

Steinmetz stared at him across 240,000 miles of space. "How could they know about the Jersey Colony?"

The President paused to look at Hudson, who was standing out of camera range. Hudson shook his head.

"The Selenos lunar photo probes," answered the President, omitting any reference to them being manned. "One managed to send its data back to the Soviet Union. We think it showed the Jersey Colony. We also have reason to believe the Russians suspect you destroyed the probes from the lunar surface."

An uneasy apprehension showed in Steinmetz's eyes. "You think they plan to attack us, is that it?"

"Yes, Eli, I do," said the President. "Selenos 8, the Soviet lunar station, entered orbit around the moon three hours ago. NASA computers project it to pass up a safe landing site on the face and come down on the dark side in your block of the neighborhood. A risky gamble unless they have a definite objective."

"The Jersey Colony."

"Their lunar landing vehicle holds seven men," the President continued. "The craft requires two pilot-engineers to direct its flight. That leaves five for combat."

"There are ten of us," said Steinmetz. "Two to one, not bad odds."

"Except they'll have firepower and training on their side. These men will be the deadliest team the Russians can field."

"You paint a grim picture, Mr. President. What would you have us do?"

"You've accomplished far more than any of us had any right to expect. But the deck is stacked against you. Destroy the colony and get out before there's any bloodshed. I want you and your people safely back on earth to receive the honors you deserve."

"I don't think you quite realize what we've busted our asses to build here."

"Whatever you've done isn't worth your lives."

"We've all lived with death for six years," said Steinmetz slowly. "A few more hours won't matter."

282

"Don't throw it all away on an impossible fight," the President argued.

"Sorry, Mr. President, but you're talking to a man who lost his daddy at a little sand spit called Wake Island. I'll put it to a vote, but I already know the outcome. The other guys won't cut and run any more than I will. We'll stay and fight."

The President felt proud and defeated at the same time. "What weapons do you have?" he asked wearily.

"Our arsenal consists of one used rocket launcher, which is down to its last shell, an M-14 National Match rifle, and a twenty-two-caliber target pistol. We brought them for a series of gravity experiments."

"You're outclassed, Eli," the President said miserably. "Can't you realize that?"

"No, sir. I refuse to quit on a technicality."

"What technicality?"

"The Russians are the visitors."

"So what?"

"That makes us the home team," said Steinmetz slyly. "And the home team always has the advantage."

"They've landed!" exclaimed Sergei Kornilov, smashing a fist into one hand. "Selenos 8 is on the moon!"

Below the VIP observation room, on the floor of the Soviet Mission Control Center, the engineers and space scientists burst into wild cheering and applause.

President Antonov held up a glass of champagne. "To the glory of the Soviet Union and the party."

The toast was repeated by the Kremlin officials and high-ranking military officers crowded in the room.

"To our first stepping-stone on our quest of Mars," toasted General Yasenin.

"Here, here!" replied a chorus of deep voices. "To Mars."

Antonov set his empty glass on a tray and turned to Yasenin, his face abruptly serious. "How soon before Major Leuchenko makes contact with the moon base?" he asked.

"Allowing for time to secure the spacecraft systems, make a reconnaissance of the terrain, and position his men for the assault, I would say four hours."

283

"How far away is the landing site?"

"Selenos 8 was programmed to touch down behind a low range of hills less than three kilometers from where Selenos 4 detected the astronauts," answered the general.

"That seems quite close," said Antonov. "If the Americans tracked our descent, Leuchenko has lost all opportunity for surprise."

"There is little doubt they have realized what we're up to."

"You're not concerned?"

"Our advantage lies in Leuchenko's experience and superior fire-power, Comrade President." Yasenin's face wore the expression of a boxing manager who had just sent his fighter into the ring against a one-armed man. "The Americans are faced with a no-win situation."

47

MAJOR GRIGORY LEUCHENKO LAY STRETCHED in the fine, gray dust of the moon's surface and stared at the desolate wasteland spread beneath the pitch-black sky. He found the silent and ghostly landscape similar to the arid desert of Afghanistan's Seistan Basin. The gravel plains and rolling mound-shaped hills gave little definition. It reminded him of a great sea of plaster of paris, yet it seemed strangely familiar to him.

He fought off an urge to vomit. He and his men were all suffering from nausea. There had been no time to train for the weightless environment during the journey from earth, no weeks or months to adjust as had the cosmonauts of the Soyuz missions. They were given only a few hours' instruction on how to operate the life-support systems of their lunar suits, a brief lecture on conditions they could expect to find on the moon, and a briefing on the location of the American colony.

He felt a hand squeeze his shoulder through his lunar suit. He spoke into his helmet's internal transmitter without turning.

"What have you got?"

Lieutenant Dmitri Petrov pointed toward a flat valley running between the sloping walls of two craters about a thousand meters to the left. "Vehicle tracks and footprints, converging into that shadow below the left crater's rim. I make out three, maybe four small buildings."

"Pressurized greenhouses," said Leuchenko. He set a pair of boxlike binoculars on a small tripod and settled the wide viewing piece around the faceplate of his helmet. "Looks like vapor issuing out of the crater's sloping side." He paused to adjust the focus. "Yes, I can see it clearly now. There's an entrance into the rock, probably an

285

airlock with access to their interior facility. No sign of life. The outer perimeter appears deserted."

"They could be hiding in ambush," said Petrov.

"Hide where?" asked Leuchenko, sweeping the open panorama. "The scattered rocks are too small to shield a man. There are no breaks in the terrain, no indication of defense works. An astronaut in a bulky white lunar suit would stand out like a snowman in a field of cinders. No, they must be barricaded inside the cave."

"Not a wise defensive position. All to our advantage."

"They still have a rocket launcher."

"That has little effect against men spread in a loose formation."

"True, but we'll have no cover and we can't be sure they don't have other weapons."

"A heavy concentration of fire inside the cave entrance might force their hand," suggested Petrov.

"Our orders are not to cause any unnecessary destruction to the facility," said Leuchenko. "We'll have to move in—"

"Something is moving out there!" Petrov cried.

Leuchenko stared through the binoculars. An odd-looking open vehicle had appeared from behind one of the greenhouses and was traveling in their direction. A white flag, attached to an antenna, hung limply in the airless atmosphere. He watched until it stopped fifty meters away and a figure stepped out onto the lunar soil.

"Interesting," said Leuchenko thoughtfully. "The Americans want to parley."

"Might be a trick. A ruse to study our force."

"I don't think so. They wouldn't make contact under a flag of truce if they were acting from a position of strength. Their intelligence people and tracking systems on earth warned them of our arrival, and they must realize they're outgunned. Americans are capitalists. They look at everything from a business viewpoint. If they can't make a fight for it, they'll try to strike a deal."

"You going out?" asked Petrov.

"No harm in talking. He doesn't appear armed. Perhaps they can be persuaded to bargain their lives for an intact colony."

"Our orders were to take no prisoners."

"I haven't forgotten," said Leuchenko tensely. "We'll cross that bridge when we've achieved our objective. Tell the men to keep the American in their sights. If I raise my left hand, give the order to fire."

He handed his automatic weapon to Petrov and rose lightly to his feet. His lunar suit, rifle, and life-support backpack, containing an

286

oxygen recharger and water recharger for cooling, added 194 pounds to Leuchenko's body weight for a total of almost 360 earth pounds. But his lunar weight was only 60 pounds.

He moved toward the lunar vehicle in the half-walking, half-hopping gait typical when moving under the light gravitational pull of the moon. He quickly approached the lunar vehicle and halted about five meters away.

The American moon colonist was leaning unconcernedly against a front wheel. He straightened, knelt on one knee, and wrote a number in the lead-colored dust.

Leuchenko understood and turned his radio receiver to the frequency indicated. Then he nodded.

"Are you receiving me?" the American asked in badly mispronounced Russian.

"I speak English," replied Leuchenko.

"Good. That will save any misunderstanding. My name is Eli Steinmetz."

"You are the United States moon base leader?"

"I head up the project, yes."

"Major Grigory Leuchenko, Soviet Union."

Steinmetz moved closer and they stiffly shook hands. "It seems we have a problem, Major."

"One neither of us can avoid."

"You could turn around and hike back to your lunar lander," said Steinmetz.

"I have my orders," Leuchenko stated in a firm tone.

"You're to attack and capture my colony."

"Yes."

"Is there no way we can prevent bloodshed?"

"You could surrender."

"Funny," said Steinmetz. "I was about to ask the same of you."

Leuchenko was certain Steinmetz was bluffing, but the face behind the gold-tinted visor remained unreadable. All Leuchenko could see was his own reflection.

"You must realize that your people are no match for mine."

"In a knock-down, drag-out firefight you'd win," agreed Steinmetz. "But you can remain outside your landing craft only for a few hours before you must go back and replenish your breathing systems. I reckon you've already used up two."

"We have enough left to accomplish the job," Leuchenko said confidently.

287

"I must warn you, Major. We have a secret weapon. You and your men will surely die."

"A crude bluff, Mr. Steinmetz. I would have expected better from an American scientist."

Steinmetz corrected him. "Engineer, there's a difference."

"Whatever," said Leuchenko impatiently. As a soldier, he was out of his element in wordy negotiations. He was anxious for action. "It's senseless to carry this conversation any further. You would be wise to send your men out and turn over the facility. I'll guarantee your safety until you can be returned to earth."

"You're lying, Major. Either your people or mine will have to be erased. There can be no losers left to tell the world what happened here."

"You're wrong, Mr. Steinmetz. Surrender and you will be treated fairly."

"Sorry, no deal."

"Then there can be no quarter."

"I expected none," said Steinmetz, his tone grim. "You attack and the waste of human lives will be on your shoulders."

Anger rose within Leuchenko. "For one who is responsible for the deaths of nine Soviet cosmonauts, Mr. Steinmetz, you're hardly in a position to lecture me on human life."

Leuchenko couldn't be certain, but he swore Steinmetz tensed. Without waiting for a reply, he turned on his heels and loped away. He looked over his shoulder and saw that Steinmetz stood there for several seconds before slowly reentering the lunar vehicle and driving back to the colony, trailing a small cloud of gray dust behind the rear wheels.

Leuchenko smiled to himself. In two more hours, three at the most, his mission would be successfully achieved. When he reached his men, he studied the layout of the craggy surface in front of the moon base through the binoculars again. Finally, when he was satisfied there were no American colonists lurking amid the rocks, Leuchenko gave the order to spread out in loose formation and advance. The elite Soviet fighting team moved forward without an inkling that Steinmetz's inventive trap was set and waiting.

48

AFTER STEINMETZ RETURNED to the entrance of Jersey Colony's subterranean headquarters, he leisurely parked the lunar vehicle and shuffled slowly inside. He took his time, almost feeling Leuchenko's eyes probing his every movement. Once out of view of the Russians, he stopped short of the airlock and quickly stepped through a small side tunnel that gradually rose through the crater's interior slope. His passage raised small clouds of dust that filled the narrow shaft, and he had to continually wipe his visor to see.

Fifty steps and a minute later he crouched and crawled into an opening that led to a small shelf camouflaged by a large gray cloth perfectly matched to the surrounding surface. Another suited figure was lying on his stomach, gazing through the telescopic sight of a rifle.

Willie Shea, the colony's geophysicist, did not notice another presence until Steinmetz eased down beside him. "I don't think you made much of an impression," he said with a bare hint of a Boston twang. "The Slavs are about to attack the homestead."

From the elevated vantage point Steinmetz could clearly see Major Leuchenko and his men advancing across the valley. They came on like hunters stalking their prey, making no attempt to use the high ground of the crater's sides. The loose shale would have made the going too slow. Instead, they jumped across the flat ground in zigzag patterns, throwing themselves prone every thirty or forty feet, taking advantage of every boulder, every broken contour of the land. An expert marksman would have found the twisting and dodging figures nearly impossible to hit.

"Put a shot about ten feet in front of the point man," said Steinmetz. "I want to observe their reaction."

"If they're monitoring our frequency, we'll give away our every move," protested Shea.

"They haven't got time to hunt for our frequency. Shut up and shoot."

Shea shrugged inside his lunar suit, peered through the crosshairs of his scope, and squeezed off a round. The gunshot was strangely silent because there was no air on the moon to carry the sound waves.

A puff of dust kicked up ahead of Leuchenko and he immediately dropped to the ground. His men followed suit and stared over the sights of their automatic weapons, waiting expectantly for more fire. But nothing happened.

"Did anyone see where it came from?" Leuchenko demanded.

The replies were negative.

"They're sighting for range," said Sergeant Ivan Ostrovski. A hardened veteran of the Afghanistan fighting, he could not believe he was actually in combat on the moon. He swept a pointed finger over the ground about two hundred meters ahead. "What do you make of those colored rocks, Major?"

For the first time Leuchenko spied several boulders scattered in a ragged line across the valley, stained with bright orange paint. "I doubt if it has anything to do with us," he said. "Probably put there for some sort of experiment."

"I think the fire came on a downward angle," said Petrov.

Leuchenko took the binoculars from his hip pack, set them on the tripod, and carefully scanned the side and rim of the crater. The sun was a blazing white but with no air to spread the light an astronaut standing in the shadows of a rock formation would be almost invisible.

"Nothing shows," he said finally.

"If they're waiting for us to close the gap, they must be conserving a small supply of ammunition."

"We'll know in another three hundred meters what kind of reception they've planned," muttered Leuchenko. "Once we come under cover of the greenhouses we'll be out of sight of the cave entrance." He rose to one knee and waved his arm forward. "Fan out and keep alert."

The five Soviet fighters leaped to their feet and scrambled on. As they reached the orange rocks another shot struck the fine sand in front of them and they flung themselves prone, a jagged line of white

290

figures, face visors flashing in the intense rays of the sun.

Only a hundred meters separated them from the greenhouses, but nausea was draining their energy. They were as tough as any fighting men in the world, but they were combating space sickness in tandem with an alien environment. Leuchenko knew he could count on them to go far beyond their limits of endurance. But if they didn't force their way into the safe atmosphere of the colony within the next hour, there was little chance of them making it back to their landing craft before their life-support systems gave out. He gave them a minute to rest while he made another examination of the ground ahead.

Leuchenko was an old hand at sniffing out traps. He had come within a hair of being killed on three different patrols in ambushes laid by the Afghan rebels, and he had learned the fine art of scenting danger the hard way.

It wasn't what his eyes could see; it was what they couldn't see that rang a warning bell in his head. The two shots didn't fit a wild pattern. They struck him as deliberately placed. A crude warning? No, it had to mean something else, he speculated. A signal perhaps?

The confining pressure suit and helmet irritated him. He longed for his comfortable and efficient combat gear, but fully realizing they could not protect his body from the frying heat and the cosmic rays. For at least the fourth time the bile rose in his throat and he gagged as he forced himself to swallow it.

The situation was hellish, he thought angrily. Nothing was to his liking. His men were exposed in the open. He'd been given no intelligence on the Americans' weapons except the reported rocket launcher. Now they were under attack by small-arms fire. Leuchenko's only consolation was that the colonists seemed to be using a rifle or maybe even a pistol. If they possessed a full automatic firearm, they could have cut down the Soviets a hundred meters back. And the rocket launcher. Why hadn't they tried it before now? What were they waiting for?

What bothered him most was the total lack of movement by the colonists. The greenhouses, equipment, and small laboratory modules sitting around the entrance to the cave appeared deserted.

"Unless you see a target," he ordered, "hold your fire until we reach cover. Then we'll regroup and storm the main quarters inside the hill."

Leuchenko waited until each of his four men acknowledged and then he motioned them on.

Corporal Mikhail Yushchuk was about thirty meters behind and to

291

one side of the man on his left. He stood and began running in a crouching position. He had taken only a few steps when he felt a stinging sensation in his kidney. Then the sudden thrust of pain was repeated. He reached around and grasped the small of his back just below his support system pack. His vision began to blur and his breath came in gasps as his pressurized suit began to leak. He sank to his knees and stared dumbly at his hand. The glove was drenched in blood that was already steaming and coagulating under the roasting heat from the sun.

Yushchuk tried to warn Leuchenko, but his voice failed. He crumbled into the gray dust, his eyes dimly recognizing a figure in a strange space suit standing over him with a knife. Then his world went black.

Steinmetz witnessed Yushchuk's death from his vantage point and issued a series of sharp commands into his helmet's transmitter. "Okay, Dawson, your man is ten feet left and eight feet ahead of you. Gallagher, he's twenty feet to your right and moving forward. Steady, steady, he's cutting right into Dawson. Okay, nail him."

He watched two of the colonists materialize as if by magic and attack one of the Soviets who was lagging slightly behind his comrades.

"Two down, three to go," Steinmetz muttered softly to himself.

"I've got my sights set on the point man," said Shea. "But I can't promise a clean hit unless he freezes for a second."

"Lay another shot, only closer this time to get them on the ground again. Then stay on him. If he gets wise, he could cut our guys down before they could close on him. Blast his ass if he so much as turns his head."

Shea silently aimed his M-14 and pulled off another shot, which struck less than three feet in front of the lead man's boots.

"Cooper! Snyder!" Steinmetz barked. "Your man is flat on the ground twenty feet ahead and to your left. Take him, now!" He paused to scan the position of the second remaining Russian. "Same goes for Russell and Perry, thirty feet directly in front. Go!"

The third member of the Soviet combat team never knew what hit him. He died while hugging the ground for cover. Eight of the colonists were now closing the pincers from the rear of the Russians, whose concentration was focused on the colony.

Suddenly Steinmetz froze. The man behind the leader swung around just as Russell and Perry leaped at him like offensive tackles charging a quarterback.

Lieutenant Petrov spotted the converging shadows as he rose to his feet for the final dash to the greenhouses. He instinctively twisted around in an abrupt corkscrew motion as Russell and Perry crashed into him. A cold professional, he should have fired and brought them down. But he hesitated a split second too long out of astonishment. It was as if the Americans had risen up out of the moon's surface like spectral demons. He managed to snap off a shot that drilled one of his assailant's upper arms. Then a knife flashed.

Leuchenko's eyes were trained toward the colony ahead. He was unaware of the slaughter going on behind him until he heard Petrov gasp out a warning. He spun around and stood rooted in shocked awe.

His four men were stretched out in a lifeless sprawl on the lunar gravel. Eight American colonists had appeared out of nowhere and were rapidly encircling him. Sudden hatred burst within him, and he thrust his weapon into firing position.

A bullet thumped into his thigh and he tilted sideways. Tensed in sudden pain, he squeezed off twenty rounds. Most of them flew wide into the lunar desert, but two found their mark. One of the colonists fell backward and another dropped to his knees clutching his shoulder.

Then another bullet tore into his neck. He held on to the trigger, spewing rounds until the clip ran dry, his shots flying wild.

He cursed as he crumpled limply to the ground. "Damn the Americans!" he shouted inside his helmet. He thought of them as devils who didn't play the game according to the rules. He lay on his back, staring up at the faceless forms standing above him.

They parted as another member of the colonists approached and knelt down beside Leuchenko.

"Steinmetz?" Leuchenko asked weakly. "Can you hear me?"

"Yes, I'm on your frequency," answered Steinmetz. "I can hear you."

"Your secret weapon ... how did you make your people appear from nothing?"

Steinmetz knew he would be talking to a dead man within seconds.

293

"An ordinary shovel," he replied. "Since we all have to wear pres-surized lunar suits with self-contained life supports, it was a simple matter to bury the men in the soft soil."

"They were marked by the orange rocks?"

"Yes, from a hidden platform on the crater's side I could direct when and where to attack you from the rear."

"I do not wish to be buried here," Leuchenko murmured. "Tell my nation...tell them to bring us home someday."

It was close, but Steinmetz got it in. "You'll all go home," he said. "That's a promise."

In Russia a grim-faced Yasenin turned to President Antonov. "You heard," he said through clenched lips. "They're gone."

"They're gone," Antonov repeated mechanically. "It was as though Leuchenko's last words came from across the room."

"His communications were relayed by the two crewmen on the lunar landing craft direct to our space communications center," explained Kornilov.

Antonov moved away from the window overlooking the mission control room and sat down heavily in a chair. For such a large bear of a man he seemed shrunken and withered. He looked down at his hands and shook his head sadly.

"Poor planning," he said quietly. "We threw Major Leuchenko and his men's lives away and achieved nothing."

"There was no time to plan a proper mission," Yasenin offered lamely.

"Under the circumstances, we did all that was possible," added Kornilov. "We still have the glory of the first Soviet men to walk on the moon."

"The luster has already faded." Antonov's voice was leaden with defeat. "The Americans' incredible accomplishment will bury any propaganda value of our achievement."

"Perhaps we can still stop them," Yasenin said bitterly.

Kornilov stared at the general. "By sending up a better prepared fighting force?"

"Exactly."

"Better yet, why not wait until they return?"

Antonov looked at Kornilov with curious eyes. "What are you suggesting?"

"I've been speaking to Vladimir Polevoi. He's informed me that

294

the GRU's listening center in Cuba has intercepted and identified the voice and video transmissions from the American moon colony to a location outside of Washington. He's sending copies of the communications by courier. One of them reveals the scheduled departure of the colonists for earth."

"They're returning?" asked Antonov.

"Yes," replied Kornilov. "According to Polevoi, they intend to link up with the American space station in forty-six hours, then return to the Kennedy spaceport at Cape Canaveral on the shuttle *Gettysburg*."

Antonov's face brightened. "Then we still have a chance to stop them?"

Yasenin nodded. "They can be destroyed in deep space before they dock at the space station. The Americans wouldn't dare retaliate after we confront them with the crimes they've committed against us."

"Better to reserve our retribution as leverage," said Kornilov thoughtfully.

"Leverage?"

Kornilov smiled enigmatically. "The Americans have a saying, 'The ball is in our court.' It is they who are on the defensive. The White House and the State Department are probably drafting a reply to our expected protest this minute. I propose we sidestep the accepted routine and remain silent. Do not play the role of a victimized nation. Instead, we use our leverage and cause an event."

"What kind of event?" asked Antonov, straightening with interest.

"The seizure of the vast amount of data carried by the returning moon colonists."

"By what means?" Yasenin demanded.

The smile left Kornilov's face and his expression went dead serious. "We force the *Gettysburg* to crash-land in Cuba."

PART IV

The Gettysburg

49

PITT WAS GOING MAD. The two days of inactivity were the most agonizing he had ever known. There was little for him to do but eat, exercise, and sleep. He had yet to be called on to participate in the training exercises. Hourly, he cursed Colonel Kleist, who bore Pitt's onslaughts with stoic indifference, explaining with tight-lipped patience that his Cuban Special Forces team could not assault Cayo Santa María until he pronounced them fit and ready. And no, he would not speed up the timetable.

Pitt worked off his frustration by taking long swims to the outer reef and climbing a steep rock face whose summit looked out over the surrounding sea.

San Salvador, the smallest of the Bahamas, was known to old mariners as Watling Island, after a zealot buccaneer who flogged members of his crew who did not observe the Sabbath. It is also believed to be the island where Columbus first stepped ashore in the New World. With a picturesque harbor and a lush interior blued by freshwater lakes, few tourists gazing at its beauty would have guessed it contained a huge military training complex and missile observation installation.

The CIA staked out its claim on a remote beach called French Bay at the southern tip of the island. There was no road linking the covert training center with Cockburn Town and the main airport. The only way in or out was by small boat through the surrounding reefs or by helicopter.

Pitt rose shortly before sunrise on the morning of his third day on the island and swam strongly for half a mile, and then worked his way back to shore, free-diving among the coral formations. Two hours later, he walked from the warm water and stretched out on the beach, overwhelmed by a surge of helplessness as he stared over the sea toward Cuba.

A shadow fell across his body, and he sat up. A dark-skinned man stood over him, dressed comfortably in a loose-fitting cotton shirt and shorts. His slick, night-black hair matched an enormous moustache. Sad eyes stared from a face wrinkled from long exposure to wind and sun, and when he smiled his lips barely moved.

"Mr. Pitt?"

"Yes."

"We haven't been formally introduced, but I'm Major Angelo Quintana."

Pitt came to his feet and they shook hands. "You're leading the mission."

Quintana nodded. "Colonel Kleist tells me you've been riding him pretty hard."

"I left friends who may be fighting to stay alive."

"I also left friends in Cuba, Mr. Pitt. Only they lost their battle to live. My brother and father died in prison merely because a member of their local block committee, who owed my family money, accused them of counterrevolutionary activities. I sympathize with your problem, but you do not have a monopoly on grief."

Pitt did not offer condolences. Quintana struck him as a man who didn't dwell on sorrow. "As long as I believe there is still hope," he said firmly, "I'm not about to stop pushing."

Quintana gave him an easy smile. He liked what he saw in Pitt's eyes. This was a man who could be trusted when things got tight. A hardnose who did not know the definition of failure.

"So you're the one who made the ingenious escape from Velikov's headquarters."

"A ton of luck played a heavy role."

"How would you describe the morale of the troops guarding the compound?"

"If you mean mental condition, I'd have to say they were bored to the gills. Russians aren't used to the draining humidity of the tropics. Overall they seemed sluggish."

"How many patrolling the island?"

"None that I could see."

"And the guardhouse at the front gate?"

300

"Only two."

"A canny man, Velikov."

"I gather you respect him for making the island appear deserted."

"You gather right. I would have expected a small army of guards and the usual Soviet security measures. But Velikov doesn't think like a Russian. He designs like an American, refines like a Japanese, and expedites like a German. The man is one shrewd operator."

"So I've heard."

"I'm told you met him."

"We've had a couple of conversations."

"What was your impression of him?"

"He reads the *Wall Street Journal*."

"That all?"

"He speaks better English than I do. His nails are clean and trimmed. And if he's read half the books and magazines in his library he knows more about the United States and its taxpayers than half the politicians in Washington."

"You're probably the only Westerner running around loose who's ever seen him face to face."

"It was no treat, believe me."

Quintana thoughtfully scraped one toe in the sand. "Leaving such a vital installation so lightly guarded is an open invitation for infiltration."

"Not if Velikov knows you're coming," said Pitt.

"Okay, the Cuban radar network and the Russian spy satellites can spot every plane and boat within fifty miles. An air drop or a landing from the sea would be impossible. But an underwater approach could squeeze under their detection grids with ease." Quintana paused and grinned. "In your case the vessel was too tiny to show up on a radarscope."

"My inventory of oceangoing yachts was marginal," Pitt said lightly. Then he turned serious. "You've overlooked something."

"Overlooked what?"

"Velikov's brain. You said he was a shrewd operator. He didn't build a fortress bristling with landmines and concrete bunkers for one simple reason: he didn't have to. You and Colonel Kleist are bleeding optimists if you think a submarine or your SPUD, or whatever you call it, can penetrate his security net."

Quintana's eyebrows narrowed. "Go on."

"Underwater sensors," explained Pitt. "Velikov must have ringed the island with sensors on the sea floor that can detect the movement

301

of a submarine's hull against a water mass and the cavitation of its propellers."

"Our SPUT was designed to slip through such a system."

"Not if Velikov's marine engineers bunched the sensing units a hundred yards apart. Nothing but a school of fish could swim past. I saw the trucks in the compound's garage. With ten minutes' warning Velikov could put a security force on the beach that would slaughter your men before they stepped foot out of the surf. I suggest you and Kleist reprogram your electronic war games."

Quintana subsided into silence. His precisely conceived landing plan began to crack and shatter before his eyes. "Our computers should have thought of that," he said bitterly.

"They don't create what they're not taught," Pitt replied philosophically.

"You realize, of course, this means we have to scrub the mission. Without the element of surprise there isn't the slightest hope of destroying the installation and rescuing Mrs. LeBaron and the others."

"I disagree."

"You think you're smarter than our mission computers?"

"I escaped Cayo Santa María without detection. I can get your people in the same way."

"With a fleet of bathtubs?" Quintana said sarcastically.

"A more modern variation comes to mind."

Quintana looked at Pitt in deep speculation. "You've got an idea that might turn the trick?"

"I most certainly have."

"And still meet the timetable?"

"Yes."

"And succeed?"

"You feel safer if I underwrote an insurance policy?"

Quintana sensed utter conviction in Pitt's tone. He turned and began walking toward the main camp. "Come along, Mr. Pitt. It's time we put you to work."

50

FIDEL CASTRO SAT slouched in the fighting chair and gazed pensively over the stern of a forty-foot cabin cruiser. His shoulders were harnessed and his gloved hands loosely clutched the heavy fiberglass rod, whose line trailed from a huge reel into the sparkling wake. The dolphin bait was snatched by a passing barracuda, but Castro didn't seem to mind. His thoughts were not on marlin.

The muscular body that once earned him the title "Cuba's best school athlete" had softened and expanded with age. The curly hair and the barbed-wire beard were gray now, but the revolutionary fire in his dark eyes still burned as brightly as it did when he came down from the mountains of the Sierra Maestra thirty years ago.

He wore only a baseball cap, swimming trunks, old sneakers, and sunglasses. The stub of an unlit Havana drooped from one corner of his lips. He turned and shielded his eyes from the brilliant tropical sunlight.

"You want me to cease *internacionalismo?*" he demanded above the muffled roar of the twin diesels. "Renounce our policy of spreading Cuba's influence abroad? Is that what you want?"

Raúl Castro sat in a deckchair, holding a bottle of beer. "Not renounce but quietly bring down the curtain on our commitments abroad."

"My brother the hardline revolutionary. What brought on your about-face?"

"Times change," Raúl said simply.

Cold and aloof in public, Fidel's younger brother was witty and congenial in private. His hair was black, slick, and closely trimmed above the ears. Raúl viewed the world from a pixie face through dark, beady eyes. A narrow moustache stretched across his upper lip, the pointed tips ending precisely above the corners of his mouth.

Fidel rubbed the back of one hand against a few drops of sweat that clung to his eyebrows. "I cannot write off the enormous cost in money and the blood of our soldiers. And what of our friends in Africa and the Americas? Do I write them off like our dead in Afghanistan?"

"The price Cuba was paid for our involvement in revolutionary movements outweighs the gains. So we made friends in Angola and Ethiopia. What will they ever do for us in return? We both know the answer is nothing. We have to face it, Fidel, we made mistakes. I'll be the first to admit mine. But for God's sake, let's cut our losses and return to building Cuba into a great socialist nation to be envied by the third world. We'll achieve far more by having them copy our example than by giving them our people's blood."

"You're asking me to turn my back on our honor and our principles."

Raúl rolled the cool bottle across his perspiring forehead. "Let's look at the truth, Fidel. We've thrown principles overboard before when it was in the best interests of the revolution. If we don't shift gears soon and vitalize our stagnating economy, the people's discontent might turn to unrest, despite their love for you."

Fidel spat the cigar stub over the boat's transom and motioned to a deckhand for another. "The U.S. Congress would love to see the people turn against me."

"The Congress doesn't bother me half as much as the Kremlin," said Raúl. "Everywhere I look I find a traitor in Antonov's pocket. I can't even trust my own security people anymore."

"Once the President and I agree to the U.S.–Cuban pact and sign it, our Soviet fair-weather friends will be forced to release their tentacles from around our necks."

"How can you finalize anything when you refuse to sit down and negotiate with him?"

Fidel paused to light a fresh cigar brought by the deckhand. "By now he's probably made up his mind that my offer to sever our links with the Soviet Union in return for United States economic aid and open trade agreements is genuine. If I appear too eager for a meeting, he'll only set impossible preconditions. Let him stew for a while. When he realizes I'm not crawling over the White House doormat, he'll lower his sights."

"The President will be even more eager to come to terms when he learns of the reckless encroachment by Antonov's cronies into our government."

Fidel held up the cigar to make his point. "Exactly why I have sat back and allowed it to happen. Playing on American fears of a Soviet stooge figureheading a puppet regime is all to our advantage."

Raúl emptied the beer bottle and tossed it over the side. "Just don't wait too long, big brother, or we'll find ourselves out of a job."

"Never happen." Fidel's face creased in a cocksure smile. "I am the glue that holds the revolution together. All I have to do is go before the people and expose the traitors and the Soviet plot to undermine our sacred sovereignty. And then, as President of the Council of Ministers, you will announce the cutting of all ties to the Kremlin. Any discontent will be replaced with national rejoicing. With one swing of the ax I'll have cut the massive debt to Moscow and removed the U.S. trade embargo."

"Better be soon."

"In my speech during the Education Day celebration."

Raúl checked the calendar on his watch. "Five days from now."

"A perfect opportunity."

"I'd feel better if we could test the President's mood toward your proposal."

"I'll leave it to you to contact the White House and arrange for a meeting with his representatives during the Education Day festivities."

"Before your speech, I hope."

"Of course."

"Aren't you tempting fate, waiting until the last moment?"

"He'll take me up on it," said Fidel through a cloud of smoke. "Make no mistake. My gift of those three Soviet cosmonauts should have shown him my good intentions."

Raúl scowled. "Could be he has already sent us his reply."

Fidel turned and glared at him. "That is news to me."

"I didn't come to you because it was only a blind guess," said Raúl nervously. "But I suspect the President used Raymond LeBaron's airship to smuggle in an envoy behind the back of Soviet intelligence."

"Good Christ, wasn't it destroyed by one of our patrol helicopters?"

"A stupid blunder," confessed Raúl. "There were no survivors."

Fidel's face mirrored confusion. "Then why is the State Department accusing us of imprisoning Mrs. LeBaron and her crew?"

"I've no idea."

"Why am I kept in the dark on these matters?"

"The report was sent but not read, like so many others. You have become a difficult man to reach, big brother. Your attention to detail is not what it used to be."

Fidel furiously reeled in the line and undid the harness to the fighting chair. "Tell the captain to turn the boat toward the harbor."

"What do you intend to do?"

Fidel cut a wide smile around the cigar. "Go duck hunting."

"Now? Today?"

"As soon as we get to shore I'm going to hole up at my country retreat outside Havana, and you're coming with me. We'll remain secluded, taking no calls and meeting with no one until Education Day."

"Do you think that wise, leaving the President hanging, shutting ourselves off from the Soviet internal threat?"

"What harm can it do? The wheels of American foreign relations turn like the wheels of an ox cart. With his envoy dead, he can only stare at a wall and wait for my next exchange. As for the Russians, the opportunity isn't ripe for them to make their move." He lightly punched Raúl on the shoulder. "Cheer up, little brother. What could possibly happen in the next five days that you and I can't control?"

Raúl vaguely wondered too. He also wondered how he could feel as chilled as a tomb under a blazing Caribbean sun.

Shortly after midnight, General Velikov stood stiffly beside his desk as the elevator doors spread and Lyev Maisky strode into the study.

Velikov greeted him coolly. "Comrade Maisky. An unexpected pleasure."

"Comrade General."

"Can I offer you any refreshments?"

"This damnable humidity is a curse," replied Maisky, wiping a hand over his brow and studying the sweat on his fingers. "I could use a glass of iced vodka."

Velikov picked up a phone and issued a curt order. Then he gestured toward a chair. "Please, make yourself comfortable."

Maisky fell wearily into a soft leather chair and yawned from jet lag. "I'm sorry you weren't warned of my coming, General, but Comrade Polevoi thought it best not to risk interception and decoding of your new instructions by the U.S. National Security Agency's listening facilities."

306

Velikov raised his eyebrow in a practiced motion and gave Maisky a wary stare. "New instructions?"

"Yes, a most complicated operation."

"I hope the chief of the KGB isn't ordering me to postpone the Castro assassination project."

"Not at all. In fact, I've been asked to tell you the ships with the required cargoes for the job will arrive in Havana Harbor half a day ahead of schedule."

Velikov nodded gratefully. "We can use the extra time."

"Have you encountered any problems?" asked Maisky.

"Everything is running smoothly."

"Everything?" Maisky repeated. "Comrade Polevoi was not happy about the escape of one of your prisoners."

"He need not worry. A fisherman found the missing man's body in his nets. The secret of this installation is still secure."

"And what of the others? You must know the State Department is demanding their release from Cuban officials."

"A crude bluff," Velikov replied. "The CIA hasn't a shred of proof the intruders are still alive. The fact that Washington is demanding their release from the Cubans instead of us proves they're shooting in the dark."

"The question is, What are they shooting at?" Maisky paused and removed a platinum cigarette holder from his breast pocket. He lit a long, unfiltered cigarette and exhaled the smoke toward the ceiling. "Nothing must delay Rum and Cola."

"Castro will speak as promised."

"Can you be sure he won't suddenly change his mind?"

"If history repeats itself, we're on firm ground. *El jefe máximo*, the big boss, hasn't turned down a chance to make a speech yet."

"Barring accident, sickness, or hurricane."

"Some things are beyond human control, but I don't intend to fail."

A uniformed guard appeared with a chilled bottle of vodka and a glass resting in a bed of ice. "Only one glass, General? You're not joining me?"

"Perhaps a brandy later."

Velikov waited patiently until Maisky had consumed a third of the bottle. Then he took the leap.

"May I ask the deputy of the First Chief Directorate to enlighten me on this new operation?"

"Of course," Maisky said sociably. "You are to use whatever electronic capability under your command to force the United

States space shuttle down in Cuban territory."

"Did I hear you correctly?" asked Velikov, stunned.

"Your orders, which come from Comrade President Antonov, are to break into the computerized guidance control sensors of the space shuttle *Gettysburg* between its earth reentry and approach to Cape Canaveral and direct it to land on our military airfield at Santa Clara."

Frowning, baffled, Velikov openly stared at Maisky as if the KGB deputy were mad. "If I may say so, that's the craziest scheme the directorate has ever conceived."

"Nevertheless, it has all been worked out by our space scientists," Maisky said airily. He rested his foot on a large accountant's-type briefcase. "The data are all here for programming your computers and training your staff."

"My people are communications engineers." Velikov looked totally lost and sounded the same way. "They don't know anything about space dynamics."

"They don't have to. The computers will do it for them. What is most important is that your equipment here on the island have the capability to override the Houston Space Control Center and take command of the shuttle."

"When is this act supposed to take place?"

"According to NASA, the *Gettysburg* begins her earth reentry roughly twenty-nine hours from now."

Velikov simply nodded his head. The shock had quickly melted away and he regained total control, calm, mind clicking, the complete professional. "Of course, I'll give you every cooperation, but I don't mind saying it will take more than an ordinary miracle to accomplish the unbelievable."

Maisky downed another glass of vodka and dismissed Velikov's pessimism with a wave of the hand. "Faith, General, not in miracles, but in the brains of Soviet scientists and engineers. That's what will put America's most advanced spacecraft on the runway in Cuba."

Giordino stared dubiously at the plate sitting on his lap. "First they feed us slop and now it's sirloin steak and eggs. I don't trust these bastards. They probably spiced it with arsenic."

"A cheap shot to build us up before they tear us down again," said Gunn, ravenously digging into the meat. "But I'm going to ignore it."

"This is the third day the goon in room six has left us alone. Something smells."

"You'd prefer having another rib broken?" Gunn muttered between mouthfuls.

Giordino probed the eggs with his fork, gave in, and tried them. "They're probably fattening us up for the kill."

"I hope to God they've laid off Jessie too."

"Sadists like Gly get turned on beating women."

"Have you ever wondered why Velikov is never present during Gly's punch parties?"

"Typical of the Russians to let a foreigner do their dirty work, or maybe he can't stand the sight of blood. How should I know?"

Suddenly the door was flung open and Foss Gly stepped into the cell. The thick, protruding lips parted in a smile, and the pupils of his eyes were deep, black, and empty.

"Enjoying your dinner, gentlemen?"

"You forgot the wine," Giordino said contemptuously. "And I like my steak medium rare."

Gly stepped closer and, before Giordino could guess his intentions, swung his fist in a vicious backhand against Giordino's rib cage.

Giordino gasped, and his entire body jerked in a convulsive spasm. His face went ashen, and yet, incredibly, he gave a lopsided grin, blood rolling through the hairs of his stubbled chin from where his teeth had bitten his lower lip.

Gunn rose up from his cot on one arm and heaved his plate of food at Gly's head, the eggs spattering the side of the torturer's face, the half-eaten meat scoring a bull's-eye across the mouth.

"A stupid reaction," Gly said, his voice a furious whisper. "One you'll regret." He reached down, grabbed Gunn's shattered ankle, and gave it a sickening twist.

Gunn clenched his fists, eyes glazed in pain, but uttered no sound. Gly stepped back and studied him, seemingly fascinated. "You're tough, very tough, for a little man."

"Crawl back in your hole, slime," Giordino gasped, still catching his breath.

"Stubborn, stubborn," Gly sighed wearily. For a quick second his eyes took on a pensive look, then the black emptiness returned, as cold and evil as if chiseled on a statue. "Ah, yes, you distracted me. I came to deliver news of your friend Dirk Pitt."

"What about him?"

"He tried to escape and was drowned."

"You're lying," said Gunn.

"A Bahamian fisherman found him. The American consulate has already identified the body, or what was left after the sharks were finished with it." Then Gly wiped the egg from his face, removed the steak from Giordino's plate, dropped it on the floor, and ground his boot in it. *"Bon appétit, gentlemen."*

He walked from the cell and locked the door behind him.

Giordino and Gunn looked at each other in long silence, a sudden realization growing within them. Then their faces lit up with broad grins that quickly turned into laughter.

"He did it!" Giordino cried, his elation overcoming his pain. "Dirk made it home free!"

51

THE GLAMOUR EXPERIMENTS on the space station *Columbus* centered on the manufacture of exotic medicines, the growth of pure crystals for computer semiconductor chips, and gamma ray observation. But the bread-and-butter activity of the forty-ton settlement on the fringe of the last frontier was the repair and service of satellites.

Jack Sherman, commander of the station, was in the cylinder-shaped maintenance module helping a team of engineers jockey a satellite into a repair cradle when a voice came through the central speaker. "You available, Jack?"

"I'm here."

"Can you come to the command module?"

"What's up?"

"We've got some joker breaking into our communications channel."

"Pipe it down here."

"Better you should come up."

"Give me a couple of minutes."

The satellite secured and the airlock closed, Sherman peeled off his pressure suit and slipped his boots into a pair of slotted rails. Then he walked in a sliding motion through the weightless environment to the brain center of the station.

His chief communications and electronics engineer simply nodded at his approach. "Listen to this." He spoke into a microphone mounted in a control panel. "Please identify yourself again."

There was a slight pause and then: "*Columbus*, this is Jersey Colony. We request permission to dock at your station."

The engineer turned and looked up at Sherman. "What do you think? Must be some weirdo on earth."

Sherman leaned over the panel. "Jersey Colony, or whatever you call yourself, this is a closed NASA channel. You are interfering with

311

space communications procedures. Please break off."

"No way," came the strange voice. "Our lunar transfer vehicle will rendezvous with you in two hours. Please advise us on docking procedures."

"Lunar what?" Sherman's face tightened in anger. "Houston Control, do you copy?"

"We copy," came a voice from the Houston Space Control Center. "What do you make of it?"

"We're trying to get a fix on it, *Columbus*. Please stand by."

"I don't know who you are, fella," snapped Sherman, "but you're in deep trouble."

"The name is Eli Steinmetz. Please have medical assistance standing by. I have two injured men on board."

Sherman pounded a fist on the back of the engineer's chair. "This is crazy."

"Who am I communicating with?" asked Steinmetz.

"This is Jack Sherman, commander of the *Columbus*."

"Sorry about the abrupt intrusion, Sherman, but I thought you'd been informed of our arrival."

Before Sherman could reply, Houston Control returned. "*Columbus*, his signals are not coming from earth, repeat, not coming from earth. They originate in space beyond you."

"All right, you guys, what's the gag?"

The voice of NASA's director of Flight Operations broke in. "No gag. Jack, this is Irwin Mitchell. Prepare your crew to receive Steinmetz and his colonists."

"What colonists?"

"About time someone from the 'inner core' showed up," said Steinmetz. "For a minute there, I thought we'd have to crash the front gate."

"Sorry, Eli. The President thought it best to keep things quiet until you reached *Columbus*."

"Will someone please tell me what's going on?" Sherman demanded in exasperation.

"Eli will explain when you meet him," answered Mitchell. Then he addressed Steinmetz. "How are the wounded?"

"Resting comfortably, but one will require major surgery. A bullet is lodged near the base of the brain."

"You heard, Jack," said Mitchell. "Alert the crew of the shuttle. They may have to advance their departure."

"I'll take care of it," Sherman said. His voice settled and the tone was calm, but he was far too intelligent not to be bewildered. "Just where in hell does this...this Jersey Colony come from?"

"Would you believe the moon?" Mitchell replied.

"No," said Sherman flatly. "I damned well wouldn't."

The Theodore Roosevelt Room in the West Wing of the White House was once called the Fish Room because it contained aquariums and fishing trophies of Franklin Delano Roosevelt. Under Richard Nixon it was furnished in Queen Anne and Chippendale style and used for staff meetings and occasional press conferences.

The walls and carpet were in light and dark shades of terra-cotta. A painting of the Declaration of Independence hung on the east wall over a carved wooden mantel. Sternly surveying the room from the south wall, Teddy Roosevelt sat astride a horse in a portrait painted in Paris by Tade Styka. The President preferred this intimate room over the more formal Cabinet Room for important discussions partly because there were no windows.

He sat at the head of the conference table and scribbled on a note pad. On his left sat Secretary of Defense Jess Simmons. Next to him came CIA Director Martin Brogan, Dan Fawcett, and Leonard Hudson. Douglas Oates, the Secretary of State, sat immediately to his right, followed by National Security Adviser Alan Mercier and Air Force General Allan Post, who headed up the military space program.

Hudson had spent over an hour briefing the President's men on the history of the Jersey Colony. At first they sat there stunned and silent. Then the excitement set in and they fired a barrage of questions that Hudson fielded until the President ordered lunch served in the room.

The utter astonishment gave way to enthusiastic compliments for Hudson and his "inner core," which slowly faded to grim reality at the report on the conflict with the Soviet cosmonauts.

"Once the Jersey colonists return safely to Cape Canaveral," said the President, "perhaps I can appease Antonov by offering to share some of the immense data accumulated by Steinmetz and his team."

"Why should we give away anything?" demanded Simmons. "They've stolen enough of our technology as it is."

"No denying their thievery," replied the President. "But if our positions were reversed, I wouldn't allow them to get away with killing fourteen of our astronauts."

"I'm on your side, Mr. President," said Secretary of State Oates.

"But if the shoe was indeed on your foot, what course of retribution could you take?"

"Simple," said General Post. "If I were Antonov, I'd order the *Columbus* blasted out of the sky."

"An abhorrent thought, but one we have to take seriously," said Brogan. "The Soviet leaders must feel they have a divine right to destroy the station and everyone on board."

"Or the shuttle and its crew," Post added.

The President stared at the general. "Can *Columbus* and *Gettysburg* be shielded?"

Post gave a slight shake of his head. "Our X-ray laser defense system won't be operational for another fourteen months. While in space, both the station and the shuttle are vulnerable to the Soviet Union's Cosmos 1400 killer satellites. We can provide solid protection for the *Gettysburg* only after she passes through earth's atmosphere."

The President turned to Brogan. "How do you see it, Martin?"

"I don't think they'll target *Columbus*. They'd be leaving themselves wide open for us to retaliate against their new Salyut 10 station. I say they'll try for the shuttle."

An icy silence settled over the Roosevelt Room as every man present struggled with his own thoughts. Then Hudson's face took on an enlightened expression, and he rapped his pen against the table surface.

"We've overlooked something," he said in a level tone.

"Like what?" asked Fawcett.

"The true purpose behind their attack on Jersey Colony."

Brogan took the lead. "To save face by destroying all trace of our breakthrough in space."

"Not destroy but steal," Hudson said fervently. "Murdering the colonists wasn't an eye-for-an-eye punishment. Jess Simmons hit on it. To the Kremlin's way of thinking it was vital to seize the base intact in order to help themselves to the technology, the data, and the results of billions of dollars and twenty-five years of work. That was their goal. Revenge was secondary."

"He makes a valid point," said Oates. "Except that with the colonists on their way to earth, Jersey Colony is up for grabs."

"By using our lunar transfer vehicle we can have another crew on site within two weeks," said Hudson.

"The two cosmonauts who are sitting in Selenos 8," Simmons said.

314

"What's to stop them from simply walking in and taking over the abandoned colony?"

"I'm sorry," Hudson answered. "I forgot to mention that Steinmetz transported the five dead Russians back to the lunar lander and loaded them on board. Then he forced the surviving crew to lift off and return to earth by threatening to scatter them over the moon's surface with the last rocket in his launcher."

"The sheriff cleaning up the town," Brogan said admiringly. "I can't wait to meet this guy."

"Not without cost," said Hudson quietly. "Steinmetz is bringing back two seriously wounded men and one body."

"What is the name of the dead man?" asked the President.

"Dr. Kurt Perry, a brilliant biochemist."

The President nodded at Fawcett. "Let's see that he receives a proper ceremony."

There was a slight pause, and then Post brought the discussion back on track. "Okay, if the Soviets didn't get Jersey colony, what are they left with?"

"The *Gettysburg*," Hudson answered. "The Russians still have a chance at pirating a treasure trove of scientific data."

"By snatching the shuttle out of the air?" Simmons stated sarcastically. "News to me they have Buck Rogers on their side."

"They don't need him," Hudson retorted. "It's technically possible to program a deviation into the flight guidance systems. The computers can be fooled into sending the wrong signal to the drive elevons, the thrusters, and other equipment to control the *Gettysburg*. There are a thousand different way to nudge the shuttle off its course a few degrees. Depending on the distance from touchdown, it could be thrown off as far as a thousand miles from the Kennedy spaceport at Cape Canaveral."

"But the pilots can override the automated system and land on manual control," protested Post.

"Not if they're conned into thinking Houston Control is monitoring their return flight path."

"Is this possible?" asked the President incredulously.

Alan Mercier nodded. "Providing the Soviets have local transmitters with the capacity to overpower the shuttle's internal electronics and jam all signals from Houston Control."

The President exchanged grim looks with Brogan.

"Cayo Santa María," Brogan muttered miserably.

"An island north of Cuba containing a powerful transmission and listening facility with the necessary muscle to do the job," the President explained to the others.

"Maybe they haven't caught on that our colonists have left the moon," Fawcett said hopefully.

"They know," replied Hudson. "Once their eavesdropping satellites were aimed toward Jersey Colony, they've monitored every one of our transmissions."

"We'll have to come up with a plan to neutralize the island's equipment," suggested Post.

Brogan smiled. "Just so happens there is an operation in the works."

Post smiled back. "If you're scheming what I'm thinking, all I'd like to know is *when*."

"There is talk—purely a rumor, mind you—that Cuban military forces are going to launch an attack-and-destroy mission sometime after midnight tonight."

"And the departure time of the shuttle for home?" asked Alan Mercier.

"0500 tomorrow," Post answered.

"That settles it," said the President. "Inform the commander of *Columbus* to hold *Gettysburg* on the docking platform until we can guarantee its safe return."

Everyone around the table seemed satisfied for the moment, except Hudson. He had the look of a boy who had just lost his puppy to the county dogcatcher.

"I just wish," he muttered to no one in particular, "it was all that easy."

52

VELIKOV AND MAISKY stood on a balcony three levels above the electronic listening center and looked down on a small army of men and women who manned the sophisticated electronic receiving equipment. Twenty-four hours a day, giant antennas on Cuba intercepted United States civilian telephone calls and military radio signals, relaying them to Cayo Santa María, where they were fed into the computers for decoding and analysis.

"A truly superb job, General," said Maisky. "The reports on your installation have been far too modest."

"A day doesn't go by when we don't continue the expansion," Velikov said proudly. "Besides the business end of the complex there is a well-supplied dining room and a physical conditioning center with exercise equipment and a sauna. We even have an entertainment room and a barber shop."

Maisky's gaze rose to two screens, each ten by fifteen feet, on different walls. The left screen contained computer-generated displays while the right showed various data and intricate graphs.

"Have your people discovered the status of the moon colonists yet?"

The general nodded and picked up a telephone. He spoke a few words into the receiver while looking down on the busy equipment floor. A staff member at a console looked up and waved a hand. Then the two screens went dark for a brief instant and returned to life with a new data display.

"A complete rundown," said Velikov, pointing to the right screen. "We can monitor almost everything that is transmitted between their astronauts and Houston Control. As you can see, the moon colonists' lunar transporter docked three hours ago at the space station."

Maisky was fascinated as his eyes traveled over the display information. He could not bring himself to accept the fact that American intelligence undoubtedly knew as much if not more about Soviet space efforts.

"Do they transmit in code?" he asked.

"Occasionally, if it is a military mission, but NASA usually talks to their astronauts quite openly."

"As you can see on the data display, the Houston Ground Control Center has ordered the *Gettysburg* to postpone its scheduled departure for tomorrow morning."

"I don't like the look of that."

"I see nothing suspicious. The President probably wants time to mount a massive propaganda campaign to announce another American space triumph."

"Or they may be wise to our intentions." Maisky then became quiet, lost in thought. His eyes had a worried look, and he clasped and unclasped his hands nervously.

Velikov looked at him with amusement. "If this in any way upsets your plans, I could break in on Houston Control's frequency and issue a false command."

"You can do that?"

"I can."

"Simulate an order for the shuttle to depart the space station for reentry?"

"Yes."

"And deceive the commanders of the station and the shuttle into believing they're hearing a familiar voice?"

"They'll never detect the difference. Our computerized synthesizers have more than enough taped transmissions to perfectly imitate voice, accent, and verbal mannerisms of at least twenty different officials of NASA."

"What's to stop Houston Control from countermanding the order?"

"I can scramble their transmissions until it's too late for them to stop the shuttle. Then, if the instructions you gave us from our space scientists are correct, we'll override the craft's flight systems and bring her down at Santa Clara."

Maisky looked at Velikov long and steadily. Then he said, "Do it."

The President was dead asleep when the phone beside his bed softly chimed. He rolled over and read the luminous dial on his

318

wristwatch. Ten minutes after one in the morning. Then he answered. "Go ahead."

The voice that replied was Dan Fawcett's. "Sorry to wake you, Mr. President, but something has come up that I thought you'd want to know about."

"I'm listening. What is it?"

"I've just received a call from Irwin Mitchell at NASA. He said the *Gettysburg* has cast off from *Columbus* and is orbiting in preparation for reentry."

The President sat bolt upright, waking his wife beside him. "Who gave the order?" he demanded.

"Mitchell can't say. All communication between Houston and the space station is down because of some strange interference."

"Then how has he confirmed the shuttle's departure?"

"General Fisher has been tracking and monitoring *Columbus* at the Space Operations Center in Colorado Springs since Steinmetz left Jersey Colony. The sensitive cameras at the center caught the movement when *Gettysburg* left the station's dock. He called me as soon as he was informed."

The President pounded the mattress in dismay. "Damn!"

"I took the liberty of alerting Jess Simmons. He's already scrambled two Air Force tactical squadrons into the air to fly escort and protect the shuttle as soon as she drops through the atmosphere."

"How much time do we have before the *Gettysburg* lands?"

"From initial descent preparation to touchdown, about two hours."

"The Russians are behind this."

"The general consensus," acknowledged Fawcett. "We can't be sure yet, but all indications point to Cuba as the source of Houston's radio interference problem."

"When does Brogan's special team hit Cayo Santa María?"

"0200 hours."

"Who's leading them in?"

"One moment while I look up the name in yesterday's CIA report." Fawcett left the line for no more than thirty seconds before he returned. "The mission is being directed by Marine Colonel Ramon Kleist."

"I know the name. Kleist was a Congressional Medal of Honor winner."

"Here's something else."

"What?"

"Kleist's men are being guided by Dirk Pitt."

The President sighed almost sadly. "He's already given too much. Is his presence absolutely required?"

"It was Pitt or nobody," said Fawcett.

"Can they destroy the jamming center in time?"

"In all honesty, I'd have to say it's a toss-up."

"Tell Jess Simmons to stand by in the War Room," said the President solemnly. "If anything goes wrong, I fear the only alternative left for us to keep the *Gettysburg* and her valuable cargo out of Soviet hands is to shoot her down. Do you read me, Dan?"

"Yes, sir," Fawcett said, his face suddenly white. "I'll give him your message."

53

"ALL STOP," ORDERED KLEIST. He rechecked the readings on the Navstar satellite instrument and tapped a pair of dividers on a flattened chart. "We're seven miles due east of Cayo Santa María. This is close as we dare move the SPUT."

Major Quintana, wearing mottled gray and black battle dress, stared at the yellow mark on the chart. "Should take us about forty minutes to swing around to the south and land from the Cuban side."

"The wind is calm and the sea is only running at two feet. Another blessing is no moon. It's pitch black topside."

"Good as well as bad news," said Quintana heavily. "Makes us tough to spot, but we won't be able to see any wandering guards either. Our main problem, as I see it, is not having an exact fix on the compound. We could land miles from it."

Kleist turned and stared at a tall, commanding figure leaning against a bulkhead. He was dressed in the same night battle fatigues as Quintana. The piercing green eyes met Kleist's stare.

"You still can't pinpoint the location?"

Pitt straightened, smiled his congenial indifferent smile, and said simply, "No."

"You're not very encouraging," Quintana said nastily.

"Maybe, but at least I'm honest."

Kleist spoke with forbearance. "We regret, Mr. Pitt, that visual conditions were not ideal during your escape. But we'd be grateful if you were a bit more specific."

Pitt's smile faded. "Look, I landed in the middle of a hurricane and left in the middle of the night. Both events took place on the opposite side of the island from where we're supposed to land. I didn't measure distances, nor did I sprinkle breadcrumbs along my trail. The land was flat, no hills or streams for landmarks. Just palm

321

trees, brush, and sand. The antenna was a half mile west of the village. The compound, a good mile beyond. Once we strike the road the compound will be to the left. That's the best I can offer."

Quintana gave a resigned nod. "Under the circumstances we can't ask for more than that."

A crewman dressed sloppily in cutaway jeans and T-shirt stepped through the hatchway into the control room. He silently handed a decoded communication to Kleist and left.

"Better not be a last-minute cancellation," Pitt said sharply.

"Far from it," Kleist muttered. "More like a new twist."

He studied the message a second time, a frown crossing his normally impassive face. He handed it to Quintana, who stared at the wording and then tightened his lips in annoyance before passing the paper to Pitt. It read:

SPACE SHUTTLE GETTYSBURG HAS DEPARTED STATION AND ORBITING IN PREPARATION FOR REENTRY. ALL CONTACT LOST. YOUR TARGET'S ELECTRONICS HAVE PENETRATED GUIDANCE COMPUTERS AND TAKEN COMMAND. EXPECT COURSE DEVIATION TO SET CRAFT DOWN IN CUBA AT 0340. SPEED CRITICAL. DIRE CRISIS IF COMPOUND NOT DESTROYED IN TIME. LUCK.

"Nice of them to warn us at the last minute," said Pitt grimly. "0340 is less than two hours away."

Quintana looked at Kleist severely. "Can the Soviets actually do this thing and get away with it?"

Kleist wasn't listening. His gaze returned to the chart and he made a little pencil line that marked a course to the southern shore of Cayo Santa María. "Where approximately do you put the antenna?"

Pitt took the pencil and made a tiny dot on the sperm-shaped island at the base of the tail. "A wild guess at best."

"All right. We'll equip you with a small waterproof radio sender and receiver. I'll convert the position on the chart and program it into the Navstar computer, then maintain a fix on your signal and guide you in."

"You won't be the only one who can put a fix on us."

"A small gamble, but one that will save valuable time. You should be able to blow the antenna and cut off their radio command of the *Gettysburg* much faster than fighting your way inside the compound and destroying its brain center."

"Makes sense."

322

"Since you agree," said Kleist quietly, "I suggest you gentlemen shove off."

The special-purpose underwater transporter looked nothing like any submarine Pitt had ever seen. The craft was slightly over three hundred feet long and shaped like a chisel turned sideways. The horizontal wedgelike bow tapered quickly to an almost square hull that ended abruptly at a boxed-off stern. Her upper deck was completely smooth without any projections.

No man stood at her helm. She was totally automated with nuclear power that turned twin propellers or, when required, soundless pumps that took in water from the forward momentum and thrust it silently through vents along the sides.

The SPUT was specifically designed for the CIA to support covert arms smuggling, undercover agent infiltration, and hit-and-run raids. She could travel as deep as eight hundred feet at fifty knots, but also had the capability of running onto a beach, spreading her bows, and disgorging a two-hundred-man landing force with several vehicles.

The ship broke the surface, her flat deck only two feet above the black water. Quintana's team of Cuban exiles scrambled from the hatches and quickly began lifting the water Dashers that were passed up from below.

Pitt had ridden a Dasher at a resort in Mexico. A water-propulsion vehicle, it was manufactured in France for seaside recreation. Called the sports car of the sea, the sleek little machine had the look of two torpedoes attached side by side. The operator lay back with each leg stretched out in one of the twin hulls and controlled the movement with an automobile-type steering wheel. Power came from a high-performance battery that could propel the craft by means of water jets over smooth seas at twenty knots for three hours before recharging.

After Pitt proposed using them to cruise under the Cuban radar network, Kleist hurriedly negotiated a special purchase from the factory and arranged to have them flown by Air Force transport to San Salvador within fifteen hours.

The early morning air was warm and a light rain squall passed over. As each man slipped into his Dasher, he was shoved across the wet deck, over the low freeboard, and into the sea. Shaded blue lights had been mounted in the sterns so each man could follow the one in front.

Pitt took a few moments and stared into the darkness toward Cayo Santa María, desperately hoping he wasn't too late to save his friends. An early gull wheeled crying over his head, invisible in the murky sky.

Quintana gripped him by the arm. "You're next." He paused and stared through the gloom. "What in hell is that?"

Pitt held up a wooden shaft in one hand. "A baseball bat."

"What do you need that for? You were issued an AK-74."

"It's a gift for a friend."

Quintana shook his head in bewilderment. "Let's get going. You'll lead off. I'll bring up the rear and catch stragglers."

Pitt nodded and eased into his Dasher and adjusted a tiny receiver in one ear. Just before the SPUT crew pushed him over the side Colonel Kleist bent down and shook Pitt's hand. "Get them to the target," he said tensely.

Pitt gave him a sober grin. "I aim to."

Then his Dasher was in the water. He adjusted the power lever to half speed and eased clear of the ship. There was no use in turning to check if the others were following. He couldn't have seen them anyway. The only light came from the stars, and they were too dim to sparkle the water.

He increased speed and studied the luminescent dial of the compass strapped to one wrist. He maintained a heading of due east until Kleist's voice came through his earpiece: "Bear 270 degrees."

Pitt made the correction and kept on the course for ten miles, keeping a few knots below the Dasher's full speed to allow the men behind to close up if they strayed out of line. He was certain the sensitive underwater sensors would pick up the raiding party's approach, but he counted on the Russians to dismiss the readings on their recording instruments as a school of fish.

A long way off to the south toward Cuba, a good four miles perhaps, a searchlight from a patrol boat blazed on and swept the water like a scythe, cutting the night, searching for intruding vessels. The far-off glow dimly lit them up, but they were two small and low in the water to be seen at that distance.

Pitt received a new bearing from Kleist, and altered course to the north. The night was as dark as a crypt, and he could only hope the other thirty men were hugging his stern. The Dasher's twin bows dipped into a series of rising waves, tossing spray into his face, and he tasted the strong saltiness of the sea.

The slight turbulence from the Dasher's passage through the water caused flecks of sparkling phosphorus that briefly flashed like an armada of fireflies before dying in his wake. Pitt was finally beginning to relax a bit when Kleist's voice came through his ear again: "I put you about two hundred yards from shore."

Pitt slowed his little boat and eased ahead cautiously. Then he stopped, drifting with the current. He waited, eyes strained against the dark, tense and listening. Five minutes went by, and Cayo Santa María's outline vaguely loomed ahead, black and ominous. The surf was nearly nonexistent on the inside waters of the island, and its soft lapping on the beach was the only sound he could hear.

He gently pressed the power pedal and went forward dead slow, ready to turn hard and speed out to sea if they were detected. Seconds later, the Dasher bumped noiselessly into the sand. Immediately Pitt stepped out and dragged the light craft across the beach and into the underbrush beneath a line of palm trees. Then he waited until Quintana and his men rose up like wraiths and silently grouped around him in a tight knot, indistinct blurs in the gloom, thankful to a man their feet were on solid land again.

As insurance against Murphy's law, Quintana took precious time to account for every man and briefly check his equipment. Finally satisfied, he turned to Pitt. "After you, amigo."

Pitt took a reading from the compass, and then led the way inland on a slight angle to his left. He held the baseball bat out in front of him like a blind man with a cane. Less than two hundred feet from the staging area, the end of the bat met with the electrified fence. He stopped abruptly and the man in his rear bumped into him.

"Easy!" Pitt hissed. "Pass it on, we're at the fence."

Two men with shovels came forward and attacked the soft sand. In no time they had excavated a hole that was large enough to push a small burro through.

Pitt crawled under first. For a moment he was uncertain which way he should go. He hesitated, sniffing at the wind. Then, suddenly, he knew exactly where he was.

"We screwed up," he murmured to Quintana. "The compound is only a few hundred yards to our left. The antenna is a good mile in the opposite direction."

"How can you tell?"

"Use your nose. You can smell exhaust fumes from the diesel engines that run the generators."

Quintana inhaled deeply. "You're right. A breeze is carrying it from the northwest."

325

"So much for a quick solution. It'll take your men a good half hour to reach the antenna and set the charges."

"Then we'll go for the compound."

"Safer to play both ends against the middle. Send your strongest runners to blow the antenna and the rest of us will try for the electronics center."

Quintana took less than a second to make up his mind. He went through the ranks and quickly selected five men. He returned with a small, indistinct figure whose head hardly reached Pitt's shoulders.

"This is Sergeant López. He'll need directions to the antenna."

Pitt stripped the compass off his wrist and handed it to the sergeant. López didn't speak English and Quintana had to translate. The little sergeant was a quick study. He repeated Pitt's instructions flawlessly in Spanish. Then López flashed a smile, gave a curt order to his men, and vanished into the night.

Pitt and the rest of Quintana's force took off at a run. The weather began to deteriorate. Clouds blanketed the stars, and the raindrops that splattered against the palm fronds made a strange drumming sound. They wound through trees gracefully curved from the fury of hurricane winds. Every few yards someone stumbled and fell but was helped up by others. Soon their breathing came more heavily and the sweat flowed down their bodies and soaked their battle fatigues. Pitt set a fast pace, driven on by desperate anticipation of finding Jessie, Giordino, and Gunn still alive. His mind remained remote from the discomfort and growing exhaustion by envisioning the agonies Foss Gly must have inflicted on them. His ugly thoughts were interrupted when he stepped out of the underbrush onto the road.

He turned left toward the compound, making no attempt at stealth or concealment, using the flat surface to make time. The feel of the land felt more familiar to Pitt now. He slowed to a walk and whispered for Quintana. When he felt a hand on one shoulder, he gestured at a dim light barely visible through the trees. "The guardhouse at the gate."

Quintana slapped Pitt's back in acknowledgment and gave instructions in Spanish to the next man in line, who slipped away toward the light.

Pitt didn't have to ask. He knew the security guards manning the gate had only another two minutes to live.

He skirted the wall and crept into the culvert, vastly relieved to find the bars still bent as he had left them. They scrambled through and wormed their way to the air vent above the compound's motor pool. This was as far as Pitt was supposed to go. Kleist's firm instructions were for him to guide Quintana's force to the air vent and go no further. He was to step out of the way, return alone to the landing beach, and wait for the others to withdraw.

Kleist should have guessed that when Pitt offered no argument the orders were not about to be carried out, but the colonel had too many problems on his mind to become suspicious. And good old Pitt, quite naturally, had been the very model of cooperation when he laid out a diagram of the entry into the compound.

Before Quintana could reach out and stop him, Pitt dropped through the vent onto the support girder over the parked vehicles and disappeared like a shadow down the exit shaft to the cells far below.

54

DAVE JURGENS, flight commander of the *Gettysburg*, was mildly disturbed. He shared the elation with everyone in the space station at the unexpected arrival of Steinmetz and his men from the moon. And he found nothing amiss in the sudden orders to carry the colonists to earth as soon as their scientific cargo could be loaded into the shuttle's payload bay.

What disturbed him was the abrupt demand by Houston Control to make a night landing at Cape Canaveral. His request to wait a few hours until the sun rose was met with a cold refusal. He was given no reason why NASA officials had suddenly reversed their strict policy of daylight touchdowns for the first time in nearly thirty years.

He looked over at his copilot, Carl Burkhart, a twenty-year veteran of the space program. "We won't have much of a view of the Florida swamps on this approach."

"You see one alligator, you've seen them all," the laconic Burkhart replied.

"Our passengers all tucked in?"

"Like corn in a bin."

"Computers programmed for reentry?"

"Set and ticking."

Jurgens briefly scanned the three TV screens in the center of the main panel. One gave the status on all the mechanical systems, while the other two gave data on trajectory and guidance control. He and Burkhart began to run through the de-orbit and entry procedure checklist.

"Ready when you are, Houston."

"Okay, Don," replied ground control. "You are go for de-orbit burn."

"Out of sight, out of mind," said Jurgens. "Is that it?"

"We don't read, come again."

328

"When I left earth, my name was Dave."

"Sorry about that, Dave."

"Who's on the line?" asked Jurgens, his curiosity aroused.

"Merv Foley. You don't recognize my resonant vowel sounds?"

"After all our scintillating conversations, you've forgotten my name. For shame."

"A slip of the tongue," said the familiar voice of Foley. "Shall we cut the small talk and get back to procedures."

"Whatever you say, Houston." Jurgens briefly pressed his intercom switch. "Ready to head home, Mr. Steinmetz?"

"We're all looking forward to the trip," Steinmetz answered.

In the Spartan living quarters below the flight deck and cockpit the shuttle specialists and Jersey colonists were packed together in every foot of available space. Behind them the sixty-foot-long payload bay was loaded two-thirds full with data records, geological specimens, cases containing the results of more than a thousand medical and chemical experiments—the bonanza accumulated by the colonists that would take scientists two decades to fully analyze. The bay also carried the body of Dr. Kurt Perry.

The *Gettysburg* was traveling through space backward and upside down at over 15,000 knots per hour. The small reaction-control jets were fired and joggled the craft over from orbit as thrusters pitched it to a nose-high attitude so the insulated belly could absorb the reentry friction of the atmosphere. Over Australia, two secondary engines burned briefly to slow the shuttle's orbit speed from twenty-five times the speed of sound. Thirty minutes later, they hit the atmosphere shortly before Hawaii.

As the atmosphere grew denser, the heat turned the *Gettysburg's* belly a vivid orange. The thrusters lost their effectiveness and the elevons and the rudder began to clutch the heavier air. The computers controlled the entire flight. Jurgens and Burkhart had little to do except monitor the TV data and systems indicators.

Suddenly a warning tone sounded in their headsets and a master alarm light came on. Jurgens quickly reacted by punching a computer keyboard to call up details of the problem while Burkhart notified ground control.

"Houston, we have a warning light."

"We read nothing here, *Gettysburg*. All systems look great."

"Something is going on, Houston," persisted Burkhart.

"Can only be computer error."

"Negative. All three navigation and guidance computers agree."

"I have it," said Jurgens. "We're showing a course error."

The cool voice at the Johnson Space Center returned. "Disregard, Dave. You're right on the beam. Do you copy?"

"I copy, Foley, but bear with me while I go to the backup computer."

"If it will make you happy. But all systems are go."

Jurgens quickly punched a request for navigation data from the backup computer. Less than thirty seconds later he hailed Houston.

"Merv, something's fishy. Even the backup shows us coming down four hundred miles south and fifty east of Canaveral."

"Trust me, Dave," Foley said in a bored tone. "All tracking stations show you on course."

Jurgens looked out his side window and saw only blackness below. He switched off his radio and turned to Burkhart. "I don't give a damn what Houston says. We're off our approach course. There's nothing but water under us when we should be seeing lights over the Baja California peninsula."

"Beats me," said Burkhart, shifting restlessly in his seat. "What's the plan?"

"We'll stand by to take over manual control. If I didn't know better, I'd swear Houston was setting us down in Cuba."

"She's coming in like a kite on a string," said Maisky, his expression wolfish.

Velikov nodded. "Three more minutes and the *Gettysburg* will be past the point of no return."

"No return?" Maisky repeated.

"To bank and still glide to the runway at the Kennedy Space Center."

Maisky rubbed the palms of his hands together in nervous anticipation. "An American space shuttle in Soviet hands. This has to be the intelligence coup of the century."

"Washington will scream like a village of raped virgins, demanding we return it."

"They'll get their billion-dollar super-machine back. But not before our space engineers have explored and photographed every square inch of her."

"And then there's the wealth of information from their moon colonists," Velikov reminded him.

330

"An incredible feat, General. The Order of Lenin will be in this for you."

"We're not out of the woods yet, Comrade Maisky. We cannot predict the President's reaction."

Maisky shrugged. "His hands are tied if we offer to negotiate. Our only problem as I see it is the Cubans."

"Not to worry. Colonel General Kolchak has placed a screen of fifteen hundred Soviet troops around the runway at Santa Clara. And, since our advisers are in command of Cuba's aircraft defenses, the shuttle has a clear path to land."

"Then she's as good as in our hands."

Velikov nodded. "I think you can safely say that."

The President sat in a bathrobe behind his desk in the Oval Office, chin lowered, elbows on the arms of his chair. His face was tired and drawn.

He looked up abruptly and said, "Is it certain, Houston can't make contact with the *Gettysburg?*"

Martin Brogan nodded. "That's the word from Irwin Mitchell at NASA. Their signals are being drowned out by outside interference."

"Is Jess Simmons standing by at the Pentagon?"

"We have him on a direct line," answered Dan Fawcett.

The President hesitated, and when he spoke it was in a whisper. "Then you'd better tell him to order the pilots in those fighters to stand by."

Fawcett nodded gravely and picked up the phone. "Any word from your people, Martin?"

"The latest is they've landed on the beach," Brogan said helplessly. "Beyond that, nothing."

The President felt weighted with despair. "My God, we're trapped in limbo."

One of four phones rang and Fawcett snatched it up. "Yes, yes, he's here. Yes, I'll tell him." He replaced the receiver in its cradle, his expression grim. "That was Irwin Mitchell. The *Gettysburg* has deviated too far south to reach Cape Canaveral."

"She might still make a water landing," said Brogan without enthusiasm.

"Providing she can be warned in time," added Fawcett.

The President shook his head. "No good. Her landing speed is

331

over two hundred miles an hour. She'd tear herself to pieces."

The others stood silent, searching for the right words. The President swiveled in his chair and faced the window, sick at heart.

After a few moments he turned to the men standing expectantly around his desk. "God help me for signing a death warrant on all those brave men."

55

PITT DROPPED OUT of the exit shaft and hit the corridor at a dead run. He twisted the handle and threw open the door to the cell that housed Giordino and Gunn with such a force that he nearly tore it from the hinges.

The tiny room was empty.

The noise betrayed him. A guard rushed around the corner from a side passage and stared at Pitt in astonishment. That split-second hesitation cost him. Even as he was lifting the barrel of his weapon, the baseball bat caught him on the side of the head. Pitt had grabbed the unfortunate guard around the waist and was dragging him into a convenient cell before he hit the floor. Pitt threw him on a bed and looked down into the face of the young Russian who had escorted him to Velikov's study. The boy was breathing normally, and Pitt figured the damage was no more than a concussion.

"You're lucky, kid. I never shoot anyone under the age of twenty-one."

Quintana was just coming out of the exit shaft as Pitt locked the guard in the cell and took off running again. He did not bother to be careful of concealing his presence. He would have welcomed the chance to bash the head of another guard. He reached the door to Jessie's cell and kicked it open.

She was missing too.

Dread swept through him like a wave. He plunged on through the corridors until he came to room six. There was nothing inside but the stench of torture.

Dread was replaced by cold, ungovernable rage. Pitt became someone else, a man without conscience or moral code, no longer in control of his emotions, a man for whom danger was merely a force to be ignored. Fear of dying had totally ceased to exist.

Quintana hurried up to Pitt and clutched his arm. "Damn you, get back to the beach! You know the orders—"

He got no further. Pitt shoved the stubby barrel of the AK-74 into Quintana's gut and slowly pushed him back and against a wall. Quintana had stood face to face with death many times before this moment, but staring at the ice-cold expression on the craggy face, seeing the pure look of murderous indifference in the green eyes, he knew he had one foot in a coffin.

Pitt did not speak. He pulled back the gun, raised the baseball bat to his shoulder, and pushed his way through Quintana's men. Suddenly he halted in his tracks and turned back. "The elevator is this way," he said quietly.

Quintana motioned his men to follow. Pitt took a fast head count. There were twenty-five, including himself. He hurried toward the elevator that rose to the upper levels. No more guards appeared in their way. The passages were deserted. With the prisoners dead, Pitt reasoned, Velikov probably saw no purpose in stationing more than one guard in the lower storage area.

They reached the elevator and he was about to push the Up button when the motors began to hum. He motioned everyone against the wall. They waited, listening to the elevator stop at a level above, hearing a murmur of voices and soft laughter. They stood frozen and watched the interior light shine through the crack between the doors as it descended.

It was all over in ten seconds. The doors opened and two technicians in white coats stepped outside and died without the slightest whisper of a sound from knives thrust into their hearts. Pitt was amazed at the efficiency of the act. None of the Cubans wore the slightest expression of remorse in their eyes.

"Decision time," said Pitt. "The elevator can hold only ten men."

"Only fourteen minutes until the space shuttle lands," Quintana said urgently. "We've got to find and cut off the compound's power source."

"There are four levels above us. Velikov's study is on the top. So are the living quarters. Take your pick of the other three."

"Like drawing to an inside straight."

"What else," Pitt said quickly. "We're also bunched-up fish in a barrel. My advice is to split up into three groups and take each level. You'll cover more territory faster."

"Sounds good," Quintana hastily agreed. "We've come this far with-

334

out a greeting. They won't be expecting visitors to pop up on the inside at the same time in different areas."

"I'll go with the first eight men to level two and send the elevator down for the next team, who will hit level three, and so on."

"Fair enough." Quintana wasted no time arguing. He hurriedly selected eight men and ordered them into the elevator with Pitt. Just before the doors closed he snapped, "You stay alive, damn you!"

The ride up seemed endless. None of the men looked into the eyes of the others. A few dabbed at the sweat trickling down their faces. Some scratched at imagined itches. All had a finger poised on a trigger.

At last the elevator settled to a stop and the door parted. The Cubans poured out into an operations room staffed by nearly twenty Soviet GRU officers and four women who were also in uniform. Most died behind their desks in a hail of gunfire, dying in dazed disbelief. In a few seconds the office resembled a charnel house with blood and tissue sprayed everywhere.

Pitt took no time to see more. He punched the Level 1 button on the panel and rose alone in the elevator to Velikov's study. Pressing his back against the front wall, weapon in the raised position, he stole one quick glance around the opening doors. The sight inside the study struck him with a mixed force of elation and savage anger.

Seven GRU officers were siting in a semicircle, watching in rapt fascination as Foss Gly performed his sadistic act. They seemed oblivious to the muted thump of gunfire from the level below, their senses deadened, Pitt concluded, by the emptied contents of several wine bottles.

Rudi Gunn lay off to one side, his face nearly battered into pulp, trying desperately out of some burning pride to hold up his head in contempt. One officer held a small automatic pistol on a bleeding Al Giordino who was tied in a metal chair. The brawny little Italian sagged forward with his head almost on his knees, shaking it slowly from side to side as if to clear his vision and rid himself of the pain. One of the men lifted his leg and kicked Giordino in the side, knocking him and the chair sideways to the floor. Raymond LeBaron sat beside and slightly behind Gly. The once dynamic financier had the look of a man who was worn to a shadow, his spirit torn from his body. The eyes were sightless, the face expressionless. Gly had pressured and twisted him into a decaying vegetable.

Jessie LeBaron knelt in the center of the room, staring at Gly in defiance. Her hair had ben crudely lopped short. She clutched a blanket around her shoulders. Ugly red welts and dark bruises covered her exposed legs and arms. She looked to be beyond suffering, her mind deadened to any further pain. Despite her pitiful appearance she was incredibly beautiful, with a serenity and poise that were remarkable.

Foss and the other men turned at the arrival of the elevator, but seeing that it was apparently empty, they turned back to their sport.

Just as the doors began to close Pitt stepped into the room with an almost inhuman icy calm, his AK-74 held at eye level, the muzzle erupting fire.

His first carefully aimed shots took the man who had kicked Giordino onto the floor. The second blast struck the chest of the bemedaled officer seated next to Gunn, pitching him backward into a bookcase. The third and fourth bursts swept away three men sitting in a tight group. He was swinging the gun barrel in an arc, lining up on Foss Gly, but the massively built turncoat reacted more quickly than the others.

Gly yanked Jessie to her feet and held her in front of him as a shield. Pitt delayed just long enough for the seventh Russian, who was sitting almost at his elbows, to unholster an automatic pistol and snap off a wild shot.

The bullet struck the breech of Pitt's gun, shattered it, and then ricocheted into the ceiling. Pitt raised the useless weapon and sprang at the same moment he saw the muzzle flash from the second shot. Everything seemed to slow down. Even the frightened expression on the Russian's face as he squeezed the trigger for the third time, but the blast never came. The frame of the AK-74 sliced the air and caved the side of his head in.

At first Pitt thought the second bullet had missed, but then he felt the blood dripping down his neck from the nick taken out of his left ear. He stood there rooted, his fury still burning as Gly rudely shoved Jessie sprawling on the carpet.

A satanic grin spread across Gly's evil face along with an expression of unholy expectation. "You came back."

"Very perceptive—for a cretin, that is."

"I promised you would die slowly when we met again," said Gly menacingly. "Have you forgotten?"

"No, I didn't forget," said Pitt. "I even remembered to bring a big club."

Pitt had no doubts that Gly meant to crush the life out of him with his massive hands. And he knew that his only real advantage, besides the bat, was a total lack of fear. Gly was used to seeing his victims helpless and naked, intimidated by his brute strength. Pitt's lips matched the satanic grin, and he began to stalk Gly, observing with cold satisfaction the look of confusion in his opponent's eyes.

Pitt went into a baseball crouch and swung the bat, aiming for a low pitch, and struck Gly in the knee. The blow smashed Gly's kneecap and he grunted in pain but didn't go down. He recovered in the blink of an eye and lurched at Pitt, receiving a blow in the ribs that knocked the breath from his body with an agonized gasp. For a moment he stood still warily watching Pitt, feeling the broken ribs, sucking painful intakes of air.

Pitt stepped back and lowered the bat. "Does the name Brian Shaw do anything for you?" he asked calmly.

The twisted look of hate slowly changed to puzzlement. "The British agent? You knew him?"

"Six months ago, I saved his life on a tugboat in the Saint Lawrence River. Remember? You were crushing him to death when I came up from behind and brained you with a wrench."

Pitt relished the savage glare in Gly's eyes.

"That was you?"

"A final thought to take with you," Pitt said, smiling fiendishly.

"The confession of a dead man." There was no contempt, no insolence in Gly's voice, just simple belief.

Without another word the two men began circling each other like a pair of wolves, Pitt with the bat raised, Gly dragging his injured leg. An eerie quiet settled over the room. Gunn struggled through a sea of pain to reach the fallen automatic pistol, but Gly caught the movement out of the corner of one eye and kicked the gun aside. Still tied to the chair, Giordino struggled weakly against his bonds in helpless frustration, while Jessie lay rigid, staring in morbid fascination.

Pitt took a step forward and was in the act of swinging when one foot slipped in the blood of a slain Russian. The bat should have caught Gly on the side of his head, but the arc was thrown off by six inches. On reflex Gly threw up his arm and absorbed the impact with king-size biceps.

The wooden shaft quivered in Pitt's hands as if he had struck it against a car bumper. Gly lashed out with his free hand, grabbed the end of the bat, and heaved like a weightlifter. Pitt gripped the handle for dear life as he was lifted into the air like a small child and slung halfway across the room against a wall of bookshelves, where he crashed to the floor amid an avalanche of leather-bound volumes.

Sadly, despairingly, Jessie and the others knew Pitt could never shake off the jarring collision with the wall. Even Gly relaxed and took his time about approaching the body on the floor, triumph fairly glowing on his gargoyle face, lips spread in sharkish anticipation of the extermination to come.

Then Gly stopped and stared incredulous as Pitt rose up from under a mountain of books like a quarterback who had been sacked, dazed, and slightly disoriented but ready for the next play. What Pitt knew, and no one else realized, was that the books had cushioned his impact. He hurt like hell but suffered no crippling damage to flesh and bone. Lifting the bat he moved to meet the advancing iron man, and rammed the blunt end with all his strength into the sneering face.

But he misjudged the giant's unholy strength. Gly side-stepped and met the bat with his fist, knocking it aside and taking advantage of Pitt's forward momentum to clench iron arms around his back. Pitt twisted violently and brought his knee up into Gly's groin, a savage blow that would have doubled over any other man. But not Gly. He gave a slight gasp, blinked, and then increased the pressure in a vicious bear hug that would crush the life out of Pitt.

Gly stared unblinking into Pitt's eyes from a distance of four inches. There wasn't the slightest display of physical exertion on his face. The only expression was the sneer that was locked in place. He lifted Pitt from his feet and kept squeezing, anticipating the contorted terror that would spread across his victim's face just before the end.

The air was choked off from Pitt's lungs and he gasped for breath. The room began to blur as the pain inside his chest ruptured into flaming agony. He could hear Jessie screaming, Giordino shouting something, but he couldn't distinguish the words. Through the pain his mind remained curiously sharp and clear. He refused to accept death and coldly devised a simple way to cheat it.

One arm was free, while the other, the one still clutching the baseball bat, was caught in Gly's relentless grip. The black curtain was beginning to drop over his eyes for the last time, and he realized death was only seconds away when he performed his last desperate act.

He brought up his hand until it was even with Gly's face and thrust the full length of the thumb into one eye, driving inward through the skull and twisting deeply into the brain.

338

Shock wiped the sneer off Gly's face, the shock of atrocious pain and unbelief. The dark features contorted in an anguished mask, and he instinctively released his arms from around Pitt and threw his hands up to his eye, filling the air with a horrible scream.

In spite of the terrible injury, Gly remained on his feet, thrashing around the room like a crazed animal. Pitt could not believe the monster was still alive, he almost believed Gly was indestructible — until a deafening roar drowned the agonized cries.

Once, twice, three times, calmly and quite coldly, Jessie pulled the trigger on the fallen automatic pistol and shot Foss Gly in the groin. The shells thudded into him, and he staggered backward a few steps, then stood grotesquely for a few moments as if held by puppet strings. Finally he collapsed and crashed to the floor like a falling tree. The one eye was still open, black and as evil in death as it had been in life.

56

MAJOR GUS HOLLYMAN was flying scared. A career Air Force pilot with almost three hundred hours of flight time, he was suffering acute pangs of doubt, and doubt was one of a pilot's worst enemies. Lack of confidence in himself, his aircraft, or the men on the ground could prove deadly.

He couldn't bring himself to believe his mission to shoot down the space shuttle *Gettysburg* was anything more than a crazy exercise dreamed up by some egghead general with a fetish for far-out war games. A simulation, he told himself for the tenth time, it had to be a simulation that would terminate at the last minute.

Hollyman stared up at the stars through the canopy of the F-15E night attack fighter and wondered if he could actually obey an order to destroy the space shuttle and all those on board.

His eyes dropped to the instruments that glowed on the panel in front of him. His altitude was just over 50,000 feet. He would have less than three minutes to close on the rapidly descending space shuttle and lock in before firing a radar-guided Modoc missile. He automatically went through the procedure in his mind, hoping it would get no further than a mental event.

"Anything yet?" he asked his radar observer, a gum-chewing lieutenant named Regis Murphy.

"Still out of range," replied Murphy. "The last update from the space center in Colorado puts her altitude at twenty-six miles, speed approximately six thousand and slowing. She should reach our sector in five minutes, forty seconds, at a speed of twelve hundred."

Hollyman turned and scanned the black sky behind, spotting the faint exhaust glow of the two aircraft following his tail. "Do you copy, Fox Two?"

"Roger, Fox Leader."

"Fox Three?"

"We copy."

A cloud of oppression seemed to fill Hollyman's cockpit. None of this was right. He hadn't dedicated his life to defending his country, hadn't spent years in intensive training, simply to blast an unarmed aircraft carrying innocent scientists out of the air. Something was horribly wrong.

"Colorado Control, this is Fox Leader."

"Go ahead, Fox Leader."

"I request permission to terminate exercise, over."

There was a long pause. Then: "Major Hollyman, this is General Allan Post. Do you read me?"

So this was the egghead general, Hollyman mused. "Yes, General, I read you."

"This is not an exercise. I repeat, this is not an exercise."

Hollyman did not mince words. "Do you realize what you're asking me to do, sir?"

"I'm not asking, Major. I'm giving you a direct order to bring down the *Gettysburg* before she lands in Cuba."

There had been no time for a full briefing when Hollyman was ordered to scramble his flight into the air. He was stunned and bewildered at Post's sudden revelation. "Forgive me for asking, General, but are you acting by higher command? Over."

"Is a directive straight from your Commander in Chief in the White House good enough for you?"

"Yes, sir," he said slowly. "I guess it is."

God, Hollyman thought despairingly, there was no getting around it.

"Altitude twenty-two miles, nine minutes to touchdown." Burkhart was reading off the instruments for Jurgens. "We've got lights off to our right."

"What's going down, Houston?" asked Jurgens, his face set in a frown. "Where in hell are you putting us?"

"Stay cool," replied the impassive voice of Flight Director Foley. "You're lined up just fine. Just sit tight and we'll bring you in."

"Radar and navigation indicators say we're touching down in the middle of Cuba. Please cross-check."

"No need, *Gettysburg*, you're on final approach."

"Houston, I'm not getting through to you. I repeat, where are you setting us down?"

There was no reply.

"Listen to me," said Jurgens in near desperation. "I'm going to full manual."

"Negative, Dave. Remain in auto. All systems are committed to the landing site."

Jurgens clenched his fists in futility. "Why?" he demanded. "Why are you doing this?"

There was no reply.

Jurgens looked over at Burkhart. "Move the speed brakes back to zero percent. We're going on TAEM.* I want to keep this ship in the air as long as I can until we get some straight answers."

"You're only prolonging the inevitable by a couple of minutes," said Burkhart.

"We can't just sit here and accept this."

"It's out of our hands," Burkhart replied miserably. "We've no place else to go."

The real Merv Foley sat at a console in the Houston control center in helpless rage. His face, the color of chalk, showed an expression of incredulity. He pounded a fist against the edge of the console.

"We're losing them," he muttered hopelessly.

Irwin Mitchell of the "inner core" stood directly behind him. "Our communications people are doing the best they can to get through."

"Too damned late!" Foley burst out. "They're on final approach." He turned and grabbed Mitchell by the arm. "For Christ's sake, Irv, beg the President to let them land. Give the shuttle to the Russians, let them take whatever they can get out of it. But in the name of God don't let those men die."

Mitchell stared up dully at the data display screens. "Better this way," he said, his voice vague.

"The moon colonists—those are your people. After all they've achieved, the years of struggling just to stay alive in a murderous environment, you can't simply write them off this close to home."

"You don't know those men. They'd never allow the results of their efforts to be given away to a hostile government. If I was up there

*Terminal-area energy management, a process for conserving speed and altitude.

and Eli Steinmetz was down here, he wouldn't hesitate to blow the *Gettysburg* to ashes."

Foley looked at Mitchell for a long moment. Then he turned away and buried his head in his hands, stricken with grief.

57

Jessie lifted her head and gazed at Pitt, the coffee-brown eyes misted, teardrops rolling past the bruises on her cheeks. She was shuddering now, shuddering from the death around her and immense relief. Pitt unashamedly embraced her, saying nothing, and gently removed the gun from her hand. Then he released her, quickly cut Giordino's bonds, gave Gunn a reassuring squeeze on the shoulder, and stepped up to the huge wall map.

He rapped his knuckles against it, gauging the thickness. Then he moved back and lashed out with his foot at the center of the Indian Ocean. The hidden panel gave way, swung on its hinges, and smashed against the wall.

"I'll be back," he said, and disappeared into a passageway.

The interior was well lit and carpeted. He rushed incautiously, the gun held out in front of him. The passage was air-conditioned and cool, but the sweat was flowing through his pores more heavily than ever before. He rubbed a sleeve over his forehead, blocking his view for a brief moment, and almost died.

At that exact moment he reached a cross passage, and like a scene from an old Mack Sennett silent movie he collided with two guards who were walking around the corner.

Pitt crashed through them, knocking them to the sides, then whirled and dropped to the floor. The advantage of surprise was on his side. The guards hadn't expected to meet a foe so close to General Velikov's study. Pitt did. The automatic in his hand spat four times before the startled guards had a chance to trigger their rifles. He leaped to his feet while they were still falling.

For two seconds, perhaps three—it seemed an hour—he stared at the inert figures, curiously unaffected by their death but stunned that it all happened so fast. Mentally and emotionally he was exhausted,

344

physically he felt reasonably fit. He sucked in deep lungfuls of air until his mind struggled through the haze, and he turned it to figuring which passage ran toward the electronic center of the compound.

The side passages had concrete floors, so he stuck with the one with the carpet and forged ahead. He had run only fifty feet when his brain cells finally came back on line and he cursed his sluggishness for not thinking to snatch one of the guard's rifles. He pulled out the clip of the automatic. It was empty, only one shell remained in the chamber. He wrote off the mistake and kept going.

It was then he saw a backwash of light ahead and heard voices. He slowed and ghosted up to a portal and peered out with the wariness of a mouse peeking from a knothole for a cat.

Six feet away was a railing on a balcony overlooking a vast room crammed with banks of computers and consoles stretched in neat rows beneath two large data display screens. At least ten technicians and engineers sat and calmly monitored the array of electronics while another five or six stood in agitated conversation.

The few uniformed guards who were present were crouched at one end of the room, their rifles aimed at a heavy steel door. A barrage of gunfire was coming from the other side, and Pitt knew Quintana and his men were about to break through. Now he was really sorry he hadn't taken the guns from the dead guards. He was about to turn and run back for them when a thunderous roar engulfed the room, followed by a great shower of dust and debris as the shattered door twisted crazily and burst into jagged fragments.

Before the cloud settled, the Cubans charged through the opening, guns blazing. The first three inside the room went down from the fire of the guards. Then the Russians seemed to melt away before the murderous onslaught. The din inside the concrete-walled room was deafening, but even so, above it all Pitt could hear the screams of the wounded. Most of the technicians hid under their consoles. Those who resisted were unmercifully shot down.

Pitt moved out along the balcony, keeping his back flattened against the wall. He saw two men standing about thirty feet away, staring in rapt horror at the carnage below. He recognized one of them as General Velikov and began edging closer, stalking his prey. He had only moved a short distance when Velikov pulled back from the balcony railing and turned. He looked at Pitt blankly for an instant, and his eyes widened in recognition, and then incredibly he smiled. The man seemed to have no nerves at all.

Pitt raised the automatic and took deliberate aim.

Velikov moved with the swiftness of a cat, jerking the other man in front of him, a fraction of a second before the hammer fell on the cartridge.

The bullet caught Lyev Maisky in the chest. The deputy chief of the KGB stiffened in shock and stood there staring in petrified astonishment before staggering backward and tumbling over the railing to the floor below.

Pitt unconsciously pulled the trigger again, but the gun was empty. In a futile gesture he threw it at Velikov, who easily deflected it with an arm.

Velikov nodded, his face revealing more curiosity than fear. "You're an amazing man, Mr. Pitt."

Before Pitt could reply or take a step, the general lurched sideways through an open door and slammed it shut. Pitt threw himself against the door, but he was too late. The lock was on the inside and Velikov had snapped the latch. There would be no kicking this one in. The heavy bolt was firmly embedded in a metal frame. He raised his fist to punch the door, thought better of it, swung around and ran down a stairway to the floor below.

He crossed the room through the confusion, stepping over the bodies until he reached Quintana, who was emptying the magazine of his AK-74 into a bank of computers.

"Forget that!" Pitt shouted in Quintana's ear. He gestured to the radio console. "If your men haven't destroyed the antenna, let me try to make contact with the shuttle."

Quintana lowered his rifle and looked at him. "The controls are in Russian. Can you operate it?"

"Never know till I try," said Pitt. He sat at the radio console and quickly studied the confusing sea of lights and switches labeled in the Cyrillic alphabet.

Quintana leaned over Pitt's shoulder. "You'll never find the right frequency in time."

"You Catholic?"

"Yes. Why?"

"Then call up the saint who guides lost souls and pray this thing is already set on the shuttle's frequency."

Pitt placed the tiny headset over one ear and kept pressing switches until he received a tone. Then he adjusted the microphone and pressed what he guessed and fervently hoped was the Transmit switch.

"Hello, *Gettysburg*, do you read me? Over." Then he pushed what he was sure was the Receive switch.

Nothing.

He tried a second, and a third. "*Gettysburg*, do you read? Over."

He pushed a fourth switch. "*Gettysburg. Gettysburg*, please respond," Pitt implored. "Do you read me? Over."

Silence, and then: "This is *Gettysburg*. Who the hell are you? Over."

The sudden reply, so clear and distinct, surprised Pitt, and he took nearly three seconds to answer.

"Not that it matters, the name is Dirk Pitt. For the love of God, *Gettysburg*, sheer off. I repeat, sheer off. You are on a glide path for Cuba."

"So what else is new?" said Jurgens. "I can only keep this bird in the air a few more minutes and must make a touchdown attempt at the nearest landing strip. We've run out of options."

Pitt did not reply immediately. He closed his eyes and tried to think. Suddenly something clicked in his mind.

"*Gettysburg*, can you possibly make Miami?"

"Negative. Over."

"Try for the Key West Naval Air Station. It lies at the tip of the Keys."

"We copy. Our computers show it one hundred ten miles north and slightly east of us. Very doubtful. Over."

"Better to pile it up in the water than hand it to the Russians."

"That's easy for you to say. We've got over a dozen people on board. Over."

Pitt wrestled with his conscience for a moment, struggling whether or not to play God. Then he said urgently, "*Gettysburg*, go for it! Go for the Keys."

He couldn't have known it but Jurgens was about to make the same decision. "Why not? What have we got to lose but a billion-dollar airplane and our lives. Keep your fingers crossed."

"When I go off the air you should be able to reestablish communications with Houston," said Pitt. "Good luck, *Gettysburg*. Come home safe. Out."

Pitt sat there, drained. There was a strange silence in the devastated room, a silence only intensified by the low moans of the wounded. He looked up at Quintana and smiled thinly. His part in the act was over, he thought vaguely, all that was left was to gather up his friends and return home.

But then his mind recalled the La Dorada.

58

THE *GETTYSBURG* MADE A FAT target as she glided quietly through the night. There was no glow from the exhaust pods of her dead engines, but she was lit from bow to tail by flashing navigation lights. She was only a quarter of a mile ahead and slightly below Hollyman's attack fighter. He knew now that nothing could save the shuttle and the men inside. Her fiery end was only seconds away.

Hollyman went through the mechanical motions of planning his attack. The visual displays on his forward panel and windshield showed the necessary speed and navigation data along with the status and firing cues of his missile delivery systems. A digital computer automatically tracked the space shuttle, and he had little to do except press a button.

"Colorado Control, I am locked on target."

"Roger, Fox Leader. Four minutes to touchdown. Begin your attack."

Hollyman was torn by indecision. He felt such a wave of revulsion that he was temporarily incapable of movement, his mind sick with the realization of the terrible act he was about to commit. He had nurtured a forlorn hope the whole thing was some horrible mistake and the *Gettysburg*, like a condemned convict about to be executed in an old movie, would be saved by a last-minute reprieve from the President.

Hollyman's distinguished career in the Air Force was finished. Despite the fact he was carrying out orders, he would forever be branded as the man who blasted the *Gettysburg* and her crew out of the sky. He experienced a fear and an anger he had never known before.

He could not accept his lot as hard luck, or that fate chose him to play executioner. He softly cursed the politicians who made the military decisions, and who had brought him to this moment.

"Repeat, Fox Leader. Your transmission was garbled."

"Nothing, Control. It was nothing."

"What is your delay?" asked General Post. "Begin your attack immediately."

Hollyman's fingers hovered over the fire button. "God forgive me," he whispered.

Suddenly the digits on his tracking display began to change. He studied them briefly, drawn by curiosity. Then he stared at the space shuttle. It appeared to be rolling.

"Colorado Control!" he shouted into his microphone. "This is Fox Leader. *Gettysburg* has broken off her approach heading. Do you copy? *Gettysburg* is banking left and turning north."

"We copy, Fox Leader," replied Post, relief evident in his voice. "We have the course change on our tracking display. Take up position and stay with shuttle. Those guys are going to need all the moral support they can get."

"With pleasure," said Hollyman gleefully. "With pleasure."

A pall of silence hung over the Johnson Space Center control room. Unaware of the near-fatal drama played out by the Air Force, the ground team of four controllers and a growing crowd of NASA scientists and administrators hung in a purgatory of gloom. Their tracking network displayed the sudden turn to the north by the shuttle, but it could have merely indicated a roll or an S-turn in preparation for landing.

Then with startling abruptness, Jurgens' voice cracked the silence. "Houston, this is *Gettysburg*. Do you read? Over."

The control room erupted in a pandemonium of cheering and applause. Merv Foley reacted swiftly and replied. "Roger, *Gettysburg*. Welcome back to the fold."

"Am I talking to the real Merv Foley?"

"If there are two of us, I hope they catch the other guy quick before he signs our names to a lot of checks."

"You're Foley, all right."

"What is your status, Dave? Over."

"Are you tracking?"

"All systems have been go except communications and guidance control since you departed the space station."

"Then you know our altitude is 44,000 feet, speed 1,100. We're going to try for a touchdown at Key West Naval Air Station, over."

Foley looked up at Irwin Mitchell, his face strained.

Mitchell nodded and lightly tapped Foley's shoulder. "Let's pull out all the stops and bring those guys home."

"She's a good four hundred miles outside the cross-range," said Foley dejectedly. "We've got a hundred-ton aircraft with a descent rate of 10,000 feet a minute on a glide slope seven times steeper than a commercial airliner's. We'll never do it."

"Never say never," Mitchell replied. "Now tell them we're getting on it. And try to sound cheerful."

"Cheerful?" Foley took a few seconds to brace himself, and then he pressed the Transmit switch. "Okay, Dave, we're going to work on the problem and get you to Key West. Are you on TAEM? Over."

"Affirmative. We're pulling every trick in the book to conserve altitude. Our normal pattern approach will have to be deleted to extend our reach, over."

"Understood. All air and sea rescue units in the area are being alerted."

"Might not be a bad idea to let the Navy know we're dropping in for breakfast."

"Will do," Foley said. "Stand by."

He punched in tracking data on the display screen of his console. The *Gettysburg* was dropping past 39,500 feet, and she still had eighty miles to go.

Mitchell walked over, his eyes staring at the trajectory display on the giant wall screen. He adjusted his headset and called Jurgens.

"Dave, this is Irwin Mitchell. Go back to auto. Do you copy? Over."

"I copy, Irv, but I don't like it."

"Better the computers handle this stage of the approach. You can go back to manual ten miles from touchdown."

"Roger, out."

Foley looked up at Mitchell expectantly. "How close?" was all he asked.

Mitchell took a deep breath. "Paper thin."

"They can do it?"

"If the wind doesn't get temperamental, they stand a hairline chance. But if it veers into a five-knot crosswind, they buy the farm."

There was no fear in the cockpit of the *Gettysburg*. There was no time for it. Jurgens followed the descent trajectory on the computer

350

display screens very closely. He flexed his fingers like a piano player before a concert, anxiously awaiting the moment he took over manual control for the final landing maneuvers.

"We've got an escort," said Burkhart.

For the first time, Jurgens turned his eyes from the instruments and gazed out the windows. He could just make out an F-15 fighter flying alongside about two hundred yards away. As he watched, the pilot switched on his navigation lights and waggled his wings. Two other aircraft in formation followed suit. Jurgens reset his radio to a military frequency.

"Where did you guys come from?"

"Just cruising the neighborhood for girls and spotted your flying machine," answered Hollyman. "Anything we can do to assist? Over."

"Got a towrope? Over."

"Fresh out."

"Thanks for hanging around, out."

Jurgens felt a small measure of comfort. If they fell short of Key West and had to ditch, at least the fighters could stand by and guide rescuers to their position. He turned his attention back to the flight indicators and idly wondered why Houston hadn't put him in communication with the Key West Naval Air Station.

"What in hell do you mean Key West is shut down?" Mitchell shouted at a white-faced engineer standing at his side, who was holding a phone. Without waiting for an answer, Mitchell grabbed the receiver. "Who am I talking to?" he demanded.

"This is Lieutenant Commander Redfern."

"Are you fully aware of the seriousness of this situation?"

"It has been explained, sir, but there is nothing we can do. A fuel tanker crashed into our power lines earlier this evening and blacked out the field."

"What about your emergency generators?"

"The diesel-engine power source ran fine for about six hours and then failed from a mechanical problem. They're working on it now and should have it back in service in an hour."

"That's too damned late," Mitchell snapped. "The *Gettysburg* is two minutes away. How can you guide them in on the final approach?"

"We can't," answered the commander. "All our equipment is shut down."

351

"Then line the runway with car and truck headlights, anything that will illuminate the surface."

"We'll do our best, sir, but with only four men on flight line duty this time of the morning it won't be much. I'm sorry."

"You're not the only one who's sorry," Mitchell grunted, and slammed down the phone.

"We should have the runway on visual by now," said Burkhart uneasily. "I see the city lights of Key West but no sign of the air station."

For the first time, a faint gleam of sweat appeared on Jurgens' brow. "Damned odd we haven't heard from their control tower."

At that moment, Mitchell's strained voice broke in. "*Gettysburg*, Key West station has a power outage. They are making an effort to light the runway with vehicles. We are directing your approach from the east to land on a westerly heading. Your runway is seven thousand feet. If you overshoot you wind up in a recreation park. Do you copy? Over."

"Roger, Control. We copy."

"We show you at 11,300 feet, Dave. Speed 410. One minute, ten seconds and six miles to touchdown. You are go for full manual, over."

"Roger, going to manual."

"Do you have the runway on visual?"

"Nothing yet."

"Excuse the interruption, *Gettysburg*." It was Hollyman cutting in on the NASA frequency. "But I think my boys and I can play Rudolph to your sleigh. We'll go ahead and light the way, over."

"Much obliged, little buddy," said Jurgens gratefully.

He watched as the F-15s accelerated past, dropped their noses, and pointed them toward Key West. They fell into line as if playing follow the leader and switched on their landing lights. At first the brilliant rays only reflected on water, and then they lit up a salt flat before sweeping up the naval air station runway.

The effort of concentration showed on Jurgens' face. The shuttle went right where he aimed it, but it was never meant to soar through the air like a paper glider. Burkhart read out the airspeed and altitude so Jurgens could center his attention on flying.

"*Gettysburg*, you are three hundred feet under minimum," said Foley.

"If I pull up another inch, she'll stall."

The runway seemed to take forever to grow larger. The shuttle

352

was only four miles out, but it looked like a hundred. Jurgens believed he could make it. He had to make it. Every brain cell in his skull willed the *Gettysburg* to hang in the air.

"Speed 320, altitude 1,600, three miles to runway," reported Burkhart. His voice had a trace of hoarseness.

Jurgens could see the flashing lights from the fire and rescue equipment now. The fighters were hovering above him, shining their landing lights on the concrete ribbon 1.5 miles long by 200 feet wide.

The shuttle was eating up her glide slope. Jurgens flared her out as much as he dared. The landing lights glinted on the shoreline no more than ninety feet below. He held on to the last possible second before he pushed the switch and deployed the landing gear. Normal landing procedure required the wheels to touch 2,760 feet down the runway, but Jurgens held his breath, hoping against hope that they would even reach the concrete.

The salt flat flashed past under the blinding beams and was lost in the darkness behind. Burkhart gripped his seat rests and droned off the diminishing numbers.

"Speed 205. Main gear at ten feet...five feet...three feet...two feet...one, contact."

The four huge tires of the main landing gear thumped on the hard surface and protested at the sudden friction with a puff of smoke. A later measurement would show that Jurgens touched the shuttle down only forty-seven feet from the end of the runway. Jurgens gently pitched the bow down until the nose wheel made contact and then pushed both brake pedals. He rolled the spacecraft to a stop with a thousand feet to spare.

"They made it!" Hollyman whooped over his radio.

"*Gettysburg* to Houston Control," said Jurgens with an audible sigh. "The wheels have stopped."

"Magnificent! Magnificent!" shouted Foley.

"Congratulations, Dave," added Mitchell. "Nobody could have done it better."

Burkhart looked over at Jurgens and said nothing, simply gave a thumbs-up sign.

Jurgens sat there, his adrenaline still flowing, basking in his triumph over the odds. His weary mind began to wander and he found himself wondering who Dirk Pitt was. Then he pressed the intercom switch.

"Mr. Steinmetz."

"Yes, Commander?"

"Welcome back to earth. We're home."

353

59

PITT TOOK ONE QUICK comprehensive look as he stepped back into Velikov's study. Everyone was kneeling, clustered around Raymond LeBaron, who was stretched out on the floor. Jessie was holding his hand and murmuring to him. Gunn looked up at Pitt's approach and shook his head.

"What happened?" Pitt asked blankly.

"He jumped to his feet to help you and caught the bullet that cut your ear," Giordino replied.

Before kneeling, Pitt stared down a moment at the mortally wounded millionaire. The clothing that covered the upper abdomen bloomed in a spreading stain of crimson. The eyes still had life and were focused on Jessie's face. His breath came in rapid and shallow pants. He tried to raise his head and say something to her, but the effort was too great and he fell back.

Slowly Pitt sank on one knee beside Jessie. She turned and looked at him with tears trickling down her discolored cheeks. He stared back at her briefly without speaking. He could think of nothing to say to her, his mind was played out.

"Raymond tried to save you," she said huskily. "I knew they could never completely turn him inside out. In the end he came back."

LeBaron coughed, a strange rasping kind of cough. He gazed up at Jessie, his eyes dulled, face white and drained of blood. "Take care of Hilda," he whispered. "I leave everything in your hands."

Before he could say more, the room trembled as the rumble of explosives came from deep below; Quintana's team had begun destroying the electronic equipment inside the compound. They would have to leave soon, and there would be no taking Raymond LeBaron with them.

Pitt thought of all the newspaper stories and magazine articles glorifying the dying man on the carpet as a steel-blooded power merchant who could make or break executive officers of giant corporations or high-level politicians in government, a wizard at manipulating the financial markets of the world, a vindictive and cold man whose trail was littered with the bones of competing businesses he had crushed and their thousands of employees who were cast out on the streets. Pitt had read all that, but all he saw was a dying old man, a paradox of human frailty, who had stolen his best friend's wife and then killed him for a fortune in treasure. Pitt could feel no pity for such a man, no flicker of emotion.

Now the slender thread holding LeBaron on to life was about to break. He leaned over and placed his lips close to the old power broker's ear.

"La Dorada," Pitt whispered. "What did you do with her?"

LeBaron looked up, and his eyes glistened for an instant as his clouding mind took a final look at the past. His voice was faint as he summoned up the strength to answer. The words came almost as he died.

"What did he say?" asked Giordino.

"I'm not sure," replied Pitt, his expression bewildered. "It sounded like 'Look on the main sight.'"

To the Cubans across the bay on the main island the detonations sounded like distant thunder and they paid no attention. No spouting volcano of red and orange lit the horizon, no fiery column of flame reaching hundreds of feet through the black sky attracted their curiosity. The sounds came strangely muffled as the compound was destroyed from within. Even the belated destruction of the great antenna went without notice.

Pitt helped Jessie to the staging area on the beach, followed by Giordino and Gunn, who was carried on a stretcher by the Cubans. Quintana joined them and dropped all caution as he shined a pencil-thin flashlight in Pitt's face.

"You'd better get a patch on that ear."

"I'll survive until we reach the SPUT."

"I had to leave two men behind, buried where they'll never be found. But there are still more going out than came in. Some of you will have to double up on the water Dashers. Dirk, you carry Mrs. LeBaron. Mr. Gunn can ride with me. Sergeant López can—"

"The sergeant can ride alone," Pitt interrupted.

"Alone?"

"We left a man behind too," said Pitt.

Quintana quickly swept the narrow beam at the others. "Raymond LaBaron?"

"He won't be coming."

Quintana gave a slight shrug, bowed his head at Jessie, and said simply, "I'm sorry." Then he turned away and began assembling his men for the trip back to the mother ship.

Pitt held Jessie close to him and spoke gently. "He asked you to take care of his first wife, Hilda, who still lives."

He couldn't see the surprise on her face, but he could feel her body tense.

"How did you know?" she asked incredulously.

"I met and talked with her a few days ago."

She seemed to accept that and did not ask him how he came to be at the rest home. "Raymond and I went through the ceremony and played out our roles as man and wife, but he could never completely give up or divorce Hilda."

"A man who loved two women."

"In different, special ways. A tiger in business, a lamb on the home front, Raymond was lost when Hilda's mind and body began to deteriorate. He desperately needed a woman to lean on. He used his influence to fake her death and place her in a rest home under a former married name."

"Your cue to walk on the scene." He did not like being cold, but he was not sorry.

"I was already part of his life," she said without hurt. "I was one of the senior editors of the *Prosperteer*. Raymond and I had carried on an affair for years. We felt comfortable together. His proposal bordered on a business proposition, a staged marriage of convenience, but it soon grew into more, much more. Do you believe that?"

"I've no talent for rendering verdicts," Pitt replied quietly.

Quintana detached himself from the shadows and touched Pitt's arm. "We're moving out. I'll take the radio receiver and lead off." He moved close to Jessie and his voice softened. "Another hour and you'll be safe. Do you think you can hold on a little longer?"

"I'll be fine. Thank you for your concern."

The Dashers were dragged across the beach and set in the water. At Quintana's command everyone mounted and set off across the black water. This time Pitt brought up the rear as Quintana, headset in place, homed in on the SPUT from headings transmitted by Colonel Kleist.

They left an island of dead in their wake. The huge compound was reduced to great broken slabs of concrete that crumbled inward. The vast array of electronic equipment and the ornate furnishings smoldered like the dying core of a volcano deep beneath the sun-bleached coral sand. The giant antenna lay in a thousand twisted pieces, shattered beyond any possible repair. Within hours hundreds of Russian soldiers, led by agents of the GRU, would be crawling over the ruins, searching and sifting the sands for incriminating evidence of the forces responsible for the destruction. But the only bits and pieces their probing investigation would turn up pointed directly to the cunning mind of Fidel Castro and not the CIA.

Pitt kept his eyes locked on the shaded blue light of the Dasher straight in front of him. They were going against the tide now and the tiny craft nosed into the wave troughs and bounced over the crests like a roller coaster. Jessie's added weight slowed their speed, and he kept the accelerator pressed against its stop to keep from falling behind.

They had only traveled about a mile when Pitt felt one of Jessie's hands loosen from his waist.

"Are you all right?" he asked.

His answer was the feel of a cold gun muzzle against his chest just beneath the armpit. He dipped his head very slowly and looked down under his arm. There was indeed the black outline of an automatic pistol pressed into his rib cage, a 9-millimeter Makarov, and the hand that held it was rock steady.

"If I'm not being too forward," he said in genuine surprise, "may I ask what's on your mind?"

"A change in plan," she replied, her voice low and tense. "Our job is only half done."

Kleist paced the deck of the SPUT as Quintana's team of raiders were lifted on board and the Dashers quickly stowed through a large hatch and down a ramp to the cavernous cargo bay. Quintana circled the ship, riding herd until there was no one left in the water; only then did he climb onto the low deck.

"How did it go?" Kleist asked anxiously.

"As they say on Broadway, a smash hit. The destruction was complete. You can tell Langley the GRU is off the air."

"Nice work," said Kleist. "You'll receive a fat bonus and long vacation. Courtesy of Martin Brogan."

"Pitt deserves a major share of the credit. He led us straight into the parlor before the Russians woke up. He also went on the radio and warned off the space shuttle."

"Unfortunately, there are no brass bands for part-time help," said Kleist vaguely. Then he asked, "And what of General Velikov?"

"Presumed dead and buried in the rubble."

"Any casualties?"

"I lost two men." He paused. "We also lost Raymond LeBaron."

"The President won't be happy when he hears that news."

"More of an accident really. He made a very brave but foolhardy attempt to save Pitt's life and was shot for his effort."

"So the old bastard went out a hero." Kleist stepped to the edge of the deck and peered into the darkness. "And what of Pitt?"

"A slight wound, nothing serious."

"And Mrs. LeBaron?"

"A few days' rest and some cosmetics to cover the bruises, and she'll look as good as new."

Kleist turned briskly. "When did you see them last?"

"When we left the beach. Pitt was carrying her on his Dasher. I kept the speed low so they could keep up."

Quintana couldn't see it, but Kleist's eyes turned fearful, fearful with the sudden realization that something was terribly amiss. "Pitt and Mrs. LeBaron have not come on board."

"They must have," Quintana said uneasily. "I'm the last one in."

"Neither has been accounted for," said Kleist. "They're still out there somewhere. And since Pitt didn't carry the radio receiver on the return trip, we can't guide them home."

Quintana put a hand to his forehead. "My fault. I was responsible."

"Maybe, maybe not. If something went wrong, if his Dasher broke down, Pitt would have called out, and you would have surely heard him."

"We might pick them up on radar," Quintana offered hopefully.

Kleist doubled his fists and rapped them together. "We'd better hurry. It's suicide to drift around here much longer."

He and Quintana hurried down the ramp to the control room. The radar operator was sitting in front of a blank scope. He looked up as the two officers flanked his sides, their faces strained.

"Raise the antenna," ordered Kleist.

358

"We'll be targeted by every radar unit on the Cuban coast," the operator protested.

"Raise it!" Kleist demanded sharply.

Topside, a section of the deck parted and a directional antenna unfolded and rose on the top of a mast that telescoped nearly fifty feet into the sky. Below, six pairs of eyes watched as the screen glowed into life.

"What are we looking for?" asked the operator.

"Two of our people are missing," answered Quintana.

"They're too small to show on the screen."

"What about computer enhancement?"

"We can try."

"Go for it."

After half a minute, the operator shook his head. "Nothing within two miles."

"Increase the range to five."

"Still nothing."

"Go to ten."

The operator ignored the radar screen and stared intently at the enhanced computer display. "Okay, I have a tiny object that's a possible. Nine miles southwest, bearing two-two-two degrees."

"They must be lost," muttered Kleist.

The radar operator shook his head. "Not unless they're blind or plain stupid. The skies are clear as crystal. Any tenderfoot Boy Scout knows where the North Star lies."

Quintana and Kleist straightened and stared at each other in mute astonishment, unable to fully comprehend what they knew to be true. Kleist was the first to ask the inescapable question.

"Why?" he asked dumbly. "Why would they deliberately go to Cuba?"

PART V

The Amy Bigalow

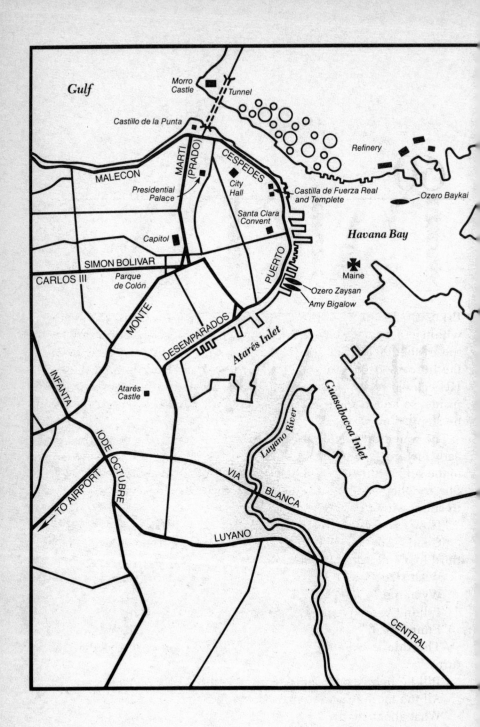

Gulf

Morro
Castle

Tunnel

Castillo de la Punta

MALECON

MARTI
(PRADO)

CESPEDES

City
Hall

Refinery

Presidential
Palace

Castilla de Fuerza Real
and Templete

Ozero Baykai

Santa Clara
Convent

Havana Bay

Capitol

SIMON BOLIVAR

PUERTO

CARLOS III

Parque
de Colón

Maine

MONTE

Ozero Zaysan

Amy Bigalow

DESEMPARADOS

Atarés Inlet

INFANTA

Atarés
Castle

Guasabacoa Inlet

Luyano River

IODE OCTUBRE

VIA
BLANCA

TO AIRPORT

LUYANO

CENTRAL

60

PITT AND JESSIE EVADED a prowling Cuban patrol boat and were within a thousand yards of the Cuban shoreline when the battery on the Dasher died. He pulled the drain plugs, and they swam away as the little sport craft slipped under the sea and sank to the bottom. His combat boots were a tight fit and allowed little water to seep inside, so he left them on, well aware they would be essential once he stepped on shore.

The water felt comfortably warm and the waves remained low. An early morning quarter-moon slipped over the horizon two hours ahead of the sun. With the added light Pitt could easily keep Jessie in view. She coughed as if she had taken in some water but appeared to be treading without effort.

"How's your backstroke?" he asked.

"Good." She sputtered and spit for a moment and said, "I took third in an all-state high school meet."

"What state?"

"Wyoming."

"I didn't know Wyoming had a swimming pool."

"Funny man."

"The tide is running in our favor, so let's get moving before it turns."

"It'll be light soon," she said.

"All the more reason to make shore and find cover."

"What about sharks?"

363

"They never breakfast before six o'clock," he said impatiently. "Now come on, no more talk."

They set off with the elementary backstroke, arms thrown back, legs thrusting in a whip kick. The incoming tide pushed them along at close to a knot, and they made good time. Jessie was a strong swimmer. She matched Pitt stroke for stroke, staying right alongside him. He marveled at her endurance after all she had been through the past six days and felt pity for the aches and exhaustion he knew she was suffering. But he could not allow her to slack off now, not until they reached shore and found a small measure of safety.

She had not offered a reason for forcing him to turn for Cuba, and Pitt had not asked. He didn't have to be clairvoyant to know she had a definite purpose in mind that went beyond mere insanity. This lady had very definite ideas and the stubbornness to back them up. He could have disarmed her by capsizing the Dasher during a fast turn on the down slope of a wave, and he was also reasonably certain she wouldn't have pulled the trigger if he had refused.

But it was business as usual for Pitt. "In for a penny, in for a pound / It's love that makes the world go round." Only he wasn't in love—attracted, yes, but not swept away. Curiosity overrode any passionate urge. He could never resist sticking his foot through a door to the unknown. And then there was the lure of the La Dorada treasure. LeBaron's clue was meager, but the statue had to be some- where in Cuba. The only snag was that he could easily get killed.

Pitt stopped and dove straight down, touching bottom at what he reckoned was ten feet. He reached out and accidentally brushed one of Jessie's legs as he surfaced. She shrieked, thinking she was being attacked by something big with a triangular fin, unseeing eyes, and a mouth that only a dentist could appreciate.

"Quiet!" he rasped. "You'll alert every guard patrol for miles."

"Oh, God, it was you!" she groaned in dazed fright.

"Keep it low," he murmured close to her ear. "Sound carries over water. We'll rest awhile and watch for signs of activity."

There was no answer from her, simply a light touch of her hand on his shoulder in agreement. They treaded water for several min- utes, peering into the darkness. The dim moonlight softly illuminated the coastline of Cuba, the narrow strip of white sand and the dark shadows of the growth behind. About two miles to their right they could see lights from cars passing on a road that cut close to the shore. Five miles beyond an incandescent glow revealed a small port city.

364

Pitt could not detect any indication of movement. He gestured forward and began swimming again, using a breaststroke this time so he could keep his eyes trained ahead. Heights and shapes, angles and contours became nebulous silhouettes as they moved closer. After fifty yards he extended his feet downward and touched sand. He stood and the water came up to his chest.

"You can stand," he said softly.

There was a momentary pause, then she whispered tiredly, "Thank heavens, my arms feel like lead."

"As soon as we reach the shallows you lie still and take it easy. I'm going to scout around."

"Please be careful."

"Not to worry," he said, breaking into a wide grin. "I'm getting the hang of it. This is the second enemy beach I've landed on tonight."

"Are you ever serious?"

"When the occasion demands. Like now, for instance. Give me the gun."

She hesitated. "I think I lost it."

"You think?"

"When we went in the water..."

"You dropped it."

"I dropped it," she repeated in innocent regret.

"You don't know what a joy it's been working with you," Pitt said in abject exasperation.

They swam the remaining distance in silence until the low surf diminished and it was only a few inches deep. He motioned for Jessie to stay put. For the next minute Pitt lay rigid and unmoving, then abruptly, without a word, he leaped to his feet, ran across the sand, and vanished into the shadows.

Jessie fought to keep from nodding off. Her whole body was going numb from exhaustion, and she gratefully became aware that the pain from the bruises caused by Foss Gly's hands were fading away. The soothing lap of the water against her lightly clad body relaxed her like a sedative.

And then she froze, fingers digging into the wet sand, her heart catching in her throat.

One of the bushes had moved. Ten, maybe twelve yards away, a dark mass detached itself from the surrounding shadows and advanced along the beach just above the tideline.

It was not Pitt.

The pale light from the moon revealed a figure in a uniform carrying a rifle. She lay paralyzed, acutely aware of her naked help-lessness. She pressed her body into the sand and slid backward slowly into deeper water, an inch at a time.

Jessie shrank in a vain attempt to make herself smaller as the beam from a flashlight suddenly speared the dark and played on the beach above the waterline. The Cuban sentry swept the light back and forth as he walked toward her, intently examining the ground. With a fearful certainty Jessie realized that he was following footprints. She felt a sudden anger at Pitt for leaving her alone, and for leaving a trail that led straight to her.

The Cuban approached within ten yards and would have seen the upper outline of her shape if he had only turned a fraction in her direction. The beam stopped its sweep and held steady, probing at the impressions left by Pitt on his dash across the beach. The guard swung to his right and crouched, aiming the flashlight into the bordering undergrowth. Then, inexplicably, he spun around to his left and the beam caught Jessie full in its glare. The light blinded her.

For a second the Cuban stood startled, then his free hand lifted the barrel of the automatic rifle that was was slung over his shoulder and he pointed the muzzle directly at Jessie. Too terrified to speak, she clamped her eyes closed as if the mere act would shut out the horror and impact of the bullets.

She heard a faint thud, followed by a convulsive grunt. The bullets never came. There was only a strange silence, and then she sensed the light had gone out. She opened her eyes and stared vaguely at a pair of legs that stood ankle deep in the water, straddling her head, and through them she saw the inert body of the Cuban sentry stretched out on the sand.

Pitt leaned down and gently hoisted Jessie to her feet. He smoothed back her dripping hair and said, "It seems I can't turn my back for a minute without you getting into trouble."

"I thought I was dead," she said, as her heartbeat gradually slowed.

"You must have thought the same thing at least a dozen times since we left Key West."

"Fear of death takes a while to get used to."

Pitt picked up the Cuban's flashlight, hooded it in his hand, and began stripping off the uniform. "Fortunately he's a short little rascal, about your size. Your feet will probably swim in his boots, but better too large than too small."

"Is he dead?"

"Just a small dent in the skull from a rock. He'll come around in a few hours."

She wrinkled her nose as she caught the thrown fatigue uniform. "I don't think he ever bathed."

"Launder it in the sea and put it on wet," he said briskly. "And be quick about it. This is no time to play fashionable rich bitch. The sentry at the next post will wonder why he hasn't shown up. His relief and sergeant of the guard are bound to come along pretty soon."

Five minutes later Jessie stood dripping in the uniform of a Cuban armed forces patrol guard. Pitt was right, the boots were two sizes too big. She lifted her damp hair and neatly tucked it under the cap. She turned and stared at Pitt as he emerged from the trees and bushes carrying the Cuban's rifle and a palm frond.

"What did you do with him?" she asked.

"Stashed him a ways inland under a bush." Pitt's voice betrayed a sense of urgency. He pointed at a tiny beam of light about a quarter of mile down the beach. "They're coming. No time for a volleyball game. Get a move on."

He roughly pushed her toward the trees and followed, walking backward brushing away their footprints with the palm frond. After nearly seventy yards, he dropped the frond and they hurried through the jungle growth, putting as much distance between them and the beach as possible before daylight.

They had covered five miles when the eastern sky began to brighten from black to orange. A sugarcane field rose up out of the fading darkness, and they skirted its border until it ended beside a paved two-lane highway. No headlights played on the asphalt in either direction. They walked along the shoulder, ducking into the brush whenever a car or truck approached. Pitt noticed that Jessie's steps were beginning to falter and her breathing was coming in rapid gasps. He halted, placed his handkerchief over the lens of the flashlight, and shone it in her face. He didn't require the credentials of a sports physician to see that she was done in. He put his arm around her waist and pushed on until they reached the steep sides of a small ravine.

"Catch your breath, I'll be right back."

Pitt dropped down the slope into a dry creek bed that threaded a jagged course around a low hill littered with large boulders and scrub pine. It passed under the highway through a concrete pipe three feet in diameter and spread into a fenced pasture on the other side. He scrambled back up to the road, silently took Jessie's hand, and led her stumbling and sliding to the gravelly bottom of the ravine. He flicked the beam of the flashlight inside the drainpipe.

"The only vacant room in town," he said in a voice as cheerful as he could make it under the circumstances.

It was no penthouse suite, but the curved bottom of the pipe held a good two inches of soft sand, and it was a safer haven than Pitt could have hoped for. Any pursuing guards who eventually came on their trail and followed it to the highway would assume the landing party met a prearranged ride.

Somehow they managed to find a comfortable position in the cramped darkness. Pitt set the gun and flashlight within easy reach and finally relaxed.

"Okay, lady," he said, his words echoing through the drainpipe. "I think the time has come for you to tell me what in hell we're doing here."

But Jessie didn't answer.

Oblivious to her clammy, ill-fitting uniform, oblivious even to aching feet and sore joints, she was curled in a fetal position sound asleep.

61

"DEAD? ALL DEAD?" Kremlin boss Antonov repeated angrily. "The entire facility destroyed and no survivors, none at all?"

Polevoi nodded heavily. "The captain of the submarine that detected the explosions and the colonel in command of the security forces sent ashore to investigate reported that they found no one alive. They retrieved the body of my chief deputy, Lyev Maisky, but General Velikov has yet to be found."

"Were secret codes and documents missing?"

Polevoi was not about to put his head on the block and take responsibility for an intelligence disaster. As it was, he stood within a hair of losing his lofty position and quickly becoming a forgotten bureaucrat in charge of a labor camp

"All classified data were destroyed by General Velikov's staff before they died fighting."

Antonov accepted the lie. "The CIA," he said, brooding. "They're behind this foul provocation."

"I don't think we can make the CIA the scapegoat on this one. The preliminary evidence points to a Cuban operation."

"Impossible," Antonov snapped. "Our friends in Castro's military would have warned us well in advance of any ambitious plan to attack the island. Besides, a daring and imaginative operation of this magnitude goes far beyond any Latin brain."

"Perhaps, but our best intelligence minds do not believe the CIA was remotely aware of our communications center on Cayo Santa María. We haven't uncovered the slightest indication of surveillance. The CIA is good, but its people are not gods. They could not have possibly planned, rehearsed, and carried out the raid in the few short hours from the time the shuttle left the space station until it suddenly veered off our programmed flight path to Cuba."

"We lost the shuttle too?"

"Our monitoring of the Johnson Space Center revealed that it landed safely in Key West."

"With the American moon colonists," he added flatly.

"They were on board, yes."

For seconds, too furious to react, Antonov sat there, his lips taut, unblinking eyes staring into nothingness. "How did they do it?" he growled at last. "How did they save their precious space shuttle at the last minute?"

"Fool's luck," said Polevoi, again relying on the Communist dogma of casting blame elsewhere. "Their asses were saved by the devious interference of the Castros."

Antonov's eyes suddenly focused on Polevoi. "As you've so often reminded me, Comrade Director, the Castro brothers can't go to the toilet without the KGB knowing how many squares of paper they use. You tell me how they suddenly crawled in bed with the President of the United States without your agents becoming aware of it."

Polevoi had unwittingly dug himself into a hole and now he shrewdly climbed out of it by switching the course of the briefing. "Operation Rum and Cola is still in progress. We may have been cheated out of the space shuttle and a rich source of scientific data, but it is an acceptable loss compared to gaining total mastery of Cuba."

Antonov considered Polevoi's words, and swallowed the bait. "I have my doubts. Without Velikov to direct the operation its chances for success are cut in half."

"The general is no longer crucial to Rum and Cola. The plan is ninety percent complete. The ships will enter Havana Harbor tomorrow evening, and Castro's speech is set for the following morning. General Velikov performed admirably in laying the groundwork. Rumors of a new CIA plot to assassinate Castro have already been spread throughout the Western world, and we have prepared evidence showing American involvement. All that's left to do is push a button."

"Our people in Havana and Santiago are alerted?"

"They're prepared to move in and form a new government as soon as the assassination is confirmed."

"And the next leader?"

"Alicia Cordero."

Antonov's mouth hung half open. "A woman, you're telling me? We're naming a woman to rule Cuba after Fidel Castro's death?"

370

"The perfect choice," said Polevoi firmly. "She is secretary of the Central Committee and secretary of the Council of State. Most important, she is a close confidante of Fidel and is idolized by the people for the success of her family economic programs and fiery oratory. She has a charm and charisma that matches Fidel's. Her loyalty to the Soviet Union is unquestionable, and she will have the total backing of the Cuban military."

"Who work for us."

"Who belong to us," Polevoi corrected.

"So we are committed."

"Yes, Comrade President."

"And then?" Antonov prompted.

"Nicaragua, Peru, Chile, and yes, Argentina," said Polevoi, warming to his subject. "No more messy revolutions, no more bloody guerrilla movements. We infiltrate their governments and subtly erode from within, careful to arouse no hostility from the United States. When they finally wake up it will be too late. South and Central America will be solid extensions of the Soviet Union."

"And not the party?" Antonov asked reproachfully. "Are you forgetting the glory of our Communist heritage, Polevoi?"

"The party is the base to build upon. But we cannot continue to be chained to an archaic Marxist philosophy that has taken a hundred years to prove unworkable. The twenty-first century is only a decade away. The day of cold realism is now. I quote you, Comrade President, when you said, 'I envision a new era of socialism that will wipe the hated scourge of capitalism from the earth.' Cuba is the first step in fulfilling your dream of a world society dominated by the Kremlin."

"And Fidel Castro is the barrier in our path."

"Yes," said Polevoi with a sinister smile. "But only for another forty-eight hours."

Air Force One lifted off from Andrews Air Force Base and turned south over the historic hills of Virginia. The early morning sky was clear and blue with only a few scattered thunderclouds. The Air Force colonel, who had piloted the Boeing jet under three Presidents, leveled off at 34,000 feet and gave the arrival time at Cape Canaveral over the cabin intercom.

"Breakfast, gentlemen?" asked the President, motioning toward a small dining compartment recently modified into the plane. His wife

371

had hung a Tiffany lampshade over an art deco table, lending an informal, relaxed atmosphere. "Our galley can provide champagne if anyone wishes to celebrate."

"I wouldn't mind a hot cup of black coffee," said Martin Brogan. He sat down and removed a file from his briefcase before sliding it under the table.

Dan Fawcett pulled up a chair beside him, while Douglas Oates sat opposite, next to the President. A white-coated Air Force sergeant served guava juice, the President's favorite, and coffee. Each man gave his order and relaxed, waiting for the President to launch the conversation.

"Well," he said, smiling, "we've got a lot to get through before we land at the Cape and congratulate everyone. So let's get started. Dan, fill us in on the status of the *Gettysburg* and the moon colonists."

"I've been on the phone all morning with NASA officials," said Fawcett, excitement evident in his tone. "As we all know, Dave Jurgens put the spacecraft down in Key West by the skin of his teeth. A remarkable job of flying. The naval air station has been closed to all air and car traffic. The gates and fences are under heavy Marine guard. The President has ordered a temporary news blackout on the situation until he can announce the existence of our new moon base."

"The reporters must be screaming like wounded vultures," said Oates, "demanding to know why the shuttle made an unscheduled arrival so far off course."

"That goes without saying."

"When do you plan to make the announcement?" asked Brogan.

"In two days," replied the President. "We need time to sort out the immense implications and debrief Steinmetz and his people before we throw them to the news media."

"If we delay any longer," added Fawcett, "someone in the White House press corps is bound to hit on a leak."

"Where are the moon colonists now?"

"Undergoing tests at the Kennedy Space Center medical facility," answered Fawcett. "They were flown out of Key West along with Jurgens' crew shortly after the *Gettysburg* touched down."

Brogan looked at Oates. "Any word from the Kremlin?"

"Only silence so far."

"Be interesting to see how they react to having their nationals shot down for a change."

"Antonov is a wily old bear," said the President. "He'll reject a propaganda blitz accusing us of murdering his cosmonauts in favor of secret talks where he'll demand restitution in the form of shared scientific data."

"Will you give it to him?"

"The President is morally bound to comply," said Oates.

Brogan looked appalled, and so did Fawcett.

"This is not a political matter," Brogan said in a low voice. "There is nothing in the book that says we have to throw away secrets vital to our national defense."

"We're cast as the villains this time around, not the Russians," protested Oates. "We're within inches of a SALT IV agreement to halt all future nuclear missile placement. If the President ignored Antonov's claims, the Soviet negotiators would take one of their famous walks only hours before signing the treaty."

"You may be right," said Fawcett. "But everyone connected with the Jersey Colony didn't struggle for two decades just to give it all away to the Kremlin."

The President had followed this exchange without interrupting. Now he held up a hand. "Gentlemen, I am not about to sell out the store. But there is an enormous wealth of information we can share with the Russians and the rest of the world in the interests of humanity. Medical findings, geological and astronomical data must be freely passed around. However, you may rest easy. I'm not about to compromise our space and defense programs. That area will remain firmly in our hands. Do I make myself clear?"

Silence descended on the dining compartment as the steward delivered three steaming plates of eggs, ham, and hotcakes. He refilled the coffee cups. As soon as he returned to the galley, the President sighed deeply and looked at the table in front of Brogan.

"You're not eating, Martin?"

"I usually skip breakfast. Lunch is my big meal."

"You don't know what you're missing. These hotcakes are light as a feather."

"No, thanks. I'll just stick with coffee."

"While the rest of us dig in, why don't you brief us on the Cayo Santa María operation."

Brogan took a sip from his cup, opened the file, and condensed the contents in a few concise statements. "A special combat team under the command of Colonel Ramon Kleist and led by Major Angelo Quintana landed on the island at 0200 hours this morning. By 0430 the Soviet radio jamming and listening facility, including its antenna, was destroyed and all personnel terminated. The timing

373

was most fortunate, as the final radio transmission warned off the *Gettysburg* only minutes before it would have landed on Cuban soil."

"Who gave the warning?" interrupted Fawcett.

Brogan stared across the table and smiled. "He gave his name as Dirk Pitt."

"My God, the man is everywhere," the President exclaimed.

"Jessie LeBaron and two of Admiral Sandecker's NUMA people were rescued," Brogan continued. "Raymond LeBaron was killed."

"Is that confirmed?" asked the President, his expression turned solemn.

"Yes, sir, it was confirmed."

"A great pity. He deserved recognition for his contribution to the Jersey Colony."

"Still, the mission was a great success," Brogan said quietly. "Major Quintana recovered a wealth of intelligence material, including the Soviets' latest codes. It arrived only an hour ago. Analysts at Langley are sifting through it now."

"Congratulations are in order," said the President. "Your people performed an incredible feat."

"You may not be so hasty with praise, Mr. President, after you hear the full story."

"Okay, Martin, let's have it."

"Dirk Pitt and Jessie LeBaron..." Brogan paused and gave a dejected shrug of his shoulders. "They didn't return to the mother ship with Major Quintana and his men."

"Were they killed on the island along with Raymond LeBaron?"

"No, sir. They departed with the others, but veered away and headed for Cuba."

"Cuba," the President repeated in a soft voice. He looked across the table at Oates and Fawcett, who stared back incredulously. "Good lord, Jessie is still trying to deliver our reply to the proposed U.S.–Cuban pact."

"Is it possible she can somehow make contact with Castro?" asked Fawcett.

Brogan shook his head doubtfully. "The island is teeming with security forces, police and militia units who check every mile of road. They'd be arrested inside an hour, assuming they get past patrols on the beach."

"Maybe Pitt will get lucky," Fawcett muttered hopefully.

"No," said the President gravely, his features shrouded with concern. "The man has used up whatever luck he had."

374

In a small office at the CIA headquarters at Langley, Bob Thornburg, chief documents analyst, sat with his feet crossed on his desk and read through a pile of material that had been flown in from San Salvador. He puffed a veil of blue pipe smoke and translated the Russian typing.

He quickly scanned three folders and picked up a fourth. The title intrigued him. The phrasing was peculiarly American. It was a covert action named after a mixed drink. He quickly glanced through to the end and sat there a moment, stunned. Then he set the pipe in an ashtray, removed his feet from the desktop, and read the contents of the folder more carefully, picking it apart sentence by sentence and making notes on a yellow legal pad.

Nearly two hours later, Thornburg picked up his phone and dialed an internal number. A woman answered, and he asked for the deputy director.

"Eileen, this is Bob Thornburg. Is Henry available?"

"He's on another line."

"Have him ring me first chance, this is urgent."

"I'll tell him."

Thornburg assembled his notes and was restudying the folder for the fifth time when the chime of his phone interrupted him. He sighed and picked up the receiver.

"Bob, this is Henry. What have you got?"

"Can we meet right away? I've just been going over part of the intelligence data from the Cayo Santa María operation."

"Something of value?"

"Let's say it's a blockbuster."

"Can you give me a hint?"

"Concerns Fidel Castro."

"What no good is he up to now?"

"He's going to die the day after tomorrow."

62

As soon as Pitt woke up he looked at his watch. The time was 12:18. He felt refreshed, in good spirits, even optimistic.

When he reflected on it, Pitt found his cheerful outlook grimly amusing. His future was not exactly bright. He had no Cuban currency or identification papers. He was in a Communist country without even one friendly contact or an excuse for being there. And he was wearing the wrong uniform. He would be lucky if he made it through the day without getting shot as a spy.

He reached over and gently shook Jessie by the shoulder. Then he crawled from the drainage pipe, warily surveyed the area, and began doing stretching exercises to relieve his stiff muscles.

Jessie opened her eyes and woke up slowly, languidly, from a deep luxurious sleep, gradually fitting her world into perspective. Uncurling and extending her arms and legs like a cat, she moaned softly at the pain, but was thankful it spurred her mind into motion.

She thought of silly things at first—who to invite to her next party, planning a menu with her chef, reminding the gardener to trim the hedges bordering the walks—and then memories of her husband began passing in front of her inner eye. She wondered how a woman could work and live with a man for twenty years and still not come to grips with his inner moods. Yet she more than anyone saw Raymond LeBaron simply as a human being no worse or no better than other men, and with a mind that could radiate compassion, pettiness, brilliance, or ruthlessness almost on cue to suit the moment.

She closed her eyes tightly to shut out his death. Think of someone or something else, she told herself. Think of how to survive the next few days. Think of... Dirk Pitt.

Who was he, she wondered. What kind of man? She looked at him through the drainpipe as he bent and flexed his body and for the first time since meeting him felt a sexual attraction toward him. It was ridiculous, she reasoned, she was older by at least fifteen years. And besides, he had not shown any interest in her as a desirable woman, never once cast a suggestive insinuation or made a flirtatious overture. She decided Pitt was an enigma, the type of man who intrigued women, incited them to wanton behavior, but could never be owned or beguiled by their feminine ploys.

Jessie was snapped back to reality as Pitt leaned into the pipe and smiled. "How are you feeling?"

She looked away nervously. "Battered but ready to meet the day."

"Sorry about not having breakfast ready," he said, his voice hollow through the pipe. "The room service leaves much to be desired hereabouts."

"I'd sell my soul for a cup of coffee."

"According to a road sign I spotted a few hundred yards up the road, we're ten kilometers from the next town."

"What time is it?"

"Twenty minutes to one."

"The day is half gone," she said, rolling to her hands and knees, and beginning to crawl toward the light. "We have to get moving."

"Stay where you are."

"Why?"

He didn't answer, but returned and sat down beside her. He gently took her face in his hands and kissed her mouth.

Jessie's eyes widened, and then she returned his kiss hungrily. After a long moment, he pulled back. She waited expectantly, but he made no further move, just sat there and stared into her eyes.

"I want you," she said.

"Yes."

"Now."

He drew her to him, pressing against her body, and kissed her again. Then he broke away from her. "First things first."

She gave him a hurt, curious look. "Like what things?"

"Like why did you hijack me to Cuba?"

"You have a strange sense of timing."

"I don't usually conduct foreplay in a drainpipe either."

"What do you want to know?"

"Everything."

"And if I don't tell you?"

He laughed. "We shake hands and part company."

For a few seconds she lay against the side of the pipe, considering

377

how far she would get without him. Probably no farther than the next town, the first suspicious policeman or security guard. Pitt seemed an incredibly resourceful man. He had proven that several times over. There was no avoiding the hard fact that she needed him more than he needed her.

She tried to find the right words to explain, an introduction that made some kind of sense. Finally she gave up and blurted it out. "The President sent me to meet with Fidel Castro."

His deep green eyes examined her with honest curiosity. "That's a good start. I'd like to hear the rest."

Jessie took a deep breath and continued.

She revealed Fidel Castro's genuine offer of a pact and his bizarre manner of sending it past the watchful eyes of Soviet intelligence.

She told of her secret meeting with the President after the unexpected return of the *Prosperteer* and his request for her to convey his reply by retracing her husband's flight in the blimp, a guise Castro would have recognized.

She admitted the deception in recruiting Pitt, Giordino, and Gunn, and she asked Pitt's forgiveness for a plan gone wrong by the surprise attack from the Cuban helicopter.

And last, she described General Velikov's narrowing suspicion of the true purpose behind the botched attempt to reach Castro and his demand for answers through Foss Gly's torture methods.

Pitt listened to the whole story without comment.

His response was the part she dreaded. She feared what he would say or do now that he had discovered how he had been used, lied to, and misled, battered bloody and nearly killed on several occasions for a mission he knew nothing about. She felt he had every right to strangle her.

She could think of nothing further to say except "I'm sorry."

Pitt did not strangle her. He held out his hand. She grasped it, and he pulled her toward him. "So you conned me all up and down the line," he said.

God, those green eyes, she thought. She wanted to dive into them. "I can't blame you for being angry."

He embraced her for several moments silently.

"Well?"

"Well what?"

"Aren't you going to say something?" she asked timidly. "Aren't you even mad?"

He unbuttoned the shirt of the uniform and lightly touched her

378

breasts. "Lucky for you I'm not one to harbor a grudge."

Then they made love as the traffic rumbled over the highway above.

Jessie felt incredibly calm. The warm feeling had stayed with her for the last hour as they walked openly along the road's shoulder. It spread like an anesthetic, deadening her fear and sharpening her confidence. Pitt had accepted her story and agreed to help her reach Castro. And now she walked along beside him as he led her through the backcountry of Cuba as though he owned it, feeling secure and warm in the afterglow of their intimacy.

Pitt scrounged some mangoes, a pineapple, and two half-ripened tomatoes. They ate as they walked. Several vehicles, mostly trucks loaded with sugarcane and cirtrus fruits, passed them. Once in a while a military transport carrying militia swept by. Jessie would tense and look down at her tightly laced boots nervously while Pitt lifted his rifle in the air and shouted "*Saludos amigos!*"

"A good thing they can't hear you clearly," she said.

"Why is that?" he asked in mock indignation.

"Your Spanish is awful."

"It always got me by at the dog races in Tijuana."

"It won't do here. You'd better let me do the talking."

"You think your Spanish is better than mine?"

"I can speak it like a native. I can also converse fluently in Russian, French, and German."

"I'm continually amazed at your talents," Pitt said sincerely. "Did Velikov know you spoke Russian?"

"We'd have all been dead if he had."

Pitt started to say something and suddenly gestured ahead. They were rounding a curve, and he pointed at a car parked by the highway. The hood was up and someone was leaning over the fender, his head and shoulders lost in the engine compartment.

Jessie hesitated, but Pitt took her by the hand and tugged her along. "You handle this," he said softly. "Don't be frightened. We're both in military uniform, and mine belongs to an elite assault force."

"What should I say?"

"Play along. This may be a chance to get a ride."

Before she could protest, the driver heard their feet on the gravel and turned at their approach. He was a short man in his fifties with thick black hair and dark skin. He was shirtless and wore only shorts

379

and sandals. Military uniforms were so common in Cuba he scarcely gave them any notice. He flashed a broad smile. "*Hola.*"

"Having motor trouble?" Jessie asked in Spanish.

"Third time this month." He gave a helpless shrug. "She just stopped."

"Do you know the problem?"

He held up a short length of wire that had rotted apart in three different places and was barely hanging together by its insulation. "Runs from the coil to the distributor."

"You should have replaced it with a new one."

He looked at her suspiciously. "Parts for old cars like this one are impossible to find. You must know that."

Jessie caught her mistake and, smiling sweetly, quickly played on Latin *machismo*. "I'm only a woman. What would I know about mechanics?"

"Ah," he said, smiling graciously, "but a very pretty woman."

Pitt paid little attention to the conversation. He was walking around the car, examining its lines. He leaned over the front end and studied the engine for a moment. Then he straightened and stepped back.

"A fifty-seven Chevy," he said admiringly in English. "One damned fine automobile. Ask him if he has a knife and some tape."

Jessie's mouth dropped open in shock.

The driver looked at him uncertainly, unsure of what to do. Then he asked in broken English, "You no speak Spanish?"

"Faith and what's the matter?" Pitt boomed. "Haven't you ever laid eyes on an Irishman before?"

"Why an Irelander wearing a Cuban uniform?"

"Major Paddy O'Hara, Irish Republican Army, on assignment as an adviser to your militia."

The Cuban's face lit up like a camera flash, and Pitt was pleased to see that the man was duly impressed.

"Herberto Figueroa," he said, offering his hand. "I learn English many years ago when the Americans were here."

Pitt took it and nodded at Jessie. "Corporal María López, my aide and guide. She also interprets my fractured Spanish."

Figueroa dipped his head and noticed Jessie's wedding ring. "Señora López." He tilted his head to Pitt. "She understand English?" pronouncing it "chee unnarstan Englaise?"

"A little," Pitt answered. "Now then, if you can give me a knife and some tape, I think I can get you going again."

"Sure, sure," said Figueroa. He pulled a pocketknife from the glove

380

compartment and found a small roll of friction tape in a toolbox in the trunk.

Pitt reached down into the engine, cut a few excess lengths of wire from the spark plug leads, and spliced the ends back together. Then he did the same with the extra pieces until he had a wire that stretched from the coil to the distributor.

"Okay, give her a try."

Figueroa turned the ignition key and the big 283-cubic-inch V-8 coughed once, twice, and settled into a throaty roar.

"*Magnífico!*" shouted Figueroa happily. "Can I give you a ride?"

"How far you going?"

"Havana. I live there. My sister's husband died in Nuevitas. I went to help her with the funeral. Now I'm on my way home."

Pitt nodded to Jessie. This was their lucky day. He tried to picture the shape of Cuba, and he rightly calculated that Havana was very nearly two hundred miles to the northeast as the crow flies, more like three hundred by road.

He held the front seat forward as Jessie climbed in the rear. "We're grateful to you, Herberto. My staff car developed an oil leak and the engine froze up about two miles back. We were traveling to a training camp east of Havana. If you can drop us off at the Ministry of Defense, I'll see that you get paid for your trouble."

Jessie's jaw dropped and she stared at Pitt with a classic expression of distaste. He knew that in her mind she was calling him a cocky bastard.

"Your bad luck is my good luck," said Figueroa, happy at the prospect of picking up a few extra pesos.

Figueroa spun gravel on the shoulder as he quickly moved onto the asphalt, shifting through the gears until the Chevy was spinning along at a respectable seventy miles an hour. The engine sounded smooth, but the body rattled in a dozen places and the exhaust fumes leaked through the rusted floorboards.

Pitt stared at Jessie's face in the rearview mirror. She seemed uncomfortable and out of her element. A limousine was more to her liking. Pitt positively enjoyed himself. For the moment, his love of old cars overcame any thoughts of danger.

"How many miles do you have on her?" he asked.

"Over six hundred and eighty thousand kilometers," Figueroa answered.

"She's still got good power."

"If the Yankees ever dropped their trade embargo, I might be able

381

to buy new parts and keep her going. But she can't last forever."

"Do you have any trouble at the checkpoints?"

"I'm always waved on through."

"You must have influence. What do you do in Havana?"

Figueroa laughed. "I'm a cabdriver."

Pitt did not try to suppress a smile. This was even better than he had hoped. He sat back and relaxed, enjoying the scenery like a tourist. He tried to apply his mind to LeBaron's cryptic direction to the treasure of La Dorada, but his thinking was clouded with remorse.

He knew that at some time, somewhere along the road he might have to take what little money Figueroa carried and steal his cab. Pitt hoped he would not have to kill the friendly little man in the bargain.

63

THE PRESIDENT RETURNED to the White House from the Kennedy Space Center late in the evening and went directly to the Oval Office. After secretly meeting with Steinmetz and the moon colonists and hearing the enthusiastic reports of their explorations, he felt exhilarated. Sleep was forgotten as he walked into his office alone, inspired to plan a new range of space goals.

He sat down behind the big desk and opened a lower drawer. He lifted out a walnut humidor and removed a large cigar. He peeled off the cellophane, stared a moment at the dark brown, tightly wrapped leafy cover, and inhaled the heady aroma. It was a Montecristo, the finest cigar Cuba made, and banned from American import by the trade embargo on Cuban goods.

The President relied on an old trusted school pal to smuggle him a box every two months from Canada. Even his wife and closest aides were unaware of his cache. He clipped one end and exactingly lit the other, wondering as he always did what kind of uproar the public would raise if they discovered his clandestine and slightly illegal indulgence.

Tonight he did not give a damn. He was riding high. The economy was holding, and Congress had finally got around to passing tough budget cuts and a flat-tax law. The international scene had entered a cooling-off period, however temporary, and his popularity polls showed him up five percentage points. And now he was about to make a political profit on his predecessors' foresight, just as Nixon did after the success of the Apollo program. The stunning success of the moon colony would be the high-water mark of his administration.

His next goal was to enhance his image on Latin American affairs. Castro had cracked open the door with his offer of a treaty. Now, if the President could slip his foot over the threshold before it slammed shut again, he might have a fighting chance to neutralize Marxist influence in the Americas.

The prospects appeared gloomy at the moment. It was most likely that Pitt and Jessie LeBaron had been either shot or arrested. If they had not, then it was only a matter of hours before the inevitable happened. The only course of action was to slip someone else into Cuba to make contact with Castro.

His intercom buzzed. "Yes?"

"Sorry to interrupt you, Mr. President," said a White House operator, "but Mr. Brogan is calling and he says it is urgent he speak with you."

"It's quite all right. Please put him on."

There was a slight click and Martin Brogan said, "Did I catch you in bed?"

"No, I'm still up. What's on your mind that couldn't wait until tomorrow's briefing?"

"I'm still at Andrews Field. My deputy was waiting for me with a translated document that was taken from Cayo Santa María. It contains some pretty hot material."

"Can you fill me in?"

"The Russians are going to knock off Castro the day after tomorrow. The operation is code-named 'Rum and Cola.' It details the complete takeover of the Cuban government by Soviet agents."

The President watched the blue smoke from the Havana cigar curl toward the ceiling. "They're making their move sooner than we figured," he said thoughtfully. "How do they intend to eliminate Castro?"

"The wild part of the plan," said Brogan. "The GRU arm of the KGB intends to blitz the city along with him."

"Havana?"

"A damned good chunk of it."

"Jesus Christ, you're talking a nuclear bomb."

"I've got to be honest and say the document does not state the exact means, but it's quite clear that some kind of explosive device is being smuggled into the harbor by ship that can level four square miles."

Depression settled around the President and dampened his high spirits. "Does the document give the name of the ship?"

"It mentions three ships but none by name."

"And when is the blast supposed to be set off?"

"During an Education Day celebration. The Russians are counting on Castro making an unscheduled appearance and giving his usual two-hour harangue."

"I can't believe Antonov is a party to such horror. Why not send in a local team of hit men and gun Castro down? What's to be gained by taking a hundred thousand innocent victims with him?"

"Castro is a cult figure to the Cubans," explained Brogan. "A cartoon Communist to us maybe, but a revered god to them. A simple assassination will ignite an overwhelming ground swell of resentment against the Soviet-backed parties who replace him. But a major disaster—that would give the new leaders a rallying cry and a cause to incite the people to close ranks behind a new government, particularly if it was proven the United States was the culprit, specifically the CIA."

"I still can't conceive of such a monstrous scheme."

"I assure you, Mr. President, everything is spelled out in black and white." Brogan paused to scan a page of the document. "Odd thing, it's vague about the details of the explosion, but very specific in listing the step-by-step propaganda campaign to blame us. It even lists the names of the Soviet cohorts and the positions they are to move into after they seize control. You may be interested to learn that Alicia Cordero is to be the new President."

"God help us. She's twice the fanatic Fidel is."

"In any case, the Soviets win and we lose."

The President laid the cigar in an ashtray and closed his eyes. The problems never end, he mused. One begets another. The triumphs of office do not last very long. The pressure and the frustrations never let up.

"Can our Navy stop those ships?" he asked.

"According to the schedule, two of them have already docked in Havana," answered Brogan. "The third should be entering the harbor any hour. I had the same idea but we're an inch early and a mile late."

"We must have the names of those ships."

"I've already got my people checking on all shipping arrivals in Havana Harbor. They should have identification within the hour."

"Of all the times for Castro to hide out," the President said in exasperation.

"We found him."

"Where?"

"At his country retreat. He's cut off all contact with the outside world. Even his closest advisers and the Soviet bigwigs can't reach him."

"Who do we have on our team who can meet him face to face?"

Brogan grunted. "No one."

"There must be somebody we can send in."

"If Castro was in a communicative mood, I can think of at least ten people on our payroll who could get through the front gate. But not as things stand now."

The President toyed with the cigar, fumbling for inspiration. "How many Cubans can you trust in Havana who work the docks and have maritime experience?"

"I'd have to check."

"Guess."

"Off the top of my head, maybe fifteen or twenty."

"All right," the President said. "Round them up. Have them get on board those ships somehow and find which one is carrying the bomb."

"Someone who knows what he's doing will have to defuse it."

"We'll cross that bridge when we learn where it's hidden."

"A day and a half isn't much time," Brogan said glumly. "Better we concentrate on sorting out the mess afterward."

"You'd better get the show moving. Keep me informed every two hours. Turn everyone you've got in the Cuban department loose on this thing."

"What about warning Castro?"

"My job. I'll handle it."

"Good luck, Mr. President."

"Same to you, Martin."

The President hung up. His cigar had gone out. He relit it, then picked up the phone again and placed a call to Ira Hagen.

64

THE GUARD WAS YOUNG, no more than sixteen, eager and dedicated to Fidel Castro and committed to revolutionary vigilance. He glowed with self-importance and official arrogance as he swaggered to the car window, rifle slung tightly over one shoulder, and demanded to see identification papers.

"It had to happen," Pitt muttered under his breath.

The guards at the first three checkpoints had lazily waved Figueroa through when he flashed his taxi driver's permit. They were *campesinos* who chose the routine of a military career over a dead-end life of working in the fields or factories. And like soldiers in every army of the world, they found sentry duty tedious, eventually losing all suspicions except when their superiors arrived for an inspection.

Figueroa handed the youngster his permit.

"This only covers the Havana city borders. What are you doing in the country?"

"My brother-in-law died," Figueroa said patiently. "I went to his funeral."

The guard bent down and looked through the driver's open window. "Who are these others?"

"Are you blind?" Figueroa snapped. "They're military like you."

"We have orders to be on the watch for a man wearing a stolen militia uniform. He is suspected of being an imperialist spy who landed on a beach one hundred miles east of here."

"Because *she* is wearing a militia uniform," said Figueroa, pointing to Jessie in the backseat, "you think the Yankee imperialists are sending women to invade us?"

"I want to see their identification papers," the guard persisted.

Jessie rolled down the rear window and leaned out. "This is Major O'Hara of the Irish Republican Army, on assignment as an adviser.

I'm Corporal López, his aide. Enough of this nonsense. Pass us through."

The guard kept his eyes on Pitt. "If he's a major, why isn't he showing his rank?"

For the first time it occurred to Figueroa that there was no insignia on Pitt's uniform. He stared at Pitt, a doubtful frown spreading across his face.

Pitt sat there without taking part in the exchange. Then he slowly turned and gazed into the guard's eyes and gave him a friendly smile. When he spoke his voice was soft, but it carried total authority.

"Get this man's name and rank. I wish to have him commended for his attention to duty. General Raúl Castro has often said Cuba needs men of this caliber."

Jessie translated and watched with relief as the guard stood erect and smiled.

Then Pitt's tone turned glacial, and so did his eyes. "Now tell him to stand clear or I'll arrange to have him sent as a volunteer to Afghanistan."

The young guard seemed to shrink perceptibly as Jessie repeated Pitt's words in Spanish. He stood lost, undecided what to do as a long black car pulled up and stopped behind the old cab. Pitt recognized it as a Zil, a seven-seater luxury limousine built in Russia for high-ranking government and military officials.

The Zil's driver honked his horn impatiently, and the guard seemed frozen with indecision. He turned and stared pleadingly at another guard, but his partner was occupied with traffic traveling in the other direction. The limousine's driver honked again and shouted out his side window.

"Move that car aside and let us pass!"

Then Figueroa got into the act and began yelling at the Russians. "Stupid Russo, shut up and take a bath! I can smell you from here!"

The Soviet driver pushed open his door, leaped from behind the wheel, and shoved the guard aside. He was built like a bowling pin, huge, beefy body and small head. His rank indicated that he was a sergeant. He stared at Figueroa through eyes burning with malice.

"Idiot," he snarled. "Move this wreck."

Figueroa shook his fist in the Russian's face. "I'll go when my countryman tells me to."

"Please, *please*," Jessie pleaded, shaking Figueroa's shoulder "We don't want any trouble."

"Discretion isn't a Cuban virtue," Pitt murmured. He cradled the assault rifle in his arms with the muzzle pointed at the Russian and eased the door open.

Jessie turned and peered cautiously through the rear window at the limousine, just in time to see a Soviet officer, followed by two armed bodyguards, climb from the backseat and gaze with an amused smile at the shouting match taking place beside the taxicab. Jessie's mouth dropped open and she gasped.

General Velikov, looking tired and haggard, and wearing a badly fitted borrowed uniform, approached from the rear of the Chevrolet as Pitt slid out of his seat and stepped around the front end before Jessie could warn him.

Velikov's attention was focused on his driver and Figueroa, and he paid scant notice to what appeared to be another Cuban soldier emerging from the other side of the car. The argument was heating up as he came alongside.

"What is the problem?" he asked in fluent Spanish.

His answer did not come from his driver, but from a totally unexpected source.

"Nothing we can't settle like gentlemen," Pitt said acidly in English.

Velikov stared at Pitt for a long moment, the amused smile dying on his lips, his face as expressionless as ever. The only sign of astonished recognition was a sudden hardness of the flat cold eyes.

"We are survivors, are we not, Mr. Pitt?" he replied.

"Lucky. I'd say we were lucky," Pitt answered in a steady voice.

"I congratulate you on your escape from the island. How did you manage it?"

"A makeshift boat. And you?"

"A helicopter concealed near the installation. Fortunately, your friends failed to discover it."

"An oversight."

Velikov glanced out of the corner of his eye, noting with irritation the relaxed stance of his bodyguards. "Why have you come to Cuba?"

Pitt's hand tightened around the rifle's grip, muzzle pointing in the sky just above Velikov's head, finger poised on the trigger. "Why bother to ask when you've established the fact I'm a habitual liar?"

"I also know you only lie if there is a purpose. You didn't come to Cuba to drink rum and lie in the sun."

"What now, General?"

"Look around you, Mr. Pitt. You're hardly in a position of strength. The Cubans do not take kindly to spies. You would be wise to lay down your gun and place yourself under my protection."

"No, thank you. I've been under your protection. His name was Foss Gly. You remember him. He got high by pounding his fists on flesh. I'm happy to report he's no longer in the pain business. One of his victims shot him where it hurts most."

"My men can kill you where you stand."

"It's obvious they don't understand English and haven't got any idea of what's being said between us. Don't try to alert them. This is what's known as a Mexican standoff. You so much as pick your nose and I'll put a bullet up the opposite nostril."

Pitt glanced around him. Both the Cuban checkpoint guard and the Soviet driver were listening dumbly to the English conversation. Jessie was crouched down in the backseat of the Chevy, only the top of the fatigue cap showing above the side window. Velikov's guards stood lax, their eyes and minds turning to the landscape, automatic pistols snapped securely in their holsters.

"Get in the car, General. You'll be riding with us."

Velikov stared coldlly at Pitt. "And if I refuse?"

Pitt stared back with grim conviction. "You die first. Then your bodyguards. After them, the Cuban sentries. I'm prepared to kill. They're not. Now, if you please..."

The Soviet bodyguards stood rooted and looked on in rapt amazement as Velikov silently followed Pitt's gesture and entered the front passenger's seat. He turned briefly and gazed curiously at Jessie.

"Mrs. LeBaron?"

"Yes, General."

"You're with this madman?"

"I am."

"But why?"

Figueroa opened his mouth to interrupt, but Pitt roughly shouldered the Soviet driver aside, firmly gripped the friendly Cuban's arm, and pulled him from the car.

"This is as far as you go, *amigo*. Tell the authorities we abducted you and hijacked your taxi." Then he passed his rifle to Jessie through the open window and angled his long frame behind the wheel. "If the general so much as twitches, shoot him through the head."

Jessie nodded and placed the gun barrel against the base of Velikov's skull.

Pitt shifted the Chevy into first gear and accelerated smoothly as if he was on a Sunday drive, watching the figures at the checkpoint through the rearview mirror. He was gratified to see that they milled around in confusion, not sure of what to do. Then Velikov's driver and bodyguards finally woke up to what was happening, ran to the black limousine, and took up the chase.

Pitt skidded to a stop and took the gun from Jessie. He fired several shots at a pair of telephone wires where they ran through insulators at the top of a pole. The car was burning rubber on the asphalt before the parted ends of the wire dropped to the ground.

"That should buy us half an hour," he said.

"The limousine is only a hundred yards behind and gaining." Jessie's voice was high-pitched and apprehensive.

"You'll never shake them" said Velikov calmly. "My driver is an expert at high speeds, and the car is powered by a seven-liter 425-horsepower engine."

For all of Pitt's offhandedness and casual speech there was an icy competence and an unmistakable air about him of someone who knew exactly what he was doing.

He offered Velikov a reckless smile and said, "The Russians haven't built a car that can take a 'fifty-seven Chevy."

As if to hammer home the point he mashed the gas pedal to the floor and the tired old car seemed to reach into the depths of her worn parts for a burst of power she hadn't known in thirty years. The big roaring lump of iron could still go. She gathered speed and ate up the highway, the steady roar of her squat V-8 meant business.

Pitt's entire mind was concentrated on his driving and on studying the road two, even three turns ahead. The Zil clung tenaciously to the smokescreen that poured from the Chevy's tailpipe. He threw the car around a series of hairpin turns as they climbed through forested hills. He was skirting the fine edge of disaster. The brakes were awful and did little but smell and smoke when Pitt stood on them. Their lining was gone and metal ground against metal inside the drums.

At ninety miles an hour a front-wheel wobble set in with eyeball-rattling proportions. The steering wheel shuddered in Pitt's hands. The shock absorbers were long gone and the Chevy sponged around the bends, leaning precariously, tires screeching like wild turkeys.

Velikov sat stiff as wood, his eyes trained straight ahead, one hand gripping the door handle with white knuckles as if ready to eject before the inevitable crash.

Jessie was frankly terrified, closing her eyes as the car drifted and swayed wildly along the road. She braced her knees on the back of the front seat to keep from being thrown from side to side and stead-

391

ied the rifle aimed at Velikov's lower hairline.

If Pitt was aware of the considerable anguish he was causing his passengers, he gave no sign of it. A half-hour head start was the most he could hope for before the Cuban sentries made contact with their superiors and reported the kidnapping of the Soviet general. A helicopter would be the first sign the Cuban military was closing in and preparing a trap. When and how far ahead they would set up a roadblock was a matter of pure conjecture. A tank or a small fleet of armored cars suddenly appearing around a hidden curve and the ride would be over. Only Velikov's presence forestalled a massacre.

The driver of the Zil was no lightweight. He gained on Pitt in the turns, but dropped back in the straights as the burning acceleration of the old Chevy took hold. Out of the corner of one eye Pitt caught a small sign indicating they were approaching the port city of Cárdenas. Houses and small roadside businesses began to hug the highway and the traffic increased.

He glanced at the speedometer. The wavering needle hovered around 85. He backed off until it dropped to 70, keeping the Zil at bay as he weaved in and out of the traffic, one hand heavy on the horn. A policeman made a futile attempt to wave him to the curb as he careened around the Plaza Colón and a high bronze statue of Columbus. Luckily the streets were broad and he had little trouble staying clear of pedestrians and other vehicles.

The city lay just inland of a shallow, circular bay, and as long as he kept the sea on his right he figured he was still heading toward Havana. Somehow he managed to stay on the main road, and less than ten minutes later the car was flying from the major portion of the city and entering the countryside again.

During the high-speed run through the streets the Zil had closed to within fifty yards. One of the bodyguards leaned out the window and fired his pistol.

"They're shooting at us," Jessie announced in the tone of someone who was emotionally washed out.

"He's not aiming at us," Pitt replied. "They're trying for our tires."

"You're as good as caught," said Velikov. Those were the first words he had uttered in fifty miles. "Give it up. You can't get away."

"I'll quit when I'm dead." Pitt's cool composure was staggering.

It was not the answer Velikov was expecting. If all Americans were like Pitt, he thought, the Soviet Union was in for a rough time. Velikov prided himself on his skills in manipulating men, but this was clearly one man he would never dent.

They soared over a dip in the road and landed heavily on the other side. The muffler was torn away and the sudden thunder of exhaust was startling, almost shattering in its unexpected fury of sound. Their eyes began to water from the fumes, and the interior of the car became a steam bath under the combined onslaught of the heat from the engine and humid climate outside. The floorboards were almost hot enough to melt the soles of Pitt's boots. Between the noise and the heat, he felt as though he were working overtime in a boiler room.

The Chevy was becoming a mechanical bedlam. The teeth on the transmission were ground down to their nubs, and they howled in protest at the high revolutions. Strange knocking sounds began to emanate from the engine's bowels. But she was still vicious, and with that old deep-throated Chevy sound, she barreled along almost as if she knew this would be her last ride.

Pitt had carefully slowed ever so slightly and allowed the Russian driver to pull up within three car lengths. Pitt swung the Chevy back and forth across the road to throw off the bodyguard's aim. He eased his foot off the accelerator a hair until the Zil had come within twenty feet of the Chevy's rear bumper.

Then Pitt stood on the brakes.

The sergeant driving the Zil was good, but he wasn't that good. He snapped the steering wheel to the left and almost swung clear. But there was no time and even less distance. The Zil crashed into the rear of the Chevy with a scream of steel and an eruption of glass, crushing the radiator against the engine as the tail end whipped around in a corkscrew motion.

The Zil, madly out of control, and now nothing but three tons of metal bent on its own destruction, sideswiped a tree and caromed across the road to smash into an empty, broken-down bus at a speed of eighty miles an hour. Orange flame burst from the car as it flipped crazily end over end for over a hundred yards before coming to rest on its roof, all four tires still spinning. The Russians were trapped inside and had no hope of escape as the orange flames transformed into a thick cloud of black smoke.

The faithful, battered Chevy was still running on little but mechanical guts. Steam and oil were streaming from under the hood, second gear was gone along with the brakes, and the twisted rear bumper was dragging on the road, throwing out a spray of sparks.

The plume of smoke would draw the searchers. The net was closing. The next mile, the next curve in the highway, might reveal a roadblock. Pitt was sure a helicopter would appear any minute over the treetops bordering the road. Now was the time to ditch the car. It was senseless to play on his luck any longer. Like a bandit running from a posse, the time had come to trade horses.

He slowed down to fifty as he approached the outskirts of the city of Matanzas. He spotted a fertilizer plant and turned into the parking lot. Stopping the dying Chevy under a large tree, he looked around, and not seeing anyone, killed the engine. The crackling of burning metal and hissing steam replaced the ear-blasting drone of the exhaust.

"What's your next scheme?" asked Jessie. She was coming back on balance now. "You *do* have another scheme up your sleeve, I hope."

"The Artful Dodger has nothing on me," said Pitt with a reassuring grin. "Sit tight. If our friend the general hiccups, kill him."

He walked through the parking lot. It was a weekday and it was filled with the workers' cars. The stench from the plant had a sickening smell about it that filled the air for miles. He stood near the main gate as a stream of trucks loaded with ammonium sulphate, potassium chloride, and animal manure rumbled into the plant and trucks carrying the processed fertilizer in paper bags drove out. He had an idea and strolled casually down the dirt road that led to the highway. He waited for about fifteen minutes until a Russian-built truck filled with raw manure turned in and headed for the plant. He stood in the middle of the road and waved it to a stop.

The driver was alone. He looked down from the cab questioningly. Pitt motioned him out and pointed vigorously under the truck. Curious, the driver stepped to the ground and crouched down next to Pitt, who was staring intently at the drive shaft. Seeing nothing wrong, the driver turned just as Pitt chopped him on the back of the neck.

The driver went limp and Pitt caught him over a shoulder. He heaved the unconscious Cuban into the truck's cab and quickly climbed in. The engine was running and he shifted it into gear and drove toward the tree that shielded the Chevy from the air.

"Everyone climb aboard," he said, jumping down from the cab.

Jessie shrank back in disgust. "God, what's in there?"

"The polite word is manure."

"You expect me to wallow in filth?" demanded Velikov.

"Not only wallow," Pitt replied, "you're going to bury yourselves in it." He took the assault rifle from Jessie and prodded the general none too gently in the kidneys. "Up you go, General. You've probably rubbed many a KGB victim in slime. Now it's your turn."

Velikov shot Pitt a malignant look, and then climbed into the back of the truck. Jessie reluctantly followed as Pitt began stripping off the driver's clothes. They were several sizes too small and he had to leave the shirt unbuttoned and the pants fly unzipped to get into them. He quickly slipped his combat fatigues on the Cuban and dragged him up into the back with the others. He handed the rifle back to Jessie. She needed no instructions and placed the muzzle against Velikov's head. He found a shovel in a rack beside the cab and began to cover them.

Jessie gagged and fought to keep from retching. "I don't think I can take this."

"Be thankful it came from horses and cattle and not the city sewer."

"That's easy for you to say, you're driving."

When they were all invisible but could still breathe, Pitt returned to the cab and drove the truck back to the highway. He paused before turning as a flight of three military helicopters whirled overhead and a transport convoy of armed troops sped in the direction of the wrecked Zil.

Pitt waited and then turned left onto the highway. He was about to enter the city limits of Matanzas when he came to a roadblock manned by an armored car and nearly fifty soldiers, all looking very grim and purposeful.

He stopped and held out the papers he had taken off the driver. His scheme worked even better than he had imagined. The guards never came near the obnoxious-smelling truck. They waved him through, glad to see him on his way and happy to breathe fresh air again.

An hour and a half later the sun had fallen in the west and the lights of Havana twinkled to life. Pitt arrived in the city and drove up the Via Blanca. Except for the truck's aroma, he felt safely anonymous in the noisy, bustling, rush-hour traffic. He also felt more secure entering the city during the evening.

With no passport and no money his only option was to make contact with the American mission at the Swiss Embassy. They could take Jessie off his hands and keep him hidden until his passport and entry papers were sent by diplomatic courier from Washington. Once he became an official tourist, he could search for the riddle of the La Dorada treasure.

Velikov presented no problem. Alive, the general was a dangerous menace. He would go on murdering and torturing. Dead, he was only a memory. Pitt decided to kill him with one quick shot in a deserted alley. Anyone curious enough to investigate would simply chalk the blast up to a backfire from the truck.

He turned into a narrow road between a row of deserted warehouses near the dock area and stopped the truck. He left the engine running and stepped to the rear of the truck. As he climbed over the tailgate, he saw Jessie's head and arms protruding from the load of manure. Blood was seeping from a small gash in her temple and her right eye was swelling and turning purple. The only signs of Velikov and the Cuban driver were hollowed-out indentations where Pitt had buried them.

They were gone.

He eased her out of the muck and brushed it away from her cheeks. Her eyes fluttered open and focused on him, and after a moment she slowly shook her head from side to side. "I'm sorry, I messed things up."

"What happened?" he asked.

"The driver came to and attacked me. I didn't yell to you for help because I was afraid we might arouse suspicion and be stopped by police. We wrestled for the gun and it was lost over the side of the truck. Then the general grabbed my arms and the driver beat me until I passed out." Something suddenly occurred to her and she looked around wildly. "Where are they?"

"Must have jumped from the truck," he answered. "Can you remember where or how long ago it took place?"

The effort of concentration showed on her face. "I think it was about the time we were coming into the city. I recall hearing the sound of heavy traffic."

"Less than twenty minutes ago."

He helped her to the side of the truck bed and gently lowered her to the ground. "Best if we leave the truck here and catch a cab."

"I can't go anywhere smelling like this," she said in surprise. "And look at you. You look ridiculous. Your whole front end is open."

Pitt shrugged. "Oh, well, I won't be arrested for indecent exposure. I still have my shorts on."

"We can't catch a cab," she said in exasperation. "We don't have any Cuban pesos."

"The American mission at the Swiss Embassy will take care of it. Do you know where they're located?"

"It's called the Special Interests Section. Cuba has the same setup in Washington. The building faces the water on a boulevard called the Malecón."

"We'll hide out until it gets dark. Maybe we can find a water faucet and clean you up. Velikov will launch a full-scale search of the city for us. They'll probably watch the embassy, so we'll have to figure a way to sneak in. You feel strong enough to start walking?"

"You know something," she said with a pained smile, "I'm getting awfully tired of you asking that question."

65

IRA HAGEN STEPPED OFF the aircraft and entered the terminal of
José Martí Airport. He had prepared himself for a hassle with the
immigration officials, but they simply glanced at his diplomatic passport and passed him through with a minimum of formality. As he
walked to the baggage claim, a man in a seersucker suit hailed him.

"Mr. Hagen?"

"I'm Hagen."

"Tom Clark, chief of the Special Interests Section. I was alerted
to your arrival by Douglas Oates himself."

Hagen measured Clark. The diplomat was an athletic thirty-five
or so, with a tan face, Errol Flynn moustache, thinning red hair neatly
combed forward to hide the spreading bare front, blue eyes, and a
nose that had been broken more than once. He pumped Hagen's
hand heartily a good seven times.

"I don't suppose you greet many Americans down here," said Hagen.

"Very few since President Reagan placed the island off limits to
tourists and businessmen."

"I assume you've been apprised of the reason for my visit."

"Better we wait and discuss it in the car," said Clark, nodding
toward an unobtrusive fat woman sitting nearby with a small suitcase
on her lap.

Hagen didn't need a blueprint to recognize a stakeout with a disguised receiver that recorded their every word.

After close to an hour, Hagen's suitcase was finally cleared and
they made for Clark's car, a Lincoln sedan with a driver. A light rain
was falling, but Clark was prepared with an umbrella. The driver
placed the suitcase in the trunk and they set off toward the Swiss
Embassy, where the U.S. Special Interests Section was housed.

Hagen had honeymooned in Cuba several years before the revolution and he found that Havana looked much the same as he remembered it. The pastel colors of the stucco buildings gracing the palm-lined avenues seemed faded but little changed. It was a nostalgic trip. The streets were teeming with 1950s automobiles, makes that stirred old memories—Kaisers, Studebakers, Packards, Hudsons, and even one or two Edsels. They mingled with the newer Fiats from Italy and Ladas from Russia.

The city thrived, but not with the passions of the Batista years. The beggars, prostitutes, and slums were gone, replaced with an austere shabbiness that was the hallmark of Communist countries. Marxism was a wart on the rectum of mankind, Hagen decided.

He turned to Clark. "How long have you been in the diplomatic service?"

"Never," Clark answered. "I'm with the company."

"CIA."

Clark nodded. "If you prefer."

"That line about Douglas Oates?"

"For the benefit of the airport eavesdropper. I was informed of your mission by Martin Brogan."

"Where do you stand on finding and disarming the device?"

Clark smiled darkly. "You can call it a bomb. No doubt a low-yield bomb, but having enough punch to level half of Havana and start a firestorm that will incinerate every flimsy house and hut in the suburbs. And no, we haven't found it. We've got an undercover team of twenty men probing the dock areas and the three ships in question. Nothing has turned up. They might as well be looking for a shoe in a swamp. The celebration ceremonies and parade are less than eighteen hours away. It would take an army of two thousand searchers to find the bomb in time. And to make matters worse, our tiny force is handicapped by having to work around Cuban and Russian security measures. As things look, I'd have to say the detonation is inevitable."

"If I can get through to Castro and give him the President's warning—"

"Castro won't talk to anybody," said Clark. "Our most trusted officials in the Cuban government—we own five who hold top-level positions—can't make contact. I hate to say it, but your job is more hopeless than mine."

"Are you going to evacuate your people?"

There was a look of deep sadness in Clark's eyes. "No. We're all going to stay on this thing to the end."

Hagen was silent as the driver turned off the Malecón and through the entrance of what had once been the United States Embassy but was now officially occupied by the Swiss. Two guards in Swiss Army uniforms swung open the high iron gate.

Suddenly, with no warning, a taxicab whipped directly behind the limousine and followed it through the gate before the startled guards could react and push it closed. The cab was still rolling when a woman in a militia uniform and a man clad in rags jumped out. The guards quickly recovered and came running over as the stranger confronted them, crouching in a part-boxing, part-judo stance. They stopped, fumbling for their holstered automatic pistols. The delay was enough for the woman to yank open a rear door to the Lincoln and climb in.

"Are you American or Swiss?" she demanded.

"American," replied Clark, as stunned by the disgusting aroma that hung on her as by her abrupt appearance. "What do you want?"

Her answer was entirely unexpected. She began to laugh hysterically. "American or Swiss. My God, I sound like I'm asking for cheese."

The chauffeur finally woke up to the intrusion, leaped from the car, and grabbed her around the waist.

"Wait!" ordered Hagen, seeing that the woman's face was badly bruised. "What's going on?"

"I'm an American," she blurted after gaining a measure of control. "My name is Jessie LeBaron. Please help me."

"Good lord," Hagen muttered. "You're not Raymond LeBaron's wife?"

"Yes. Yes, I am." She motioned wildly at the struggle that was erupting in the driveway of the embassy. "Stop them. He's Dirk Pitt, special projects director for NUMA."

"I'll handle it," said Clark. By the time he was able to intercede, Pitt had flattened one guard and was wrestling with the other. The Cuban cab driver danced about wildly waving his arms and shouting for his fare. Several plainclothes policemen also added to the confusion by appearing from nowhere on the street side of the closed gate and demanding that Pitt and Jessie be turned over to them. Clark ignored the police, stopped the fight, and paid off the driver. Then he led Pitt over to the Lincoln.

"Where in hell did you come from?" Hagen asked. "The President thought you were either dead or arrested—"

"Not now!" Clark interrupted. "We'd better get out of sight before the police forget the sanctity of the embassy and turn ugly."

He quickly hustled everyone inside and through a corridor to the American section of the building. Pitt was shown to a spare room where he could take a shower and shave. One of the staff who was about his size lent him some casual clothes. Jessie's uniform was burned in the trash, and she thankfully bathed off the stench of the manure. A Swiss Embassy doctor gave her a thorough examination and treated her cuts and bruises. He arranged for a hearty meal and ordered her to rest for a few hours before being interviewed by Special Interests Section officials.

Pitt was escorted to a small conference room. As he entered, Hagen and Clark rose and formally introduced themselves. They offered him a chair and everyone got comfortable around a heavy-legged table hand-carved from pine.

"We haven't time for lengthy explanations," said Clark without preamble. "Two days ago, my superiors at Langley briefed me about your planned covert raid on Cayo Santa María. They confided in me so I would be prepared if it failed and there was fallout here in Havana. I was not told of its success until Mr. Hagen—"

"Ira," Hagen cut in.

"Until Ira just now showed me a top-secret document taken from the island installation. He also has a directive from Martin Brogan and the President asking me to be on the lookout for you and Mrs. LeBaron. I was ordered to notify them immediately in the event you were caught and arrested."

"Or executed," Pitt added.

"That too," acknowledged Clark.

"Then you also know why Jessie and I cut out and came to Cuba."

"Yes. She carries an urgent message from the President to Castro."

Pitt relaxed and slouched in his chair. "Fine. My part in the affair is finished. I'd appreciate it if you could arrange to fly me back to Washington after I've had a few days to take care of some personal business."

Clark and Hagen exchanged stares, but neither could look Pitt square in the eyes.

"Sorry to screw up your plans," said Clark. "But we have a crisis on our hands, and your experience with ships might prove helpful."

"I'd be no good to you. I'm washed out."

"Can we take a few minutes and tell you what we're dealing with here?"

"I'm willing to listen."

Clark nodded, satisfied. "Okay, Ira has come direct from the President. He's better qualified to explain the situation than I am." He turned to Hagen. "You've got the floor."

Hagen took off his coat, removed a handkerchief from his hip pocket, and wiped his perspiring forehead. "The situation is this, Dirk. Do you mind if I call you Dirk?"

"It's my name."

Hagen was an expert judge of men, and he liked what he saw. This guy didn't seem the type who could be conned. There was also a look about him that suggested trust. Hagen laid the cards on the table and spelled out the Russian plot to murder the Castros and assume control of Cuba. He waded through the details in concise terms, explaining how the nuclear explosive was smuggled into the harbor and the projected time of its detonation.

When Hagen finished, Clark outlined the operation to find the bomb. There was no time to bring in a highly trained nuclear-device search team, nor would the Cubans allow them to step foot in the city. He had only twenty men with the most primitive radiation-detection equipment. He had the horrifying responsibility of leading the search, and it didn't require much imagination for him to get across the futility of his substandard efforts. Finally he paused.

"Do you follow me, Dirk?"

"Yes..." Pitt said slowly. "I follow. Thank you."

"Any questions?"

"Several, but one is uppermost in my mind. What happens to all of us if this thing isn't found and disarmed?"

"I think you know the answer," said Clark.

"Okay, but I want to hear it from you."

Clark's face took on the look of a mourner at a funeral. "We all die," he said simply.

"Will you help us?" asked Hagen.

Pitt looked at Clark. "How much time is left?"

"Roughly sixteen hours."

Pitt rose from his chair and began pacing the floor, his instincts beginning to sift through the maze of information. After a minute of silence as Hagen and Clark watched him expectantly, he suddenly leaned across the table and said, "I need a map of the dock area."

One of Clark's staff quickly produced one.

Pitt smoothed it out on the table and peered at it. "You say you can't alert the Cubans?" he asked as he studied the docking facilities of the bay.

"No," Hagen replied. "Their government is riddled with Soviet agents. If we were to warn them, they'd ignore it and squelch our search operation."

"What about Castro?"

"Penetrating his security and warning him is my job," said Hagen.

"And the United States receives the blame."

"Soviet disinformation will see to that."

"May I have a pencil, please?"

Clark obliged and sat back quietly while Pitt made a circle on the map.

"My guess is the ship with the bomb is docked in the Antares Inlet."

Clark's eyebrows raised. "How could you know that?"

"The obvious place for an explosion to cause the most damage. The inlet cuts almost into the heart of the city."

"Good thinking," said Clark. "Two of the suspected ships are docked there. The other is across the bay."

"Give me a rundown on the vessels?"

Clark examined the page of the document pertaining to the ship arrivals. "Two belong to the Soviet Union merchant fleet. The third sails under Panamanian registry and is owned by a corporation run by Cuban anti-Castro exiles."

"The last is a phony front set up by the KGB," said Hagen. "They'll claim the Cuban exiles are an arm of the CIA, making us the villains of the destruction. There won't be a nation in the world who will believe our noninvolvement."

"A sound plan," said Clark. "They'd hardly use one of their own vessels to carry the bomb."

"Yes, but why destroy two ships and their cargoes for no purpose?" asked Pitt.

"I admit it doesn't add up."

"Ships' names and cargoes?"

Clark extracted another page from the document and quoted from it. "The *Ozero Zaysan*, Soviet cargo ship carrying military supplies and equipment. The *Ozero Baykai*, a 200,000-ton oil tanker. The bogus Cuban-operated ship is the *Amy Bigalow*, bulk carrier with a cargo of 25,000 tons of ammonium nitrate."

Pitt stared at the ceiling as if mesmerized. "The oil tanker, is she the one moored across the bay?"

"Yes, at the oil refinery."

"Have any of the cargoes been unloaded?"

Clark shook his head. "There has been no activity around the two

403

cargo carriers, and the tanker still sits low in the water."

Pitt sat down again and gave the other two men in the room a cold, hard stare. "Gentlemen, you've been had."

Clark looked at Pitt in dark speculation. "What are you talking about?"

"You overestimated the Russians' grandstand tactics and underestimated their cunning," said Pitt. "There is no nuclear bomb on any of those ships. For what they plan to do, they don't need one."

66

COLONEL GENERAL VIKTOR KOLCHAK, chief of the fifteen thousand Soviet military forces and advisers based on Cuban soil, came from behind his desk and embraced Velikov warmly.

"General, you don't know how glad I am to see you alive."

"The feeling is mutual, Colonel General," said Velikov, returning Kolchak's bear hug.

"Sit down, sit down, we have much to discuss. Whoever was behind the destruction of our island surveillance facility will pay. A communication from President Antonov assures me he will not take this outrage sitting down."

"No one agrees more than me," said Velikov. "But we have another urgent matter to discuss."

"Care for a glass of vodka?"

"I can do without," Velikov replied brusquely. "Rum and Cola takes place tomorrow morning at ten-thirty. Are your preparations complete?"

Kolchak poured a small shot of vodka for himself. "Soviet officials and our Cuban friends are discreetly slipping out of the city in small groups. Most of my military forces have already left to begin sham maneuvers forty miles away. By dawn, all personnel, equipment, and important documents will have been quietly evacuated."

"Leave some behind," Velikov said casually.

Kolchak peered over his rimless glasses like a grandmother hearing a four-letter word from a child. "Leave what behind, General?"

Velikov brushed off the derisive look. "Fifty Soviet civilian personnel, wives and families, and two hundred of your military forces."

"Do you know what you're asking?"

"Precisely. We cannot lay blame on the CIA for a hundred thousand deaths without suffering casualties ourselves. Russians dying beside

405

Cubans. We'll reap propaganda rewards that will go far in smoothing the path for our new government."

"I can't bring myself to throw away the lives of two hundred and fifty countrymen."

"Conscience never bothered your father when he cleared German mine fields by marching his men over them."

"That was war."

"Only the enemy has changed," Velikov said coldly. "We have been at war with the United States since 1945. The cost in lives is small compared to increasing our hold in the Western Hemisphere. There is no room for argument, General. You will be expected to do your duty."

"I don't need the KGB lecturing me on my duty to the motherland," Kolchak said without rancor.

Velikov shrugged indifferently. "We all do our part. Getting back to Rum and Cola; after the explosion your troops will return to the city and assist in medical and relief operations. My people will oversee the orderly transition of government. I'll also arrange for international press coverage showing benevolent Soviet soldiers caring for the injured survivors."

"As a soldier I have to say I find this entire operation abhorrent. I can't believe Comrade Antonov is a party to it."

"His reasons are valid, and I for one do not question them."

Kolchak leaned against the edge of his desk, his shoulders sagging. "I'll have a list made up of those who will stay."

"Thank you, Colonel General."

"I assume all preparations are complete?"

Velikov nodded. "You and I will accompany the Castro brothers to the parade reviewing stand. I will be carrying a pocket transmitter that will detonate the explosives in the primary ship. When Castro begins his usual marathon speech, we will make an unobtrusive exit to a waiting staff car. Once we are safely out of range—allowing about thirty minutes to drive fifteen miles—I'll activate the signal and the blast will follow."

"How do we explain our miraculous escape?" Kolchak asked sarcastically.

"First reports will have us dead and missing. Later, we'll be discovered among the injured."

"How badly injured?"

"Just enough to look convincing. Torn uniforms, a little blood, and some artificial wounds covered by bandages."

406

"Like two hooligans who vandalized the dressing rooms of a theater."

"Hardly the metaphor that comes to mind."

Kolchak turned and sadly looked out the window of his headquarters over the busy city of Havana.

"Impossible to believe that tomorrow at this time," he said in a morbid tone, "all this will be a smoldering, twisted sea of misery and death."

The President worked at his desk late. Nothing was cut-and-dried, black or white. The job of Chief Executive was one compromise after another. His wins over Congress were diluted by tacked-on amendments, his foreign policies picked apart by world leaders until little remained of the original proposals. Now he was trying to save the life of a man who had viewed the United States as his number one enemy for thirty years. He wondered what difference any of it would make two hundred years from now.

Dan Fawcett walked in with a pot of coffee and sandwiches. "The Oval Office never sleeps," he said with forced cheerfulness. "Your favorite, tuna with bacon." He offered the President a plate and then poured the coffee. "Can I help you with anything?"

"No thanks, Dan. Just editing my speech for tomorrow's news conference."

"I can't wait to see the faces of the press corps when you lay the existence of the moon colony on them, and then introduce Steinmetz and his people. I previewed some of the videotapes they brought back of their lunar experiments. They're incredible."

The President set the sandwich aside and thoughtfully sipped the coffee. "The world is upside down."

Fawcett paused in midbite. "Pardon?"

"Think of the terrible incongruity. I'll be informing the world of man's greatest modern achievement at the same time that Havana is being blown off the map."

"Any late word from Brogan since Pitt and Jessie LeBaron popped up at our Special Interests Section?"

"Not in the past hour. He's keeping a vigil at his office too."

"How in the world did they ever manage it?"

"Two hundred miles through a hostile nation. Beats me."

The direct phone line to Langley rang. "Yes."

"Martin Brogan, Mr. President. Havana reports that searchers have not yet detected a positive radioactive reading in any of the ships."

"Did they get on board?"

"Negative. Security is too heavy. They can only drive by the two ships tied to the docks. The other one, an oil tanker, is moored in the bay. They circled it in a small boat."

"What are you telling me, Martin? The bomb was unloaded and hidden in the city?"

"The ships have been under tight surveillance since arriving in the harbor. No cargo has come off."

"Maybe the radiation can't leak through the steel hulls of the ships."

"The experts at Los Alamos assure me it can. The problem is our people in Havana are not professional radiation experts. They're also hamstrung having to use commercial Geiger counters that aren't sensitive enough to measure a light reading."

"Why didn't we get qualified experts with the right equipment in there?" the President demanded.

"It's one thing to send in one man on a diplomatic mission with a small suitcase like your friend Hagen. It's something else to smuggle a team with five hundred pounds of electronic equipment. If we had more time, something might have been arranged. Covert boat landings and parachute drops stand little chance through Cuba's defense screen. Smuggling by ship is the best method, but we're talking at least a month's preparation."

"You make it sound like we're a guy with an unknown disease and no known cure."

"That about sums it up, Mr. President," said Brogan. "About all we can do is sit and wait...and watch it happen."

"No, I won't have that. In the name of humanity we have to do something. We can't let all those people die." He paused, feeling a knot growing in his stomach. "God, I can't believe the Russians will actually set off a nuclear bomb in a city. Doesn't Antonov realize he's plunging us deeper into a morass there can be no backing out of?"

"Believe me, Mr. President, our analysts have run every conceivable contingency through computers. There is no easy answer. Asking the Cubans to evacuate the city through our radio networks will accomplish nothing. They'll simply ignore any warnings coming from us."

"There is still hope Ira Hagen can get to Castro in time."

"Do you really think Fidel will take Hagen at face value? Not very likely. He'll think it's only a plot to discredit him. I'm sorry, Mr. President, we have to steel ourselves against the disaster, because there isn't a damned thing we can do about it."

The President wasn't listening anymore. His face reflected grim despair. We put a colony on the moon, he thought, and yet the world's inhabitants still insist on murdering each other for asinine reasons.

"I'm calling a cabinet meeting tomorrow early, before the moon colony announcement," he said in a defeated voice. "We'll have to create a plan to counter Soviet and Cuban accusations of guilt and pick up the pieces as best we can."

67

LEAVING THE SWISS EMBASSY was ridiculously easy. A tunnel had been dug twenty years before that dropped over a hundred feet below the streets and sewer pipes, far beneath any shafts Cuban security people might have sunk around the block. The walls were sealed to keep out water, but silent pumps were kept busy draining away the seepage.

Clark led Pitt down a long ladder to the bottom, and then through a passage that ran for nearly two city blocks before ending at a shaft. They climbed up and emerged in a fitting room of a women's dress shop.

The shop had closed six hours earlier and the window displays effectively blocked any view of the interior. Sitting in the storeroom were three exhausted, haggard-looking men who gave barely a sign of recognition to Clark as he entered with Pitt.

"No need to know real names," said Clark. "May I present Manny, Moe, and Jack."

Manny, a huge black with a deeply trenched face, wearing an old faded green shirt and khaki trousers, lit a cigarette and merely glanced at Pitt with world-weary detachment. He looked like a man who had experienced the worst of life and had no illusions left.

Moe was peering through spectacles at a Russian phrase book. He wore the image of an academic—lost expression, unruly hair, neatly sculptured beard. He silently nodded and gave an offhand smile.

Jack was the stereotype Latin out of a 1930s movie—flashing eyes, compact build, fireworks teeth, triangular moustache. All he was missing was a bongo drum. He gave the only words of recognition. "*Hola,* Thomas. Come to pep-talk the troops?"

"Gentlemen, this is...ah...Sam. He's come up with an angle that throws new light on the search."

"It better be damned well worth it to drag us off the docks," grunted Manny. "We've got little time to waste on asshole theories."

"You're no closer now to finding the bomb than you were twenty-four hours ago," Clark said patiently. "I suggest you listen to what he has to say."

"Screw you," Manny said. "Just when we found a way to slip on board one of the freighters, you call us back."

"You could have searched every inch of those ships and never found a ton-and-a-half nuclear device," said Pitt.

Manny turned his attention to Pitt, eyes traveling from feet to hair, like a linebacker sizing up an opposing halfback. "Okay, smartass, where's our bomb?"

"Three bombs," Pitt corrected, "and none of them nuclear."

There was silence in the room. Everyone but Clark appeared skeptical.

Pitt pulled the map from under his shirt and unfolded it. He borrowed some pins from a mannikin and stuck it on one wall. He was not put off by the indifferent attitude of the group of CIA agents. His eyes showed him these men were alert, precise, and competent. He knew they possessed a remarkable variety of skills and the absolute determination of men who did not take failure lightly.

"The *Amy Bigalow* is the first link in the holocaust chain. Her cargo of twenty-five thousand tons of ammonium nitrate—"

"That's nothing but *fertilizer*," said Manny.

"—is also a highly volatile chemical," Pitt continued. "If that amount of ammonium nitrate were to explode, its force would be far greater than the bombs dropped on Hiroshima and Nagasaki. They were air drops and much of their destructive power was lost in the atmosphere. When the *Amy Bigalow* blows at ground level, most of her power will sweep through Havana like a hurricane of molten lava. The *Ozero Zaysan*, whose manifest claims she's carrying military supplies, is probably crammed to the top of her holds with munitions. She'll unleash her destructive horror in a sympathetic explosion with the *Amy Bigalow*. Next, the *Ozero Baykai* and her oil will ignite, adding to the devastation. Fuel storage tanks, refineries, chemical plants, any factory with volatile materials, will go up. The conflagration can conceivably last for days."

Outwardly, Manny, Moe, and Jack appeared uncomprehending, the expressions on their faces inscrutable. Inwardly, they were stunned by the unthinkable horror of Pitt's vision of hell.

Moe looked at Clark. "He's on dead center, you know."

411

"I agree. Langley misread the Soviets' intent. The same results can be achieved without resorting to nuclear terror."

Manny rose and clasped Pitt's shoulders between two great clamshell hands. "Man, I gotta hand it to you. You really know where the crap flows."

Jack spoke up for the first time. "Impossible to unload those ships before the celebration tomorrow."

"But they can be moved," said Pitt.

Manny considered that for a moment. "The freighters might clear the harbor, but I wouldn't bet on getting the tanker under way in time. We'd need a tug just to shove her bows toward the channel."

"Every mile we put between those ships and the harbor means a hundred thousand lives spared," said Pitt.

"Might give us extra time to look for the detonators," said Moe.

"If they can be found before we reach open sea, so much the better."

"And if not," Manny muttered grimly, "we'll all be committin' suicide."

"Save your wife the cost of a funeral," said Jack with a death's-head smile. "There won't be anything left to bury."

Moe looked doubtful. "We're way short of hands."

"How many ship's engineers can you scrape up?" asked Pitt.

Moe nodded across the room. "Manny there used to be a chief engineer. Who else can you name, Manny?"

"Enrico knows his way around an engine room. So does Hector when he's sober."

"That's three," said Pitt. "What about deckhands?"

"Fifteen, seventeen including Moe and Jack," answered Clark.

"That's twenty, and I make twenty-one," said Pitt. "What about harbor pilots?"

"Every one of them bastards is in Castro's pocket," snorted Manny. "We'll have to steer the ships clear ourselves."

"Wait just a damned minute," interjected Moe. "Even if we overpowered the security force guarding the docks, we'd still have the ships' crews to fight."

Pitt turned to Clark. "If your people take care of the guards, I'll eliminate the crews."

"I'll personally lead a combat team," replied Clark. "But I'm curious as to how you intend to accomplish your end of the bargain."

"Already done," Pitt said with a wide grin. "The ships are abandoned. I'll guarantee that the crews have been quietly evacuated to a safe place outside the destruction zone."

"The Soviets might spare the lives of their own people," said Moe. "But they'd hardly give a damn about the foreign crew on the *Amy Bigalow.*"

"Sure, but on the other hand, they couldn't risk a nosy crewman hanging around while the detonating device was placed in position."

Jack thought a moment, then said, "Two and two make four. This guy is sharp."

Manny gazed at Pitt with a newfound respect in his eyes. "You with the company?"

"No, NUMA."

"Second-guessed by an amateur," Manny sighed. "Time to take my pension."

"How many men do you estimate are patrolling the ships?" Clark asked him.

Manny took out a soiled handkerchief and blew his nose like a honking goose before answering. "About a dozen guarding the *Bigalow.* Same number around the *Zaysan.* A small patrol boat is moored next to the oil tanker. Probably no more than six or seven in her crew."

Clark began to pace back and forth as he spoke. "So that's it. Gather up your crews. My team will take out the guards and protect the operation. Manny, you and your men will get the *Amy Bigalow* under way. Moe, take the *Ozero Zaysan.* The tugboat is your department, Jack. Just make sure there isn't an alarm when you pirate it. We've got six hours of daylight left. Let's make good use of every minute." He stopped and looked around. "Any questions?"

Moe raised a hand. "After we make open water, what happens to us?"

"Take your ship's motor launch and beat it as fast and as far as you can before the explosions."

No one made a comment. They all knew their chances bordered on hopeless.

"I'd like to volunteer to go with Manny," said Pitt. "I'm pretty fair with a helm."

Manny came to his feet and slapped a hand on Pitt's back that knocked the wind from him. "By God, Sam, I think I might learn to like you."

Pitt gave him a heavy stare. "Let's hope we live long enough to find out."

413

68

THE *AMY BIGALOW* lay moored alongside a long modern wharf that had been built by Soviet engineers. Beyond her, a few hundred yards across the dock channel, the cream-colored hull of the *Ozero Zaysan* sat dark and deserted. The lights of the city sparkled across the black waters of the harbor. A few clouds drifted down from the mountains, crossing the city and heading out to sea.

The Russian-built command car turned off the Boulevard Desemparados, followed by two heavy military trucks. The convoy moved slowly through the dock area and stopped at the boarding ramp of the *Amy Bigalow*. A sentry stepped from inside a guard shack and cautiously approached the car.

"Do you have permission to be in this area?" he asked.

Clark, wearing the uniform of a Cuban colonel, gave the sentry an arrogant stare. "Send for the officer of the guard," he ordered sharply. "And say *sir* when you address an officer."

Recognizing Clark's rank under the yellowish, sodium vapor lights that illuminated the waterfront, the sentry stiffened to attention and saluted. "Right away, sir. I'll call him."

The sentry ran back to the guard shack and picked up a portable transmitter. Clark shifted in his seat uneasily. Deception was vital, strong-arm tactics fatal. If they had stormed the ships with guns blazing, alarms would have sounded throughout the city's military garrisons. Once alerted, and with their backs to the wall, the Russians would have been forced to set off the explosions ahead of schedule.

A captain came through a door of a nearby warehouse, paused a moment to study the parked column, and then walked up to the passenger side of the command car and addressed Clark.

"Captain Roberto Herras," he said, saluting. "How can I help you, sir?"

"Colonel Ernesto Pérez," replied Clark. "I've been ordered to relieve you and your men."

Herras looked confused. "My orders were to guard the ships until noon tomorrow."

"They've been changed," Clark said curtly. "Have your men assemble for departure back to their barracks."

"If you don't mind, Colonel, I wish to confirm this with my commanding officer."

"And he'll have to call General Melena, and the general is asleep in bed." Clark stared at him with narrowed, cold eyes. "A letter attesting to your insubordination won't look good when your promotion to major comes due."

"Please, sir, I'm not refusing to obey a superior."

"Then I suggest you accept my authority."

"Yes, Colonel. I—I'm not doubting you…" He caved in. "I'll assemble my men."

"You do that."

Ten minutes later Captain Herras had his twenty-four-man security force lined up and ready to move out. The Cubans took the change of guard willingly. They were all happy to be relieved and returned to their barracks for a night's sleep. Herras did not seem to notice that the colonel's men remained hidden inside the darkness of the lead truck.

"This your entire unit?" asked Clark.

"Yes, sir. They're all accounted for."

"Even the men guarding the next ship?"

"Sorry, Colonel. I left sentries at the boarding ramp to make sure no one boarded until your men were dispersed. We can drive by and pick them up as we leave."

"Very well, Captain. The rear truck is empty. Order them to board. You can take my car. I'll have my aide pick it up later at your headquarters."

"That's good of you, sir. Thank you."

Clark had his hand on a tiny .25-caliber silenced automatic that was sitting loose in his pants pocket, but he left it in place. The Cubans were already climbing over the tailgate of the truck under the direction of a sergeant. Clark offered his seat to Herras and casually strolled toward the silent truck containing Pitt and the Cuban seamen.

The vehicles had turned around and were leaving the dock area when a staff car carrying a Russian officer drove up and stopped. He leaned out the window of the rear seat and stared, a suspicious frown on his face.

"What's going on here?"

Clark slowly approached the car and passed around the front end, assuring himself that the only occupants were the Russian and his driver.

"Changing of the guard."

"I know of no such orders."

"They came from General Velikov," said Clark, halting no more than two feet from the rear door. He could now see the Russian was also a colonel.

"I've just come from the general's headquarters to inspect security. Nothing was said about changing the guard." The colonel opened the door as if to get out of the car. "There must be a mistake."

"No mistake," said Clark. He pressed the door shut with his knees and shot the colonel between the eyes. Then he coldly put two bullets in the back of the driver's head.

Minutes later the car was set in gear and rolled into the dark waters between the wharves.

Manny led the way, followed by Pitt and four Cuban merchant seamen. They rushed up the boarding ramp to the main deck of the *Amy Bigalow* and split up. Pitt climbed the ladder topside while the rest dropped down a companionway to the engine room. The wheelhouse was dark, and Pitt left it that way. He spent the next half hour checking the ship's electronic controls and speaker system with a flashlight until he had every lever and switch firmly planted in his mind.

He picked up the ship's phone and rang the engine room. A full minute went by before Manny answered.

"What in the hell do you want?"

"Just checking in," said Pitt. "Ready when you are."

"You got a long wait, mister."

Before Pitt could reply, Clark stepped into the wheelhouse. "You talking to Manny?" he asked.

"Yes."

"Get him up here, now."

Pitt passed on Clark's brusque command, and received a barrage of four-letter words before ringing off.

Less than a minute later, Manny burst through the door reeking

416

of sweat and oil. "Make it quick," he snapped to Clark. "I got a problem."

"Moe has it even worse."

"I already know. The engines have been shut down."

"Are yours in running shape?"

"Why wouldn't they be?"

"The Soviet crew took sledgehammers to every valve on the *Ozero Zaysan*," said Clark heavily. "Moe says it would take two weeks to make repairs."

"Jack will have to tow him out to sea with the tug," Pitt said flatly.

Manny spat through the wheelhouse door. "He'll never make it back in time to move the oil tanker. The Russians ain't blind. They'll catch on to the game soon as the sun comes up."

Clark nodded his head in slow understanding. "I fear he's right."

"Where do you stand?" Pitt asked Manny.

"If this tub had diesels, I could start her up in two hours. But she's got steam turbines."

"How much time do you need?"

Manny looked down at the deck, his mind running over the lengthy and complicated procedures. "We're starting with a dead plant. First thing we did was get the emergency diesel generator going and light off the burners in the furnace to heat the fuel oil. The lines have to be drained of condensation, the boilers fired up, and the auxiliaries put on line. Then wait for the steam pressure to rise enough to operate the turbines. We're looking at four hours—providin' everything goes right."

"Four hours?" Clark felt dazed.

"Then the *Amy Bigalow* can't clear the harbor before daylight," said Pitt.

"That wraps it." There was a tired certainty in Clark's voice.

"No, that doesn't wrap it," said Pitt firmly. "If we get even one ship past the harbor entrance we cut the death toll by a third."

"And we all die," added Clark. "There'll be no escape. Two hours ago I'd have given us a fifty-fifty chance of surviving. Not now, not when your old friend Velikov spots his monstrous plan steaming over the horizon. And lest we forget the Soviet colonel sitting on the bottom of the bay, he'll be missed before long and a regiment will come looking for him."

"And there's that captain of the security guards," said Manny. "He'll wise up damned quick when he catches hell for leaving his duty area without proper orders."

The thump of heavy diesel engines slowly amplified outside and a ship's bell gave off three muted rings.

Pitt peered through the bridge windows. "Jack's coming alongside with the tug."

He turned and faced the lights of the city. They reminded him of a vast jewelry box. He began to think of the multitude of children who went to bed looking forward to the holiday celebrations. He wondered how many of them would never wake up.

"There's still hope," he said at last. Quickly he outlined what he thought would be the best solution for reducing the devastation and saving most of Havana. When he finished, he looked from Manny to Clark. "Well, is it workable?"

"Workable?" Clark was numb. "Myself and three others holding off half the Cuban Army for three hours? It's downright homicidal."

"Manny?"

Manny stared at Pitt, trying to make something of the craggy face that was barely visible from the lights on the wharf. Why would an American throw away his life for people who would shoot him on sight? He knew he'd never find the answer in the darkened wheelhouse of the *Amy Bigalow,* and he shrugged in slow finality.

"We're wastin' time," he said as he turned and headed back to the ship's engine room.

69

THE LONG BLACK LIMOUSINE eased to a quiet stop at the main gate of Castro's hunting lodge in the hills southeast of the city. One of the two flags mounted on the front bumper symbolized the Soviet Union and the other marked the passenger as a high-ranking military officer.

The visitors' house outside the fenced estate was the headquarters for Castro's elite bodyguard force. A man in a tailored uniform but showing no insignia walked slowly up to the car. He looked at the shadowed form of a big Soviet officer sitting in the darkness of the backseat and at the identification that was held out the window.

"Colonel General Kolchak. You do not have to prove yourself to me." He threw a wavelike salute. "Juan Fernández, chief of Fidel's security."

"Don't you ever sleep?"

"I'm a night owl," said Fernández. "What brings you here at this ungodly hour?"

"A sudden emergency."

Fernández waited for further elaboration, but none came. He began to feel uneasy. He knew that only a critical situation could bring the Soviets' highest-ranking military representative out at three-thirty in the morning. He wasn't sure how to deal with it.

"I'm very sorry, sir, but Fidel left strict orders not to be disturbed by anyone."

"I respect President Castro's wishes. However, it's Raúl I must speak with. Please tell him I'm here on a matter of extreme urgency that must be dealt with face to face."

Fernández mulled over the request for a moment and then nodded. "I'll phone up to the lodge and tell his aide you're on your way."

"Thank you."

Fernández waved to an unseen man in the visitors' house and the

419

electronically operated gate swung open. The limousine drove up a curving road that hugged the hills for about two miles. Finally, it pulled up in front of a large Spanish-style villa that overlooked a panorama of dark hills dotted by distant lights.

The driver's boot crunched on the gravel drive as he stepped around to the passenger's door. He did not open it but stood there for nearly five minutes, casually observing the guards that patrolled the grounds. At last, Raúl Castro's chief of staff came yawning through the front door.

"Colonel General, what an unexpected pleasure," he said without enthusiasm. "Please come in. Raúl is on his way down."

Without replying, the Soviet officer heaved his bulk from the car and followed the aide over a wide patio and into the foyer of the lodge. He held a handkerchief over his face and snorted into it. His driver came also, keeping a few steps behind. Castro's aide stood aside and gestured toward the trophy room. "Please make yourselves comfortable. I'll order some coffee."

Left alone, the two stood silently with their backs to the open doorway and stared at an army of boar heads mounted on the walls and the dozens of stuffed birds perched around the room.

Raúl Castro soon entered in pajamas and silk paisley robe. He halted in midstride as his guests turned and faced him. His brows knitted together in surprise and curiosity.

"Who the devil are you?"

"My name is Ira Hagen, and I bear a most important message from the President of the United States." Hagen paused and nodded at his driver, who doffed her cap, allowing a mass of hair to fall to her shoulders. "May I present Mrs. Jessie LeBaron. She's endured great hardship to deliver a personal reply from the President to your brother regarding his proposed U.S.–Cuban friendship pact."

For a moment the silence in the room was so total that Hagen became conscious of the ticking of an elaborate grandfather clock standing against the far wall. Raúl's dark eyes darted from Hagen to Jessie and held.

"Jessie LeBaron is dead," he said in quiet astonishment.

"I survived the crash of the blimp and torture by General Peter Velikov." Her voice was calm and commanding. "We carry documented evidence that he intends to assassinate you and Fidel tomorrow morning during the Education Day celebration."

The directness of the statement, the tone of authority behind it, made an impression on Raúl.

420

He hesitated thoughtfully. Then he nodded. "I'll wake Fidel and ask him to listen to what you have to say."

Velikov watched as a file cabinet from his office was jostled onto a handcart and taken by elevator down to the fireproof basement of the Soviet Embassy. His second-ranking KGB officer entered the disarranged room, brushed some papers from a chair, and sat down.

"Seems a shame to burn all of this," he said tiredly.

"A new and finer building will rise from the ashes," said Velikov with a cunning smile. "Gift of a grateful Cuban government."

The phone buzzed and Velikov quickly answered. "What is it?"

The voice of his secretary replied. "Major Borchev wishes to talk to you."

"Put him on."

"General?"

"Yes, Borchev, what's your problem?"

"The captain in command of waterfront security has left his post along with his men and returned to their base outside the city."

"They left the ships unguarded?"

"Well... not exactly."

"Did they or did they not desert their post?"

"He claims he was relieved by a guard force under the command of a Colonel Ernesto Pérez."

"I issued no such order."

"I'm aware of that, General. Because if you had, it would have most certainly come to my attention."

"Who is this Pérez and what military unit is he assigned to?"

"My staff has checked Cuban military files. They find no record of him."

"I personally sent Colonel Mikoyan to inspect security measures around the ships. Make contact and ask him what in hell is happening down there."

"I've tried to raise him for the past half hour," said Borchev. "He doesn't respond."

Another line buzzed, and Velikov placed Borchev on hold.

"What is it?" he snapped.

"Juan Fernández. General, I thought you should know that Colonel General Kolchak just arrived for a meeting with Raúl Castro."

"Not possible."

"I checked him through the gate myself."

421

This new development added fuel to Velikov's confusion. A stunned look gripped his face and he expelled his breath in an audible hiss. He had only four hours' sleep in the last thirty-six and his mind was becoming woolly.

"You there, General?" asked Fernández anxiously at the silence.

"Yes, yes. Listen to me, Fernández. Go to the lodge and find out what Castro and Kolchak are doing. Listen in to their conversation and report back to me in two hours."

He didn't wait for an acknowledgment, but punched into Borchev's line. "Major Borchev, form a detachment and go to the dock area. Lead it yourself. Check out this Pérez and his relief force and report back to me as soon as you find out anything."

Then Velikov buzzed his secretary. "Get me Colonel General Kolchak's headquarters."

His deputy straightened in the chair and stared at him curiously. He had never seen Velikov in a state of nervousness before.

"Something wrong?"

"I don't know yet," Velikov muttered.

The familiar voice of Colonel General Kolchak suddenly burst from the other end of the phone line. "Velikov, how are things progressing with the GRU and KGB?"

Velikov stood stunned for several moments before recovering. "Where are you?"

"Where am I?" Kolchak repeated. "Trying to clear classified documents and equipment from my headquarters, the same as you. Where did you think I was?"

"I just received a report you were meeting with Raúl Castro at the hunting lodge."

"Sorry, I haven't mastered being in two places at the same time," said Kolchak imperturbably. "Sounds to me your intelligence agents are starting to see ghosts."

"Most strange. The report came from a usually reliable source."

"Is Rum and Cola in any danger?"

"No, it is continuing as planned."

"Good. Then I take it the operation is running smoothly."

"Yes," Velikov lied with a fear tainted by uncertainty, "everything is under control."

70

THE TUGBOAT WAS CALLED the *Pisto* after a Spanish dish of stewed red peppers, zucchini, and tomatoes. The name was appropriate, as her sides were streaked red with rust and her brass coated with verdigris. Yet, despite the neglect to her outer structure, the big 3,000-horsepower diesel engine that throbbed in her bowels was as bright and glossy as a polished bronze sculpture.

Hands gripping the big teakwood wheel, Jack stared through the moisture-streaked windows at the gigantic mass looming up in the blackness. She was as cold and dark as the other two carriers of death tied to the docks. No navigation lights indicated her presence in the bay, only the patrol boat that circled her 1,100-foot length and 160-foot beam served as a warning for other craft to stay clear.

Jack eased the *Pisto* abreast of the *Ozero Baykai* and cautiously edged toward the aft anchor chain. The patrol boat quickly spotted them and came alongside. Three men rushed from the bridge and manned a rapid-fire gun on the bow. Jack rang the engine room for All Stop, an act that was strictly for show as the tug's bow wave was already dying away to a ripple.

A young lieutenant with a beard leaned out of the wheelhouse of the patrol boat and raised a bullhorn.

"This is a restricted area. You don't belong here. Move clear."

Jack cupped his hands to his mouth and shouted, "I've lost all power to my generators and my diesel just died on me. Can you give me a tow?"

The lieutenant shook his head in exasperation. "This is a military boat. We do not give tows."

"Can I come aboard and use your radio to call my boss? He'll send another tug to tow us clear."

"What's wrong with your emergency battery power?"

"Worn out." Jack made a gesture of helplessness. "No parts for repair. I'm on the waiting list. You know how it is."

The boats were so close now they were almost touching. The lieutenant laid aside the bullhorn and replied in a rasping voice, "I cannot allow that."

"Then I'll have to anchor right here until morning," Jack replied nastily.

The lieutenant angrily threw up his hands in defeat. "Come aboard and make your call."

Jack dropped down a ladder to the deck and jumped across the four-foot gap between the boats. He looked around him with a slow, salty indifference, carefully noting the relaxed attitude of the three-man gun crew, the mate standing by the helm casually lighting a cigar, the tired look on the lieutenant's face. The only man who was missing, he knew, was the engineer below.

The lieutenant came up to him. "Make it quick. You're interfering with a military operation."

"Forgive me," said Jack slavishly, "but it's not my doing."

He reached forward as if wanting to shake hands and pumped two bullets from a silenced automatic into the lieutenant's heart. Then he calmly shot the helmsman.

The trio around the bow gun crumpled and died under a flight of three precisely aimed arrows, fired by Jack's crew with crossbows. The engineer never felt the bullet that struck him in the temple. He fell over the boat's diesel engine, lifeless hands gripping a rag and a wrench.

Jack and his crewmen carried the bodies below and then swiftly opened all drain plugs and sea cocks. They returned to the tug and paid no more attention to the sinking patrol boat as it drifted away on the tide into the darkness.

There was no gangway down, so a pair of grappling hooks were thrown over the tanker's deck railing. Jack and two others clambered up the sides and then hauled up portable acetylene tanks and a cutting torch.

Forty-five minutes later the anchor chains were cut away and the little *Pisto*, like an ant trying to move an elephant, buried her heavy rope bow fender against the huge stern of the *Ozero Baykai*. Inch by inch, almost imperceptibly at first, and then yard by yard the tug began nudging the tanker away from the refinery and toward the middle of the bay.

· · ·

Pitt observed the slothful movement of the *Ozero Baykai* through a pair of night glasses. Fortunately the ebb tide was working in their favor, pulling the behemoth farther from the core of the city.

He had found a self-contained breathing unit and searched the holds for any sign of a detonating device, but could find nothing. He came to the conclusion it must have been buried somewhere under the ammonium nitrate in one of the middle cargo holds. After nearly two hours, he climbed to the main deck and thankfully breathed in the cool breeze off the sea.

Pitt's watch read 4:30 when the *Pisto* came about and returned to the docks. She made straight for the munitions ship. Jack backed her in until Moe's men hauled in the tow wire that was unreeled from the great winch on the stern of the tug and made fast to the *Ozero Zaysan*'s aft bollards. The lines were cast off, but just as the *Pisto* prepared to pull, a military convoy of four trucks came roaring onto the wharf.

Pitt dropped down the gangway and hit the dock at a dead run. He dodged around a loading crane and stopped at the stern line. He heaved the fat, oily rope off the bollard and let it fall in the water. There was no time to cast off the bow line. Heavily armed men were dropping from the trucks and forming into combat teams. He climbed the gangway and engaged the electric winch that lifted it level with the deck to prevent any assault from the wharf.

He snatched up the bridge phone and rang the engine room. "Manny, they're here" was all he said.

"I've got vacuum and enough steam in one boiler to move her."

"Nice work, my friend. You shaved off an hour and a half."

"Then let's haul ass."

Pitt walked over to the ship's telegraph and moved the pointers to Stand By. He threw the helm over so the stern would swing away from the pier first. Then he rang for Dead Slow Astern.

Manny rang back from the engine room and Pitt could feel the engines begin to vibrate beneath his feet.

Clark realized with sudden dismay that his small group of men were greatly outnumbered and any escape route cut off. He also discovered that they were not up against ordinary Cuban soldiers but an elite force of Soviet marines. At best he might gain a few minutes' grace—enough time for the ships to move clear of the docks.

He reached into a canvas bag hanging from his belt and took out a grenade. He stepped from the shadows and lobbed the grenade into the rear truck. The explosion came like a dull thump, followed by a brilliant flash of flame as the fuel tank burst. The truck seemed to blossom outward, and men were thrown across the dock like fiery bowling pins.

He ran through the dazed and disorganized Russians, leaping over the screaming injured who were rolling around the dock desperately trying to douse their flaming clothing. The next detonations came in rapid succession, echoing across the bay, as he heaved three more grenades under the remaining trucks.

Fresh flame and clouds of smoke billowed above the roofs of the warehouses. The marines frantically abandoned their vehicles and scrambled for their lives out of the holocaust. A few were galvanized into action and began firing into the darkness at anything that vaguely resembled a human form. The ragged fusillade mingled with the sound of shattering glass as the windows of the warehouses were blown away.

Clark's small team of six fighters held their fire. The few shots that came in their direction went over their heads. They waited as Clark mingled in the disorganized melee, unsuspected in his Cuban officer's uniform, cursing in fluent Russian and ordering the marines to regroup and charge up the wharf.

"Form up! Form up!" he shouted excitedly. "They're running away. Move, damn you, before the traitors escape!"

He broke off suddenly as he came face to face with Borchev. The Soviet major's mouth fell open in total incredulity and before he could close it Clark grabbed him by the arm and hurled him over the dock into the water. Fortunately, no one took notice amid the confusion.

"Follow me!" Clark yelled, and began running up the dock where it passed between two warehouses. Individually, and in groups of four or five, the Soviet marines raced after him, crouching and zig-zagging in highly trained movements across the wharf, laying down a sheet of fire as they advanced.

They seemed to have overcome the paralyzing shock of surprise and were determined to retaliate against their unseen enemy, never knowing they were escaping from one nightmare and entering another. No one questioned Clark's orders. Without their commander

426

to tell them otherwise, the noncoms exhorted their men to follow the officer in the Cuban uniform who was leading the attack.

When the marines had dodged their way between the warehouses, Clark threw himself flat as though hit. It was the signal for his men to open up. The Soviets were hit from all sides. Many were cut off their feet. They made perfect targets, silhouetted by the blazing pyre of the trucks. Those who survived the scything sweep of death returned the fire. The staccato crash of sound was deafening as shells thudded into wooden walls and human flesh or missed and richocheted, whining into the night.

Clark rolled violently toward the cover of a packing crate, but was struck in the thigh and again by a bullet that passed through both wrists.

Badly battered, but still fighting, the Soviet marines began to pull back. They made a futile attempt to break out of the dock area and reach the safety of a concrete wall running along the main boulevard, but two of Clark's men laid down a hail of fire that stopped them in their tracks.

Clark lay there behind the crate, blood streaming from shattered veins, his life draining away, and he was helpless to stop it. His hands hung like broken tree limbs, and there was no feeling in his fingers. Blackness was already closing in when he dragged himself to the edge of the pier and stared out over the harbor.

The last sight his eyes were to ever see was the outline of the two cargo ships against the lights on the opposite shore. They were swinging clear of the docks and turning toward the harbor entrance.

71

WHILE THE BATTLE WAS RAGING on the wharf, the little *Pisto* took the tow and began pulling the *Ozero Zaysan* into the harbor stern first. Struggling mightily, she buried her huge single propeller in the oily water and boiled it into a cauldron of foam.

The 20,000-ton vessel began to move, her formless bulk animated by orange flames as she slipped into open water. Once free of the docks Jack made a wide 180-degree sweep, pivoting the munitions ship until her bow faced the harbor entrance. Then the tow wire was released and winched in.

In the wheelhouse of the *Amy Bigalow* Pitt gripped the helm and hoped something would give. He tensed, scarcely daring to breathe. The still-fastened bowline came taut and creaked from the tremendous stress placed on it by the backing vessel and stoutly refused to snap. Like a dog straining at a leash, the *Amy Bigalow* tucked her bow slightly, increasing the tension. The rope held, but the bollard was torn from its dock mountings with a loud crunch of splintered wood.

A tremor ran through the ship and she gradually began to back away into the harbor. Pitt put the wheel over and slowly the bows came around until she had turned broadside to the receding dock. The vibration from the engine smoothed out and soon they were quietly gliding astern with a light wisp of smoke rising from the funnel.

The whole waterfront seemed to be ablaze, the flames from the burning trucks casting an eerie, flickering light inside the wheelhouse. All hands except Manny came up from the engine room and stood by on the bow. Now that he had room to maneuver, Pitt spun the wheel hard to starboard and rang Slow Ahead on the telegraph.

428

Manny answered and the *Amy Bigalow* lost sternway and began to creep slowly forward.

The stars in the east were beginning to lose their sparkle as the shadowy hull of the *Ozero Zaysan* drew abeam. Pitt ordered All Stop as the tugboat came about under the bows. The *Pisto*'s crew flung up a light heaving rope that was tied to a graduated series of heavier lines. Pitt watched from the bridge as they were hauled on board. Then the thick tow cable was taken up by a forward winch and made fast.

The same act was repeated on the stern, only this time with the port anchor chain from the dead and drifting *Ozero Zaysan*. After the chain was winched across, its links were tied to the after bits. The two-way connection was made. The three vessels were now tethered together, with the *Amy Bigalow* in the middle.

Jack gave a blast on the *Pisto*'s air horn, and the tug began to ease ahead, taking up the slack. Pitt stood on the bridge wing and stared aft. When one of Manny's men signaled that the tow chain on the stern was taut, Pitt gave a slight pull on the steam whistle and swung the telegraph to Full Ahead.

The final step in Pitt's plan had been completed. The oil tanker was left behind, floating nearer the oil storage tanks on the opposite shore of the harbor, but a good mile farther from the more populated center of the city. The other two ships and their deadly cargoes were gathering way in their dash for the open sea, the tugboat adding her power to that of the *Amy Bigalow* to raise the speed of the marine caravan.

Behind them the great column of smoke and flame spiraled up into the early blue of morning. Clark had bought them enough time for a fighting chance, but he had paid with his life.

Pitt did not look back. His eyes were drawn like a magnet on the beacon from the lighthouse above the gray walls of Morro Castle, that grim fortress guarding the entrance to Havana Harbor. It lay three miles away, but it seemed thirty.

The die was cast. Manny raised power to the other engine and the twin screws thrashed the water. The *Amy Bigalow* began to pick up speed. Two knots became three. Three became four. She beat toward the channel below the lighthouse like a Clydesdale in a pulling contest.

They were forty minutes away from reaching home free. But the warning was out and the unthinkable was yet to come.

429

Major Borchev dodged the burning embers that fell and hissed in the water. Floating there under the pilings, he could hear the roar of automatic weapons fire and see the flames leap into the sky. The dirty water between the docks felt tepid and reeked of dead fish and diesel oil. He gagged and vomited up the foul backwash he had swallowed when the strange Cuban colonel shoved him over the side.

He swam for what seemed a mile before he found a ladder and climbed to the top of an abandoned pier. He spat out the disgusting taste and jogged toward the burning convoy.

Blackened and smoldering bodies littered the dock. The gunfire had stopped after Clark's few surviving men escaped in a small outboard boat. Borchev walked cautiously through the carnage. Except for two wounded men who had taken refuge behind a forklift, the rest were dead. His entire detachment had been wiped out.

Half crazed with anger, Borchev staggered among the victims, searching, until he came upon the body of Clark. He rolled the CIA agent over on his back and looked down into sightless eyes.

"Who are you?" he demanded senselessly. "Who do you work for?"

The answers had died with Clark.

Borchev took the limp body by the belt and dragged it to the edge of the pier. Then he kicked it into the water.

"See how you like it!" he shouted insanely.

Borchev wandered aimlessly amid the massacre for another ten minutes before he regained his balance. He finally realized he had to report to Velikov. The only transmitter had melted inside the lead truck, and he began to run around the waterfront, feverishly hunting for a telephone.

He found a sign on a building identifying a dockworkers' recreation room. He lunged at the door and smashed it open with his shoulder. He fumbled along the wall, found the light switch, and turned it on. The room was furnished with old stained sofas. There were checkerboards and dominoes and a small refrigerator. Posters of Castro, Che Guevara haughtily smoking a cigar, and a somber Lenin stared down from one wall.

Borchev entered the office of a supervisor and snatched up the telephone on a desk. He dialed several times without getting through. Finally he raised the operator, cursing the retarded efficiency of the Cuban phone system.

430

The clouds above the eastern hills were beginning to glow orange and the sirens of the city's fire squads were converging on the waterfront when he was finally connected to the Soviet Embassy.

Captain Manuel Pinon stood on the bridge wing of the Russian-built Riga-class patrol frigate and steadied his binoculars. He had been awakened by his first officer soon after the fighting and conflagration had broken out in the commercial dock area. He could see little through the binoculars because his vessel was moored to the naval dock around a point just below the channel and his vision was blocked by buildings.

"Shouldn't we investigate?" asked his first officer.

"The police and fire crews can handle it," answered Pinon.

"Sounds like gunshots."

"Probably a warehouse blaze that's ignited military supplies. Better we stay clear of the fireboats." He handed the glasses to the first officer. "Keep a watch on it. I'm going back to bed."

Pinon was just about to enter his stateroom when his first officer came running up the passageway.

"Sir, you'd better return to the bridge. Two ships are attempting to leave the harbor."

"Without clearance?"

"Yes, sir."

"Could be they're moving to a new mooring."

The first officer shook his head. "Their heading is taking them into the main channel."

Pinon groaned. "The gods are against me getting any sleep."

The first officer grinned sardonically. "A good Communist does not believe in gods."

"Tell that to my white-haired mother."

On the bridge wing once again, Pinon yawned and peered through the early-morning haze. Two ships under tow were about to enter the Entrada Channel for open seas.

"What in hell—" Pinon refocused the glasses. "Not a flag, not a navigation light showing, no lookouts on the bridge—"

"Nor do they respond to our radio signals requesting their intent. Almost looks like they're trying to sneak out."

"Counterrevolutionary scum trying to reach the United States," Pinon growled. "Yes, that must be it. Can't be anything else."

"Shall I give the order to cast off and get under way?"

431

"Yes, immediately. We'll come around across their bows and block their way."

Even as he spoke, the first officer's hand was reaching for the siren switch that whooped the crew to action stations.

Ten minutes later the thirty-year-old ship, retired by the Russian Navy after it had been replaced by a newer, modified class of frigate, drifted broadside across the channel. Her four-inch guns turned and aimed almost point-blank at the rapidly approaching phantom vessels.

Pitt gazed at the blinking signal lamp on the frigate. He was tempted to turn on the radio, but it was agreed upon from the beginning that the convoy would remain silent in case an alert port authority official or security post receiver happened to tune in on the same frequency. Pitt's international Morse code was rusty, but he deciphered the message as "Stop immediately and identify."

He kept a sharp eye on the *Pisto*. He was aware that any sudden evasive move would have to originate with Jack. Pitt called down to the engine room and alerted Manny to the frigate blocking their course, but the brass telegraph pointers remained locked on Full Ahead.

They were so close now he could see the Cuban naval ensign standing stiffly in the offshore breeze. The vanes on the signal lamp flipped up and down again. "Stop immediately or we will open fire."

Two men appeared on the stern of the *Pisto* and frantically began reeling out more cable. At the same time the tug lost way, made a sharp turn to starboard, and heaved to. Then Jack stepped out of the wheelhouse and hailed the frigate through a bullhorn.

"Give way, you sea cow's ass. Can't you see I have a tow?"

Pinon ignored the insult. He expected no less from a tug captain. "Your movement is unauthorized. I am sending over a boarding party."

"I'll be damned if I let any candy-ass Navy boy step foot on my ship."

"You'll be dead if you don't," Pinon replied in good humor. He was uncertain now whether this was a mass escape attempt by dissidents, but the strange actions of the tug and unlit ships required an investigation.

He leaned over the bridge railing and ordered the ship's motor cutter and boarding crew to lower away. When he turned back to face the unidentified convoy, he froze in horror.

Too late. In the dusky light he had failed to see that the ship behind the tug was not a dead tow. It was under way and boring down on the frigate at a good eight knots. He stared dazedly for several seconds before his reeling mind took hold.

"Full ahead!" he shrieked. "Guns fire!"

His command was followed by a deafening blast as shells streaked across the narrowing gap, tore into the bow and superstructure of the *Amy Bigalow*, and exploded in a burst of flame and shattered steel. The port side of the wheelhouse seemed to melt away as if ripped open by a junkyard mangling machine. Glass and debris felt like pellets out of a shotgun. Pitt ducked and kept his grip on the wheel with a determination tied to blind stubbornness. He was lucky to emerge with only a few cuts and a bruised thigh.

The second salvo blew away the chart room and sliced the forward mast in two. The top half fell over the side and was dragged for a hundred feet before the cables parted and it floated clear. The funnel was shattered and turned to scrap, and a shell burst inside the starboard anchor locker, scattering a cloud of salt-rusted links like shrapnel.

There would be no third salvo.

Pinon stood absolutely still, hands tightly clenched on the bridge rail. He stared up at the menacing black bows of the *Amy Bigalow* as they rose ponderously over the frigate, his face white and his eyes sick with a certainty that his ship was about to die.

The frigate's screws beat the water in a frenzy, but they could not push her out of the way soon enough. There was no question of the *Amy Bigalow* missing and no doubt as to Pitt's intentions. He was compensating and cutting the angle toward the frigate's midsection. Those of the crew who were topside and could see the approaching disaster gazed numb with horror before finally reacting and throwing themselves over the sides.

The *Amy Bigalow*'s sixty-foot-high stem slashed through the frigate just forward of her rear turret, shredding the plates and penetrating the hull for nearly twenty feet. Pinon's ship might have survived the collision and made shore before settling in the water, but with a terrible screech of grinding steel the bow of the *Amy Bigalow* rose up from the gaping wound until her barnacled keel was exposed. She hung there for an instant, and then dropped, crushing the frigate in two and pile-driving the stern section out of sight beneath the surface.

Instantly, the sea poured into the amputated stern, sweeping through the twisted bulkheads and flooding the open compartments. As the cataract surged into the doomed frigate's hull she quickly began to settle astern. Her dying agony did not last long. By the time the *Ozero Zaysan* was towed over the collision site, she was gone, leaving a pitiful few of her crew struggling in the water.

72

"YOU WALKED INTO A TRAP?" Velikov's voice came flat and hard over the phone.

Borchev felt uncomfortable. He couldn't very well admit that he was one of the only three survivors out of forty and lacked even a scratch. "An unknown force of at least two hundred Cubans opened fire with heavy equipment before we could evacuate the trucks."

"You certain they were Cubans?"

"Who else could have planned and carried it out? Their commanding officer was wearing a Cuban Army uniform."

"Pérez?"

"Can't say. We'll need time to make an identification."

"Might have been a blunder by green troops who opened fire out of stupidity or panic."

"They were far from stupid. I can recognize highly trained combat troops when I see them. They knew we were coming and laid a well-prepared ambush."

Velikov's face went completely blank and then quickly reddened. The assault on Cayo Santa María passed before his eyes. He could scarcely contain his rage. "What was their objective?"

"A delaying action to take possession of the ships."

Borchev's answer staggered Velikov. He felt as if his body had turned to ice. The questions came spilling out of his mouth. "The Rum and Cola operation ships were seized? Are they still moored to their docks?"

"No, a tugboat towed off the *Ozero Zaysan*. The *Amy Bigalow* steamed clear under her own power. I lost sight of them after they rounded the point. A little later I heard what sounded like naval gunfire near the entrance channel."

Velikov had heard the rumble of heavy guns too. He stared at a

435

blank wall with unbelieving eyes, trying to envision the circle of men dogging his intricately planned operations. He refused to believe that intelligence units loyal to Castro had the knowledge and expertise. Only the long arm of the Americans and their Central Intelligence Agency could have destroyed Cayo Santa María and wrecked his scheme to terminate the Castro regime. Only one individual could have been responsible for the leak of information.

Dirk Pitt.

A deep look of concentration tensed Velikov's face. The mud was clearing from the water. He knew what he had to do in the little time left.

"Are the ships still in the harbor?" he demanded of Borchev.

"If they were trying to escape to the sea, I'd put them somewhere in the Entrada Channel."

"Find Admiral Chekoldin and tell him I want those ships stopped and headed back to the inner harbor."

"I thought all Soviet naval ships have stood out to sea."

"The admiral and his flagship aren't due to depart until eight o'clock. Don't use the telephone. Convey my request in person and stress the urgency."

Before Borchev could reply, Velikov threw down the receiver and rushed to the main entrance of the embassy, ignoring the busy staff preparing for evacuation. He ran outside to the embassy limousine and shoved aside the chauffeur, who was standing by to drive the Soviet ambassador to safety.

He turned the ignition key and threw the transmission into drive the instant the engine fired. The rear wheels spun and shrieked furiously as the car leaped out of the embassy courtyard into the streets.

Two blocks later Velikov was stopped dead.

A military roadblock barred his way. Two armored cars and a company of Cuban soldiers stretched across the broad boulevard. An officer stepped up to the car and shone a flashlight in the window.

"May I see your identification papers, please?"

"I am General Peter Velikov, attached to the Soviet Military Mission. I'm in a great hurry to reach Colonel General Kolchak's headquarters. Stand aside and let me pass."

The officer studied Velikov's face for a moment as if satisfying himself. He switched off the flashlight and motioned for two of his men to enter the backseat. Then he came around and climbed into the front passenger's seat.

436

"We've been waiting for you, General," he said in a cold but courteous tone. "Please follow my directions and turn left at the next cross street."

Pitt stood, feet slightly apart, both hands on the helm, his craggy face thrust forward, as he watched the lighthouse at the harbor entrance slip past with terrible slowness. His whole mind and body, every nerve was concentrated on moving the ship as far away from the populated city as possible before the ammonium nitrate was detonated.

The water turned from gray-green to emerald and the ship started to roll slightly as it plowed into the swells marching in from the sea. The *Amy Bigalow* was taking in water through her ripped bow plates, but she still answered her helm and chased after the tailing wake of the tugboat.

His whole body ached from exhaustion. He drove himself on with sheer willpower. The blood from the cuts he received from the blast of the frigate's guns had hardened into dark red streaks down his face. He was oblivious to the sweat and the clothes sticking to his body.

He closed his eyes for a moment and wished he was back in his hangar apartment with a Bombay gin martini, sitting in a steaming shower. God, he was tired.

A sudden gust of wind blew in through the shattered bridge windows and he opened his eyes again. He studied the shorelines both port and starboard. The hidden gun emplacements around the harbor remained silent and there were still no signs of aircraft or patrol vessels. Despite the battle with the naval frigate no alarm had been given. The confusion and lack of intelligence among the Cuban military security forces were working in their favor.

The still sleeping city lingered behind as if tied to the trailing ship's stern. The sun was up now and the convoy in naked view up and down the coast.

A few more minutes, a few more minutes, he said in his mind over and over.

Velikov was ordered to stop on a quiet corner near Cathedral Square in old Havana. He was led into a shabby building with dusty and cracked windows, past glass cases displaying faded posters of 1940s

437

movie stars staring at the camera while seated at the bar inside.

A one-time watering hole patronized by wealthy American celebrities, Sloppy Joe's was now only a dingy hole in the wall, long forgotten except by an elderly few. Four people were seated off to one side of the tarnished and neglected bar.

The interior was dark and smelled of disinfectant and decay. Velikov didn't recognize his hosts until he was halfway across the unswept floor. Then he stopped short and stared unbelieving, a sudden nausea growing within him.

Jessie LeBaron was sitting between a strange fat man and Raúl Castro. The fourth party stared back ominously.

"Good morning, General," said Fidel Castro. "I'm happy you could join us."

73

PITT'S EARS PICKED UP the drone of an aircraft. He released his hold on the wheel and stepped to the door of the bridge wing.

A pair of helicopter gunships were beating along the shore from the north. His gaze swung back to the harbor entrance. A gray warship was charging through the channel at full speed, throwing up a big bow wave. A Soviet destroyer this time, pencil-thin, forward guns trained on the creeping, defenseless death ships. The chase that nobody could win was on.

Jack stepped out onto the deck of the tugboat and looked up at the broken, twisted wreck of the *Amy Bigalow*'s bridge. He marveled that anyone was still alive and manning the helm. He made a gesture to his ear and waited until a hand waved back in understanding. He watched as a crewman hurried to the freighter's stern and gave the same signal to Moe on board the *Ozero Zaysan*. Then he returned inside and called out on the radio.

"This is *Pisto*. Do you read? Over."

"Loud and clear," replied Pitt.

"I've got you," Moe added.

"This is as good a time as any to tie your helms and abandon ship," said Jack.

"Good riddance," Moe snorted. "Let these hell buckets go up by themselves."

"We'll leave our engines running at full ahead," said Pitt. "What about the *Pisto*?"

"I'll man her a few more minutes to make sure the ships don't circle back to shore," replied Jack.

"Better not be late. Castro's boys are coming through the slot."

"I see them," said Jack. "Good luck. Out."

Pitt locked the helm in the Dead Ahead position and called up

Manny. The tough chief engineer needed no urging. He and his men were swinging the ship's motor launch out in its davits three minutes later. They scrambled aboard and were beginning to lower it when Pitt jumped over the railing and dropped in.

"Almost left you behind," shouted Manny.

"I radioed the destroyer and told her to stand clear or we'd blow up the munitions ship."

Before Manny could reply, there was an echoing thunderlike rumble. A few seconds later a shell plunged into the sea fifty yards in front of the *Pisto*.

"They didn't buy your bill of goods," Manny grunted. He started the boat's engine and engaged the gearbox to equal the ship's headway when they hit the water. The falls were cast off and they were thrown broadside into the wash, almost swamping the launch. The *Amy Bigalow* swept past on her final voyage, deserted and destined for obliteration.

Manny turned and saw that Moe and his crew were lowering the *Ozero Zaysan*'s launch. It smashed into a swell and was thrown against the steel sides with such force that the seams on the starboard side were sprung and the bottom half awash, drowning the engine.

"We've got to help them," said Pitt.

"Right you are," Manny agreed.

Before they could come about, Jack had appraised the situation and yelled through his bullhorn, "Leave them be. I'll pick them up after I cut loose. Look to yourselves and head for shore."

Pitt took the pilot's chair from a crewman who had smashed his fingers in the davit ropes. He sheered the launch toward the tall buildings lining the Malecón waterfront and crammed the throttle against its stop.

Manny was looking back at the tug and the drifting launch that carried Moe's crew. His face went gray as the destroyer fired again and twin columns of water straddled the *Pisto*. The spray crashed down on her upper works, but she shook off the deluge and plowed on.

Moe turned away with a feeling of dread that he did not show. He knew he would never see his friends alive again.

Pitt was gauging the distance between the retreating ships and the shore. They were still close enough for the explosives to devastate a major share of Havana, he judged grimly, way too close.

•   •   •

"Did President Antonov agree to your plan for my assassination?" Fidel Castro asked.

Velikov stood with arms crossed. He was not offered a chair. He glared back at Castro with cold contempt. "I am a ranking military office of the Soviet Union. I demand to be treated accordingly."

The black, angry eyes of Raúl Castro flashed. "This is Cuba. You don't demand anything here. You're nothing but KGB scum."

"Enough, Raúl, enough," cautioned Fidel. He looked at Velikov. "Don't toy with us, General. I've studied your documents. Rum and Cola is no longer a secret."

Velikov played out his hand. "I'm fully aware of the operation. Another vicious CIA attempt to undermine the friendship between Cuba and the Soviet Union."

"If that is so, why didn't you warn me?"

"There was no time."

"You found time enough to clear out Russian nationals," Raúl snapped. "Why were you running away at this time in the morning?"

A look of arrogance crossed Velikov's face. "I won't bother to answer your questions. Need I remind you I have diplomatic immunity. You have no right to interrogate me."

"How do you intend to set off the explosives?" asked Castro calmly.

Velikov stood silent. The corners of his lips turned up slightly in a smile at the sound of the distant rumble of heavy gunfire. Fidel and Raúl exchanged glances, but nothing was said between them.

Jessie shuddered as the tension mounted in the small barroom. For a moment she wished she was a man so she could beat the truth out of the general. She suddenly felt sick and wanted to scream because of the costly time that was drifting away.

"Please tell them what they want to know," she begged. "You can't stand there and allow thousands of children to die for a senseless political cause."

Velikov did not argue. He remained unmoved.

"I'll be happy to take him out back," said Hagen.

"You needn't soil your hands, Mr. Hagen," said Fidel. "I have experts in painful interrogation waiting outside."

"You wouldn't dare," Velikov snapped.

"It is my duty to warn you that if you do not halt the detonation you'll be tortured. Not with simple injections like political prisoners at your mental hospitals in Russia, but unspeakable tortures that will continue day and night. Our finest medical specialists will keep you alive. No nightmare can do justice to your suffering, General. You

441

will scream until you can scream no more. Then, when you are little more than a vegetable without sight, speech, or hearing, you will be transported and dumped in a slum somewhere in North Africa where you will survive or die, and where no one will rescue or pity a crippled beggar living in filth. You will become what you Russians call a nonperson."

Velikov's shell cracked, but very thinly. "You waste your breath. You are dead. I am dead. We are all dead."

"You're mistaken. The ships carrying the munitions and ammonium nitrate have been removed from the harbor by the very people you blame. At this minute agents of the CIA are sailing them out to sea where the explosive force will only kill the fish."

Velikov quickly pressed his slim advantage. "No, *Señor Presidente,* it is you who are mistaken. The sound of guns you heard a few moments ago came from a Soviet vessel stopping the ships and turning them back inside the harbor. They may explode too early for your celebration speech, but they will still accomplish the end results."

"You're lying," Fidel said uneasily.

"Your reign as the great father of the revolution is over," said Velikov, his voice sly and baiting. "I'll gladly die for the Russian motherland. Will you sacrifice your life for Cuba? Maybe when you were young and had nothing to lose, but you're soft now and too used to having others do your dirty work for you. You've got the good life and you're not about to let it slip away. But it's finished. Tomorrow you'll only be another photograph on a wall and a new president will sit in your place. One whose loyalties extend to the Kremlin."

Velikov stepped back a few paces and took out a small case from his pocket.

Hagen recognized it immediately. "An electronic transmitter. He can send a signal to detonate the explosives from here."

"Oh, God!" Jessie cried despairingly. "Oh, my God, he's going to do it, he's really going to do it."

"Don't bother to call your bodyguards," said Velikov. "They'll never react in time."

Fidel stared at him with cold bleak eyes. "Remember what I said."

Velikov stared back contemptuously. "Can you really picture me screaming in agony in one of your dirty prisons?"

"Give me the transmitter and you will be free to leave Cuba unharmed."

"And return to Moscow a cowardly figure? I think not."

"It's on your head," said Fidel, his expression a curious blend of anger and fear. "You know your fate if you detonate the explosives and live."

"Little chance of that," Velikov sneered. "This building sits less than five hundred yards from the harbor channel. There will be nothing left of us." He paused, his face as hard as a chiseled gargoyle. Then he said, "Goodbye, *Señor Presidente.*"

"You bastard—" Hagen leaped over the table in an incredible display of agility for his huge bulk and was only inches away from Velikov when the Russian pressed the transmitter's Activate switch.

74

THE *AMY BIGALOW* VAPORIZED.

The *Ozero Zaysan* waited only a fraction of a second longer before blowing herself out of existence. The combined force of the volatile cargoes inside the two ships threw up a mountainous column of fiery debris and smoke that thrust five thousand feet into the tropical sky. A vast vortex opened in the sea as a gigantic geyser of maddened water and steam shot up into the smoke and then burst outward.

The brilliant red-white glare flashed across the water with the blinding intensity of ten suns, followed by a thunderous clap that lashed and flattened the wave tops.

The sight of the gallant little *Pisto* as the blast flung her two hundred feet into the air like a disintegrating skyrocket was locked forever in Pitt's mind. He watched stunned as her shredded remains along with Jack and his crew splattered into the maelstrom like burning hail.

Moe and his crew in the drifting launch simply vanished off the face of the sea.

The explosive fury blew the two helicopter gunships out of the air. Seagulls within two miles were crushed by the concussion. The propeller from the *Ozero Zaysan* whirled across the sea and smashed into the control castle of the Soviet destroyer, killing every man on the bridge. Twisted steel plates, rivets, chain links, and deck gear pelted the city, tearing through walls and roofs like cannon shells. Telephone poles and streetlights were lashed and broken off at the base.

Hundreds of people perished in their beds while still asleep. Many were terribly gashed by flying glass or crushed by pancaked ceilings. Early-morning workers and pedestrians were picked up off their feet and crushed against buildings.

The shock wave struck the city with twice the force of any recorded hurricane, flattening wooden structures near the shore as though they were paper toys, collapsing storefronts, shattering a hundred thousand windows, and hurling parked automobiles into buildings.

Inside the harbor the monstrous *Ozero Baykai* went up.

At first, flames shot from her hull like blowtorches. Then the whole oil tanker burst open in a giant fireball. A surge of flaming oil swamped the surrounding waterfront structures and launched a chain reaction of explosions from combustible cargoes sitting on the docks. Fiery metal plunged into oil and gas storage tanks on the east side of the harbor. One after another they blew up like a time-sequence fireworks display, spewing gigantic black smoke clouds over the city.

An oil refinery exploded, then a chemical company blew, followed by blasts at a paint company and fertilizer plant. Two nearby freighters, under way and heading for sea, collided, caught fire, and began to blaze. A fiery hunk of steel from the destroyed tanker plummeted into one of ten railroad tank cars containing propane and sent them up like a string of firecrackers.

Another blast...then another...and another.

Four miles of waterfront were turned into a holocaust. Ashes and soot covered the city like a black snowfall. Few stevedores working the docks survived. Fortunately, the refineries and the chemical plant were nearly abandoned. Loss of life would have been many times higher if it had not been a national holiday.

The worst of the disaster inside the harbor was past, but the nightmare still facing the rest of the city had yet to arrive.

An immense fifty-foot tidal wave rose up out of the vortex and hurtled toward shore. Pitt and the others stared in awe as the green and white mountain roared after them. They sat there waiting, no panic, just staring and waiting for the frail little launch to become a shattered piece of wreckage and the water their tomb.

The seawall along the Malecón was only thirty yards away when the horizontal avalanche engulfed the launch. The crest curled and burst right over them. It tore Manny and three men from their seats, and Pitt watched them sail through the crashing spray like roof shingles in a tornado. The seawall rushed closer but the momentum of the wave lifted the launch over the top and slung it across the wide boulevard.

Pitt clutched the helm with such strength that it was torn away from its mounting and he was swept clear. He thought this was the

445

end, but with a conscious effort of will he took a deep breath and held it as he was pulled under. As if in a dream he could look down through the strangely clear and demoniac water, seeing cars tumbling in crazy gyrations as if thrown by a giant hand.

Buried deep in the boiling turmoil, he felt strangely detached. It struck him as ludicrous that he was about to drown on a city street. His desire for life still clung tenaciously, but he did not struggle senselessly and waste precious oxygen. He went lax and vainly tried to peer through the froth, his mind somehow working with uncanny clarity. He knew that if the wave swept him against a concrete building the rushing tons of water would mash him into the same consistency as a watermelon dropped from an airplane.

His fear would have been heightened if he had seen the launch smash into the second story of an apartment building that housed Soviet technicians. The impact collapsed the hull as if the planking were no stronger than an eggshell. The four-cylinder diesel engine was tossed through a broken window by the cascade and ended up in a stairwell.

Mercifully, Pitt was swept into a narrow side street like a log through a chute. The flood carried everything before it in a great tumbling mass of wreckage. But even as it curled around the buildings strong enough to withstand the onslaught, the wave was already beginning to die. Within seconds the leading edge would reach its high mark and then recede, the retreating torrent sucking human bodies and loose debris back to the sea.

Pitt began to see stars as his brain starved for oxygen. His senses began to shut down one by one. He felt a jarring blow as his shoulder struck a fixed object. He whipped an arm around it, trying to hang on, but he was thrust forward by the force of the wave. He ran into another flat surface, and this time he reached out and clutched it in a death grip, not recognizing it as a sign over a jeweler's shop.

The thinking, feeling equipment of his body slowed and shut down as if its electrical current had switched off. His head was pounding and blackness was covering the stars bursting behind his eyes. He existed only on instinct, and soon even that would desert him.

The wave had reached its outer limit and began to fall in on itself, rushing back to the sea. It was too late for Pitt, he was slipping away from consciousness. His brain somehow managed to send out one last message. An arm clumsily jammed its way between the sign and its support shaft that protruded from the building, and wedged there.

446

Then his bursting lungs could take no more, and he began to drown.

The great rumble from the explosions echoed away into the hills and sea. There was no sunlight over the city, no real sunlight. It was hidden by a smoke-blackened pall of incredible density. The whole harbor seemed afire; the docks, ships, storage tanks, and three square miles of oil-coated water were bristling with orange and blue flame that streaked up into the dark canopy.

The dreadfully wounded city began to shake off the shock and stagger to its feet. Sirens began to match the noisy intensity of the crackling fires. The tidal wave had flowed back into the Gulf of Mexico, dragging a great mass of splintered debris and bodies in its wake.

Survivors began to stumble dazed and injured into the streets, like bewildered sheep, shocked at the enormous devastation around them, wondering what had happened. Some wandered in shock, unfeeling of their wounds. Others stared dumbly at the huge piece of the *Amy Bigalow*'s rudder that had crashed through the bus station and mashed four of the vehicles and several people who were waiting to board.

A piece of the *Ozero Zaysan*'s forward mast was found embedded in the center of Havana Stadium's soccer field. A one-ton winch landed in a wing of University Hospital and squashed the only three beds not occupied in a forty-bed ward. It was to be widely talked about as only one of a hundred miracles that happened that day. A great boon to the Catholic Church and a small setback to Marxism.

Rescue parties began to form as firefighters and police converged on the waterfront. Army units were called out along with the militia. There was panic amid the chaos at first. The military forces turned their backs on rescue work and manned island defenses under the mistaken belief the United States was invading. The injured seemed to be everywhere, some screaming in pain, most hobbling or walking away from the flaming harbor.

The earthshaking quake died with the shock waves. The ceiling of Sloppy Joe's had fallen in, but the walls still stood. The barroom was a shambles. Wooden beams, fallen plaster, overturned furniture, and broken bottles lay scattered under a thick cloud of dust. The

447

swinging door had been ripped from its hinges and hung at a crazy angle over Castro's bodyguards, who lay groaning under a small hill of bricks.

Ira Hagen hoisted himself painfully to his feet and shook his head to clear it from the ringing of the concussion. He wiped his eyes to penetrate the dust cloud and clutched a wall for support. He looked up through the now open ceiling and saw pictures still hanging on the walls of the floor above.

His first thought was of Jessie. She was lying partially under the table that still stood in the center of the room. Her body was crumpled in a curled position. Hagen knelt and gently turned her over.

She lay motionless, appearing lifeless under the coating of white plaster dust, but there was no blood or serious wounds. Her eyes were half open and she groaned. Hagen smiled with relief and removed his coat. He folded and placed it under her head.

She reached up and grasped his wrist more tightly than he believed possible and stared up at him.

"Dirk is dead," she whispered.

"He might have survived," said Hagen softly, but there was no optimism in his tone.

"Dirk is dead," she repeated.

"Don't move," he said. "Just lie easy while I check out the Castros."

Then he rose unsteadily and began searching through the fallen debris. The sound of coughing came from his left and he climbed over the rubble until he bumped into the bar.

Raúl Castro was hanging on to the raised edge of the bar with both hands, dazed and in shock, hacking the dust from his throat. Blood was trickling from his nose and a nasty cut on his chin.

Hagen marveled at how close everyone had been sitting before the explosions and how scattered they were now. He uprighted a fallen chair and helped Raúl to sit down.

"Are you all right, sir?" Hagen asked, genuinely concerned.

Raúl nodded weakly. "I'm all right. Fidel? Where is Fidel?"

"Sit tight. I'll find him."

Hagen moved off through the rubble until he found Fidel Castro. The Cuban leader was on his stomach and twisted sideways, shoulders propped up by one arm. Hagen stared in fascination at the scene on the floor.

Castro's eyes were trained on an upturned face only a foot away. General Velikov was spread-eagled on his back, a large beam crushing his legs. The expression on his face was a mixture of defiance and apprehension. He stared up at Castro through eyes bitter with the taste of defeat.

There was not a flicker of emotion in Castro's expression. The plaster dust made him look as though he were sculpted in marble. The rigidity of the face, masklike, the total concentration, was almost inhuman.

"We live, General," he murmured triumphantly. "We both live."

"Not right," Velikov uttered through clenched teeth. "We should all be dead."

"Dirk Pitt and the others somehow got the ships through your naval units and out to sea," explained Hagen. "The destructive force of the explosion was only one-tenth of what it might have been if they remained in the harbor."

"You have failed," said Castro. "Cuba remains Cuba."

"So near and yet—" Velikov shook his head resignedly. "And now for the revenge you vowed to take on me."

"You will die for every one of my countrymen you murdered," Castro promised, in a voice as cold as an open grave. "If it takes a thousand deaths or a hundred thousand. You will suffer them all."

Velikov grinned crookedly. He seemed to have no nerves at all. "Another man, another time, and you will surely be killed, Fidel. I know. I helped create five alternative plans in case this one failed."

449

PART VI

Eureka! the La Dorada

75

November 8, 1989
Washington, D.C.

MARTIN BROGAN WALKED into the early-morning cabinet meeting late. The President and the men seated around the large kidney-shaped table looked up expectantly.

"The ships were detonated four hours ahead of schedule," he informed them while still standing.

His announcement was greeted with solemn silence. Every man at the table had been told of the unbelievable plan by the Soviets to remove Castro, and the news struck them more as an inevitable tragedy than a shocking catastrophe.

"What are the latest reports on loss of life?" asked Douglas Oates.

"Too early to tell," replied Brogan. "The whole harbor area is in flames. The deaths could conceivably total in the thousands. The devastation, however, is not nearly as severe as we first projected. It appears our agents in Havana seized two of the ships and sailed them out of the harbor before they exploded."

As they listened in contemplative quiet, Brogan read from the initial reports sent from the Special Interests Section in Havana. He recounted the details of the plan to move the ships and the sketchy details of the actual operation. Before he had finished, one of his aides entered and slipped him an updated report. He scanned it silently and then read the first line.

"Fidel and Raúl Castro are alive." He paused to gaze at the President. "Your man, Ira Hagen, says he is in direct contact with the Castros and they have requested any assistance we can offer in the way of disaster relief, including medical personnel and supplies,

453

firefighting equipment, food and clothing, and also morgue and embalming experts."

The President looked at General Clayton Metcalf, chairman of the Joint Chiefs of Staff. "General?"

"After your call last night, I alerted Air Transport Command. We can begin the airlift as soon as the people and supplies arrive at the airfields and are loaded on board."

"Any approach by American military aircraft had better be coordinated or the Cubans will cut loose with their surface-to-air missiles," pointed out Secretary of Defense Simmons.

"I'll see to it a line of communication is opened with their Foreign Ministry," said Secretary of State Oates.

"Better make it clear to Castro that any relief we send is organized under the umbrella of the Red Cross," added Dan Fawcett. "We don't want to scare him into slamming the door."

"An angle we can't overlook," said the President.

"Almost a crime to take advantage of a terrible disaster," mused Oates. "Still, we can't deny it's a heaven-sent opportunity to cement relations with Cuba and defuse revolutionary fever throughout the Americas."

"I wonder if Castro has ever studied Símon Bolívar?" the President asked no one in particular.

"The Great Liberator of South America is one of Castro's idols," replied Brogan. "Why do you ask?"

"Then perhaps he's finally heeded one of Bolívar's quotations."

"Which quotation is that, Mr. President?"

The President looked from face to face around the table before answering. "'He who serves a revolution plows the sea.'"

76

THE CHAOS SLOWLY SUBSIDED and the rescue work began as the population of Havana recovered from the shock. Hurricane emergency procedures were put into operation. Army and militia units along with paramedics sifted through the rubble, lifting the bodies of the living into ambulances and the dead into trucks.

The Santa Clara convent, dating from 1643, was taken over as a temporary hospital and quickly filled. The wards and corridors of University Hospital soon overflowed. The elegant old Presidential Palace, now the museum of the revolution, was turned into a morgue.

Injured people walked the streets bleeding, staring vacantly or searching desperately for loved ones. A clock on top of a building in Cathedral Square of old Havana sat frozen at 6:21. Some residents who had fled their homes during the havoc began to drift back. Others who had no homes to return to walked through the streets, picking their way around the bodies, carrying small bundles containing salvaged possessions.

Every fire unit for a hundred miles streamed into the city and vainly fought the fires spreading throughout the waterfront. A tank of chlorine gas exploded, adding its poison to the ravages of the blaze. Twice the hundreds of firefighters had to run for cover when a change of wind whipped the blistering heat in their faces.

Even while the rescue operations were being organized, Fidel Castro launched a purge of disloyal government officials and military officers. Raúl personally directed the roundup. Most had abandoned the city, having been forewarned of Rum and Cola by Velikov and the KGB. One by one they were arrested, each one stunned by the news the Castro brothers were still alive. By the hundreds they were transported under heavy guard to a secret prison compound deep in the mountains, never to be seen again.

At two o'clock in the afternoon the first U.S. Air Force heavy cargo plane landed at Havana's international airport. Soon a constant stream of aircraft were arriving. Fidel Castro was on hand to greet the volunteer doctors and nurses. He personally saw to it that Cuban relief committees stood by to receive the supplies and cooperate with the incoming Americans.

By early evening, Coast Guard and firefighting vessels from the port of Miami began to stream over the smoke-filled horizon. Bulldozers, heavy equipment, and oil-fire experts from Texas moved into the fiery wreckage along the harbor and wasted no time in attacking the flames.

Despite past political differences the imagination of the United States and Cuba seemed to leap to the occasion and everyone worked together closely on the specific emergencies to be met.

Admiral Sandecker and Al Giordino stepped off a NUMA jet late in the afternoon. They hitched a ride on a truck, loaded with bed linen and military cots, as far as a distribution depot, where Giordino hot-wired and *borrowed* an abandoned Fiat.

The false sunset from the flames tinted their faces red through the windshield as they gazed incredulously at the gigantic smoke cloud and great sea of fire.

After nearly an hour of winding their way through the city and being directed by police through complicated detours to avoid streets choked with debris and rescue vehicles, they finally reached the Swiss Embassy.

"We have our job cut out," said Sandecker, staring at the ruined buildings and the wreckage littering the wide boulevard of the Malecón.

Giordino nodded sadly. "He may never be found."

"Still, we owe it to him to try."

"Yes," Giordino said heavily. "We owe Dirk that."

They turned and walked through the battered entrance of the embassy and were directed to the communications room of the Special Interests Section.

The room was jammed with news correspondents, waiting their turn to transmit reports of the disaster. Sandecker shouldered his way through the throng and found a heavyset man dictating to a radio operator. When the man finished, Sandecker tapped him on the arm.

"You Ira Hagen?"

"Yes, I'm Hagen." The hoarse voice matched the tired lines in the face.

"Thought so," said Sandecker. "The President described you in some detail."

Hagen patted his rotund stomach and forced a smile. "I'm not hard to pick out in a crowd." Then he paused and looked at Sandecker strangely. "You say the President—"

"I met with him four hours ago in the White House. My name is James Sandecker and this is Al Giordino. We're with NUMA."

"Yes, Admiral, I know the name. What can I do for you?"

"We're friends of Dirk Pitt and Jessie LeBaron."

Hagen closed his eyes for a second and then gazed at Sandecker steadily. "Mrs. LeBaron is one hell of a woman. Except for a few small cuts and bruises, she came out of the explosion in good shape. She's helping out at an emergency hospital for children in the old cathedral. But if you're looking for Pitt, I'm afraid you're wasting your time. He was at the helm of the *Amy Bigalow* when she blew up."

Giordino suddenly felt sick at heart. "There's no chance he might have escaped?"

"Of the men who fought off the Russians on the docks while the ships slipped out to sea, only two survived. Every one of the crew on board the ships and tugboat is missing. There's little hope any of them made it clear in time. And if the explosions didn't kill them, they surely must have drowned in the tidal wave."

Giordino clenched his fists in frustration. He turned and faced away so the others couldn't see the tears rimming his eyes.

Sandecker shook his head in sorrow. "We'd like to make a search of the hospitals."

"I hate to sound heartless, Admiral, but you'd do better to look in the morgues."

"We'll do both."

"I'll ask the Swiss to arrange a diplomatic pass so you can move freely about the city."

"Thank you."

Hagen looked at both men, his eyes filled with compassion. "If it's any consolation, your friend Pitt was responsible for saving a hundred thousand lives."

Sandecker stared back, a sudden proud look on his face. "And if you knew Dirk Pitt, Mr. Hagen, you'd have expected no less."

457

77

WITH NOT MUCH OPTIMISM, Sandecker and Giordino began looking for Pitt in the hospitals. They stepped over countless wounded who lay in rows on the floors as nurses administered what aid they could and teams of exhausted doctors labored in the operating rooms. Numerous times they stopped and helped move stretcher cases before continuing the hunt.

They could not find Pitt among the living.

Next they searched through the makeshift morgues, some with trucks waiting in front containing bodies stacked four and five deep. A small army of embalmers worked feverishly to prevent the spread of disease. The dead lay everywhere like cordwood, their faces bare, staring vacantly at the ceilings. Many were too burned and mutilated to identify and were later buried in a mass ceremony in the Colón cemetery.

One harried morgue attendant showed them the remains of a man reported to have been washed in from the sea. It was not Pitt, and they failed to identify Manny because they did not know him.

The early-morning sun rose over the ravaged city. More injured were found and carried to the hospitals, more dead to the morgues. Troops with fixed bayonets walked the streets to prevent looting. Flames still raged in the dock area, but the firefighters were making headway. The vast cloud still bloomed black in the sky, and airline pilots reported that easterly winds had carried it as far as Mexico City.

Sickened by the sights they witnessed that night, Sandecker and Giordino were glad to see daylight again. They drove to within three blocks of Cathedral Plaza and were stopped by wreckage blocking the streets. They walked the rest of the way to the temporary children's hospital to find Jessie.

She was soothing a small girl who was whimpering as a doctor encased a slim brown leg in a cast. Jessie looked up at the admiral and Giordino as they approached. Unconsciously her eyes wandered over their faces, but her weary mind did not recognize them.

"Jessie," said Sandecker softly. "It's Jim Sandecker and Al Giordino."

She looked at them for a few seconds and then it began to register. "Admiral. Al. Oh, thank God you've come." She whispered something in the girl's ear, and then stood and embraced them both, crying uncontrollably.

The doctor nodded at Sandecker. "She's been working like a demon for twenty hours straight. Why don't you see to it she takes a breather."

Each man took an arm and eased her outside. They gently lowered her to a sitting position on the cathedral steps.

Giordino sat down in front of Jessie and looked at her. She was still dressed in combat fatigues. The camouflage pattern was now blotched with bloodstains. Her hair was damp with perspiration and tangled, her eyes red from the pervasive smoke.

"I'm so glad you found me," she said finally. "Did you just arrive?"

"Last night," replied Giordino. "We've been looking for Dirk."

She gazed blankly at the great smoke cloud. "He's gone," she said as if in a trance.

"The bad penny always turns up," Giordino muttered absently.

"They're all gone—my husband, Dirk, so many others." Her voice died.

"Is there coffee anywhere?" said Sandecker, changing the tack of the conversation. "I think we could all use a cup."

Jessie nodded weakly toward the entrance to the cathedral. "A poor woman whose children are badly injured has been making some for the volunteers."

"I'll get it," said Giordino. He rose and disappeared inside.

Jessie and the admiral sat there for several moments, listening to the sirens and watching the flames leap in the distance.

"When we return to Washington," Sandecker said at last, "if I can help in any way..."

"You're most kind, Admiral, but I can manage." She hesitated. "There is one thing. Do you think that Raymond's body might be found and shipped home for burial?"

"I'm sure after all you've done, Castro will cut through any red tape."

"Strange how we became drawn into all this because of the treasure."

459

"The La Dorada?"

Jessie's eyes stared at a group of figures walking toward them in the distance, but she gave no sign of seeing them. "Men have been beguiled by her for nearly five hundred years, and most have died because of their lust to own her. Stupid... stupid to waste lives over a statue."

"She is still considered the greatest treasure of them all."

Jessie closed her eyes tiredly. "Thank heavens it's hidden. Who knows how many men would kill for it."

"Dirk would never climb over someone's bones for money," Sandecker said. "I know him too well. He was in it for the adventure and the challenge of solving a mystery, not for profit."

Jessie did not reply. She opened her eyes and finally took notice of the approaching party. She could not see them clearly. One of them seemed seven feet tall through the yellow haze from the smoke. The others were quite small. They were singing, but she couldn't make out the tune.

Giordino returned with a small board holding three cups. He stopped and stared for a long moment at the group threading their way through the rubble in the plaza.

The figure in the middle wasn't seven feet tall, but a man with a small boy perched on his shoulders. The boy looked frightened and tightly laced his hands around the man's forehead, obscuring the upper part of his face. A young girl was cradled in one muscled arm, while the opposite hand was clutched by a girl no more than five. A string of ten or eleven other children followed close behind. They sounded as if they were singing in halting English. Three dogs trotted alongside and yapped in accompaniment.

Sandecker looked at Giordino curiously. The barrel-chested Italian blinked away the eye-watering smoke and gazed with an intense wondering expression at the strange and pathetic sight.

The man looked like an apparition, exhausted, desperately so. His clothes were in tatters and he walked with a limp. The eyes were sunken and the gaunt face was streaked with dried blood. Yet his jaw was determined, and he led the children in song with a booming voice.

"I must go back to work," said Jessie, struggling to her feet. "Those children will need care."

They were close enough now so that Giordino could make out the song they were singing.

I'm a Yankee Doodle Dandy. A Yankee Doodle do or die...

460

Giordino's jaw dropped and his eyes widened in disbelief. He pointed in uncomprehending awe. Then he threw the coffee cups over his shoulder and bounded down the steps of the cathedral like a madman.

"It's him!" he shouted.

A real live nephew of my Uncle Sam. Born on the fourth of July.

"What was that?" Sandecker shouted after him. "What did you say?"

Jessie jumped to her feet, suddenly oblivious to the wrenching fatigue, and ran after Giordino. "He's come back!" she cried.

Then Sandecker took off.

The children stopped in midchorus and huddled around the man, frightened at the sudden appearance of three people shouting and running toward them. They clung to him as life itself. The dogs closed ranks around his legs and began barking louder than ever.

Giordino halted and stood there only two feet away, not sure of what to say that was meaningful. He smiled and smiled in immense delight and relief. At last he found his tongue.

"Welcome back, Lazarus."

Pitt grinned impishly. "Hello, pal. You wouldn't happen to have a dry martini in your pocket?"

461

78

SIX HOURS LATER Pitt was sleeping like a stone in an empty alcove of the cathedral. He had refused to go down until the children were cared for and the dogs fed. Then he insisted that Jessie get some rest too.

They lay a few feet apart on double blankets that served as pads against the hard tile floor. Faithful Giordino sat in a wicker chair at the entrance of the alcove, guarding against invasion of their sleep, shushing an occasional band of children who played too close and too loud.

He stiffened at the sight of Sandecker approaching with a group of uniformed Cubans at his heels. Ira Hagen was among them, looking older and far more tired than when Giordino had last seen him, hardly twenty hours previously. The man next to Hagen and directly behind the admiral, Giordino recognized immediately. He rose to his feet as Sandecker nodded toward the sleeping figures.

"Wake them up," he said quietly.

Jessie struggled up from the depths and moaned. Giordino had to shake her by the shoulder several times to keep her from slipping back again. Still bone-tired and drugged from sleep, she sat up and shook her head to clear the blurriness.

Pitt came awake almost instantly, his mind triggered like an alarm clock. He twisted around and elbowed himself to a sitting position, eyes alert and sweeping the men standing around him in a half circle.

"Dirk," said Sandecker. "This is President Fidel Castro. He was making an inspection tour of the hospitals and was told you and Jessie were here. He'd like to talk to you."

Before Pitt could make a remark, Castro stepped forward, took his hand, and pulled him to his feet with surprising strength. The magnetic brown eyes met with piercing opaline green. Castro wore neat,

462

starched olive fatigues with a commander in chief's shoulder insignia, in contrast to Pitt, who still had on the same ragged and dirty clothes as when he arrived at the cathedral.

"So this is the man who made idiots out of my security police and saved the city," said Castro in Spanish.

Jessie translated, and Pitt made a negative gesture. "I was only one of the luckier men who survived. At least two dozen others died trying to prevent the tragedy."

"If the ships had exploded while still tied to the docks, most of Havana would now be a leveled wasteland. A tomb for myself as well as half a million people. Cuba is grateful and wishes to make you a Hero of the Revolution."

"There goes my standing in the neighborhood," muttered Pitt.

Jessie threw him a distasteful look and didn't translate.

"What did he say?" asked Castro.

Jessie cleared her throat. "Ah...he said he is honored to accept."

Castro then asked Pitt to describe the seizing of the ships. "Tell me what you saw," he said politely. "Everything you know that happened. From the beginning."

"Starting with the time we left the Swiss Embassy?" Pitt asked, his eyes narrowed in furtive but shrewd reflection.

"If you wish," answered Castro, comprehending the look.

As Pitt narrated the desperate fight on the docks and the struggle to move the *Amy Bigalow* and the *Ozero Zuysun* from the harbor, Castro interrupted with a barrage of questions. The Cuban leader's curiosity was insatiable. The report took almost as long as the actual event.

Pitt related the facts as straight and unemotionally as he could, knowing he could never do justice to the incredible courage of men who selflessly gave their lives for people of another country. He told of Clark's magnificent holding action against overwhelming odds; how Manny and Moe and their crews struggled in the dark bowels of the ships to get them under way, knowing they could be blown into atoms at any moment. He told how Jack and his crew stayed with the tugboat, towing the death ships out to sea until it was too late to escape. He wished they could all be there to tell their own stories, and he wondered what they might have said. He smiled to himself, knowing how Manny would have turned the air blue with pungent language.

463

At last Pitt told of being swept into the city by the tidal wave and blacking out, and how he regained consciousness hanging upside down from an overhead jewelry-shop sign. He related how staggering through the debris he heard a little girl crying, and pulled her and a brother from under the wreckage of a collapsed apartment building. After that he seemed to attract lost children like a magnet. Rescue workers added to his collection during the night. When no more could be found alive, a policeman directed Pitt to the children's hospital and relief center, where he was discovered by his friends.

Suddenly Pitt's voice trailed off and he dropped his hands limply to his sides. "That's all there is to tell."

Castro looked at Pitt steadily, his face filled with emotion. He stepped forward and embraced him. "Thank you," he murmured in a broken voice. Then he kissed Jessie on both cheeks and shook Hagen's hand. "Cuba thanks you all. We will not forget."

Pitt looked at Castro slyly. "I wonder if I might ask a favor?"

"You have but to name it," Castro quickly answered.

Pitt hesitated, then he said, "There is this taxi driver named Herberto Figueroa. If I were to find him a restored 'fifty-seven Chevrolet in the States and have it shipped, do you suppose you could arrange for him to take delivery. Herberto and I would both be very grateful."

"But of course. I'll personally see to it he receives your gift."

"There is one more favor," said Pitt.

"Don't push your luck," whispered Sandecker.

"What is it?" Castro asked courteously.

"I wonder if I could borrow a boat with a crane?"

79

THE BODIES OF MANNY and three of his crew were identified. Clark was fished out of the channel by a fishing boat. Their remains were flown back to Washington for burial. Nothing of Jack, Moe, and the rest ever turned up.

The fire was finally under control four days after the death ships were blown out of existence. The final, stubborn blaze would not be extinguished until a week later. Another six weeks would pass before the last of the dead were found. Many were never found at all.

The Cubans were meticulous in their accounting. They eventually compiled a complete list of casualities. The known dead came to 732. The injured totaled 3,769. The missing were calculated at 197.

At the President's urging, Congress passed an emergency aid bill of $45 million to help the Cubans rebuild Havana. The President also, as a gesture of goodwill, lifted the thirty-five-year-old trade embargo. At last Americans could legally smoke good Havana cigars again.

After the Russians were expelled, their only representation in Cuba was a Special Interests Section in the Polish Embassy. The Cuban people shed no tears at their departure.

Castro still remained a Marxist revolutionary at heart, but he was mellowing. After agreeing in principle to the U.S.–Cuban friendship pact, he unhesitantly accepted an invitation to visit with the President at the White House and make an address before Congress, although he did grumble when asked to keep his speech to twenty minutes.

At dawn on the third day after the explosions an old peeling, weather-worn vessel dropped anchor almost in the exact center of the harbor. Fireboats and salvage craft swept past her as though she were a disabled car in the center of a highway. She was a squat workboat, broad and beamy, about sixty feet in length with a small derrick on the stern whose boom extended over the water. Her crew seemed oblivious to the frenzy of activity going on around them.

Most of the flames in the dock area had been extinguished, but firemen were still pouring thousands of gallons of water on the smoldering debris inside the heat-twisted framework of the warehouses. Several blackened oil storage tanks across the harbor sputtered with stubborn flame, and the acrid pall of smoke reeked of burned oil and rubber.

Pitt stood on the bleached deck of the workboat and squinted through the smoky yellow haze at the wreck of the oil tanker. All that remained of the *Ozero Baykai* was the scorched superstructure on the stern that rose grotesque and distorted above the oily water. He turned his attention to a small compass he held in one hand.

"Is this the spot?" asked Admiral Sandecker.

"Cross bearings on the landmarks check out," Pitt answered.

Giordino stuck his head out the wheelhouse window. "The magnetometer is going crazy. We're right over a heavy mass of iron."

Jessie was sitting on a hatch. She wore gray shorts and a pale blue blouse and looked like her old luscious self.

She flashed a curious look at Pitt. "You still haven't told me why you think Raymond hid the La Dorada on the bottom of the harbor and how you know exactly where to look."

"I was stupid not catch on immediately," explained Pitt. "The words sound the same, and I misinterpreted them. I thought his last words were 'Look on the m-a-i-n s-i-g-h-t.' What he was really trying to say was 'Look on the M-a-i-n-e s-i-t-e.'"

Jessie looked confused. "Maine site?"

"Remember Pearl Harbor, the Alamo, and the *Maine*. On or about this spot in 1898 the battleship *Maine* blew up and launched the Spanish-American War."

An edge of excitement began to form inside her. "Raymond threw the statue on top of an old shipwreck?"

"Shipwreck site," Pitt corrected her. "The hulk of the *Maine* was raised and towed out to sea, where she was sunk with flag flying in 1912."

"But why would Raymond deliberately throw the treasure away?"

"It all goes back to when he and his marine salvage partner, Hans Kronberg, discovered the *Cyclops* and salvaged the La Dorada. It should have been a triumph for two friends who fought the odds together and stole the most sought-after treasure in history from a possessive sea. And it should have had a happy ending. But the tale turned sour. Raymond LeBaron was in love with Kronberg's wife."

Jessie's face tensed in understanding. "Hilda."

"Yes. Hilda. He had two motives for wanting to get rid of Hans. The treasure and a woman. Somehow he must have talked Hans into making another dive after the La Dorada was raised. Then he cut the lifeline, leaving his friend to die a horrible death. Can you imagine what it must have been like, strangling in agony deep inside a steel crypt like the *Cyclops?*"

Jessie averted her eyes. "I can't bring myself to believe you."

"You saw Kronberg's body with your own eyes. Hilda was the real key. She outlined most of the sordid story. I only had to fill in a few details."

"Raymond could never commit murder."

"He could and he did. With Hans out of the picture he went one step further. He dodged the Internal Revenue Service—who can blame him when you remember the federal government collected over eighty percent of income above $150,000 in the late fifties— and sidestepped a time-consuming lawsuit from Brazil, which would have rightly claimed the statue as a stolen national treasure. He kept quiet and set a course for Cuba. A shifty man, your lover.

"The problem he now faced was how to dispose of it. Who could afford to pay even a fraction of twenty to fifty million dollars for an art object? He was also afraid that once the word was out the current Cuban dictator, Fulgencio Batista, a racketeer of the first magnitude, would have it seized. And if Batista didn't grab it for himself, the army of Mafia hoods he invited into Cuba after the Second World War would. So Raymond decided to carve up the La Dorada and sell it bit by bit.

"Unfortunately for him, his timing was bad. He sailed his salvage boat into Havana on the same day that Castro and his rebels swarmed into town after toppling Batista's corrupt government. The revolutionary forces immediately closed down the harbors and airports to stop Batista's cronies from fleeing the country with uncountable wealth."

"LeBaron got nothing?" asked Sandecker. "He lost it all?"

"Not entirely. He realized he was trapped and it was only a question of time before the revolutionaries searched his salvage boat and found the La Dorada. His only option was to hack out whatever he

467

could carry and catch the next plane back to the States. Under cover of night he must have slipped his salvage boat into the harbor, hoisted the statue overboard, and dumped it on top of the site where the battleship *Maine* had blown up seventy years before. Naturally he planned to come back and retrieve it after the chaos died down, but Castro didn't play according to LeBaron's rules. Cuba's honeymoon with the United States soon fell apart and he could never return and raise three tons of priceless treasure under the eyes of Castro's security."

"What piece of the statue did he remove?" Jessie asked.

"According to Hilda, he pried out the ruby heart. Then, after he smuggled it home, he discreetly had it cut, faceted, and sold through brokers. Now he had enough leverage to reach the pinnacle of high finance with Hilda at his side. Raymond LeBaron had arrived in fat city."

For a long moment they were quiet, each with his own thoughts, envisioning a desperate LeBaron throwing the golden woman over the side of his boat thirty years ago.

"The La Dorada," said Sandecker, breaking the silence. "Her weight would have pushed her deep beneath the soft silt of the harbor bottom."

"The admiral has a point," said Giordino. "LeBaron failed to consider that finding her again would be a major operation."

"I admit that bothered me too," said Pitt. "He must have known that after the Army Corps of Engineers stripped and removed the main hull section of the *Maine* hundreds of tons of wreckage were left embedded in the mud, making her almost impossible to find. The most sophisticated metal detector that money can buy won't pick out one particular object in a junkyard."

"So the statue will lie down there forever," said Sandecker. "Unless someday, someone cómes along and dredges up half the harbor until he strikes it."

"Maybe not," Pitt said thoughtfully, his mind seeing something only he could see. "Raymond LeBaron was a canny character. He was also a professional salvage man. I believe he knew exactly what he was doing."

"What are you aiming at?" asked Sandecker.

"He put the statue over the side, all right. But I'm betting he very slowly lowered her feet first so she came down on the bottom standing up."

468

Giordino stared down at the deck. "Might be," he said slowly. "Might be. How tall is she?"

"About eight feet, including the base."

"Thirty years for three tons to settle in the mud..." mused Sandecker. "It's possible a couple of feet of her may still be protruding from the harbor floor."

Pitt smiled distantly. "We'll know as soon as Al and I dive down and run a search pattern."

As if on cue they all became quiet and gazed over the side into the water, oil-slicked and ash-coated, dark and secretive. Somewhere in the sinister green depths La Dorada beckoned.

80

PITT STOOD IN FULL DIVE GEAR and watched the bubbles rising from the deep and bursting on the surface. He glanced at his watch, marking the time. Giordino had been down nearly fifty minutes at a depth of forty feet. He went on watching the bubbles and saw them gradually travel in a circle. He knew that Giordino had enough air left for one more 360-degree sweep around the descent line tied to a buoy about thirty yards from the boat.

The small crew of Cubans Sandecker had recruited were very quiet. Pitt looked along the deck and saw them lined up at the rail beside the admiral, staring as though hypnotized at the glitter from the bubbles.

Pitt turned to Jessie, who was standing beside him. She hadn't said a word or moved in the last five minutes, her face tense with deep concentration, her eyes shining with excitement. She was swept up in the anticipation of seeing a legend. Then suddenly she called out. "Look!"

A dark form rose from the depths amid a cloud of bubbles, and Giordino's head broke the water near the buoy. He rolled over on his back and paddled easily with his fins until he reached the ladder. He handed up his weight belt and twin air cylinder before climbing to the deck. He pulled off his face mask and spit over the side.

"How did it go?" asked Pitt.

"Okay," Giordino answered. "Here's the situation. I made eight sweeps around the base point where the buoy's descent line is anchored. Visibility is less than three feet. We may have a little luck. The bottom is a mixture of sand and mud, so it's not real soft. The statue may not have sunk over her head."

"Current?"

"About a knot. You can live with it."

"Any obstructions?"

"A few bits and pieces of rusted wreckage protrude from the bottom, so be careful not to snag your distance line."

Sandecker came up behind Pitt and made a final check of his gear. Pitt stepped through an opening in the rail and set the air regulator's mouthpiece between his teeth.

Jessie gave his arm a gentle squeeze through the protective dry suit. "Luck," she said.

He winked at her through the face mask and then took a long step forward. The bright sunlight was diffused by a sudden burst of bubbles as he was engulfed by the green void. He swam out to the buoy and started down the descent line. The yellow nylon braid faded and vanished a few feet below in the opaque murk.

Pitt followed the line cautiously, taking his time. He paused once to clear his ears. Less than a minute later the bottom abruptly seemed to lift up toward him and meet his outstretched hand. He again paused to adjust his buoyancy compensator vest and check his watch for the time, compass for direction, and air pressure gauge. Then he took the distance line Giordino had attached to the descent line by a clip and moved out along the radius.

After swimming about twenty-four feet his hand came in contact with a knot in the line Giordino had tied to measure the outer perimeter of his last sweep. After a short distance, Pitt spied an orange stake standing in the muck that marked the starting point for his circular search pattern. Then he moved out another six-foot increment, held the line taut, and began his sweep, his eyes taking in the three-foot visibility on both sides.

The water was desolate and lifeless and smelled of chemicals. He passed over colonies of dead sea life, crushed by the concussion from the bursting oil tanker, their bodies rolling across the bottom with the tide like leaves under a gentle breeze. He had sweated inside his dry suit under the sun on the boat, and he was sweating inside it now forty feet below the surface. He could hear the sounds of the rescue boats racing back and forth across the harbor, the roar of their exhaust and cavitation of their propellers magnified by the density of the water.

Yard by yard he scanned the barren harbor until he completed a full circle. He moved the marker out and started another sweep in the opposite direction.

Divers often experience great loneliness when swimming over an underwater desert with nothing to see beyond a hand's reach. The

471

real world with people, less than fifty feet away on the surface, ceases to exist. They experience a careless abandon and an indifference toward the unknown. Their perception becomes distorted and they began to fantasize.

Pitt felt none of those things, except maybe a touch of a fantasy. He was drunk with the hunt and so absorbed in seeing the treasured statue in his mind, gleaming gold and brilliant green, that he almost missed a vague form looming up through the mist on his right.

Rapidly kicking his fins, he swam toward it. The object was round and indistinct and partly buried. The two feet that protruded from the silt were coated with slime and strands of sea growth that waved with the current.

A hundred times Pitt had wondered how he'd feel, how he would react when he confronted the golden woman. What he really felt was fear, fear that it was only a false alarm and the search might never end.

Slowly, apprehensively, he wiped away the slimy growth with his gloved hands. Tiny particles of vegetation and silt billowed in a brown swirl, obscuring the thing. He waited under an eerie silence until the cloud melted into the watery gloom.

He moved closer, floating just above the bottom, until his face was only a few inches away from the mysterious object. He stared through his face mask, his mouth suddenly going dry, his heart pounding like a calypso drum.

With a look of timeless melancholy, a pair of emerald-green eyes stared back at him.

Pitt had found La Dorada.

81

January 4, 1990
Washington, D.C.

THE PRESIDENT'S ANNOUNCEMENT of the Jersey Colony and the exploits of Eli Steinmetz and his moon team electrified the nation and caused a worldwide sensation.

Every evening for a week television viewers were treated to spectacular scenes of the lunar landscape never viewed during the brief Apollo landings. The struggle of the men to survive while constructing a livable habitat was also shown in dramatic detail.

Steinmetz and the others became the heroes of the hour. They were feted across the country, interviewed on countless television talk shows, and given the traditional ticker tape parade in New York.

The cheers for the moon colonists' triumph had the ring of old-fashioned patriotism, but the impact went deeper, broader. Now there was something tangible beyond the short, showy flights above the earth's atmosphere, a permanence in space, solid proof that man could live a life far from his home planet.

The President looked buoyant at a private dinner party he hosted in honor of the "inner core" and the colonists. His mood was far different from the first time he had confronted the men who conceived and launched the moon base. He held out a glass of champagne to Hudson, who was staring absently through the roomful of people as though it were silent and empty.

"Your mind lost in space, Leo?"

Hudson's eyes fixed on the President for a moment, and then he nodded. "My apologies. A nasty habit of mine, tuning out at parties."

"I'll bet you're hatching plans for a new settlement on the moon."

473

Hudson smiled wryly. "Actually, I was thinking of Mars."

"So the Jersey Colony is not the end."

"There will never be an end, only the beginning of another beginning."

"Congress will ride with the mood of the country and vote funding to expand the colony. But an outpost on Mars—you're talking heavy money."

"If we don't do it now, the next generation will."

"Got a name for the project?"

Hudson shook his head. "Haven't given it much thought."

"I've often wondered," the President said, "where you came up with 'Jersey Colony.'"

"You didn't guess?"

"There's the state of New Jersey, the isle of Jersey off the French coast, Jersey sweaters..."

"It's also a breed of cow."

"A what?"

"The nursery rhyme, 'Hey diddle diddle,/The cat and the fiddle,/The cow jumped over the moon.'"

The President looked blank for a moment, and then he broke out laughing. When he recovered he said, "My God, there's irony for you. Man's greatest achievement was named after a Mother Goose cow."

"She's truly exquisite," said Jessie.

"Yes, gorgeous," agreed Pitt. "You never tire of looking at her."

They gazed in rapt fascination at the La Dorada, which now stood in the East Building central court of Washington's National Gallery. The burnished golden body and the polished emerald head gleamed under the sun's rays that shone through the great skylight. The dramatic effect was awesome. Her unknown Indian sculptor had portrayed her with compelling beauty and grace. She stood in a relaxed posture, one leg in front of the other, arms slightly bent at the elbows with hands extended outward from the sides.

Her rose quartz pedestal sat atop a five-foot-high solid block of Brazilian rosewood. The missing heart had been replaced by one crafted out of crimson glass that almost matched the splendor of the original ruby.

Throngs of people stared in wonder at the dazzling sight. A line stretched outside the gallery by the mall for nearly a quarter of a mile. La Dorada even surpassed the attendance record for the King Tut artifacts.

Every dignitary in the capital appeared to pay homage. The President and his wife escorted Hilda Kronberg-LeBaron to the preopening viewing. She sat in her wheelchair, a content old lady with sparkling eyes who smiled and smiled as the President honored the two men in her past with a short dedication speech. When he lifted her out of her chair so she could touch the statue, there wasn't a dry eye in the house.

"Strange," Jessie murmured, "when you think about how it all began with the shipwreck of the *Cyclops* and ended on the shipwreck of the *Maine*."

"Only for us," Pitt said distantly. "For her it began four hundred years ago in a Brazilian jungle."

"Hard to imagine such a thing of beauty has caused so many deaths."

He wasn't listening and didn't reply.

She flashed a curious look at him. He was staring intently at the statue, his mind lost in another time, another place.

"Rich the treasure, sweet the pleasure," she quoted.

He slowly turned and looked at her, his eyes refocusing on the present. The spell was broken. "I'm sorry," he said.

Jessie couldn't help smiling. "When are you going to give it a try?"

"Try?"

"Rush off to search for La Dorada's lost city?"

"No need to rush," Pitt replied, suddenly laughing. "It's not going anywhere."